HLB

02/16

04 SEP 2018

20 AUG 2019

D0766532

Please return this book on or before the date shown above. To
renew go to www.essex.gov.uk/libraries, ring 0345 603 7628 or
go to any Essex library.

Essex County Council

Also by Debbie Johnson

Cold Feet at Christmas
Pippa's Cornish Dream
Never Kiss a Man in a Christmas Jumper

Debbie Johnson

The Birthday That Changed Everything

HARPER

Harper
An imprint of HarperCollins*Publishers* Ltd
The News Building
1 London Bridge Street
London SE1 9GF

www.harpercollins.co.uk

A paperback original 2015
1

A catalogue record for this book
is available from the British Library

ISBN: 978-0-00-815016-7

Set in Birka by Born Group using Atomik ePublisher from Easypress

Printed and bound in Great Britain by
Clays Ltd, St Ives plc

MIX
Paper from
responsible sources
FSC™ C007454

This one's for Ann Potterton and the Turkey gang – who inspired the whole idea in the first place!

PART ONE

Oxford – 39 and counting . . .

Chapter 1

I was online, buying myself a fortieth birthday present from my husband, when I discovered he was leaving me for a Latvian lap-dancer less than half my age.

Now, I like to think I'm an open-minded woman, but that definitely wasn't on my wish list.

One minute I was sipping coffee, listening to the radio and trying to choose between a new Dyson and a course of Botox, and the next it all came apart at the seams. The rug was tugged from beneath my feet, and I was left lying on my almost middle-aged backside, wondering where I'd gone wrong. All while I was listening to a band called The Afterbirth, in an attempt to understand my Goth daughter's tortured psyche.

The Internet wasn't helping my mood either. I knew the Dyson was the sensible choice, but the Botox ad kept springing into evil cyber-life whenever my cursor brushed against it. Maybe it was God's way of telling me I was an ugly old hag who desperately needed surgical intervention.

The fact that I was having to do it at all was depressing enough. As he'd left for work that morning, Simon had casually suggested I 'just stick something on the credit card'. He might as well have added 'because I really can't be arsed . . .'

He may be my husband of seventeen years, but he is a truly lazy git sometimes. We're not just talking the usual male traits – like putting empty milk cartons back in the fridge, or squashing seven metric tons of household waste into the kitchen bin to avoid emptying it – but real, hurtful laziness. Like, anniversary-forgetting, birthday-avoiding levels of hurtful.

Of course, it hadn't always been like that. Once, it had been wonderful – flawed, but wonderful. Over the last few years, though, we'd been sliding more and more out of the wonderful column, and so far into flawed that it almost qualified as 'fucked-up'.

It had happened so slowly, I'd barely noticed – a gradual widening of the cracks in the plasterwork of our marriage: different interests, different priorities. A failure on both our parts, perhaps, to see the fact that the other was changing.

With hindsight, he'd been especially switched off in recent months: spending more time at work, missing our son's sports day, and not blowing even half a gasket when Lucy dyed her blond hair a deathly shade of black. I'd put it down to the male menopause and moved on. I was far too busy pairing lost socks to give his moods too much attention anyway. Tragic but true – I'd taken things for granted as much as he had.

As I flicked between Curry's and Botox clinics, an e-mail landed. It was Simon – probably, I thought as I opened it, reminding me to iron five fresh work shirts for him. I don't know why he bothers – it's part of my *raison d'être*. If he opened that wardrobe on a Monday morning and five fresh work shirts weren't hanging there, perfectly ironed, I think we'd both spontaneously combust.

'Dear Sally,' it started, 'this is the hardest thing I've ever had to do, but I need to take a break. I have some issues I need to sort out and I can't do that at home. I won't be coming back this weekend, but I'll contact you soon so we can talk. Please don't hate me – try to understand it's not about you or anything you've done wrong, it's about me making the time to find myself. I'd really appreciate it if you could pack me a bag – you know what I'll need. And if you could explain to the children for me it would probably be for the best – you're so much better at that kind of thing. With love, Simon. PS – please don't forget to pack my work shirts.'

And at the bottom of the e-mail, rolling across the page in all its before-and-after glory, was an advert. For bloody Botox. I stared at it and gave some serious consideration to smashing the laptop to pieces with a sledgehammer.

Instead, I remained calm and in control of my senses. At least calm enough to not wreck the computer.

The only problem was what to do next. When you get news like that, especially in the deeply personal format of an e-mail, it renders you too stupefied to feel much at all. I think my brain shut down to protect itself from overload, and I did the logical thing – started making lunch. Lucy would be back from a trip to Oxford city centre soon with her friends Lucifer and Beelzebub. Well, that was my name for them. I think it was actually Tasha and Sophie, but they'd changed a lot since Reception, and I wasn't sure if they were even human any more.

They'd left earlier that morning on some sort of adventure to mark the end of the school term. They were probably sticking it to the Man by shoplifting black nail varnish from Superdrug.

My son, Ollie, was out at Warhammer club at the local library, where he took a frightening amount of pleasure in painting small figures of trolls and demons various shades of silver. He still looked like a normal fourteen-year-old, at least – apart from the iPod devices that had now permanently replaced his ears. I'd got used to raising my voice slightly when talking to him, a bit like you do with an elderly aunt at a family do, and playing ad hoc games of charades to let him know dinner was ready or it was time for school.

They'd both be coming home soon, even if Simon wasn't, and they'd be hungry, thirsty, possibly lazy, grumpy, and a variety of other dwarfs as well.

On autopilot, I opened the fridge door and pulled out some ham, mayonnaise and half a leftover chocolate log, starting to assemble a sumptuous feast. Well, maybe not that sumptuous, but pretty good for a woman who'd just been cyber-dumped.

Simon was leaving me, I thought as I chopped and spread. Leaving us. My handsome husband: orthopaedic surgeon to the stars. Or at least a few C-listers who'd knackered their knees skiing, and one overweight comedian who snapped his wrist in a celebrity break-dancing contest.

It didn't seem real. I couldn't let it be real. Our marriage had survived way too much for it to fall to pieces now. Me getting pregnant when we were both student doctors working twenty-hour days. Lucy arriving, Ollie soon after; struggling to cope on one wage as Simon carried on with his residency. The miscarriage I'd had a few years ago, which devastated us both, even though we hadn't planned any more . . . seventeen years of love and passion and anger and boredom and resentment couldn't end with an e-mail, surely?

Except I knew marriages did end, all the time. At the school where I work as a teaching assistant, the deputy head's husband had recently run off with a woman he met through an online betting website. Apparently they bonded over a game of Texas Hold 'Em and next thing she knew, he'd buggered off to Barrow-in-Furness to start a new life. And my sister-in-law Cheryl divorced my brother Davy after twenty-two years, once the kids had grown up and she realised he was only ten per cent tolerable, and ninety per cent tosser.

As you enter your forties, it feels like the bad news overtakes the good. More cheating spouses and tests on breast lumps, and a lot fewer mini-breaks to Paris. I'd seen enough marriages crumble to know the risks.

I suppose I'd always thought, maybe a bit smugly, that Simon and I were solid. Solid as a big, immovable, maybe not particularly inspiring, rock. More Scafell Pike than Kilimanjaro, but still solid.

'*Mum*,' shouted Ollie, having walked into the room without me so much as noticing his size ten feet stomping through the hallway, 'stop!'

'Stop what?' I said, wiping my hands on the tea towel. My face was wet. I hadn't even noticed I'd been crying. I wiped that with the tea towel too.

'Stop spreading mayo on that chocolate log, because it's going to taste like puke – are you going senile or what? And are you . . . crying?'

I glanced down. It looked a bit like a scene from *Close Encounters of the Third Kind*, where everybody was trying to sculpt a big hill out of mashed potato. Except ruder – because a chocolate log covered in a white creamy substance does look kind of gross.

I scraped it all into the bin and took a deep breath. The tears were still flowing. Even if my brain wasn't quite processing what was going on, my emotions had kicked in against my will. I swiped my fingers across my face to wipe the tears away, smearing my cheeks with chocolate mayo cake.

Should I tell the kids or not? Was there any point, if it wasn't real? Perhaps I needed to read that e-mail again. He had said it wasn't to do with me. That he just had some issues to work through. Maybe he'd go on a retreat to Tibet and fix himself, and all this emotion would have been for nothing.

Maybe I should wait and see what happened. What he had to say for himself. The Simon I knew, the Simon I'd loved for so long, wouldn't do this. Maybe it *was* just a rough patch. Maybe he'd come round tomorrow, see me in my finest negligee and realise the error of his ways. He'd come crying into my arms, and bury his head in my heaving bosom . . . except I don't own a negligee. Or anything more sexy than a T-shirt from the local garage that says 'Honk here for service' across the boobs.

When you've been married for seventeen years, have two teenaged children and are almost forty, you're more likely to be shopping at Mother Malone's Big Knicker Emporium than Ann Summers. Maybe that was the problem. Maybe I should have been greeting Simon at the door every night dressed in garter belts and stockings, bearing a G&T with a blow-job chaser.

'Come and sit down, Mum, I'll make you a cup of tea,' Ollie was saying, carefully taking the knife from my hands and putting it on top of the fridge. He gently placed his arm round my shoulders and guided me over to the sofa. He's already much taller than my five foot five, and it's disconcerting to have to look up at your own baby.

I realised then how seriously he was taking my newfound pallor and altered mental state – he'd actually taken his iPod earphones out, and they were dangling like silver tendrils down the front of his I Heart Tolkien T-shirt.

'What's up, Mum? You look terrible. Has there been an accident? Is it Lucy? Have you finally accepted you should have let that priest do the exorcism when you were up the duff?'

His lame attempt at humour both warmed my heart and made me feel even worse. I felt more tears welling up in my eyes, running down my face in big, fat, chocolaty drops, pooling under my chin and making my neck soggy.

I stared into space while the deluge continued, barely able to breathe between sobs, lovely Ollie patting my hand and looking slightly more hysterical with every passing moment.

He jumped up as he heard the front door slam – I don't think he'd have cared if it was a gas salesman, or a hooded figure carrying a scythe. It was the cavalry as far as he was concerned.

My own heart did an equally big jig – was it him? Was it Simon, coming home to tell me it had all been a mistake?

Telling me he was sorry? Telling me to forget all about it? I felt so impossibly weak, so impossibly broken by his proposed absence, that the thought of him walking back through that door was like being zapped by a defibrillator.

'What the fuck's going on here?' Lucy shrilled at us as she stormed into the living room. Not Simon after all. Someone much scarier.

Lucy is five foot eight, most of it legs, and does a very good storm. Hands on hips, she stared down at her weeping mother, fidgeting brother, and the tea towel smeared with the remains of mayo-on-sponge. She narrowed her eyes and threw her head back. Her hair didn't budge – probably because it was dyed midnight blue-black, straightened, and glued to her head with industrial-strength hairspray.

'Tash, Soph!' she yelled. 'Bugger off, will you? Mommy dearest is having some kind of spaz attack and I need to deal with the dramatics . . .'

I heard a very impolite sniggering from the hallway, and a slight creak of the door as the Devil's Daughters sneaked a peek at the crazy woman.

They might listen to a lot of songs about the unbearable agonies of stubbing your toe on a guitar amp, but they had no empathy with a real-life human being at all. They'd be more upset at missing an episode of *The Vampire Diaries* than seeing me in tears, and I'd known them since they were four. They departed in a fit of giggles.

Lucy looked down at me, not knowing quite how to behave for a change. Her usual loving approach – verbal abuse combined with facial representations of complete contempt

– normally served her well, but she was clearly a bit unsettled by all the tears.

'Okay, Mother, what's the big deal? I know this is probably just some stupid retarded midlife crisis, but I'll give you the benefit of the doubt – have you got cancer?'

Momentarily thrown by a worldview where having cancer was preferable to a midlife crisis, I managed to stop my sniffling and stem the torrential waterworks. Attagirl, Lucy.

'No, I haven't got cancer,' I said, feeling poor Ollie deflate slightly beside me with relief – he'd obviously feared something similar. But, unlike my darling daughter, he'd actually given a shit.

'It's your dad . . .'

'Has he got cancer?' interrupted Lucy, kicking her Converse-clad feet impatiently against the coffee table. She was dressed in leggings with black and purple hoops, and could have passed for the Wicked Witch of the West.

'And if he has got cancer, is it in some disgusting place like his testicles? Because I'm telling you now there is no way I am going to sit around listening to people discuss my dad's balls—'

'No, no, your dad's balls are fine . . . well, I suppose they are, I haven't seen them up close recently . . .'

'Oh, gross, Mum!' cried Ollie, making gagging gestures with his fingers in his throat and pretending to vomit. Lucy looked similarly disgusted at the mere mention of me in close proximity to her father's genitals. Clearly she preferred the theory that she had been hand-delivered by Satan's stork.

'Oh, just shut up, both of you!' I said. 'Your dad, and his testicles, are okay – but he's leaving us. No, that's not right.

Not us – me. He's leaving me. For a while. Just for a bit, while he gets his head together. I'm probably being dramatic for no reason. But . . . well, I only just found out. He told me today. Kind of. He e-mailed me today, actually—'

'Hang on a minute – did you say e-mail? Are you telling me he frigging *e-mailed* you to say he was doing a runner?' asked Lucy, incredulously.

'Yes, well, you know how busy he gets at work . . .'

'Oh for fuck's sake, Mum, *you*,' she replied, leaning down over the sofa and poking one of her fingers in my face so hard that I went cross-eyed, 'are such a loser! He *e-mails* you to say he's walking out and you justify it because he's busy? This isn't about him, it's about you. You're a doormat. You've got no backbone. You're just a human being made of fucking jelly. No wonder he left you – you probably bored him to death!'

Exit Lucy, stage left, in a cloud of sulphurous smoke. I could practically feel the ceiling shake as she stomped up the stairs to her room, slammed the door, and started blasting music so loudly through her speakers that nomadic tribespeople in Uzbekistan would be wondering where the party was and if they should bring a bottle.

Oh good. The Afterbirth again. My favourites.

Chapter 2

'Nobody else my arse,' said my sister-in-law Diane on the phone from Liverpool. 'There always is, Sal. It's rule number one in the big book of rules about men – they never, ever leave a woman unless there's someone else to go to, no matter how miserable they are. They treat their sex lives like a relay race – they always need to pass the baton . . .'

Phallic imagery aside, I knew she had a point. And Di should know. She was married to my brother Mark, who was pretty much the best of a bad bunch, but they'd really gone through the mill when they were younger. He'd had affairs. She'd had affairs. It got to the stage where they needed a PA to remind them of who was shagging who. Eventually all the mistresses and toy boys became a burden, and they decided to have an affair with each other instead. Two decades on, they're still married, so they must have done something right.

It was the day after my exciting e-mail treat, and the kids were handling it about as well as could be expected. Lucy was out, probably scaring toddlers in the local park as she sat having a fag in the playground with the Demon Twins. Ollie was upstairs in his room, playing Lords of Legend online.

And Simon was due to come round any minute.

'But he says he needs to find himself, Di. Don't you think there could be some truth in that? We've all been so busy for so long since the kids came along, and there's his work. What if he genuinely just needs a bit of time and space?'

'Yeah, right,' she snorted, 'of course. Let's face it, Sal, any man who spends as much time in front of the mirror as Simon does shouldn't have any problem with finding himself. And, as for his work, are we supposed to feel sorry for him because he's successful? That could've been you if things had worked out differently. I know you wouldn't be without the kids – well, not Ollie anyway – but if Mr Lover Lover Man hadn't got you knocked up when you were still a student, you'd be a doctor too.

'He couldn't have done everything he has without you at home backing him up. So don't give me that "finding myself" crap. Take my word for it, he's got some little tart he's shacking up with who gives him seven blow jobs a day and treats him like God. I know it's not really in your nature, but you need to find your inner bitch. He deserves it for dumping you by e-mail.'

'I know,' I said, 'I keep thinking I might have missed something and opening it again . . . For a while I convinced myself it wasn't real, it was some kind of freaky spam . . . Anyway, better go – he'll be here soon. Thanks for all the advice and I'll try to stay tough, okay?'

'Okay, love, you do that – and you better not have ironed those bloody shirts!'

I put the phone down, still marvelling at the thought of a woman who had the time – never mind the oral dexterity

– to give seven blow jobs a day. How would that even be possible? She'd have to go to work with him, and live under his desk. And it could be really distracting when he was in surgery – she'd have to scrub in, and even then I'm not sure it would be hygienic . . .

Had Simon and I ever reached those levels of sexual athleticism? Maybe – but if we had, we'd been too drunk to notice. I was only twenty-one when we met, and sex at that age is all about enthusiasm, not expertise. And, in our case, it was also all about the contraception. Or lack thereof. Before long I was puking my guts up on morning rounds at St Sam's, realising I was pregnant with the blob of cells that would become Lucy. She was a lot less trouble then.

I spent the next four weeks vomiting. Simon spent the next four weeks planning our wedding – or at least his mother did, as soon as she found out what was going on. She was a force to be reckoned with and we weren't left much choice. Within minutes of peeing on the pregnancy test, she told us when and where we'd be getting married. I was too tired to care really, and Simon – well, he'd come from money, and respectability, and having a bastard child in his twenties was never going to be part of the plan.

Up until now I thought we'd made the right choices. For everything I'd given up, I'd gained tenfold. A good man, two healthy children, a nice home. It was more than most people got, and I'd been content. On the whole.

But maybe I'd got it all wrong. Maybe I should have spent more time getting blow-job lessons at the local College of Sex. Seven times a day? Really, was it possible?

Simon had texted me to say he'd be round at eleven, so he must be taking a break from his BJ schedule for at least an hour. He was always on time for everything; it was a point of pride with him, so I had exactly ten minutes left. Ten minutes left to rehearse speeches I knew wouldn't come out right, as I didn't have a clue how his side of the script went. I didn't know if Diane was right about there being someone else, or how I'd cope with it if there was.

I'd got up early, exhausted after a disjointed and dream-ridden night's semi-sleep. My eyes were swollen and stinging from fatigue and tears. I'd walked the dog, cried, had a shower, cried, done the ironing, cried, and had a Force Ten row with Lucy, all before calling Diane. I'd also tried on three different outfits and rearranged my hair several times before giving up in disgust. I mean, where are the style guides on How To Look Good Dumped? Or What Not To Wear While Confronting Your Probably Cheating Husband? You never see that on bloody telly, and I bet it's not just me who needs it.

Physically, I'm not in bad nick considering I am, as my kids charmingly put it, 'halfway to dead', but I'm definitely at the stage in life where the perfection of youth is a distant memory.

I'm in a gym, but in all honesty the only pounds I lose are from my bank balance. I had been hopeful that the sheer effort of carrying round a membership card in my purse would reinstate me to my size ten glory days, but apparently not. What a con.

I still fit into a size fourteen, or at least most of me does. But I have a wobbly blancmange tummy that never left after childbirth, and my derrière is, diplomatically speaking, comfortable. My boobs are too big for their own good, and need an awful lot of help from a very strong push-up bra fairy. I'd 'let myself go', as my gran might have said.

Eventually, after a load of fretting that did nothing but get me hot and bothered, my hair had ended up in its usual slightly unruly shoulder-length bob, and I stuck with jeans and a T-shirt. I had no idea what to go for – seductive, dignified, aloof? All I felt was shattered and confused. And I knew the fact that I was focusing so hard on clothes and preparations was just a way of avoiding the ugly truth: the fact that my marriage, and life as I knew it, could be over.

I heard the key in the door, accompanied by an inappropriately cheery 'Hello!' as Simon arrived and let himself in.

He was wearing a pair of new jeans – at least jeans I'd never seen before. Skin-tight on the thighs and boot cut. His fair hair was styled slightly differently, swept straight back and gelled rather than parted in his traditional 'trust me I'm a doctor' look. And he smelled – a lot. Of some quite powerful cologne or aftershave that he'd never used around the house. He looked younger, and cooler, and actually pretty damn handsome. It was him – but not him. It was his sexier evil twin.

'You're having an affair with some little tart who gives you seven blow jobs a day and treats you like God, aren't you?' I said immediately.

I just knew – from the second he walked into the room, I could tell. It wasn't only the new style and the new smell – it was the new swagger.

He was trying desperately to hold a serious and sympathetic expression on his face, but I could see it there in his eyes: a newfound confidence, self-belief . . . happiness, I suppose. The bastard.

He sat down next to me on the sofa, taking my hand in his and looking at me with that same sympathy. The look I'd seen on his professional face so many times over the years. The one that said: 'I am the bearer of bad news, but don't worry, I'm here for you.'

'Don't lie, Simon – I can see it all over you. There's somebody else, so don't deny it. How long has it been going on?'

'Oh, Sal,' he said, 'I'm so sorry . . . I never wanted to hurt you, I really didn't . . . I wasn't looking for this. It just happened. We've drifted apart so much in recent years. I honestly don't think you're happy either . . .'

I slapped his hand away and looked straight ahead. I couldn't bear to see that sparkle he was trying to hide, the way he was sad about destroying me, but unbearably happy for himself. The emotional conundrum of the newly freed male.

'What do you mean you weren't looking for it? Did you accidentally fall into another woman's vagina, then?'

'There's no need to be crude about it, Sal; it's not like that! It's not just the sex . . .' – the never-ending, headboard-pounding, scream-out-loud sex, I added in my own mind's eye – 'it's more than that. I'm in love with her. You have to believe me when I say I'd never do anything to intentionally make you suffer, or the kids. I wouldn't be doing this if it weren't serious. But I just couldn't go on like we were any more. You must know what I mean!'

Uhm . . . no, actually. I'd been perfectly happy the way things were. Or, at least, definitely not unhappy. I obviously had a much higher boredom threshold than he did, and significantly lower expectations of how exciting family life in the suburbs was supposed to be. Simon, though, seemed to mean what he was saying, and appeared confused that I didn't 'get it' – he genuinely thought we'd both been unhappy, that this was somehow inevitable or necessary, a natural progression rather than a thunderbolt from the blue.

'So who's the lucky woman then?' I asked, focusing on the mistress straight away. The other issues – the fact that he'd seen our marriage in a totally different way to me – were too complicated to tackle just then. The fact that he was shagging someone else was, in a twisted way, more palatable.

Even as I spoke, I recognised that my tone of voice could curdle milk. I sounded like a bitter old hag, and might as well buy seven cats and stop washing right now.

'Her name is Monika,' he replied, intonating the name with such reverence that he could have been talking about the Virgin Mary. Except not in this case, it would seem, unless the Blessed Mother had taken a very unexpected turning in life. 'We met in a . . . in a hospitality venue I visited when I was on that Ortho conference in London in March.'

'The one you said was full of cranky old men talking about hip replacements over their peppered steak? And what's a "hospitality venue" anyway? Is it double-speak for a pub or a . . .'

The light slowly dawned as he started to shuffle slightly nervously next to me, casting his eyes down for the first time.

'A strip club? A strip club. You're running off with a fucking stripper. My God, Simon – could you *be* any more predictable? You're giving up your wife, your home, your kids and your bloody dog, all for the sake of someone who shakes her tits for a living?'

His head snapped up again, and I could see I'd hit a nerve. 'She's not just some slapper, you know! Back in Latvia she was training at catering school, then the opportunity came up to travel to London. She's a really intelligent girl, I'm sure she'll do very well for herself once she goes back to college!'

'In Latvia? Back to college? Please tell me you mean as a mature student . . . how old is she?'

A beat of silence. He didn't want to tell me. This was going to be bad – very bad.

'HOW OLD IS SHE?' I yelled in his face.

'Nineteen,' he mumbled, jerking his head back in shock, 'she's nineteen, all right? But that means nothing. Where she's come from, that's mature. She's been through more than most people have already. It's not easy growing up in Latvia, you know. There wasn't much money, no jobs, no way out. She needed—'

'She needed a really stupid man, Simon, that's what she needed. A really stupid man with a bit of money and his brains in his balls. And it looks like she got exactly that. It's pathetic . . . Ollie and Lucy are losing their father because you can't keep it in your pants? Have you any idea how much this is going to hurt them?'

'But it won't,' he replied, edging away from my anger. 'They'll understand, even if you don't. They're older now

– we've done a good job raising them. They've had a solid start in life, and they don't need us to be together for their sakes any more. They'll know I deserve a chance to be happy and in love – and so do you. And there's no problem with the house – obviously you'll keep that for as long as you all need it – or with money. I'll make sure you're all provided for . . .'

I was momentarily struck dumb by his use of the phrase 'together for their sakes'. Was that how he'd been feeling? Is that what our marriage had been? Had I been so stupid I hadn't noticed – or was Simon rewriting our history to justify current actions he must be ashamed of, deep down?

It was as though I was talking to a stranger – and one who certainly didn't understand at least one of his children.

'If you think for a minute that Lucy is going to accept this in any way,' I said, 'you're even dumber than you look in those sprayed-on jeans. She'll hate you for it. And I don't blame her.'

I don't know how he'd expected this conversation to go, but I was clearly not reacting the way he'd expected. He looked almost afraid as my voice rose. He stood up, retreating by several steps and taking refuge by the bay window – presumably so he'd have witnesses if I whacked him round the head with a paperweight.

'Don't worry, Simon, you're not worth it. If I'm not what you want any more, that's your choice. Before you came here today I was really hoping we could patch things up. That we could put things right – that I could try and be more like you want me to be. But without the aid of a time machine, that's obviously not going to happen. I can't believe you're leaving me for someone who's not much older than your own daughter. We've gone through all these years together and you throw it away like it means nothing . . .'

My quieter tone calmed him, and he took a step forward, holding out his hands in supplication. How could somebody so familiar, so beloved, suddenly be a complete alien? I suppose we'd taken each other so much for granted over the years that it seemed unbelievable that anything could change. Now here he was in front of me, as a totally different person. Amazing what the love of a bad woman can do for a man.

I wanted to kill him, and spit on his bleeding corpse. And I wanted him to take me in his arms and tell me he'd stay, that everything was going to be all right. I wanted the whole damn mess to just go away. I wanted my husband back. I wanted to sleep for ever. The shock of it all was starting to really kick in, and I didn't know where to put myself. The anger of my words was real – but the changing landscape of my future life was now becoming a hideous reality, a poisonous shift that I could do nothing to control or avoid.

'I'm sorry, Sal,' he said, sounding genuinely regretful. 'If there was anything I could do to make you feel better, I would . . . but I belong with Monika now. If I don't try and make a go of this, I'll never forgive myself – and I won't be much use here with you, either.'

I gulped back the sobs I could feel coming. I needed to weep and wail and beg God to help me, but that was between me and the Almighty. I'd never forgive myself if I broke down in front of Simon.

'You'd better go then,' I said, waving him towards the door. 'Leave the keys behind. Call to arrange a time to see the kids.

Your bag's in the hall. And yes, I did pack your five freshly ironed work shirts.'

With five freshly burned holes through the backs, I silently added. But he didn't need to discover that until Monday morning, did he?

Chapter 3

Oxford is a beautiful city. Full of beautiful people, leading beautiful lives. On a good day it's an inspiring place to be; surrounded by ancient, ivy-clad colleges, woodland walks, quaint bookshops and the sense of being somewhere truly special.

This, however, was not one of those good days. I'd driven into town with Lucy, planning to do some shopping, but we'd almost come to blows within minutes of arriving at the Covered Market. She wanted her nose pierced. I said no. She said I was a boring bitch. I said thank you very much Lucy and headed for the Ben's Cookies stall. She stomped along behind me, knocking dangling pigeons out of the way as we passed the butchers' stands, sizzling with fury.

Erring on the side of caution, I went for the ten-cookie box – you can never have too much chocolate chip in a time of crisis. I passed one to Lucy, hoping it might shut her up for a minute, and wandered over to a stall that was selling fresh lardy cake and tiffin as well.

'For God's sake, you're disgusting,' she said, attractively spitting out tiny chunks of chocolate as she hissed at me. 'All you do these days is eat. So he's gone – so fucking what? Did it ever occur to you that eating yourself to death might not be the answer? It's all your fault anyway . . .'

This was a rehashed version of one of her very favourite theme tunes of the last few weeks – a catchy ditty known as 'You Drove Him Away (You Stupid Selfish Cow)'. She launched loudly into an extended remix, and I noticed small crowds of backpacked tourists edging around her nervously, as though she was a terrorist attack in Emo form – a weapon of mass destruction who could go off at any minute, taking all our eardrums with her.

'And anyway,' she screeched, crumpling up her cookie wrapper and throwing it on the floor, 'it's all so fucking embarrassing! Why did he have to bugger off with some teeny trollopy Iron Curtain whore, for fuck's sake? My mates will piss themselves laughing when they hear about it! Why couldn't he just shag his secretary like any other self-respecting middle-aged fuck-up?'

I often wonder why my kids are so foul-mouthed. I'm not. Very. But Lucy is in the Premier League when it comes to swearing. We were called into school when she was six because she called the dinner lady a 'bastarding shit' for giving her beans instead of spaghetti hoops. When she was forced to apologise she said, 'I'm fucking sorry', kicked me in the shin, and ran away laughing. Simon always blamed the Liverpool side of my family, and he may be right. I suspect those Scouse Irish genes definitely play a part in it.

She was still going great guns, lecturing me on how I was a bloated pig, a nightmare to live with, and completely bereft of any redeeming qualities. For her finishing touch she told me, and the other few hundred people in the market that Saturday afternoon, that a blow-up doll had more personality than I did and was probably better in bed, too. Nice. I can't say it didn't hurt, but I understand the way Lucy ticks – loudly, and like a bomb about to blow.

She was missing her dad and hurting like hell and, short of kicking the dog, which would contravene her moral code, Ollie and I were the only victims in sight. Ollie didn't listen, and occasionally punched her in the kidneys anyway, so she was wary of him. I did listen, and as a responsible adult tried to avoid the kidney-punching thing, so I made a much better target.

I let her finish, then pointed at the wrapper on the floor. 'Pick that up and find a bin,' I said quietly, walking away. I heard her scream – full throttle – in the background. Priceless glass *objets d'art* probably shattered across the city, and shocked poodles in parks covered their ears with their paws.

'I'm going home!' she yelled after me, oblivious to the mounting concern of nearby stallholders, and strode off. Hopefully in the direction of the bus stops on Cornmarket, but entirely possibly to the nearest stockist of voodoo dolls, air rifles or nose piercings.

I clenched my eyes against tears, and reminded myself for the millionth time that she didn't mean it. Most of it. That I was the grown-up, the mother, and no matter how much I was crumbling inside, she was hurting too.

It might have been stress-induced psychosis on her part, but she was right about one thing at least – it was time to stop seeking solace in the biscuit barrel. I've never been the kind of person who loses her appetite due to heartbreak. I'm far more likely to go the other way. At tough times in my life, a multipack of Penguins has often been my only friend. If I carried on like this, I'd put on masses of weight, be the size of two Latvian lap-dancers, and feel even worse about myself than I did already.

Since Monika-gate broke, Lucy had, predictably enough, refused to see her father, and had given no consideration at all to meeting the new love of his life. Or the 'teeny trollopy whore', as she affectionately called her.

Ollie had done both and, bless him, reported back hilariously on how Dad was now dressing in Bart Simpson T-shirts and pink Crocs in an attempt to look younger. I'd tried hard not to pump him for too much information, but he's a bright boy – he gave me a full run-down before I had the chance to even consider interrogating him. 'Mum,' he said, 'I can't lie – she's not a munter. In fact she's pretty fit, if I'm honest, which feels wrong when your dad's holding her hand. But she talks weird – like a Russian villain in a spy film. With this really deep voice. So there's always the chance that she's actually a man and Dad just hasn't discovered her internal willie yet.'

Which I must admit I found strangely comforting.

I wandered along Turl Street and out on to the High, narrowly avoiding a collision with a pack of cyclists waging guerrilla warfare on pedestrians. No, this definitely wasn't one of those good days in Oxford. It was the new Oxford, setting for the new me, and my new, vastly unimproved life. The one where I felt completely and utterly alone, adrift in a sea of misery.

In fact, all the beautiful people and the beautiful buildings were just making me feel worse. For the first time I could understand the urge to take a semi-automatic weapon, climb the stairs of St Mary's Church tower, and just let rip.

I stopped outside the travel agent's, looking at the offers in the window. We hadn't booked anything for this year. Simon had been reluctant to commit to our usual two weeks in France. He said he was getting bored of it. Now I knew he wasn't just bored of France. He was bored of his entire life. He'd been gone for six weeks now – which equated to 294 blow jobs by my reckoning. That probably made things a bit less boring for him.

For me, it had been a torment of tedium combined with near paralysing anxiety. Six weeks of yo-yoing between 'I can do this' and utter desperation. Six weeks of total loneliness. Six weeks of watching mindless TV and doing household chores and wearing false smiles; my heart leaping every time the phone rang or the door was opened. Just in case he'd come home. Of worrying about the kids and worrying about me and worrying about a future I couldn't quite get a hold of.

Six weeks of total crap, in all honesty.

Maybe, I thought, I needed a holiday too.

Ollie had told me his dad and Monika were heading off to Ibiza for a week. Clubbing in San Antonio. The thought of Simon waving his forty-one-year-old hands in the air and blowing a fluorescent whistle at a beachfront rave was one of the few things that had made me crack a smile in recent days. A lesser woman than I would hope he'd overdose on E and get trampled to death by a tranny in platform heels.

The door pinged as I wandered in, and I sat down, plonking the cookie box on the seat next to me. My new life-partner.

'How can I help you today?' said the sales assistant, who had 'Nikki' printed on her name badge. Nikki had disconcertingly huge bleached-blond hair, and skin that looked like it had been marinated overnight in a vat of Bisto.

'I'm looking for a holiday,' I replied. 'I'm not quite sure what, but something special. We all need a really special holiday. So knock yourself out, Nikki – anywhere in the world, anything at all. Money,' I added, safe in the knowledge that I still had access to Simon's credit card, 'is no object.'

'Well, that's the kind of challenge we thrive on in the travel consultancy business!' she said, keeping a straight face. I was about to laugh but then I realised she meant it.

Her fingers started to fly over her keyboard, her face frowning in concentration. She was murmuring to herself as she worked; a steady subconscious flow that sounded something along the lines of 'Yes! No! All booked up! No availability there . . . maybe . . . possibly . . . Ebola virus outbreak . . . border control . . . diamond mines . . . mosquito nets . . .'

'Stop!' I said, leaning over the desk to break her concentration. I had visions of ending up on a camel-back tour of Alaska or blue-tailed-skink-watching in Cameroon.

'When I said *anything*, what I actually mean is a holiday with a beach. A swimming pool. Cocktails. Possibly the opportunity to do "Macarena"-style Euro-pop dances with waiters in restaurants. Lots of activities for the kids. Other teenagers, but nobody too scary who might teach them how to use flick knives or get one of them pregnant. And somewhere I can get a tan just like yours.'

Her face froze like a teak mask, clearly unhappy at this dull change of direction.

'Well, my tan comes from the Boots in Summertown, but I presume you're looking for somewhere a bit further afield than that?'

Suitably chastised for my lack of adventurous spirit, I watched her manicured nails go back into overdrive. Occasionally she paused to ask me a question, like how old the kids were (easy), if they liked water sports (um . . . possibly) and if I was into tennis (yes, if it involves watching men in tight white shorts at Wimbledon).

After what felt like a lifetime of waiting and watching, she finally looked up from her screen, a brilliant smile breaking out on her face. She had great teeth too – I wondered if they were from Boots as well but didn't dare ask.

'I've got it. It's in Turkey, and there are just two inter-connecting rooms left. Very nice, exclusive resort – lots of planned activities for young people, like sailing, windsurfing, water-skiing, as well as for adults. Tennis lessons. Golf if you want it. Beauty treatments, spa. If you don't mind me saying, you look a bit tired – I think this is just what you need. A perfect holiday.'

She was right. I was tired. And more than a bit . . . A perfect holiday.

Now, that sounded even better than another cookie.

PART TWO

Turkey – The Big 4-0

Chapter 4

'You mean to tell me there's no fucking hairdryer in this dump?' said Lucy, stalking round our rooms as though she'd just been stranded on a landfill site and told to lick old tins of cat food for tea. 'You told me there would be!'

'I'm sure there is, somewhere, Luce, I'll look later . . .' I answered, puffing a bit as I dragged the suitcases through the door. Ollie followed, hefting the biggest case into the corner and kicking it straight.

'I've got a solution, Lucy,' he said. 'When you've washed your hair, go down to the kitchens and stick your bloody head in the microwave.'

He accompanied this with a mime of a skull exploding.

'Ha-fucking-ha,' she said, falling backwards on to the bed and declaring she was exhausted.

I sat next to her, glancing around – two interconnecting rooms, one with a double bed for me, and the other with two singles for Lucy and Ollie. An en-suite for each, with walk-in showers big enough to live in. Whitewashed walls, wrought-iron headboards, pretty blue bedspreads, and views

33

over a sparkling turquoise bay. All of which would be worth nothing if Lucy didn't find a hairdryer soon.

As I leaned down to unzip my case, I realised that either my ears were still dodgy from the flight, or the luggage was buzzing. I walked up closer to it, straining my ears to listen, telling the kids to shut up.

'This case is buzzing . . .' I said, cautiously flipping over the name tag with one finger. Mr and Mrs Smith of Solihull, it read. Which was odd, as I was expecting it to say Mrs Summers of Oxford. I said as much out loud, and Lucy instantly snapped out of her catatonia.

'You picked up the wrong case, you fucking idiots!' she declared, jumping up with more energy than she'd shown in the last year and dashing to her own luggage to inspect it. 'But that's okay! Phew! It doesn't matter, panic over – at least you got mine right!'

'And mine,' added Ollie after checking. 'Looks like it's just you with the buzzing luggage, Mum. Should we call the bomb squad or something?'

'It's probably just one of Mum's vibrators – imagine them giving an armed escort to a Rampant Rabbit!' sniggered Lucy, loving every moment now she knew her straighteners were safe.

'I do *not* own a vibrator!' I snapped back, prodding the case with my toes to see if the buzzing stopped, 'although maybe I'll buy one when I get back, seeing as your dad has opted out of active service on that front, and I'm not quite dead yet!'

Silence from both offspring at that comment – a double-whammy reminder of the fact that not only had their father left, but their mother had sexual needs. Guaranteed killer.

I decided to open the case. It was probably just an electric shaver that had been switched on by accident or something. The bags had been through the wars, and had sat out in the sun for a lot longer than they should have while the baggage handlers enjoyed a second cup of coffee. I mean, how weird could a Mr and Mrs Smith from Solihull be?

'Yeuuw!' yelled Lucy, jumping away as I opened the lid.

'Gross!' added Ollie, so shocked he took several steps back.

'Shit!' I said, as it was the only word I could remember. The pungent aroma of overheated rubber and sweaty plastic wafted up from the case, making us all wrinkle our noses in disgust. It was like being held face-down in a ball pool after a couple of toddlers had vomited in it.

Inside Mr and Mrs Smith's suitcase was a dazzling display of sex toys. I mean, dozens of them. A stash easily big enough to start their own shop, or at least a well-stocked market stall. As the smell cleared, the three of us stared down at the contents.

Even at first glance, I could see cock rings, dildos, vibrators, whips, baby-pink butt plugs and items in gaudy cardboard boxes promising a real kinkorama. There was a Make Your Own Vagina moulding kit, some actually rather attractive-looking red vibrating pants, and a blow-up doll called Suck-Me-Dry Sally.

Ollie reached out and picked one of the boxes up, eyeing the cover photo with interest. 'Fake Pussy,' he read from the blurb. 'This pussy ain't too fussy, let it stroke your cock for the purr-fect orgasm . . .'

'Give me that!' I shrieked, grabbing it out of his hands and throwing it back into the case. Lucy, in the meantime, had lifted what looked like a tramp-red lipstick and was snorting away as she informed us that it was, in fact, a Clit Stick. Which are not words you want to hear coming from your sixteen-year-old daughter's mouth. I made a lunge for that as well, but she'd already pocketed it.

I had no idea who Mr and Mrs Smith were, but if they'd ended up with my bag, then somewhere in Turkey they were currently crying with disappointment. There was nothing more stimulating in it than a pile of trashy novels and swim-suits with control panels in the tummies. Not much that could compete with his-'n'-hers Hole Lot of Fun vibro-sticks, that's for sure.

The suitcase switch also presented some very practical problems – like the fact that I had no clothes other than the ones I was standing up in. And they were in such a state, they could probably stand up without me.

Jeans, Timberland boots and a fleece sweatshirt might not be unreasonable for four a.m. in England, but in Turkey I was likely to boil to death and die if I couldn't find an alternative.

I was already so hot and bothered I thought I might faint at a moment's notice – although that might also have been a delayed reaction to seeing the Black Beauty Joy Rider in its nine-inch glory.

I needed a shower, fresh clothes, and a glass of something very cold and very alcoholic. Not necessarily in that order. On cue, Lucy grabbed her suitcase, walked into her room, and clicked the lock shut.

'No,' she shouted, 'you can't borrow any of my clothes – you're too fat, and it's your fault I don't have a hairdryer . . .'

Chapter 5

There was a stunned silence as I walked into the Blue Bay Hotel's poolside bar to catch the last few minutes of our welcome meeting.

The rep's voice trailed off to a stammering standstill, and a gentle murmur of surprise did a noticeable Mexican wave around my fellow holiday-makers.

As I sat down, I was feeling decidedly nervous. Even under normal circumstances – without lost suitcases and the sudden appearance of sex aids – I wasn't used to doing this kind of thing on my own.

Every holiday I'd been on for the last seventeen years had been with Simon. Simon was good at social situations. He was charming and confident and always completely at home in a room full of strangers. I usually got away with being the support act, something I had rather pathetically mastered over the years. Now I was on a steep learning curve to becoming Miss Independent, and I can't say I was enjoying the climb that much.

I'd been left with two options – staying cooped up in the hotel with two surly teenagers waiting for a stray suitcase to turn up. Or finding an alternative way forward. I had things to do, people to meet. I wanted to sign up for sailing lessons, take mountain-bike rides through the hills and perfect my serve. It was kill or cure – either I'd simultaneously find my inner strength and lose a stone, or I'd drop dead of a heart attack.

More to the point, I wanted to go downstairs because I was absolutely gagging for a drink – it had been a long day. Travelling is never easy, but doing it mid-marriage collapse and accompanied by the alien beings known as teenagers is torturous.

After a few wardrobe malfunctions and a lot of swearing, I eventually found something I thought I could live with, and made my way downstairs into the midday heat. It wasn't the perfect outfit choice, but it covered my bits at least.

I sat alone; glancing around, I saw that every other table was filled with smiling couples and their children. Children who didn't hate their parents. Husbands who hadn't run off with Latvian lap-dancers.

More to the point, they were all dressed in nice, normal clothes. Colourful swimwear, sarongs, shorts, bright T-shirts – nothing more outrageous than a straw hat at a rakish angle. Their suitcases had obviously been packed by smart-casual beachwear experts.

Mine, on the other hand, had been packed by a pair of perverts from the West Midlands – which explained why I was wearing a Naughty Nurse Nancy costume, complete with shiny white plastic miniskirt and a name tag that said 'Sister Slut'.

All in all, it was a less than perfect start to my allegedly perfect holiday.

Chapter 6

As the meeting ended, I stayed put at the table for a minute until I took the first few mouthfuls of my gin and tonic.

The bar was surrounded by a luscious loop of garden, dripping with riotously coloured flowers and fringed with broad-leaved palm trees that edged down to the beach. I could see right out to sea from where I was sitting. The midday sun was blazing down, and the waves rippled gently into the horseshoe-shaped bay.

Out on the water I could see windsurfers and sailors bobbing around in the distance. Idyllic. If only I wasn't dressed like a comedy prostitute, it would be perfect.

As soon as I felt confident enough, I flip-flopped my way across the garden and over to the water's edge. It was lined with a pristine row of sun loungers, each with its own umbrella.

It's quite hard to gracefully arrange yourself into a horizontal position when you're wearing an outfit designed for swingers' parties. Even though other women were letting it all hang loose in string bikinis with bare boobs akimbo, for some reason I felt even more exposed than them.

At least I'd been able to borrow some of Ollie's flip-flops and dump the Timberlands. Lucy was no help, and very much enjoying it. Short of kicking the door in, there wasn't much I could do, except vow to get my revenge when we were home.

Ollie was far more willing to share but, much as I tried, I couldn't squeeze myself into the surfer shorts he offered. I couldn't even pull them up over my 'womanly' hips.

So here I was. Naughty Nurse Nancy catching a few rays. I was getting a bit itchy. And the top half – complete with a blue cross on the chest, presumably to show I was a medical professional – was rather too tight for comfort as well.

Still, I was caring less and less about that, and pretty much everything else, by the minute. The combination of sun, alcohol and hysteria was sluicing around to make me feel quite merry.

Before long I'd be up and dancing, leading a conga round the pool and flashing my matronly breasts at the waiters. Believe me, it had happened before. A few decades ago, to be fair, when my breasts were a lot more perky and the waiters a lot more interested. If I did a topless conga now I'd be in danger of breaking my own kneecaps.

I closed my eyes, loving the sensation of heat on my face. I listened to the lapping of the water as the tide crept in, and the occasional high-class horsey tones of the Sloane Ranger sailing instructors further along the shore. I was finally starting to relax, and wished very hard for another drink to magically appear next to me so I wouldn't have to run the gauntlet back to the bar.

'You look like you could do with one of these,' a woman's voice said, jolting me back to reality as she sat down on the lounger next to me. There were probably many things I looked like I could do with right then, including a mental-health assessment and a whole new wardrobe, but blessedly she was bearing a long tall glass clinking with ice and lime.

'Mehmet at the bar said you were on G&T. And possibly also some type of magic mushroom, but he was out of stock. I'm Allie, by the way. Allie Garrity.'

Allie was long and slim, maybe in her late forties, but clearly very fit and active. She had those lean yoga muscles in her arms and legs that went on for ever. Her hair was curly and cropped close to her head, and her gorgeous green eyes crinkled all around the edges as she smiled.

'Oh thanks! I can't tell you how much I appreciate that!' I said, almost salivating as I took the chill-frosted glass from her. 'Not that I'm an alcoholic or anything . . . but it's been the day from hell.'

'I thought so, from the amount you were drinking, and what you're wearing,' she replied, stretching out and turning on her side to face me, shading her eyes from the sun with her hand.

'Or maybe you always walk round half cut and dressed for an orgy – I'm not one to judge. It's caused quite a stir among the menfolk, though. My husband Mike's had to retire to his room for a cold shower. Men and their penises – show them a busty nurse and they all want to cry matron . . .'

'Oh my God,' I muttered, taking a quick restorative gulp of my drink. What a way to start my first holiday as a single mum.

'I don't know quite how to explain this,' I said, 'and it sounds ridiculous considering what I'm wearing, but this was the best I had. I got my suitcases mixed up. I've spoken to the airline and they've found mine, but it won't be here till tomorrow. All I had to wear was a really thick fleece and jeans, sticky and icky beyond belief. And you wouldn't believe the stuff that was in that case. Pervert's paradise.

'My other choices included a rubber dominatrix costume and a French maid thing I thought wasn't too bad, until I saw the six-inch black dildo in the front. I tried to pull it off but it wouldn't budge . . . but, well, yeah . . . with hindsight maybe I should have just used a bath towel, or done something less noticeable like come down stark naked doing the hand jive . . .'

Allie was quiet for a few moments. She was busy wiping the tears of laughter from her eyes, and snorting with hilarity. Sister Slut, stand-up comedian.

Once she'd stopped shaking with mirth, she said: 'Look, under the circumstances you probably made the right choice, and I'm sure it'll all seem hilarious one day. A crowd of us have been coming here for the last few years so I know a load of people. I'll ask around. You won't have to wear that all day, don't worry. Although the dildo thing could be fun in the buffet queue, I have to say . . . Where's the rest of your group, anyway? Is your hubbie hiding upstairs wearing arse-less lederhosen and nipple tassels?'

'No, although spookily enough, I think both those items are up there somewhere if you want to borrow them later. It was only my stuff that went missing,' I said. 'And, as for the rest of my group, well, that's another story. But as I had practically a whole bottle of gin in that last drink, I might as well tell you – my husband isn't here. He's fallen madly in love with a Latvian lap-dancer who's only three years older than our daughter. They're shacked up in what the papers would call a "love nest", three miles away from where we live, presumably having nonstop sex. The bastards.

'So tell the other women to lock up their menfolk, I'm here unchaperoned. I'm not technically on my own, but my kids are both teenagers, so I might as well be.'

'Yep, I know just what you mean,' she replied, seeming to take my tale of woe in her stride. Maybe this kind of thing was the norm where she came from. Maybe she was a marriage guidance counsellor. Maybe she was secretly shitfaced and hadn't taken in a word I'd said.

'Teenagers are like that,' she said. 'Mine's one of the good guys in private, but he still cringes every time I walk into the room, especially if he's with a girl he wants to impress – which seems to be all of them.

'I'm here with my husband,' she went on, 'the aforementioned Mike, and Max. He's seventeen, and if you keep that thing on, he'll probably try and seduce you with the first instalment of his six pack. He's very proud of it.

'But for a while I was on my own with him, so I know exactly how you feel. It's weird, isn't it? We split up when Max was twelve and I did the single-mum thing. Holidays are tough. It feels like you've sprouted two heads when you sit down for dinner and everyone else is in couples.'

'So what happened? Is this your second marriage?' I asked. We'd probably have swapped entire life stories by the time we finished our first drink together. It's a woman thing. Men can see each other in the same pub every night for thirty years and find out nothing more than what football club they support.

'Yes,' she said, 'second marriage, but to the same man. He saw the error of his wandering ways, and I still loved him. So we gave it another go; got married again the day after the decree absolute came through. Sometimes they need to know what they're losing before they realise how much they want it.'

That, of course, was only true if the man in question wasn't besotted with another woman. I didn't know if Simon would ever realise what he'd lost. At the moment he didn't seem to think he'd lost anything at all, other than a millstone round his neck. A burden of guilt that he was trying to carry: sending me odd enquiring texts, checking up on me, attempting to be mature despite his immature actions.

'But enough of all that, we're on holiday!' she said, seeing Mrs Glum take over my face. 'Try and forget all about your husband for a couple of weeks. Auntie Allie and her friends will look after you. You're not the only single parent here – you'll meet James later; he's been coming with his son on his own for years, and they love it. Max will help your kids settle in as well. He knows the place inside out. I think this year he's hoping to add a few more bars and clubs to his repertoire, though.'

She grimaced slightly with the last sentence – but in a mock-rueful way that showed she wasn't really stressed at all. I, on the other hand, was. If Lucy decided to discover the local bars, I'd have to learn the Turkish for 'how much is the bail?' fairly quickly.

'Oh God no – tell him to leave my daughter well alone, she won't appreciate it. She treats people who are nice like they have leprosy,' I said. 'I don't even defend her any more, and I gave birth to her. For a while I hoped it was just a phase, but I suspect it may actually be her personality.'

I could tell Allie wanted to protest, and declare her heart-felt belief that Lucy couldn't be all that bad – but we were spared my hysterical laughter by the sound of merriment approaching from the shore.

The noise level increased tenfold, as a miniature fleet of bright yellow kayaks headed in and beached right in front of us. It was a gang of kids and nannies, all dressed as pirates, with painted-on moustaches and colourful headdresses made of soggy cardboard.

An angelic-looking boy of about six or seven spotted Allie and ran over to her. He jumped on to her lap, soaking her to the skin and smudging black paint from his fake eye-patch on to her bikini top. She rubbed his halo of wild blond curls and gave him a quick kiss on the forehead.

'Wassup, Jake?' she asked, wiping some of the black goo out of his eyes with her fingertips.

'That's Pirate Captain Jake to you!' he shouted, leaping back down on to his bare feet and jigging about.

He looked me over with his big blue eyes.

'Who is this lady and why's she dressed so weird?' he asked Allie, his voice slipping out of his fake pirate lingo and into his own soft Irish accent.

'I'm Sally, and I'm a special pirate nurse,' I said, raising my eyebrows in what I hoped was a roguish fashion, but might have been more tipsy pantomime dame leering at Prince Charming in his tights.

'Well, the nurse at my school doesn't dress like that,' he answered.

'But she's not a pirate nurse. Bet she's just a landlubber who puts plasters on your knee and checks your hair for nits, isn't she?'

He thought about it.

'Yes,' he said, 'so . . . if you're a pirate nurse, are you wearing those plastic clothes because they're waterproof?'

I nodded – it was a better explanation than the real one, that's for sure.

'And because it's much easier to get all the blood off after a battle. It gets really messy when you have to chop off a leg or sew an ear back on. The worst is when eyeballs pop out, but at least if I'm wearing this, they just bounce straight off and I can catch them.'

He giggled a bit at the slightly scary references to gore and guts.

'That skirt is too short, though,' he said. 'You'd get blood on your knees. My daddy likes ladies in short skirts. He says it's very kind of them to let other people look at their legs in the summer, especially grumpy old men like him. One time last week in the shops there was this lady wearing a skirt a bit like yours, but with pointy white shoes that made her really tall, and he pushed our trolley right into a shelf of beans and they all fell off. He was really embarrassed and we pretended we wanted all the cans of beans in the trolley, even though I don't even like them—'

'Pirate Jake!' bellowed one of the pert blonde nannies. 'It's time to put away your paddle and get your ice cream!'

He whirled round to give me and Allie a final stab with his stick sword, then galloped off.

Hmmm. His dad was clearly an old lech, I thought, staring at hapless womenfolk in the shops. I made a mental note to avoid Jake's dad for the entirety of the holiday – an extra dose of sex maniac was something I could live without. Sex maniacs were at the heart of all my current problems.

His son, though, was a real cutie. It didn't seem so long ago that Lucy and Ollie were that age, so responsive and playful. These days they'd sell me into white slavery for a £20 iTunes gift card.

I'd been down here for over an hour, and had no idea what they were up to. I nervously did a quick check over my shoulder. The hotel looked peaceful. Its whitewashed walls were still standing. No smoke, no sirens, nobody running out of the building screaming and looking for holy water.

They must still be in their rooms, then.

Chapter 7

Allie took us both off to the restaurant for lunch, steering us towards a table for four. A waiter held a bottle of water for us, opening it with as much aplomb as you would a vintage Bollinger.

'That's Adnan, the head waiter,' said Allie, leaning forward to whisper conspiratorially as he left, 'he's got twelve kids . . . that he knows of.'

'Bloody hell!'

Our scurrilous gossip was interrupted by the arrival of an elderly lady, who stopped at our table and greeted Allie enthusiastically. She was so short and round that she could have passed as a garden gnome. A garden gnome who'd been kicked out of Gnomeland for having terrible dress sense and making the other gnomes look bad.

Head to toe she was dressed in a shade of pink so vivid I could feel it burning holes in my retinas. Her dimpled knees were peeking out beneath the hem of her shorts, and her freakishly small feet were encased in pink socks and pink trainers.

Little Miss Pink's hair was short and snowy white, tightly permed around a tanned and deeply wrinkled face.

'My, my, my! What an interesting outfit you have on, my dear!' she said, in a delicate Scottish accent. Yes, well. She had a point. So much for critiquing her look.

'Miss McTavish!' exclaimed Allie. 'Come and join us for lunch – this is Sally. She's just arrived and she's here with her kids.'

'Och, no husband?' she asked, as she sat down. Her plump pink derrière spilled over both sides of the chair until it was completely subsumed. It looked like she was floating unaided in front of the table, like a levitating pink blancmange.

'Dressed laike that and unchaperoned? How very ad*ven*turous of you, Sally! I like your style already – you'll have to tell me how you get on with all these fit young hunks!'

She chuckled disturbingly as she helped herself to a breadstick, inserted it into her puckered mouth and started to suck on it. I closed my eyes for a second and hoped the image would go away one day.

I wasn't here for fit young hunks, or overheated body parts, or sharing sex tips with the Incredible Glowing Granny. Admittedly from the looks of things she had a better love life than I did, but that applied just as well to Trappist monks who'd taken vows of celibacy. I'd given up on men. I was going to turn into a sexless old woman who wore beige cardigans and got her kicks from walking really slowly over zebra crossings.

'Sorry to disappoint you, Miss McTavish, but there won't be any of that going on. I'll be living like a nun for the next two weeks.'

'Now then, that would be an entirely different costume, wouldn't it? Maybe a spot of leather for that one, with a matching rosary for whipping naughty bottoms?' she said, her blue eyes twinkling with mischief.

Allie and I stared at her, rendered speechless, as she continued to fellate her breadstick.

'But if you're sticking to the quiet life, dearie, won't you be a wee bit lonely?' she asked, when we didn't respond.

It was a semi-serious question, and not one I was prepared to answer honestly. Because yes, I was lonely. And more than a wee bit. I felt it every time I looked at a couple holding hands. I felt it every time I saw a couple bickering. I felt it every time I saw some harassed-looking bloke putting the bins out, and every time I woke up in the morning and every time I went to sleep at night.

I felt it pretty much all of the time, in fact, which I didn't even want to admit to myself. I'd been married to the same man for seventeen years and had fully expected that to continue until one of us popped our clogs. I was so lonely I might sink in a sea of despair if I even let myself acknowledge it. I was functioning purely on autopilot, and flying straight into turbulence.

'Of course not,' I lied, 'I'll be too busy to be lonely, and I'm looking forward to spending some quality time with my children.'

Assuming they'd had personality transplants, I added silently.

Right on cue I saw Ollie and Lucy walking towards the restaurant. The need for sustenance must have driven them out into the wild to hunt.

Ollie was wearing those surfer shorts I hadn't been able to fit into earlier. They hung so low on his bony hips you could see the waistband of his almost-as-low boxers peeping out.

Lucy was in a black bikini top and black shorts. Her dyed hair was swinging loose on her shoulders and most of her face was hidden by huge dark sunglasses. I knew she'd be coated in factor 50 to maintain the ghostly white skin tone she was aiming for.

'Lucy! Ollie!' I shouted, standing up and waving my arms frantically.

Ollie grinned and waved back, meandering between the tables towards us. Lucy paused to think about it for a second then followed. She stopped a few feet behind him, facing in the opposite direction to avoid any meaningful social interaction.

'Hello, darling!' I said, hugging Ollie tightly to me and holding on so hard he couldn't pull away. I was totally over-egging the pudding to show Nympho Gnome that, far from being lonely, I was in fact a woman cherished and adored and held precious at the heart of a loving family unit.

'Do you two want to join us for lunch?' I asked, praying furiously to whichever god would listen that they needed cash – the only possible reason Lucy would give me the time of day. There was usually a sliding scale of civility depending on how much she needed.

Seconds after the words tumbled out I remembered that Simon had bunged them both a small fortune in guilt money before we left. They probably had more spare cash than I did. I could almost hear the coffin lid slamming shut on my fantasy image of normal family life.

Lucy swivelled her head slowly towards me, propping her shades up on to her hair and staring at me with narrowed, reptilian eyes. She looked like one of those Velociraptors that eats everyone in *Jurassic Park*. I stayed very still and hoped she wouldn't hone in on my heat signature.

'Why the fuck would I want to do that, Nurse Nancy? Does it look like I've suffered brain damage in the last hour? Why don't you give me a real holiday treat, and not speak to me for the next two fucking weeks, all right?'

Chapter 8

Following that latest in a long line of humiliations, I retreated to the pool. I was getting used to the feeling now. So my daughter disowned me in public? No big deal. I'd been through worse in the last few weeks and the party wasn't even over yet.

I probably had a divorce to look forward to, or Simon announcing he was becoming the father of Latvia's first ever naturally conceived sextuplets. I could picture him now, earnestly discussing his amazing virility on Eastern Europe's version of *Richard and Judy*. I was so punch drunk, I didn't even react when Lucy delivered one of her southpaw specials.

Reverting to my usual coping mechanism, I'd taken a small plate of treats from the lunch buffet to console me. Turkish delight. Yum. That was definitely going to help me lose the extra few pounds I'd gained. Despite the self-loathing, I still couldn't stop myself eating it. Food had been my only consolation since Simon left, and even though I could see the damage I was doing, I couldn't stop it. It was as though the carefully contained misery needed to leak out somewhere.

Allie followed over a few minutes later, carrying another round of drinks and apologising for Miss McTavish and her verbal probing, which had continued throughout lunch. I was counting myself lucky the probing was only verbal.

She'd covered such scintillating topics as the places sand could get if you had sex on the beach; the merits of photographing your own vagina, and the shocking price of property in Edinburgh these days. I must admit I did have to raise an eyebrow at the cost of a two-bedroomed flat in the New Town.

'Don't be daft,' I said to Allie, 'she's not your responsibility. I attract nutters wherever I go. She seems so out of place here, though.'

'Yep, I know what you mean,' Allie replied. 'No kids, no apparent interest in water sports – not that I'd dare say that word around her; who knows what it might unleash? All we know is that she's a writer, and says she finds being on holiday helpful for her research. Within minutes of meeting us, she'd found out that Mike's had the snip, and asked him if it's affected his orgasms. As if! He's just thrilled to be getting any!'

'And how did he react to that question?' I replied.

'With relish. That man never misses an opportunity to pretend he's Sid James in a *Carry On* movie. Bizarrely, it's one of the things I love most about him.'

We settled down into two sun loungers near the pool. A pool that Nurse Nancy could definitely not enter – my plastic might shrivel up. Allie saw my wistful expression and made a sympathetic clucking noise. She stood up with such purpose, I thought she might just say 'Alakazam' and a nice bikini would appear.

Instead, she waved over to a nearby sunbathing couple, motioning for them to join us. She cupped her hands over her mouth and shouted to another pair on the far side of the pool, who dutifully came over.

Before long, a small coterie of strangers had been assembled around my lounger. They stood smiling down, casting so much communal shadow over me the sun was momentarily eclipsed.

I sat up as straight as I could, almost dropping the plate of Turkish delight on to the concrete. I was sure they came in peace, but the thought crossed my mind that they could also be a lynch party out to tar and feather me under the little-known Obscene Outfits (While Abroad) Act.

'You see?' said Allie, waggling her fingers at me in a 'look, I told you so' gesture. 'She can't wear this all day, can she?'

'Oh my God no!' shrieked one of the men, dropping dramatically to his knees by my side, reaching out to finger the PVC hem in distaste.

He was wearing a salmon-pink sarong that not even David Beckham could have carried off. His hair was a suspiciously even shade of black, and his nails were beautifully manicured. Plus, as he continued to bemoan the state of my 'non-semble', as he called it, he displayed about as much subtlety as an am-dram performance of *Guys and Dolls*. Big flaming queen, anyone?

An exceptionally tall older woman with long, wild, steel-grey hair stepped forward. She was grandly preceded by a very large pair of breasts attempting to escape from two scraps of leopard print masquerading as a bikini.

'Rick! Give her some space, for goodness' sake – and stop stroking that plastic, you don't know where it's been!' she said. Charming.

I stood up and introduced myself, with a bright smile and as much enthusiasm as I could muster.

'Nice to meet you, Sally,' said the woman with the enormous knockers. 'I'm Marcia, and this is my husband, Rick.'

Even from a foot away, she smelled so much like a brewery that she should have had a 'highly flammable' sticker on her forehead.

It took a second for what she'd said to register. I might have been rendered momentarily unconscious by the second-hand alcohol fumes partying along with my own.

Did she really say 'husband'? Big pause for thought at that one – Rick was about as straight as Freddie Mercury, and only slightly less flamboyant. Marcia looked a bit older than him, and certainly plucked her eyebrows a lot less than he did, but she was all woman.

I wondered how a marriage like that could work, but 'better than mine' was the only answer I came up with.

'Hi, I'm Jenny, lovely to meet you,' said the other woman, a sporty-looking brunette in her late twenties, giving me a hearty handshake and a radiant smile. 'And this is Ian,' she added, gesturing to the buff-looking young man at her side. Ian was trying very hard not to stare at my now-sweaty cleavage, bless him. What a gent.

'Between us, Sally, we'll be able to find you some decent clothes to wear until your suitcase turns up,' said Allie, 'so just rest easy. Have another drink, chill out, and we'll all go off to our rooms to dig something up for you.'

'Yes, darling,' said Rick, giving me an air-kiss on each cheek and rubbing my shoulders reassuringly, 'don't worry about a thing – I'll have something perfect for you!'

Chapter 9

After they'd gone, I settled back down to enjoy the sun. I felt some of the tension ease away once I was alone again. Facing all those people at once had been scary. Even without Nurse Nancy's assistance, I would have found it daunting. I wasn't sure I liked me very much any more; I was so pathetic – whatever confidence I once had was nowhere to be seen these days. Getting dumped for a woman half your age will do that to you.

Now, I was just a scaredy-cat single parent to two alien beings who wouldn't even notice my dead body unless it was blocking the fridge door. Meanwhile Simon was romping his way through his midlife crisis and overdosing on presumably world-rocking sex.

Our sex life had been nowhere near world-rocking. In fact, woolly mammoths roamed the earth the last time my world so much as budged an inch. When he stopped even trying (because he was getting it elsewhere, I now realised), it had been a relief.

I could stop pretending to be asleep when he came to bed, and enjoy a rest on the wifely duties front. Now I was more than resting, I was facing eternal celibacy – which suited me just fine. At least that's what I kept telling myself – apart from in those moments at three a.m., when I was lying alone awake in bed and wishing my missing husband was there with me.

I'd noticed as I sat there baking and pondering my lack of sex life that a few more children were starting to appear in and around the pool – some escorted by nannies; some in chattering packs of their own.

Pirate Jake, my friend from earlier, was licking the very last yum of ice cream from a cone and balancing on his left leg like a stork.

I was considering whether to call him over when I heard the sound of running footsteps pounding behind me. A man dashed straight through the gap between my sun lounger and the one next door, moving so quickly he was a blur of fast-moving arms, legs and, luckily I supposed, swimming trunks.

The whirling dervish continued to the pool's edge, where he scooped up Jake in both arms and tucked him into his tummy, yelling 'Geronimo!' His momentum carried them both a couple of feet up into the air before gravity plunged them down into the water, the cone flying out of Jake's hand.

I watched the whirlpool they'd created when they went in, waiting for them to emerge again. After a couple of seconds they both bobbed back up, shaking their heads like wet dogs and screeching with laughter. Jake was holding on to his father's neck tightly enough to asphyxiate him.

They carried on playing for a while longer, splashing along to the other end of the pool Nemo-style, like father-and-son fishes.

After a lively ten minutes or so, they caroused their way back down to my end and climbed out – not even using the steps. I'm always jealous of people who can get out of pools without using the steps. When I try I look like a whale humping the side wall.

Jake grabbed his dad's hand and started walking him over to the bar, jumping up and down with excitement. He spotted me as they approached the sun loungers, and veered over, tugging his dad behind.

'Ahoy there, shipmate!' I said, saluting him sailor-style. 'How goes it?'

'I'm not a pirate any more, silly!' he said, as though I was the dumbest person who ever walked the earth. He must have been conferring with Lucy.

'Dad! This is that lady I told you about – the one with the really short dress made out of raincoats!'

Oh good. More humiliation – and doled out by a tiddler, at that. I put my game face on and smiled up at superdad, getting my first proper look at him.

He was about six foot tall, maybe a shade under. His hair was slick with water, but I thought he'd dry out to be blond. Striking blue eyes, the same shade as the cloudless Turkish sky. A strong jawline. A nose that looked as if it might have been involved in a rugby match or two when it was younger.

He was my age, possibly older, but had obviously looked after himself a lot better than I had. Broad, powerful-looking shoulders, with a perfectly defined musculature. Not an ounce of fat on a torso that wasn't quite at superhuman six-pack level, but was way better than anything I'd ever seen in real life before.

His arms looked strong enough to pick a woman up, throw her over his shoulder, and take her back to his cave for a quickie without breaking a sweat. Even if the woman in question had been intimately involved with a box of Ferrero Rocher for the last month.

I reminded myself that this was the latest in a long list of sex maniacs in my life, and that I was to avoid him at all costs. Allie had described him as a single dad – which probably meant he'd left Jake's mum for a younger model at some point, like they all seem to do. I mentally painted a skull and crossbones over his perfect chest. Beware. Toxic.

'Hi,' he said, returning my smile, 'I'm James Carver. Jake was just telling me about you. Sorry if he went on about me liking short skirts a lot – I must have sounded like a dirty old man . . .'

He had the same trace of Dublin in his voice as Jake. But on him, it was so sexy; he should have had his own late-night radio show for sad, lonely women to listen to.

It made me feel a bit wriggly. Which in turn made me feel a bit annoyed with myself.

'I'm sure you're not,' I replied, thinking exactly the opposite. He was looking at me a bit too closely for comfort, which was fair enough under the circumstances. I resisted the urge to cover myself up with my hands.

'I'm Sally,' I added belatedly. I was too well trained to be outwardly rude.

'Nice to meet you, Sally,' he said, as Jake started to tug on his hand to pull him away again, bored by the grown-ups' strange social etiquette.

'Come on now, Dad!' he said. 'You can talk to her later. You need to get me a juice right now or I am going to shrivel up and die like a salty slug!'

'Okay, okay, I'm coming . . .' James said, following him. He turned back as he was leaving, and gave me a killer grin. Good Lord, the man was perfect – it was against all the rules of nature. Where were the missing teeth or turned eyes that usually evened these things out?

'Looks like my presence is required elsewhere – let me buy you a drink later. Love the outfit, by the way,' he said.

Ha. I bet he did. I was living out every juvenile male fantasy on the planet, with the help of Mr and Mrs Smith from Solihull.

Despite my mental repulsion, I felt a little answering throb going on in Nurse Nancy's private parts. My libido, making a guest appearance at the most inappropriate of times.

I gestured to the waiter for another drink. James Carver might look like sex in Speedos, but he was, undeniably, male. And therefore a complete bastard.

Chapter 10

'I'm so fucking hot!' said Lucy, fanning herself with the *Complete Works of Sylvia Plath*.

'And what do you expect me to do about it?' answered Ollie as he buttered his toast. 'Come and blow on you?'

'No, I expect you to shut the fuck up and die, you stupid little shit,' she said, throwing her knife at his head like a spear. He swatted it aside with his hand so it clattered to the floor, then gave her what I think our American cousins refer to as 'the finger'.

Breakfast time with the Summers family.

At least they were sitting with me this morning – though, as the minutes ticked by, I wasn't so sure that was a good thing. It was like breakfasting on the Gaza Strip. I'd made a deal with them that they had to sit with me for at least one meal a day, so I could check they were alive and I could at least pretend I was relevant to their existence. Now, I was starting to regret it.

We were all a bit tired and crotchety after a busy day and a late night. I thought Ollie and Lucy might come to blows, and I was downing coffee like it was the elixir of youth.

Lucy had eaten alone at dinner, on the opposite side of the restaurant, reading something far more highbrow than the two-week-old *Hello!* magazine I'd scrounged.

Afterwards she took herself off to the beach with her book. I occasionally did a sneaky check on her, hiding behind bushes like an undercover agent on a surveillance mission.

She did nothing more extreme than strain her eyes to read by the light of the lanterns strung up on the jetty. Every now and then I'd see the flare of her lighter as she lit up one of the cigarettes she thought I didn't know about.

I'm sure I won't win any mother-of-the-year awards for turning a blind eye to that, but life hadn't exactly treated Lucy kindly recently, and I didn't have the heart to tackle her. She seemed content, and it was the first time I'd seen her still and quiet and not surgically attached to her phone for weeks.

She'd had the stress of doing her GCSEs, her dad leaving us, and on top of all that, the everyday horror of being a sixteen-year-old girl. Peaceful moments are few and far between. Plus, you know, she's a Gothly creature of the night and all that – who am I to get in the way of her midnight mojo?

Ollie, as is his nature, had found friends almost immediately, despite being the king of geekdom. He ate with a big crowd of other teenagers, then disappeared off to play pool and table football for hours on end. He reappeared now and then to check up on me, which was sweet. My big scrawny baby thought he was the man of the house now.

True to their word, Allie and her friends had come up with a range of random clothes for me. None of them fitted properly, but I felt wonderful – even if I was wearing a pair of old running shorts and a T-shirt. Even a cotton-rich blend felt like heaven next to my skin after the day I'd had.

After dinner I'd joined Allie and the others for a drink. There was a pretty terrace, laid out with tables and chairs and lit with candles, which seemed to be at the heart of the social scene of the Blue Bay Hotel. The entire Wardrobe Rescue Squad was there, apart from the younger couple, Jenny and Ian, who had gone on a 'moonlight cruise' – shorthand for a bonk-fest, I was told.

I met Mike, Allie's husband, who expressed his regret that I was no longer dressed as Nurse Nancy, but said the T-shirt was tight enough to make up for it. He was a stocky man in his fifties, with shaggy hair that couldn't decide whether it was red or grey. He had a big belly laugh that rattled the glasses on the table and made his eyes disappear into his face. And, somehow, he could deliver lecherous lines without sounding lecherous, which was quite the gift.

Rick and Marcia were there, and they both looked amazing in very different ways. Marcia, still necking down the booze like Prohibition might be round the corner, had her thick grey hair tied in a long plait down her back. She was wearing a majestic peacock-blue maxi-dress that held her boobs up on a kind of shelf. They looked like a pair of ripe melons perched on silk. Every man in the vicinity was surreptitiously sneaking a peek, while trying hard to pretend they hadn't even noticed.

Every man except Rick, that is. Perhaps because they were married, and Marcia's melons lost their novelty value a long time ago. Or perhaps because he was too busy chatting to all the handsome young barmen.

And, of course, there was James. The Probably a Bastard, and Definitely a Player. Wearing a pair of just-tight-enough Levis that showed off his arse to perfection. Bet he hadn't spent hours in his room, dislocating his neck to see if his bum looked too big. He was one of those comfy-in-their-own-skin people who always rubbed me up the wrong way. Just like Simon, in fact – so confident they'd probably not had a moment of self-doubt since they were six.

Still, the Levis did look excellent. A pair of well-used 501s, on the right backside, is one of the sexiest sights on earth. Perhaps it's a generational thing. I grew up watching those TV ads with the gorgeous hunk taking his pants off in the launderette and I don't think I've ever fully recovered. He was probably an arrogant bastard as well.

As if the jeans weren't enough of a shock to my system, his short-sleeved white shirt was showing off that golden tan and those yummy biceps. You could see them flexing every time he lifted his pint. I couldn't understand why all the other women hadn't fainted on the spot.

True to his word he did buy me a drink, and pulled a seat up by my side, but we didn't get much time to talk. It was a group affair, with tables and chairs clustered together as everyone chattered away and started to catch up on what had happened in their lives over the last year. Births, deaths, marriages – a living tableau of newspaper small ads.

James gave me a running commentary on who was who and what was what, so I'd 'feel like one of the gang'. I replied politely, trying not to encourage him. Just because I'd been dressed like a sex nurse when we first met didn't mean I was easy.

The Birthday that Changed Everything

Nothing about me was easy – especially not the strangely conflicting way I was feeling right then. One minute morose and wishing Simon was there with me; the next wondering what James would smell like if I leaned over and sniffed his neck. Confusing, yes. Easy? No.

Luckily for my blood pressure, he had to leave early to pick up Jake from the kids' club. Everyone waved him off, with a chorus of 'see you in the mornings' and 'sleep wells' and similar comments. They all seemed so comfortable together – like lifelong friends, rather than people who met each other for two weeks on holiday.

Nobody seemed to think this was weird; the same groups of people had been coming to the Blue Bay for three – or in some cases four – holidays in a row, and were like an extended family who only saw each other once a year. I felt borderline jealous, and had to give myself a bit of a telling-off – these people shared friendship. Which was something I was capable of – even if Simon had dumped me, I could still be a friend. I just needed to try a bit harder. I was only one day in – I could do this.

As James walked away, I noticed two things: how nice his backside was still looking in those jeans, and Miss McTavish giving me the beady eye. I prayed to God she wasn't about to ask me if I'd glanced at the crotch of his jeans to estimate bulge size. Which of course I had. Instead, she just gave me a wee wink and a little smile.

Maybe she was a mind-reader, or some kind of Scottish Dr Ruth-style sex guru. I should probably go to her for counselling. Lord knew, I needed it – why was I even noticing James's backside in my current emotionally crippled state?

Maybe it was a rebound thing. Or perhaps my ego needed boosting after its recent battering, and James's mildly flirtatious kindness was doing the trick, despite my best efforts to ignore him.

I couldn't deny the fact that I fancied him, but I wasn't going to act on it. It was way too soon for that kind of thing, and when I did act on it, it wasn't going to be with a holiday lothario on the prowl for sex on the beach. He was gorgeous – but not for me. Even if he was sparking off some delicious feelings in places I'd forgotten existed.

I'd been fighting off complete breakdown since Simon left. My life consisted of either crying, or mindless tasks to distract me from the pain. The house had never been so clean, and the dog had started to hide in the broom cupboard when he saw me approaching with the lead. I'd assumed that that was it for me and men: game over.

My reaction to James suggested otherwise, but still . . . it would end in tears. Mine. Whatever was causing me to notice James – backside and the rest – was a momentary blip. I was barely holding myself together surrounded by all these new people; coming to terms with my new status as a singleton. Any more stress would be too much – I'd be like that donkey in Buckaroo! and do a complete flip-out.

No. I was middle-aged, free and single – surely a cause for celebration, I'd decided, reaching for the rosé and topping up my glass.

I got so busy celebrating, in fact, that I spent my first night in Turkey completely pickled. I'd woken up half an hour ago, still dressed and desperate for the loo. Now I was popping paracetamol with my croissants as the kids bickered across the table.

'So, are you just going to lie on your fat arse all day and get shitfaced again?' asked Lucy. Ollie, the traitor, laughed out loud.

'Of course not!' I said. 'I'm getting stuck in to the activity programme today. And don't talk to me like that.'

'Yeah, right, whatever,' she said, implying, 'I know you're lying' and 'I don't give a fuck' at the same time. 'Maybe you'll try some extreme sunbathing. Or the gin Olympics.'

'No, come on, Luce, let's go and sign up for something together now, it'll be fun,' I said, standing up and dusting myself down. Today's ensemble was a very interesting combo of Jenny's shorts, which were too tight, and Marcia's bikini, which was slightly too big. Not *haute couture*, but circus clowns wouldn't stop on the street to point and laugh either.

Lucy didn't even bother to reply, so I walked off without her. I marched over to one of the reps, full of indignant outrage and determination to find the New Me.

'Hi! How are you?' said the rep – a scruffy-haired surfer dude with wide blue eyes and an accent like Prince William's.

'I'm keen,' I said, 'but I can't do anything and I'm really unfit. What do you suggest?'

He laughed. As though he thought I was joking and I'd said something really funny.

'I'm not joking,' I said, just to be clear.

'No, of course not,' he replied, busying himself looking through the piles of papers and timetables on the desk.

'What about windsurfing for beginners? That's on this afternoon, should be a nice day for it as well.'

'Yes, great, sign me up for that – what else? What about tomorrow?'

'Ummm . . . tennis? There's an assessment session first thing if you're interested?'

'Yes,' I answered, 'put me down for that. Sally Summers. But I don't need to bother with the assessment thingy. I'm rubbish, so put me in the lowest group possible. And have you got the times for yoga and Pilates and Boxercise there as well?'

Fully armed with notes, class times and a set of safety instructions which I'd never look at, I wandered back to our breakfast table, planning to wave them in Lucy's face. I'd show her what a super-fit super-mum I really was.

When I got there Ollie had already left. He'd mentioned something about snorkelling earlier and said he'd see me for lunch.

Lucy, however, was still there – sitting with a terribly good-looking teenaged boy. He had beautiful brown hair that caught auburn glints in the sun, and gorgeous green eyes.

Sylvia Plath was lying forgotten on the table. Lucy's iPod was no longer attached to her ears. She was listening to him, talking to him, and even issuing the occasional girlie giggle. I almost fainted from the shock.

'Hi!' I said as I joined them. Lucy gave me a look that made me feel about as welcome as raw sewage, but the junior hottie returned my smile and actually stood up to greet me. Good looks, and manners too. What on earth was he doing talking to Lucy?

'Hi, you must be Sally,' he said. 'I'm Max – Allie and Mike's son. I thought I'd come and see how Lucy was doing, and whether she fancied coming swimming with me later – if that's all right with you, Sally?'

I was momentarily flummoxed by the thought of Lucy requiring my permission to do anything, and apparently so was she. 'Yeah,' she said quickly, 'that sounds great! I love swimming. I'll go and get changed and meet you back downstairs, okay?'

And off she went. She started running, then remembered her cool and slowed down to a saunter. I swear there was an extra waggle in her hips as she went, like she knew she was being watched.

Weird, weird, weird. Especially as she hadn't been swimming of her own free will for the last two years.

Chapter 11

Windsurfing wasn't for another few hours, so I followed the extreme sunbathing route. I needed to rest now, in advance, as I'd be using up a lot of energy later on. Preventative napping – I'm sure it made perfect scientific sense.

Once I was creamed up, hydrated and reclining, the sun started to heat all the tension out of my bones, and I relaxed completely into a state of woozy wellbeing.

All I could hear was the gentle slapping of the water at the pool's edge, occasional laughter floating up from the beach, and the low-pitched singing of the cicadas in the palm trees. The haunting sounds of the call to prayer from the local mosque echoed around for a minute or two, reminding me that I was somewhere really quite exotic.

Perfect.

So perfect, I may possibly have drifted off to sleep for a little while. Or 'rested my eyes', as my gran used to say when she nodded off in the armchair.

I jerked roughly awake when I heard Ollie shouting 'Mum!' in a tone that implied it wasn't the first time. I leaped up, opening my eyes to be confronted by his plastic face inches from my nose.

He pulled off his snorkelling mask, laughing away at his little joke, and said: 'You were dribbling. And mumbling,' then did a running jump into the swimming pool.

I investigated my face for slobber, slapped on some more cream and turned over. I tan easily, but cooked on one side and not the other is never a good look.

I was just drifting off again when a feeling of discontent started to swirl around me. I knew Lucy was standing there before she said a word – I could sense her dark aura chilling the air.

I turned round, reluctantly, and looked up into the eye of the storm. Her black hair was wet and dripping round her shoulders. She seemed less tough without a coating of hairspray – like a tortoise without its shell.

Her stance, though, was pure street fighter. Hands on hips, glaring down at me.

'Yes?' I asked cautiously, racking my brain for something I'd done to annoy her recently. Other than breathe.

'You know it's all your fault I don't fit in here, don't you?' she said, in a quietly furious voice. From bitter experience I knew she'd get louder and louder from this point onwards. I should have dispensed earplugs to all my fellow hotel guests as soon as we'd arrived, out of common courtesy.

'Erm . . . if I just say yes, can we leave it there?' I asked, hopefully.

'I look like a freak,' she said, as if I'd never spoken, pointing at her own hair and the thick black mascara that was clumping her eyelashes together.

'I look like a freak and it's all your fucking fault! What

kind of mother helps her daughter dye her hair black? And wear the kind of clothes I wear?'

'I don't know, Lucy,' I said, 'a supportive one? And to be fair I did draw the line at that tattoo of a spider's web you wanted for your birthday—'

'Shut up!' she shouted – at about fifty per cent capacity, I'd say.

'You're a fucking nightmare! I'm sixteen! I need something to rebel against, but no, you're always too busy being Mrs Fucking Understanding Sympathetic Parent, aren't you? It's all "yes, dear, of course you can dye your hair", "yes, dear, of course you can paint your room black", "yes, dear, of course you can shoot up fucking heroin at the dinner table!"'

Cranked right up to seventy per cent now, and building to a big finale.

'For God's sake, what do I have to do in the madhouse you call our home to break the rules? Go teetotal or join the SAS? It's a joke. You're a joke. You've screwed up your own life and now you want to do the same to me! No wonder Dad left!'

She stomped off, flip-flops smacking angrily against the concrete as she headed back to our room. Time for a bit more Sylvia Plath, I suppose.

The woman lying on the next lounger was looking on in horror. She was far too polite to say anything, but her face was frozen somewhere to the south of shocked.

'I know,' I said. 'My only consolation is she'll be leaving home soon.'

I walked over to the pool's edge and shouted Ollie over. 'What's wrong with Lucy?' I asked.

'Do you want a list?' he answered. I put on my no-nonsense face and folded my arms in front of my chest.

'Okay, okay . . . I don't know. She went swimming with Max and then his mates came and it was no big deal but I think one of them might have called her Morticia.

'Don't see why that would bother her, she'd normally just break their arm, but I think it might be 'cause she likes Max so she flipped and got embarrassed. It's girl stuff, Mum – I don't understand girls. You should go talk to her.'

Yeah, right. Whatever, as Lucy might say. That was not going to happen. She'd said her piece. She currently hated me. I'd been here before, bought a shop-load of T-shirts, and knew she needed time to calm down before I went anywhere near her. A year or so should do it.

Instead, I walked to the bar. Allie was sitting there under an umbrella, her bare feet propped up on the chair opposite her, a paperback that looked to be about serial killers splayed across her lap.

She glanced up as I arrived, and cracked open one of her best smiles.

'Trouble in paradise?' she asked, raising an eyebrow and closing her book.

'Oh,' I replied. 'You heard that, did you?'

'Yes. Because I'm not deaf. Don't let it get to you – she doesn't mean it. She's probably in her room regretting it right now.'

'That's where you're wrong,' I said, looking yearningly at her cold bottle of Peroni. 'That would be what a normal human being would do. Lucy, though, will be upstairs plotting evil acts that wouldn't be out of place in that book you're reading.

But don't worry – I'm used to it. And I met your Max earlier, Allie – how lovely is he?'

'On a scale of one to ten,' she said, smiling proudly, 'he's probably a twelve. But that's what he's like now – you should have met him when his dad first left, years ago. He was a monster. He was caught shoplifting bags of Wotsits from the corner shop; got into fights at school – the works. I felt so guilty – I knew it was all because of what we, the alleged grown-ups, were doing, messing with his poor little head. I suspect that's something you understand.'

I pondered it and, while I did so, she kindly pushed her Peroni over and gestured for me to have a swig. True friendship.

'I do,' I eventually replied. 'I do feel guilty. Even though it's not me who had the affair, or me who walked out. Even though I'd be willing to try and make it work if he wanted to come home. Probably. But . . . well, it's complicated, isn't it? I didn't walk out – but maybe I switched off. Maybe I didn't give him what he needed. Maybe I didn't notice how miserable he was, because I was so busy leading our perfect suburban middle-class life. Maybe it's at least partly my fault.'

'And maybe,' said Allie, grinning across the table at me, 'he's actually just a complete wanker.'

'That is also a distinct possibility,' I answered, feeling laughter bubble up inside me.

I realised, as I drank my pilfered lager and laughed with my newfound pal, that it was the first time I'd felt genuinely amused, or even capable of anything approaching 'fun', for a very long time.

Perhaps the holiday magic was starting to work.

Chapter 12

Windsurfing looks really, really easy. I could see loads of people doing it – gliding effortlessly along in the choppy blue bay, like humans who'd been transformed into graceful swans.

All of which made it especially galling that, so far, the only technique I'd mastered was falling into the sea and coughing up litres of salt water. I couldn't get enough balance to even stand up on the board, never mind heft the sail upright.

I wanted to give up and go for a little lie-down, but my instructor, Mo, was having none of it. Mo was about thirty and must have weighed in at a good seventeen stone, half of which was made up of ratty brown dreadlocks.

'You can do it, Sally,' he said, after my third drenching. 'You'll get it eventually and then there'll be no stopping you. Concentrate. Don't let it defeat you!'

I tried again. And again. All around me, there were giant splashes, occasional shouts of triumph, and the sound of sails whooshing down to hit the water. Clearly this was a class full of people who were probably also picked last for their netball team during PE lessons.

I took a deep breath, and tried once more. A miracle occurred – I got my sail up, and managed to keep it up, clinging hard to the handle. Okay, it might have been called something like the boom; I'd already forgotten the jargon. I don't know how it happened – it was a complete fluke, like scoring a 147 in snooker when you've never picked up a stick before.

'Mo! Look!' I shouted, terrified I'd fall off again before my mentor could witness my moment of glory.

He was knee-deep in water, helping one of the other physical incompetents, but turned round to see what I was up to.

A broad grin split his round face in two, and he made a thumbs-up gesture with both hands. 'Go for it, Sally! The bay's your oyster!'

With hindsight I suspect he didn't mean quite that. What he probably meant was 'don't go further than ten feet away from me under any circumstances, but I won't bother saying it as you're bound to fall off again any second now.'

I wasn't listening anyway. I was too busy congratulating myself. I could do it! I could windsurf – and I was the first person in the beginners' class to actually be up, up and away. Unbelievable. First actual laughter with Allie, now a physical triumph. Things were looking up.

It was probably the most self-satisfied I'd felt since I got through childbirth without an epidural. If only Simon could see me now. And Ollie and Lucy. Maybe I'd get a certificate, or a prize, or possibly some sort of championship jersey and a trophy . . .

The Birthday that Changed Everything

I was gliding along, sun glinting from the sail as I went, cutting my way through the waves, moving the mast backwards and forwards to catch the breeze.

This is a piece of cake, I was thinking. I must be a natural – I'd found my sporting forte at long last. After being crap at everything from darts to horse-riding, I'd finally discovered something I could do. I was now anticipating further lessons back home, possibly competing at international level.

Pride, of course, is the traditional forerunner of a fall. Or, in my case, the onset of a panic attack. I realised, when the learners back on the shore started to look like tiny colourful ants, that I'd travelled quite a long way without really noticing what I was doing. It felt as if I was miles away. Halfway to the nearest Greek island at least.

Despite my obvious natural talent and the international windsurfing career that beckoned, I had one very big problem: I had absolutely no idea how to turn this thing around. I could head in only one direction – towards a watery death.

The instructors were back there, dealing with all the others crashing into each other and almost drowning, and I was out here. On my own. Far, far away.

Would they send out a search party when it got to dinner and I didn't show up? Would Lucy and Ollie notice I was gone at all until they needed their passports? How far away was the next Greek island anyway?

I made a few weedy attempts at twisting the sail around in the opposite direction, but that didn't work. I dipped my foot in to use as a kind of rudder, but one size-five foot against the whole ocean wasn't much use. My arms were getting tired.

My legs were starting to feel like rubber. And I was so scared I thought I might wee my pants some time soon. Where was David Hasselhoff when you needed him?

I'd just decided to jump for it and try to swim my way back, somehow dragging the board with me, when I heard a shout coming from behind.

'Sally! You okay? Can you tack?'

I recognised the voice straight away. James. Bloody typical. Of all the gin joints in all the world . . . I had to splutter into his. Drowners can't be choosers, though, so I yelled back: 'No! I can't tack! I don't even know what that is! Help! Send out a distress flare or call the coastguard or something!'

'Just jump off,' he yelled, 'and swim to me – I'm not far behind you. Don't panic – you're going to be fine.'

Easy for him to say. He was probably an expert on tacking, whatever the hell that meant – and I was presuming at that stage it was nothing to do with dressmaking.

I jumped in, holding my nose, fighting back a surge of panic as I splashed down.

James was in a small white boat, leaning over the edge and holding out his hands to me. He had his lower body stretched out over to the other side for balance.

I doggie-paddled my way over, choking afresh each time a wave hit me in the face, until I was by the side. He grabbed hold of my hands and pulled me up. I landed in a wet, undignified heap in the middle of the boat, with what felt like a wedge of wood poking up between my bum cheeks.

'Ouch!' I shrieked, wanting to leap up but only capable of throwing myself forward on to all fours. James was sitting directly in front of me, trying not to laugh. He was wearing form-fitting cycling-type shorts, and a second-skin top that made his muscles look as if they'd been coated in shiny black paint. None of which made it easy to hate him.

'Thanks,' I said, perching myself on the opposite ledge. 'I think you might have saved my life . . . or at least saved me a long swim. I kept going and going and I just couldn't turn round . . .'

'Tack,' he said, 'that's what you do to turn. I'm impressed you made it this far on your first lesson, even if you did get stuck – most beginners just fall in for an hour.'

'I know!' I answered, wringing out my hair, 'I'm made up with myself! Not sure I'll be doing it again any time soon, though. I had a few minutes before you turned up when I was petrified. I don't think a life on the ocean wave is for me really.'

As we spoke he was untying some rope, pushing a stick around, and doing something that made the sails move. As you can tell from my masterly use of the terminology, I am a sailing expert.

'I don't know about that,' he said. 'I bet you could sail this. I could show you how.'

Yeah, I thought. And I bet it was like golf or tennis in the movies, and he'd have to put his arms round me in the process.

'Erm . . . what is this anyway? A little yacht?'

'This is a dinghy. Small enough to sail single-handed, but big enough for a few more if needs be. Jake loves them – next year he might even start going out on his own.'

Even a six-year-old was better at water sports than me. Why wasn't I surprised?

'Okay, well, good for him. I need a bit of a rest, though. Give me a few minutes to dry out and then maybe I'll try. And what do we do about the gear?'

'Don't worry, they'll nip out in the speedboat and collect it later. They'll just be glad you're back. I'd like to pretend I'm your knight in shining armour, but they'd have fetched you before long. So relax – take your few minutes,' he said, a gentle smile curving those luscious lips. He went back to doing things with ropes and sticks and sails, and I did as I was told.

I stretched out my legs as far as I could, closed my eyes, and let the sun soak into my skin. It was so quiet out here. Serene, in fact, if all you had to do was act like a cat on a window ledge on a summer's day.

We were both silent for a few minutes, and I could feel from the stable bobbing of the waves that we were staying put. Perhaps he was taken aback by my beauty and unable to move. More likely I was supposed to do something to help him.

'One day,' he said, 'I'll take you out on a bigger boat. Then you can bring a blanket and just stretch out in the sun all day like that . . .'

I opened my eyes sharply and looked at him. That sounded blissful – and dangerously flirtatious.

'We could always take Jake if you need a chaperone,' he said, a hint of challenge in his voice. 'Anyway, come on, help me sail this little yacht back to shore – it's easy,' he said, before I had chance to answer.

He pointed at the stick. 'This,' he said, 'controls the tiller. You use this to steer, and turn around. When you're sailing a dinghy, you use your bodyweight as ballast, which is what stops it from capsizing. That bit there's called the dagger board. You sat on it earlier. You can see the sails yourself, and they're attached to the boom at the bottom. Watch out for it, if you don't pay attention it can whack you on the head.'

Great. Another way to injure myself. I was obviously fated not to get to shore safe and sound.

He did some strange slow-motion action that involved him feeding the stick – sorry, the tiller – behind his back, pulling on the ropes, and moving from one side of the boat to the other. All of which he did with total ease, of course. Bet he was never picked last for the netball team.

He tried to make it simple, but I was distracted by a million and one things: exhaustion, stupidity, and the lazy curl of lust in my tummy as I watched him moving and listened to him speak.

'Right – your turn,' he said.

'No. Sorry, but I'm knackered. I need you to be a knight in shining armour for a bit longer.'

'Well, when you put it like that,' he answered, laughing, 'how could a man resist? I'm going to need you to move around when I tell you to, though, okay?'

As we made our way back, he mentioned that Jake's mother took him sailing when he stayed with her for holidays. Hmm. That meant he had Jake full time, which wasn't what I'd assumed . . . I'd assumed, in all honesty, that he was a weekend dad. Shagging his way through his middle-life crisis Monday to Friday, and going to McDonald's on Saturday.

It sounded as though I'd been wrong. I hated that. Before I could find out any more, he moved quickly on to another subject.

He asked about Ollie, who he'd met that morning snorkel-ling, and about Lucy, who he hadn't met and who I hoped he never would meet, for his sake. He didn't ask about their father – showing me the same discretion he misguidedly expected himself. Probably, knowing how close these Blue Bay people were, Allie had already filled him in on the situation.

I was pleased if she had. It saved me having the whole conversation again – I was here to try and forget Simon for a while, or at least relieve the pressure of thinking about him twenty-four hours a day. I'd have been happy if she'd issued a press release about it, in fact, if it saved me having to describe my loveless state to anyone else.

Instead, we talked about Jake. About his school life. About Dublin. And, against my better judgement, I realised that I was starting to relax around him. Even enjoy his company. It was a mix of his obvious competence, his drool-inspiring voice, and the fact that he looked like a walking piece of erotica.

But I still knew that – no matter how attractive the packaging – he was a man. I was still an emotional wreck, and jumping into bed with someone really wasn't going to help at this stage, no matter how well defined their abdominal muscles.

I could still enjoy window-shopping, though, I thought, stretching my arms up into a long, languid stretch and allowing myself a few naughty thoughts. I fear I might have even purred, or at the very least sighed.

'Shit!' he shouted, out of the blue.

I snapped to – he was sitting with his head in his hands, blood trickling from between his fingers. The boom was swinging, a matching patch of red shining in the sunlight.

'Fuck, fuck, fuck,' he said, clearly in pain. The wound was a few inches above his hairline; like most scalp cuts, it was bleeding like crazy. He tried to wipe some of the blood out of his eyes, smearing it over his forearm.

I moved across to take a look.

'No!' he said. 'Stay there or we'll go over. I'm fine. It's just a scratch.'

He'd taken quite a bang, but didn't seem on the verge of passing out or falling overboard. Which was lucky for us both; we'd have been floating adrift for eternity if it had been up to me to captain the ship.

'I'll get us back then I can sort this out. Can't believe I got caught by the bloody boom,' he said.

'What happened?'

'Erm, I got momentarily distracted,' he said, nodding towards my chest. I looked down, having the awful feeling I knew exactly what I was going to see.

Yep. Two large brown boobs, enjoying the sunshine a lot more than they'd enjoyed Marcia's bloody bikini.

Chapter 13

We splashed back to shore as soon as the boat was safe in the shallows.

'Come on, up to my room,' I said, taking his hand, 'and don't argue.'

'Okay . . . but is this really the time?' he asked, looking shocked as I led him along.

'Oh shut up – your virtue's safe. I'm not planning to seduce you, I just want to get a better look at that cut.'

We made our way up the stairs to my room, stopping to answer a few enquiries as we went. James's inner macho man kicked into action. He stood there, looking as though he'd been slaughtering a pig, insisting there was nothing wrong. Men and their egos. A constant source of amazement to me.

'Can I tell them what happened?' he asked as we climbed the stairs.

'Do, and I'll kill you.'

'Okay. But that's not fair – I'd feel like less of an idiot if I could at least tell the blokes. One look at you and they'd all understand why I lost it . . .'

Even under the circumstances – gaping scalp wound, all my fault – a comment like that made my heart skip a beat. My bruised ego was lapping it up like double cream. Pathetic.

I unlocked the door, having first knocked on Lucy's room to see if she was still around. No answer. She must be out sacrificing goats in the woods.

'Come on in, 'scuse the mess,' I said, leading the way. I went over to the windows to throw open the curtains, and turned back to tidy up the bed. I needn't have bothered – a messy duvet was the last thing anyone would notice in this particular room.

'Oh, the little cow,' I said, stopping dead and gazing around in shock. My room had been transformed into Mr and Mrs Smith's house of horrors – a showcase for their amazing Range of Rubber. Stupidly, I'd left the interconnecting door open at a time when I was number one on Lucy's shit list. Served me right really.

Suck-Me-Dry Sally was fully inflated and propped up on my pillows, handcuffed to the wrought-iron headboard. She had Black Beauty between her plastic legs and was looking understandably shocked.

The butt plugs were lined up on the dresser in order of size, next to a giant jar of lubricant that said Slippery Dick on the label. Both my bedside cabinets had vibrators on them, as though I kept them there for night-time emergencies.

'Interesting room you have here,' James said, deadpan.

'None of it's mine,' I snapped back. 'It's all from the suitcase that got swapped. My cow of a daughter has been in here doing this. And it looks like the cleaners have been, too, so they'll have me down as a pervert for the rest of the holiday as well. I'd like to throttle her scrawny neck . . .'

'I'm sure the cleaners will have seen it all before. And I won't hold it against you – I was a teenager once myself; I know what they're capable of.'

It was so the right reaction. Not a sign of the nudge-nudge wink-wink I'd expected, even with severe provocation. I pulled myself together and told him to sit on the bed. The man was dripping blood on to my carpet, for goodness' sake – I could kill Lucy later.

I went to fetch my first-aid kit from the bathroom. I have the world's best first-aid kit. Occupational hazard of being a mother, a teaching assistant, and an almost-doctor.

I held back his blood-clotted hair and examined the wound. I gently cleaned it with some warm water, and probed as softly as I could to see how deep it was. James sat stoically, wincing only slightly as I poked around.

'You'll live,' I said. 'It looks much worse than it is. I don't think you'll need stitches, but I'll dress it and you'll need to wear a very attractive bandage for the next day or so. Keep your head away from blunt objects, don't swim for a while, and avoid salsa dancing because your balance might be off. If you feel sick or sleepy, let me know.'

I bustled around, getting gauze and a long strip of bandage, then stood in front of him, tilting his head slightly so I could work at a better angle.

'You seem pretty good at all this – are you a nurse in real life as well as fancy dress?'

'Nope,' I said, trimming off some tape, 'but once upon a time I was going to be a doctor. Lucy came along and it never happened. Can't say I'd be much good at open-heart surgery, but the basics like this you never forget.'

'Why don't you go back and finish your training?' he asked as I leaned in closer to apply pressure to the dressing.

I couldn't answer for a few seconds. My bikini was still damp and the air-con was on full, giving me goosebumps. I could feel his warm breath on my breasts as he spoke. His lips were only a whisper away, and the unexpected heat on cool flesh was amazingly erotic. All I'd need to do was lean forward an inch or two . . .

It was an odd moment to feel turned on, but I was, and I was sure it was obvious. I was seriously considering seeking medical help for these inappropriate rushes of lust. I wasn't usually like this. It could be early menopause.

I reminded myself to breathe, and to talk.

'Well, that was a long time ago. Lucy's sixteen now. My training is probably next to useless these days,' I replied, feeling my hands tremble slightly as I secured the dressing and started to wrap the bandage.

My patient was quiet. All I could hear – and, deliciously, feel – was his breathing against my chest.

'Am I hurting you?' I asked, pulling away slightly to look at his face. His eyes were glazed and he was struggling to focus. Maybe he had concussion after all.

'No, you're not,' he said, 'and I'd probably wouldn't say this if it wasn't for the head injury . . . but even through that bikini, your nipples look exactly like the tops of Walnut Whips . . .'

Yikes. Time to get him out of my room right now, or I was going to have to carry out a full physical.

Chapter 14

Breakfast on the Gaza Strip again. But that morning, there seemed to have been something of a ceasefire.

Ollie was chirpy as ever, his little round glasses perched on his nose, reading a book with a dragon on the cover. Lucy was uncharacteristically chatty. She'd been into town with Max and his friends the night before, giving me barely enough time to lecture her about the dangers of alcohol before she dashed off.

There was a lot of laughter and surreptitious shuffling about on the corridor outside before I finally heard the key turn in the lock. I considered bursting out to catch them in the act, but I didn't really want to see my daughter with her tongue down someone's throat. It's like world poverty – you know it's happening, but you don't necessarily want to witness it up close.

She'd wisely kept herself scarce most of the day, knowing the longer she avoided me, the less angry I'd be about the pervert's parade she'd ambushed me with. I'd spent a good half-hour packing it all up again ready for the airline people to collect, and was fairly sure a few smaller items had gone missing.

Still, seeing her smiling and laughing at breakfast made it impossible to stay mad. In fact, it had totally thrown me – that boy must be a heck of a kisser.

'So anyway,' she said, between bites of toast, 'turns out that Max is really cool. I know he seems total surfer boy, but he's read all *The Walking Dead* graphic novels, and runs an online forum on classic horror, and he's really into The Smiths as well.'

'Are you sure he's not just gay?' Ollie asked, peering up from his page.

'Shut the fuck up, John Lennon,' she answered, reassuringly. Glad to see that love hadn't quite tamed the beast.

'He says that you can wear Billabong boarders and still listen to My Chemical Romance, because why should we judge people by what they wear? It's just so true – people make assumptions about me all the time because I wear black and have this hair—'

'But all those assumptions are true,' said Ollie, bravely. 'You *are* a freak of nature who eats babies and never appears in sunlight—'

'And, Mum,' she continued, ignoring him, 'he thinks you're awesome 'cause you allow me the freedom to be myself, and don't try to make me into what you want like most parents.'

I knew these weren't her words, or her thoughts, and should probably have been worried that her Svengali was brainwashing her. But it was all so nice to hear that I conveniently put those concerns to one side to think about later. Just the day before she'd been screaming at me for allowing her too much freedom. Hey-ho.

'He also said, and I totally don't get this, let me add, that you're pretty hot for an old lady. Weird or what?'

'Gross,' said Ollie, flatteringly.

'Well, that's very nice, dear,' I said. 'Tell Max thank you. Now, this old lady needs to go off to the tennis courts – time for a lesson!'

The two of them exchanged disbelieving looks.

'Are you sure?' asked Ollie.

'Yes,' I said, 'what could possibly go wrong with a game of tennis? Even for me?'

There was no answer, so I left them to it and ambled over to the tennis block. There were four courts, and each had a coach standing outside. Some people were in proper tennis whites, but most, like me, were in normal shorts and T-shirts.

My suitcase had come home and I almost wept with joy when Tarkan the receptionist delivered it to the door. Mr and Mrs Smith's had been dispatched in return, probably minus the few items that Lucy had filched. And me, to be honest; if my hormone level continued to rise, I might need a bit of mechanical help. It was the least they owed us for the trauma, and they could always claim back on the insurance – if they dared.

As I waited, I watched the others warming up and playing. Allie had a super-cute pleated skirt on and was hitting balls like a rocket. Jenny and Ian were playing doubles against Rick and Marcia, who were both surprisingly good. I don't know why I was surprised, except all I'd seen Rick do was file his nails and ogle men's arses, and Marcia seemed permanently tanked up. On court they rocked.

James was there too, ignoring my warning about taking it easy while his head was healing. Every time he stretched to hit a high ball, his white T-shirt rode up and flashed his perfectly flat, perfectly golden tummy. And if I stood to one side, I got a fabulous rear view when he was crouching to receive serve.

Mortally embarrassed by that one comment in my bedroom the day before, he'd been a perfect gentleman ever since. He'd carefully averted his eyes from my chest whenever I was around, and switched his flirting to low. I didn't know whether I was relieved or disappointed.

I suspected I was gazing at him like one of those teenagers in a *Jackie* photo-story, but was luckily interrupted by my coach, Nathan, who looked about eighteen. I stood to, and entered the arena of dreams.

I realised as I walked on to the court that I was surrounded by teenagers. The girls were all coy giggles and push-up trainer bras, and the boys all wanted to be Novak Djokovic. I smiled politely, feeling old enough to be their grandmother. Served me right for asking to be put straight into the rubbish group.

We were paired up, and I was lucky enough to get a young thug called Sebastian. He was about thirteen and built like a brick shithouse. Even at that age he had practically no neck, and the meanest eyes I'd ever seen.

Sebastian might have been young, but he was way better at tennis than me. I suspect he'd learned it in a juvenile rehab facility where he'd been sent after biting someone's ear off.

He was less than delighted to have Granny Summers playing opposite him as well, and growled something that sounded like 'I'm going to grind you into dust' as I walked past.

First shot, I fluked a serve that not only landed in, but which the bulldog opposite couldn't reach with his junior Bluto arms. Ha, I thought, let's see who's in the dust by the end of this, you little—

'Aaaaagh!' was all I managed to think after that. Sebastian was so peeved at losing a point he whacked the ball with all his force at my head. It hit me square on the eye so hard I thought it was going to come out of the back of my skull.

The pain was incredible, and I staggered off to the side, dodging other players' balls as I tried to find the exit gate. The swines showed no mercy, and I suspect some of them deliberately aimed at me as I stumbled blindly around. I could see Sebastian grinning and making a thumbs-up sign as I did my Frankenstein walk straight into the wire fence. Shit. I was trapped on a tennis court with the war criminals of the future.

Nathan rushed over to help me out, horrified, shouting at the others to stop.

'I'm okay, I'm okay,' I said, gingerly taking my hand off my eye. Tears were streaming from it and I could already feel it swelling as the bony socket bruised up. 'But if it's okay with you, I'm going to call it a day.'

I walked over to the bar, where there were lots of 'oohs' and 'aahs' and a gratifying amount of sympathy from the staff. Mehmet shovelled a load of crushed ice into a tea towel for me and I went to sit by the pool to try and limit the damage.

Lucy was right. Extreme sunbathing was my thing. Screw all this activity crap – I was on holiday. I needed another way to find a whole new me, because if I carried on pretending to be Sporty Sally, I was going to end up in Casualty.

'Are you all right, dearie?' asked Miss McTavish, who'd appeared from nowhere and sat down beside me. Today's colour was peach – a sequined swimsuit that had a frilly skirt that went halfway down her chubby thighs, and a matching peach sun visor.

'I'm fine, Miss McTavish,' I said, 'just not much good at dodging balls. I had this idea I'd try to recreate myself a bit on this holiday . . . but so far I'm just the same old mess.'

Even to my own ears I sounded forlorn.

'Oh, you poor wee thing. It's hard when you split up with someone, isn't it? Everything you thought you knew about them, and yourself, and life, turns out to be wrong. It's like your whole future's died, but you have to carry on and pretend everything's okay for the sake of the kids.'

It was so spot-on, so absolutely right, that I felt myself welling up. I figured I could get away with it while I had an ice pack on my face. I nodded, not trusting myself to speak.

'So what went wrong then? In your marriage? Was it the sex?' she asked – straight back to her favourite subject.

'I suppose that was a big part of it,' I said quietly. I'd spent hours and days and weeks pondering that same question. Sometimes I came up with a million and one complicated answers. Sometimes I only had one – Simon was a grade-A arsehole.

'Looking back, there was a problem,' I carried on. 'Our sex life started with a bang – pregnant after some drunken fumble I can't even remember – and over the years it just . . .

went missing in action. It's like losing a sock – you know it's gone, but you can't imagine where. And you don't look too hard because you don't think it's that important.'

Between kids and work and everything else I was always tired and always busy. After spending the day chasing four-year-olds and taking abuse from psychopathic teenagers, I usually felt about as sexy as a spinal tap by bedtime.

The last thing I wanted when I was drifting off in my flannelette pyjamas was his hand 'accidentally' finding its way to my boobs, or to feel Mr Stiffy poking me hopefully in the back. Especially when he'd been out all day cutting people's knees open for Porsche money, and hadn't uttered more than a sentence to me since he'd got in.

I tried not to blame myself, but sometimes I completely understood why he'd run off. Within seconds I was usually back to wanting to saw his balls off with a blunt nail file but, if I was totally honest, he had his reasons. Even if they were egotistical, shallow and cowardly. As the old saying goes, it takes two to tango – and two to step off the dance floor completely. Given my time again, I'd play it differently. I'd try harder. I'd be better. I'd make the damn thing work.

'A missing sock!' said Miss McT, clapping her liver-spotted hands together in glee. 'What a marvellous analogy, Sally! I know just what you mean. But what it all comes down to, you know, is you not enjoying sex enough – if it had been as good as it can be, you'd have always found the energy. I didn't even discover good sex until I was in my late sixties, would you believe! My then husband was a real goer, and he taught me a trick or two, I can tell you.'

Please Lord, please, please, please don't let her tell me what any of the tricks were, I thought, especially if they involved thrombosis stockings or Ralgex massages.

'And he was delighted when I got my false teeth,' she said, popping them out a fraction to demonstrate. She bit her dentures back in, leaned a little closer, and whispered: 'I could take them out whenever I wanted – made certain acts so much more pleasant!'

I'd dropped my ice pack and was about to punch myself in the injured eye with my own trainer. Surely that couldn't hurt any more than listening to this?

'Sally! Come on, you said you were going to meet me for a drink!' I heard Mike's voice shout out. A complete lie, but more welcome than a Lottery win.

I jumped up, told Miss McT that I had to dash, and ran like the wind to the terrace.

'Sit down,' he said. 'I'd suggest a stiff drink but it is only ten a.m. I saw her do that thing with her teeth. I've already had that one and it leads nowhere good. I can't sleep at night since I met her.'

He propped his feet up on the chair opposite, rested his hands on his beer belly and squinted up into the sun. Grizzly bear in holiday mode.

'Thanks, Mike,' I said, 'she's too much, she really is. One minute she's talking quite normally, and the next you're in *The Twilight Zone*. Scary. Like my new look?'

'Yeah, that black eye's going to look great,' he answered, scratching his shaggy mess of hair. 'You should take a leaf out of my book, Sal, and just sit still and drink. It's only when people move around too much they get hurt.'

I nodded. My eye throbbed. I reapplied the ice pack.

'They're all so bloody good. I hate them. All of them. Even Rick was better than me and he's . . .' I trailed off, unwilling to commit a social faux pas.

Mike rumbled with laughter. His tummy shook, and somewhere on another continent, a new mountain range was formed.

'I know. He is, isn't he? Or at least he seems to be. None of us can figure it out and we've known them for years. They're solid, though – really kind people. And Jenny and Ian. They had a bit of bad news last year – found out they couldn't have kids – but you never see them down.'

'Oh that's terrible!' I said. 'It must be like torture coming here and being surrounded by other people's children . . .'

'That's what we thought. But they're teachers so they need to come in the hols, and they know all our kids so well, they love seeing them, especially the little ones like Jake. Don't know how they put a brave face on it myself. All sorts goes on here. Take James – looks like he has everything, doesn't he? In fact he works bloody hard, raising that kid all on his own, no help from the useless lump Jake calls a mother. Don't know if I'd have had the balls to do that on my own.'

Mike unscrewed the cap on a bottle of water and poured us both a glass.

I didn't want to ponder James, or his balls. It seemed like I'd got the wrong impression about him, and it made me feel distinctly uncomfortable. Simon had turned me into a nutter in more ways than one.

'You get to know people really quickly here, don't you?' I said, taking a sip. 'It's like it's so intense you go on a crash course in each other. I've only been here a couple of days, but I feel like I've been here for weeks. You all seem so different, but so close at the same time.'

'The bonding power of two weeks on the piss together, that is, Sal. But you're right. We see each other once a year; a few e-mails or calls in between, maybe a meet-up in London if it suits, but every August we're here again like we never left. I don't know if it happens in other places, but we just all gelled straight away – young, old, fat, thin . . . nobody cares. We might not have much in common in the real world, but here we're best mates. I bet you and Allie have already started swapping secrets, haven't you?'

I nodded, not really knowing him well enough to discuss his previously failed marriage to his current wife.

'And I know women do that better than men – but it's also this place. I have a secret theory that one day here equals two weeks in the outside world.'

'God,' I replied, grimacing. 'I'll be ancient by the time I get out home! But I know what you mean – it's intense, in a good way. And we're relaxed, and maybe a bit drunk a lot of the time, and because it's *not* the real world, we feel safe to say and do things we'd think twice about back home. To form friendships that would take for ever on the outside.'

'That's it, Sal, exactly right. Although calling it "the outside" does make it sound a bit like a prison. And talking about relationships, our Max seems quite smitten with your Lucy, you know—'

'Does he? Why?' I asked in shock. 'Sorry, I don't mean to seem like a bad mother, but she's not exactly Miss Congeniality, is she?'

We were saved further debate by the return of the conquering heroes, flushed and exhilarated from the tennis.

'All hail!' said Mike, as though reading my thoughts, and toasted them with his glass. Allie gave him a big smacker on the lips and said she was off to get changed.

James sat next to me and stole some of my water. His neck and the bit of his chest I could see were coated in a light sheen of freshly earned sweat.

'Oh dear,' he said, holding my face in his hands to get a closer look at the eye, 'maybe I need to offer some first aid now?'

'It's nothing – by the end of the day I'll probably have the matching set. There'll be a freak storm and a rogue pineapple will land on my face while I'm sunbathing.'

He laughed and removed his hands. I was glad. I'd been worried I was going to start sucking his fingers. I felt like I was fighting a losing battle: I needed a relationship like I needed viral meningitis, but my lust glands didn't seem to know that.

'We need a danger-free way to exercise. Tomorrow morning. Meet me here at nine after breakfast and we'll go for a walk. I promise nothing bad will happen to you.'

Chapter 15

By nine the next morning, I was showered, dressed, breakfasted, and fidgeting, waiting for James to drop Jake off at kids' club and take me on an adventure. My hair was back in a little ponytail, and I had multi-coloured eyes for the occasion – one my normal brown, and one a very fashionable shade of purple.

Ollie and Lucy were both still in bed. Lucy was snoring like an asthmatic hog and, as I left, Ollie was getting out his phone to video her. He'd probably have it on YouTube before the day was out and have sent the link to the entire school.

James arrived, wearing a pair of cargo-style khaki shorts and a white T-shirt. His long, muscular legs looked capable of leaping tall mountains in a single stride. Mine, on the other hand, looked more suited to a stroll to the post office to buy a book of second-class stamps.

We left the hotel, and within a few minutes were already off the beaten track. The further we got, the more the landscape changed – no more holiday complexes or bars, just dusty roads lined with whitewashed houses and the occasional small shop with boxes of melons outside.

At first I chattered away, but before long started to feel out of puff and went quiet. I was happy enough to listen to James, telling me about his work as an architect, and how he'd returned to Dublin after leaving when he was ten.

'My parents moved us to London then,' he said, 'and that's where I grew up. But they eventually went back, and when Jake was born and I was on my own with him, I went too. London was great when my life consisted of going out on the pull after work, but there comes a time when you have to grow up.'

Or grow down, in Simon's case, I thought bitterly, then damned both him and myself for letting him intrude on the day. I felt as if he was always there, lurking in the back of my mind, no matter how hard I tried to be positive and enjoy myself.

We were heading up an incline that was steep enough to keep my trap well and truly shut, so I just nodded and smiled.

We'd been on our travels for more than half an hour, passing fewer houses and more semi-derelict buildings guarded by barking dogs and rusty wheelbarrows.

James came to a halt and I stopped next to him, trying not to cry with gratitude. I looked ahead and saw nothing but a huge hill, with an incredibly steep path wrapped around its contours like a ribbon. The path seemed to be made of nothing but loose shale, and I could see rocks freefalling down.

'Right,' said James, 'just up to the top of this hill, and then we're done . . .'

My eyes widened to the size of flying saucers. Or at least the one that wasn't swollen half shut did. No way, no way at all was I going to attempt that. It would be downright dangerous. Definitely, one hundred per cent, totally not. Ever.

'Oh . . . okay,' I muttered, like the jellyfish I am.

James burst out laughing, which wasn't very gentlemanly.

'Your face is a picture,' he said, 'priceless. Don't be daft – we'd kill ourselves up there. Come on.'

Oh ha-bloody-ha I thought, stabbing him mentally in the back as I followed. We took a much more solid-looking path round the side of the hill, edging upwards so gently that even I could cope with it.

About ten minutes later we arrived at what looked to be somebody's house. There was a small courtyard laid out haphazardly with tables and chairs, glowing pink flowers trailing from the whitewashed walls, and pots of herbs lined up along the path to the front door. Over to one side was a car without wheels, and a washing line with several football kits flapping in the breeze. I could hear the obligatory dog barking somewhere behind the building.

There was stunning view down over the bay. The Aegean was like shards of blue glass, reflecting sunlight in glittering patches.

'Gorgeous, isn't it?' said James, gesturing for me to sit. A woman wearing an apron and a headscarf came bustling out of the house, trailed by twin boys of about ten.

'James! You back!' she said, hugging him. 'Where my boy Jake? And who this – girlfriend?' She eyed me up and down without shame before giving me a wink.

'You hurt, James?' she said, reaching out to twist his head roughly to one side to inspect it.

'No, no, I'm fine, it's nothing. Leyla, this is Sally, my friend. I'll bring Jake to see you soon, I promise. How are these two doing?' he asked, gesturing to the boys, who were kicking a football to each other in the gravel driveway.

'Ah, big trouble, as usual, James. Sit, sit, I bring you apple tea and cakes.'

I raised an eyebrow at James as he obeyed and sat.

'This is a bit like a Turkish greasy spoon. I found it by accident when I was out biking, and she kind of adopted us. I come back every year. She likes practising her English on us,' he said.

Leyla was back out in minutes, depositing pastries made of calories, glued together with honey. She gave James a pat on the shoulders and headed into the house, pausing only to shout at her boys in rapid-fire Turkish. The universal instruction of 'behave yourself, or else'.

As he'd dragged me halfway up the Turkish Mount Everest for this chat, I decided now would be a good time to ask some of those questions I'd been dying to get to. Plus it might do me good to focus on the imperfections of someone else's life instead of the disaster zone of my own.

'So,' I said, 'how come you ended up on your own with Jake in the first place?'

I saw him tense slightly. This was clearly not a subject he found easy to discuss. I felt embarrassed for having asked at all, as he stayed quiet and stirred his tea.

'I was going to say it's a long story,' he said at last, 'but it's not really. Just complicated – but I'm guessing you can handle a bit of complicated, can't you, Nurse Nancy?'

He smiled to break the tension. My heart flipped.

'I met Jake's mum in a club in London. She was younger than me and I should probably have known better, but she was gorgeous and wild and had this sassy New Yorker thing going on. She has these rich hippy parents who took her on safari all the time as a kid, and she ended up being a wildlife photographer. I know. Not the kind of thing I'm used to either.

'She moved into my flat while she was staying in London, and I couldn't get enough of her. I suppose I got a bit too much of her, because she ended up pregnant. She didn't want it. I did. I persuaded her to go ahead, and told her I'd raise the baby. Which is, as you can see, what I've done.'

'Goodness. Didn't she change her mind once he was born and she saw him? I can't imagine walking away at that stage.'

'She kind of did,' James continued, 'but her heart wasn't in it. She was like a caged animal in a little flat in a city. She loved Jake, but as soon as she got offered a job in the middle of nowhere, she was packed and gone. At least he was just a baby so he's never known any different.'

'But what about you? You must have been gutted.'

'I didn't have time to mope. I had a four-month-old baby to look after, and my own career. But yeah, whenever I stopped and thought about it, it hurt like hell. She's selfish and beautiful and can charm everyone she comes across into doing what she wants – including me half the time, even when I know she's manipulating me. Jake'll probably bugger off to New York as soon as he's old enough, and I'll be sat at home looking at his baby pictures wondering where the time went . . .'

'Believe me, we all do that. Haven't you met anyone else since?' I said, dipping my fingers into the calorie cake and licking off the delicious goo. I'd been so wrong about him, and I was feeling a bit guilty now. About that, and the cake.

'No. I've been too busy, and I've been concentrating on Jake, and my job. There's no room for anything else.'

'No other women? In six years?' I asked incredulously. Was there something wrong with him? I'd never known a man go without a shag for that long. One of Diane's favourite phrases was 'men need sex like they need a shit – it's a bodily function'. Not pretty, but accurate. Surely he'd have exploded by now?

He shot me an amused look. 'When I say nobody, I mean nobody serious – I'm only flesh and blood. I don't live like a monk. I've had a few friends over the years. Women who don't want a relationship, some of them in the same boat as me, too busy for it.'

'Like a subs' bench? You can call on them when you need them, but they're not playing the full game?'

'Exactly,' he answered, 'and I'm on their subs' bench too. But I can't go on like this for ever, and maybe one day I'll meet the right woman, for me and Jake. But don't, under any circumstances, tell Mike and Allie that I've been speaking about this. He'd take the piss out of me for talking about my feelings like a big girl, and Allie'd have her mates jetting out to Dublin for blind dates. Anyway, what about you?'

Me? What about me? Surely he didn't mean I should be jetting out to Dublin for blind dates?

'What happened with you and your husband?' he clarified.

'Oh. Well. He ran off with a teenager. She's from Latvia and she's a lap-dancing catering student. She's called Monika and Ollie thinks she might be a man with fake boobs.'

'Ouch. Not much I can say to that. And when did this happen?'

'Six weeks ago,' I said, staring into my tea. It was unexpectedly hard to talk about when sober.

'Jesus. You must be all over the place. How long had you been married?'

'Oh, only seventeen years or so.'

He reached out across the table to take my hands in his. I felt embarrassed and tried to avoid his eyes. Tears started to trickle down my face and he gently smoothed them off my cheeks as they fell.

'You must have been a child bride. And, for what it's worth, I think he's an idiot. Look at you – you're funny, you're brave. You've given him two children. You're sexy as hell even with a black eye. If I wasn't a dedicated relationship-free zone, I'd be chasing you round the swimming pool every night.'

I was still crying. And laughing. And wondering – he was a relationship-free zone. So was I. Did they cancel each other out, or was that just a polite way of telling me he wasn't interested? And did that even matter, as I wasn't interested either? Much.

'Thank you,' I said, managing a smile.

We were still holding hands. He was drawing little circles on my palm with his fingers, which was sending direct signals to places much further down. We were staring into each other's eyes. I was thinking that any minute now I might climb over the table and into his lap. He was starting to look slightly nervous, as though he knew exactly what I was imagining.

Luckily, the twin Ronaldos in the driveway chose that exact moment to kick their football right at us. It whacked James in the nose, ricocheted off, and crashed spectacularly on to the table-top, shattering the glasses and sending the plates crashing to the floor. Leyla came bursting out of the house waving her tea towel and screaming full blast. The boys took one look at her and legged it in the opposite direction.

'Well,' James said, screwing his eyes up in pain, 'at least it was me this time.'

Chapter 16

'How's Lucy this morning?' Allie asked at breakfast a few days later. My daughter had been out with Max the night before, as usual.

'Erm . . . fine, as far as I know. I left her comatose in bed about half an hour ago. Why? What's she done?'

Allie sighed and sat down at the table. There was no way this was going to be good.

'Her and Max had a huge row. It was about smoking . . . he's very anti, being Mr Health Nut and all, and he told her he was sick of kissing an ashtray.'

'Ouch,' I said. That would kill her. And probably me, later, when she woke up in a foul mood and went scapegoat shopping. Max and Lucy had been inseparable ever since they met, and she fairly glowed around him. She'd had boyfriends before – but, well, she'd never actually seemed to like any of them. Which wasn't saying much, as she didn't like any member of the human race – but with Max it seemed different. Real. Maybe it was just the intensity of the Blue Bay circle – but if they'd escalated to rows already, something unusual was going on.

'I know,' said Allie, 'I smoked at her age as well, and I tried to tell him it was just a phase she was going through. But being a man-in-the-making, he went ahead and said it, without thinking through the consequences.'

'Did she kick him in the balls?'

'No. Although he said he had a pair of socks shoved down there just in case. Nope, it was worse, in a way. She just gave him a look that reduced him to rubble and walked off. I think he almost wet his pants.

'He thought it over and went to look for her later. He found her crashed out on the beach. Looks like she drank a whole bottle of raki and passed out.'

I'd gone to bed early last night, exhausted by a full day of sunbathing and a long chat with Jenny. The Blue Bay Accelerated Friendship Machine – plus several pints of lager, I suspect – meant that she already knew all about my situation, and I knew about hers.

We'd sat together after dinner, watching the younger kids splash around in the pool, talking about her and Ian's work as teachers – her at the local primary, him as a secondary school geography teacher.

It was impossible to miss the yearning in her eyes as she watched Jake and his pals at play, but I hadn't felt comfortable raising the issue of her fertility until she did.

'You know,' she'd said, 'when I first found out, I never wanted to see a child again. But given my job, that would have been logistically challenging. And coming here . . . well, that's part of our routine now. We'd miss everyone too much if we stopped. So we decided we just had to be British about it – keep calm and carry on. Some days, though,' she added, gesturing at the splash-a-thon in front of us with the slight sheen of tears in her eyes, 'it's easier than others.'

I felt for her, I really did – I had two children and still mourned for the time when I was a busy mum to my young brood. These days, it was more about damage limitation – and that night had been no different.

I'd heard the usual scuffling outside just before midnight and then slept easy, knowing she was back. Turns out the scuffling was Max carrying her back to the room and tucking her in.

Shit. I really couldn't ignore this – it was one escapade too far.

'God,' I said out loud, 'I must be the worst mother in the world.'

'I think you have a way to go before you qualify for that title, Sally,' replied Allie, patting my hand reassuringly. 'You've had a lot going on, and Lucy . . . well, she's independent, isn't she?'

That was one way of putting it, I thought, before I thanked her and made my way back to the room.

Lucy was pretending to be asleep. I knew she wasn't, because I'm her mum, and I've lost track of the number of times I've snuck into her room to watch her sleeping. As a baby because I was scared she might stop breathing. As a little girl because seeing her face filled me with more love than I'd ever known before. And more recently, because it was the only time I got to look at her without having to field a mouthful of abuse.

I went to the fridge, got out a bottle of water, and sat beside her.

'Luce,' I said, 'I know you're awake, so give it up. And don't start effing and blinding at me, because I'm not going away. We need to talk. Here, drink this.'

A hand emerged from under the covers, took the water and retreated. After a few awkward horizontal gulps she emerged. Her eyes were glued together with fatigue and last night's mascara. I could smell the booze seeping out of her pores.

'Okay. Go on then. But try not to shout too fucking loud because I think I might need to go to hospital,' she said, sipping the water.

'I'm not going to shout – I'm going to talk, and you're going to listen. Now shut up until I'm finished, or I will go downstairs, borrow the loud-hailer from the sailing crew, and yell in your ears for the rest of the day.'

She grimaced in horror, but stayed quiet.

'I don't really know where to start, Luce. Maybe with the smoking – and yes, I knew anyway, so don't blame Max for dropping you in it. I've been meaning to talk to you about it for ages but, well, I suppose I haven't been the world's most switched-on mother recently.

'You know, you happily flaunt everything else in front of me – the bad attitude, the swearing. You enjoy upsetting me; it's one of your hobbies. But not once have you rubbed my nose in it about the smoking – it's the only vice you've ever hidden from me.

'I think it's because deep down you're embarrassed. You know the risks and you know what you're doing is dumb.

112

You remember my mum dying of lung cancer, and the way she looked at the end, hooked up to that oxygen tank. Not a good look, and I suspect they don't come in black either. I think you're ashamed, and that's why you've been keeping it a secret. Max was right, and you know it.'

She was silent. Unusual.

'And then there's the drinking. I know girls drink at sixteen. I was sixteen myself about a million years ago. But last night was stupid and dangerous – by drinking raki, you could have really ended up in hospital. You're not a Turkish man with chest hair and a moustache, so don't touch it again. And what if Max hadn't found you? Anything could have happened.'

She was shaking and gulping a bit. Tears – actual real-life tears – were starting to squeeze themselves out from between her crusted eyelids. I felt a bit panicky. I hadn't seen her cry for years, and I was way out of practice on the comforting mother front. If I touched her these days she tended to karate-chop my hands.

'I know,' she murmured at last, 'you're right, about all of it. And Max is really great. I threw up on him, and he still looked after me. I think I love him, Mum!'

The last few words rode on the back of a body-wrenching sob.

Oh shit, I thought. How I handled this could shape our relationship for the rest of our lives. I reached out, tentatively, to touch her shoulders, prepared for a slap.

Instead she jerked herself into my arms and started to sob on my shoulder. I stroked her hair and held her, almost crying myself. Okay, this was a mess, and I am probably a very selfish person for even thinking it – but it felt so good to have my daughter back again, to be able to touch her and console her and at least try to make her feel better.

She was weeping so hard her whole body was popping with grief. I squeezed her tighter and rubbed her back and told her I loved her.

'And I miss Dad!' she yowled, her voice full of anguish, 'even though I know he's a prick and I'm not sure I'd even want him to come back after what he's done, but I miss him!'

I took a deep breath and exhaled slowly. That arse really did have a lot to answer for. Sadly, I knew exactly what she meant – that complex blend of hating him and loving him all at the same time. No matter how selfish he'd been, he'd left a Simon-shaped hole in our lives that we were all struggling to fill.

'I know, I know . . . me too,' I said. 'Don't worry, it'll all be okay . . .'

'And Max probably never wants to see me again because I acted like a skanky alky, and he might think I'll grow up to be like you!' she bawled. Hmmm. More deep breaths, for different reasons this time.

'No, don't be silly, Luce. If he didn't care for you, he wouldn't have brought you up here like he did, would he? You both just need to apologise and see what happens next,' I said.

She pulled away, using my top to wipe her gunky eyes and blow her snotty nose on.

'You really think so?'

'Yes, I really do. Go and have a shower, take some paracetamol, and go find him. You'll work it out. And throw those fags away while you're at it.'

She nodded, drank some more water, and stopped hyperventilating.

'Thanks, Mum,' she said. I savoured the moment, knowing they'd be few and far between for the next few years. I was under no illusions that we'd be skipping off shopping together and swapping boy-talk from now on.

'So,' she said, shuffling under the blankets again, 'what about you, then? How are things with you?'

I couldn't have been more surprised if the toilet brush had asked me how I was. I was so stunned, I couldn't even formulate words. I stared at her, my mouth gawping like a malfunctioning robot. Lucy asking how I am? *Does not compute, does not compute.* She stared at me, waiting for my answer.

When it didn't come immediately, her face turned to thunder.

'Oh never mind!' she snapped. 'Typical! I spill my guts and get nothing in return – it's all one bloody way with you, isn't it? Now move your fat arse because I'm going to be sick!'

Normal service, it seemed, had been resumed.

Chapter 17

The night before my fortieth birthday was spent in the company of my newfound friends at the bar. Mike was doing a stand-up routine, sitting down, and Jenny and Ian were playing an athletic drinking-game version of ping pong. I suspected Jenny was losing on purpose just so she could get drunk. The very definition of work hard, play hard, all in one activity.

James was enjoying a night of freedom, as the kids' club was holding a pyjama party, where all the little ones spent the night on tiny roll-out mattresses and ate M&Ms until dawn.

Rick and Marcia were deep in conversation with the Ravishing McTavish. At no point did I see her slip her false teeth out, so I guessed they were safe.

I'd spent lunch with the Blue Bay's most confusing couple that day, and realised that, although they might be unusual, to say the least, they were also completely comfortable in each other's company, bantering like a pair of divas and anticipating each other's needs like mind-readers.

They were also fiercely protective of each other, and their extended holiday friends – which now seemed to include me.

'He must need a kick in the arse,' said Marcia, when we were discussing Simon's betrayal.

'Totally,' added Rick, holding his wife's hand over the table, his arm being used as an ashtray. 'Some men just don't appreciate what they've got.'

I was grateful for their support – and even though I had no idea what Rick had got, I knew he definitely appreciated it.

Ollie had succumbed to teenaged energy drain after a day of water-skiing, windsurfing and Xbox action with his friends the Ginger Twins, Carin and Christian. He'd slouched off for an early night after eating pretty much a whole pig at dinner.

And I was having one of those strange evenings where, no matter how much I drank, I stayed sober. In fact I was edging towards melancholy, and nobody likes a sad clown drunk, do they?

By 11.30 they were all hammered to varying degrees. James was holding it together, and Mike was taking the precaution of not moving from his bar stool, getting the waiters to place drinks directly into his hands.

Allie, Max and Lucy had been late-night shopping, and Allie was full of stories about what a master haggler Lucy was. I could imagine. After five minutes of that mouth, any self-respecting shopkeeper would pay her to leave so she didn't scare off the other customers.

Satisfied all was well with my offspring, I slipped off to the beach, where I sat down on the sand. The waves were gently whispering on to the shore, and the night air was still balmy. It was beautiful.

I glanced at my watch. Five minutes to go before the big 4-0 was finally upon me. I wasn't celebrating in quite the way I'd anticipated. I never got that Dyson. Or the Botox. Instead I'd lost a husband, and gained several vibrators.

I was hoping I could pull off this 'being alone' thing if I tried harder, and stopped torturing myself thinking about Simon with another woman. He'd made his choice, and it said more about him than it did me. I needed to concentrate on building a new future, now the one I'd counted on was dead and buried. Somehow, it felt appropriate to be turning forty here – the place where I'd come to lick my wounds, to try and recover. It was a fresh start, I told myself.

It was a great pep talk, but in my heart I wasn't totally buying it. I felt useless. The kids were growing up. They didn't really need me any more. I had no real career, no close friends. My whole life had been built around my family, and my husband. But now Simon was in love with someone else. I was a spare part, hanging round making sandwiches for everyone as they got on with their lives. Yeah, a melancholy drunk.

'What are you doing out here on your own?' said James, dropping down beside me and rudely interrupting my pity party. He handed me a fresh drink, which I probably didn't need.

I looked at his face in the moonlight. I could still make out the piercing blue of his eyes and his short blond hair. He smelled of something spicy and woody and subtly masculine.

'I'm waiting for my life to begin,' I said, mysteriously.

'In that case you'd better have a drink, it might take a while,' he said, smiling and reaching round to tuck my hair behind my ear, his fingers lingering on my cheek. We could have been the only two people in the world right then. I think I'd have liked that, just for an hour or two. Then the contact dropped, his hand returned to his lap, and I felt alone again.

He thought about what I'd said for a few moments.

'So – it's your fortieth?' he asked, once he'd figured it out.

I looked at my watch again. The hand clicked on to midnight.

'It's official,' I said, 'I am now forty. Can't say I feel much different . . .'

'No, I didn't after mine,' he said, 'just very hungover the next day. You should have told us. We could have done something to celebrate . . . but I suppose that's exactly what you wanted to avoid, isn't it?'

I nodded and looked out to sea again. I wasn't in what you'd call a celebratory mood.

'Well, happy birthday, Sally,' he said simply, putting his arm round my shoulders. It felt nice, and I leaned into him, resting my head on his chest. Maybe if I tried very hard, I could forget who we were for a while, and give my aching brain some rest. Enjoy the kindness of a stranger for what it was – a fleeting moment, bathed in moonlight on a foreign shore.

After a few silent minutes, he kissed me lightly on the head and held me tighter for a second.

'Do you want to come back to my room for a drink? I've got some champagne in the fridge I won at the tennis tournament . . . and you seem like you need cheering up.'

I took his hand and pulled myself up, dusting the sand from my skirt.

This, I thought, was one of two things: a friendly offer that I didn't need to worry about. Or a huge mistake in the making. I should, of course, refuse. Preserve either my dignity or my virtue, depending on which way the night went. Obviously I did neither.

'I might as well,' I replied. 'All I have back in my room are two grumpy teenagers and a multipack of Daim bars . . .'

Chapter 18

On the short walk back to his room I wondered what, exactly, I thought I was doing.

I'd resolved myself to happy celibacy for the rest of my life. I was still half in love with my crazy husband. And I hadn't had sex with anybody other than said crazy husband for the last seventeen years, and not even that much with him.

So why was I walking right into trouble? Or was I only imagining trouble? James was flirty, yes, but he'd made his views on relationships clear, and he'd made no real moves on me. Maybe in this case, a drink was just a drink. Or maybe he wanted to seduce me.

Or maybe – and this seemed most likely – I was a severely out-of-practice forty-year-old mother who hadn't seen herself as a sex kitten for almost two decades, and was very confused by the sudden appearance of an attractive man in her life.

He let us both into his room. It was free of blow-up dolls, and there was a wonderful smell of clean man coming from the shower. Even better, the lighting was low enough for me not to worry about how much my bottom spread across the bed when I sat down. I'd spent the last six weeks comparing my body – pretty unfavourably – to that of a nineteen-year-old exotic dancer. If by any remote chance this did get sexual, I was probably going to have to ask James to wear a blindfold. And not in a kinky way.

James cracked open the champagne and poured it for us. He passed my drink to me, the bubbles fizzing over the rim, then pulled his chair up close. He was facing me, and our knees touched each time one of us moved.

'Sorry it's the glasses we're supposed to keep our tooth-brushes in,' he said, 'and I can't promise it's going to taste that good, as it seems to have been made in Slovakia . . . but cheers anyway!'

We clinked glasses and drank. And looked at each other. And looked at each other some more. There was more fizz inside me than in the champagne, and the excitement of not knowing what was going to happen next threatened to rise up and smother me. I felt like I was sixteen again – but even more nervous. Did I want anything to happen between us? Should I make a move? Did he even fancy me, or was I having a Simon-inspired breakdown? The answer to all of it was 'no bloody idea'.

James was wearing a white polo shirt that hung loosely over his jeans. I could imagine leaning forward and slipping my hands under it, tracing the muscles in his tummy, running them up and over his chest, stroking his nipples until they were rigid. Then sliding them all the way back down again to see what else was getting hard . . .

'What are you thinking? You look miles away,' he said.

'Ummm . . . nothing. You don't want to know,' I answered.

'Well, I'll tell you what I was thinking,' he said, reaching forward to take the glass out of my hand, 'I was thinking about how beautiful you look. And about how much I want to lie you back on that bed, climb on top of you, and kiss you till you can't think straight. I know you're just out of a relationship, and I know you're confused, but there's no use pretending it's not on my mind. That it hasn't been on my mind since I first met you.'

Oh Lord. I suppose that answered at least one of my questions. He *did* fancy me. My brain might be perplexed by that – but my body had no doubt about how to react.

Even the thought of James on top of me had my pulse-points pounding. I could feel the pressure rising inside without him laying a finger on me. It was like we'd indulged in a week's worth of foreplay already, and my sex-starved body was ready to rumble. I hadn't been touched by another man for seventeen years, and suddenly I was desperate for it.

He edged forward and my knees parted without me telling them to, until one rock-hard thigh was wedged firmly between mine. I wanted to push closer and rub myself up against him. I was fairly throbbing with the need to, but I was frozen still with nerves.

He reached out to touch my knees, then ran his hands slowly, inch by inch upwards, pushing back my skirt as he went. He came to rest with his thumbs tracing sensual patterns on the soft flesh of my inner thighs. I was desperate for him to go further, to slip his fingers inside my knickers, then inside me. I thought I might collapse in a puddle if he didn't, and I completely forgot to breathe while I waited.

I slid forward a fraction to let him know what I wanted.

'Oh Jesus,' he muttered, his face as clouded with desire as mine. He was close, staring into my eyes, more intimate than a kiss.

He slid his fingers inside the flimsy material of my pants, stroking slowly up and down. I heard his breathing go ragged when he felt how wet I already was. He eased one long finger inside me, his thumb keeping a gentle rhythmic pressure on just right the spot. I rocked my body to and fro, feeling like I was going to explode into a million pieces any time now.

'Oh God, don't stop,' I muttered, feeling the heat flushing through me as he intuitively moved faster. My vision was a blur of black and white and nothing at all mattered apart from James and what he was doing to me. If he stopped, I'd cry, I knew I would. There was so much need in me, so much passion trying to fight its way out. I was on the very edge of what I suspected was going to be the best orgasm of my life, given to me with hardly any effort by a man I barely knew. None of which mattered – all that mattered was how good it felt.

It felt so good, in fact, that I was starting to hallucinate – I could have sworn that I could hear music in the background. Maybe a celestial choir serenading my forty-year-old sexual awakening. Or possibly – in fact definitely – my mobile phone, trilling the *William Tell* overture and vibrating away on James's dresser.

Slowly, groggy with lust, I came back to the real world.

'My phone, that's my phone,' I said.

'Just leave it, Sally,' he answered huskily, still intent on bringing the matter at hand to its hopefully glorious conclusion.

I sighed, pulled away from him and straightened down my skirt. The phone carried on insisting I answer it, and I had to – it could have been one of the kids needing me. The disappointment was shocking, as the waves of pleasure washed away from my body and I was left sitting there in disarray and disappointment. I felt like weeping.

James nodded his understanding – he had a child too, he knew where I was coming from. Not that I was coming at all, sadly.

He passed me the phone and sat back, breathing hard with frustration, as I answered it with shaking hands. I could see from the sizeable bulge in his jeans that he had a few withdrawal symptoms to deal with as well.

'Hello! Sally Sweets!' shouted the voice on the other end.

Un-fucking-believably, it was Simon. Using the nickname he'd had for me back in college, which I hadn't heard in years.

'Simon?' I said. 'Aren't you supposed to be in Ibiza?'

James heard the name, looked up, and made eye contact with me. What the hell was I supposed to do? Hang up? Throw it out the window? Tell Simon to piss off because I had a blow job to deliver? James saved me making the decision by getting up and heading, diplomatically, to the bathroom.

'I am in Ibiza! And it's beautiful! But I just wanted to call and tell you happy birthday, and tell you I love you! And I love the kids! And I love that man on the beach who gave me a bottle of water when I was really thirsty!'

'Simon, are you on drugs?' I asked. I could hear the sounds of blowing whistles and a pounding bass line in the background.

'I don't know, Sally! I might be! But I feel really good . . . and I know it's the end of your birthday, but I think I'm just in time! I love you!'

The line went dead. Simon loved me. How nice. He loved me so much, he'd even forgotten what day my birthday was on. And for that charade of a conversation, I'd pulled back from the brink of mind-blowing pleasure? I was not happy at all.

I stood up. Pulled my skirt down. Glanced in the mirror. I didn't look like I'd been interfered with. I could manage the walk of shame back to my room without anyone guessing what had been going on – apart from Miss McTavish, of course. She was probably outside, dangling a spy camera through the window right now.

James came back in. He was sipping from a bottle of water. His hair was all ruffled up and he was still slightly flushed. His jeans had returned to their natural state, though, which was probably a lot more comfortable for him.

He rubbed his hands over his face, and shook his head in disbelief.

'Saved by the bell, eh?' he said. He was right. I was thinking exactly that. I wasn't ready for this, for any of it. When it was happening, it felt spine-tinglingly good. But what about after?

I'd never been a casual sex kind of girl. Maybe I should be turning over a new leaf and shagging my way round Britain now I was single, but this wasn't the time to start. And James wasn't the person to start with – I liked him too much. I couldn't stand being another of the women on his subs' bench, no matter how much I'd enjoy playing ball with him. I was just too fragile.

Plus it seemed that Simon saying he loved me could still make me sad, and happy, and confused, all at the same time. Even if it was a drugged-up half-hearted display of affection, I knew I wasn't quite ready to put Dr Bollocks completely behind me yet.

Now James wasn't touching me, I could think more clearly. Feel more clearly. He might have got the day wrong, but I was obviously still on Simon's mind. Even out there in Ibiza with Monika, he'd been thinking of me. His Sally Sweets. He hadn't forgotten – and despite the mind-altering pleasure of a few moments ago, Simon was still my husband. The father of my kids. The man I'd been planning on spending the rest of my life with.

He still had more of a hold on me than anyone else, even if I'd misplaced that idea in the momentary madness with James. If Simon remembered me tonight, if he remembered Sally Sweets and all the good times we'd had together, maybe he'd remember that he should be home. With us.

'Yeah,' I said, smiling at him sadly. 'Saved by the bell. I'm going to head back to my room, James – thanks for . . . er . . . thanks for . . .'

'It was my pleasure,' he said, grinning, 'almost. Would you like me to walk you?'

'No, I'll be fine. Frankly I need a bit of time to cool off. See you tomorrow?'

'Yes, see you tomorrow. And Sally? Happy birthday.'

Chapter 19

I woke up disgustingly early the next morning. I'd had a difficult night, full of disjointed dreams in acid-trip Technicolor. James was kissing me and my head fell off. Then Simon appeared and the two of them started playing keepy-uppy with it. Lucy was in goal, wearing her school uniform, flicking my head away with a mermaid's tail. As my head was being kicked around, my eyes were open and I was watching it all flying past me.

I lay still as a corpse for a few minutes, before rousing myself enough to go down to breakfast for the very, very early shift. As a birthday treat, I planned to wear Mr and Mrs Smith's vibrating pants (one of the items I'd kept before handing the bag back to the airline rep), and eat a huge plate of Turkish delight with my seven cups of coffee. Happy Birthday To Me.

I saw James and Jake arrive, togged up for a day on the ocean wave. They both came over, and I gestured for them to sit.

'Dad, can I go and choose my own breakfast?' said Jake, as though it was the Holy Grail.

'Well, I'll come with you in a minute,' said James, 'in case I need you to help me carry my enormous plate of bacon and eggs. But why don't you go and get Sally some Turkish delight – she looks like she's running low.'

Jake stared at the still stacked plate before me, and nodded. He skipped off to the breakfast bar, and I watched him heaping sweets on to a saucer, counting them as he went.

'How are you this morning?' James asked, pouring himself some coffee from the pot. 'Any regrets?'

'Regrets?' I said, 'Well, I suppose it would have been interesting to see what happened next.'

'I think we both know what was going to happen next,' he said, his eyes sparkling at me over his cup, 'and it was going to be bloody brilliant. It might have changed your life, in fact.'

'Really? Isn't that a bit . . . arrogant of you?'

'No. I'm just a man who knows his own skills. Anyway, I'm taking you out to dinner tonight. It's all sorted. We can talk about it then. Or are you too chicken to be alone with me now?'

Yes, actually, I was. I was excited and terrified and feeling slightly nauseous. Part of that might be down to the Turkish delight, but part of it was because I was so confused. How could I be with James one minute and fantasising about Simon coming home the next?

Now there was this – the prospect of dinner. Together. Alone. Like . . . a date. I hadn't been on a date since Take That were popular the first time round. Yikes and double yikes. Was this a good feeling, or a bad one? Mainly it was an out-of-control one, and frankly I'd had enough of that in recent weeks.

Jake returned, bearing a piled-high plate. 'There are thirty-eight pieces there, Sally,' he said. 'I think. I got a bit lost after eighteen. And this is for you too. For your big birthday.'

He reached into his pocket and pulled out a fridge magnet that said I Heart Turkey on it.

'I thought it was a bit rubbish, but Dad said it's the thought that counts and that you'd love it anyway.'

'He was completely right, sweetie. I really wanted one of these – it's perfect. Now when I'm at home and it's cold and raining, I can look at it and think of you,' I said, giving him a hug.

'And my dad?' he said, into my shoulder.

'Yes, your dad too. Thinking about both of you will always cheer me up.'

'Come on, Jake, you'll make her cry. Time to stoke up the engines,' James said, standing up and taking him by the hand, 'and you, birthday girl – I'll see you later. No excuses.'

He walked away, quickly. Just to make sure I couldn't say no, I suppose.

I finished up my coffee and as much Turkish delight as I could eat without vomiting, then went back to the room to get ready for a hard day's sunbathing.

Nothing was stirring in the pit next door, and I'd given up trying to wake them years ago. If they went hungry, they could forage for wild shoots and leaves. Or buy a bag of crisps.

As I clicked the door shut to head down to the pool, I heard both their phones beeping to let them know they had text messages waiting. It was probably Simon, telling them he loved them, and his parents, and God, and the ice-cream man and that woman who served him a nice cup of tea on the train to Paddington one time.

Down at the pool, Allie was already lounging, lathered up in sun cream.

'Done my back in a bit,' she said, 'too much get-up-and-go. So today I'm having a lie-down-and-stay. How are you?'

'I'm forty today, actually, and so far it's been okay – I've eaten two massive plates of Turkish delight, and plan to do bugger-all for the whole day.'

'Sal! You should have told us!' she said.

'Well, I didn't want a fuss, I don't really feel like it.'

'But that's just selfish – it's a great excuse for a party for the rest of us . . . anyway, did you get some fab presents?'

Max probably ordered her custom-made Belgian chocolates iced with her name every year. I, on the other hand, had received a combination of a fridge magnet and big fat zero.

'Oh, here they come now – bet they've got something for you,' she said, nodding her head towards Lucy and Ollie, who were shambling towards us like extras from *The Walking Dead*. Both still wearing their nightwear and modelling varying degrees of bedhead. Ollie collided with a chair, so I guessed he'd lost his glasses again.

'Mum,' he said, 'happy birthday!'

He handed me two gifts, both wrapped in the lining paper from the drawers in our room and smelling like a thousand pairs of musty socks. Not a great start.

'Erm . . . thanks,' I said, opening them cautiously. Allie was peering over my shoulder, innocent in the ways of my children. I was half expecting to find the spare bog roll or the remote control for the telly.

Gift number one, which had Ollie's name scribbled on the paper, contained about six pieces of Turkish delight – still dusty with sugar, and very clearly filched from the breakfast table. I put it to one side for later – waste not, want not.

Gift number two, from Lucy, was always the one to fear. As I pulled the paper off, trying to shield it from Allie, Mr and Mrs Smith's Clit Stick fell into my hand. I'd suspected she'd kept hold of a souvenir – and, lucky me, it was now mine.

She smirked at me and said: 'Happy birthday – thought you might need this now you're a wrinklie . . .'

'What's that? A new lipstick?' said Allie, trying to look.

'Yes, that's exactly what it is,' I replied, shoving it into my bag and turning back to the kids.

'While I don't want to appear ungrateful,' I said to them both, 'you forgot, didn't you?'

Lucy shrugged and assumed her combat stance. 'So fucking what? It's not like you haven't had hundreds of birthdays before, is it? And you're the parent here – it's your job to remember *our* birthdays, because you're the one who dragged us into this world, not the other way round. Next time, tell my secretary in advance if you're going to get childish about it.'

Ollie told her to shut up, sighed, and sat down beside me.

'I'm sorry, Mum. We did forget. And that was really mean of us. Granddad and Auntie Diane both texted to remind us 'cause they know what a pair of knobs we are. I'm sorry. I'll make it up to you when we get home. And, as a birthday treat, we both plan to have every single meal with you today, instead of our friends – so you have some company.'

Goodness me – such sacrifice. I could tell Ollie expected me to fall down on my knees with gratitude, it was announced with such sincerity. And I could tell from Lucy's face she thought the whole idea was as appealing as eating her own toe-cheese.

'Well, that's very sweet of you both,' I said, lying, 'but I've already had breakfast. I can see you for lunch if you like. Maybe we can have a cake. And as for dinner, you'll have to sort yourselves out – because I'm going out with James.'

I'd been having doubts about even going – my inner wuss was fighting my inner slut – but it was worth saying just to see the shocked expressions on all their faces. Allie, because it was a juicy bit of gossip, and my kids because they never, ever expect me to have a life of my own. They were staring at me like I'd turned green and started speaking Martian.

I was starting to like this 'being forty' thing.

Chapter 20

'So,' said Allie, fixing me with a piercing-green stare as the kids retreated to their rooms to sleep for another four hours, 'is this a date? And how do you feel about it if it is?'

That, I thought, not meeting her eyes, was a very good question.

'The simple answer is, I don't know. I wasn't even sure I was going until just then. I'm . . . God, I'm confused, Allie. It's still all so fresh – Simon leaving me. It feels wrong to be even considering another man.'

'I understand that,' she replied, quietly. 'But it's just dinner. Simon has been gorging himself on the extramarital buffet for some time now. It might do you good. I went on a few dates, while Mike and I were separated.'

'And how did they go?' I asked, genuinely interested. I'd not known Allie long, but I already valued her friendship, and trusted her instincts.

'Well, they made me feel better about myself. Boosted my confidence. Made me feel a bit like singing "I'm Every Woman", that kind of thing. But, ultimately, I always ended the night wishing I was with Mike. None of them really lived up to him, and what we had together. That might be the case with you – in which case you know you're not ready for anything more. But . . . it might not. I know it's too soon for anything serious – but this doesn't have to be serious. James is a lovely guy. Just go out. Do your hair. Wear a nice dress. Have some fun.'

Everything she said made sense, and I decided to follow her advice. By the end of the day, I had convinced myself that it was all going to be super-casual, harmless, fun. That it meant nothing – even if thinking about the night before, the way James had made me feel, still sent tingles through my whole body.

Had Simon ever made me feel like that? I wasn't sure. If he had, I couldn't remember it. I was starting to realise that I was missing the security he represented as much as him. Simon made up more than half of our partnership when it came to the outside world – he was the one who did the talking, the joking, the impressing. I was his domestic sidekick. It was only coming here – being on my own, being forced to meet new people, and finding that I actually enjoyed it – that had highlighted the fact that I'd allowed myself to play second fiddle in my own life.

Despite having all day to prepare, I ended up running late – because my sister-in-law Diane called from Liverpool to wish me a happy birthday.

I was juggling the phone, my make-up, and a choice of three different outfits while she talked. Eventually, she cottoned on.

'You've met someone, haven't you?' she said, gleefully.

'No, don't be daft, I'm just getting ready for a night at the bar.'

'Bollocks!' she replied, laughing. I heard her shout out to my brother: 'Guess what, Sal's pulled!', and him laughing too. At least I was a source of entertainment for my nearest and dearest.

'No use lying. I can tell. Now, what are you wearing?'

I gave in and described my choices to her. She listened carefully, asking a few questions along the way, and said: 'The black linen trousers 'cause they're classy, and the white top with the low neck and your boostiest bra. Because that's slutty. Now, have a good night, and don't do anything I wouldn't do . . .'

Seeing as Diane had shagged half the men in Liverpool, and a few of the women, that left me quite a lot of leeway.

James was waiting for me downstairs. The Levis were back, with a pale blue cotton shirt. He had that sexy spicy smell going on again. It made my nostrils, and a few other body parts, quiver. He did a double take when he saw me – or, more accurately, my cleavage.

'You look . . . dangerous,' he said. Which was probably good – I still wasn't sure.

He turned to Jake, who was hopping on one leg by his side, eager to run away to Ian and Jenny, who were looking after him tonight. He gave his son a kiss on his curly hair, and finally let go of his hand. Jake sprinted over to the bar, and leaped straight on to Jenny's lap.

She wrapped her arms around him, and squeezed him so hard he squealed. Amid my own nerves and panic, I registered a moment of complete sympathy for the younger woman – she was clearly a natural with kids, and from what Mike had said, they were facing a future without their own. As though she knew I was thinking about her, Jenny looked up, gave me a huge smile, and made a gesture at her own breasts before giving me the thumbs-up. Great. I'd clearly made a splash in the boob department, at least.

We waved goodbye, and walked along the promenade to a cluster of bars and restaurants, choosing one right on the beach. James pulled my chair out for me to sit on, and I hovered until he went away.

'Sorry,' I said, 'I grew up with four older brothers. Pulling chairs away as I went to sit down was like a family tradition. I still get nervous now.'

That wasn't the only thing I was nervous about, now we were here, alone. I was nervous I'd choke on a piece of melon or have some stupid allergic reaction to shellfish that would make my eyes swell up like Space Hoppers. And I was nervous because I didn't know how this was going to play out. And, more confusingly, I was nervous because I had no idea how I *wanted* it to play out.

James was being flirtatious and charming and trying hard not to talk to my chest. I was flirting right back; and I soon realised we were heading straight back down last night's path, and the wine I was guzzling was acting like our sat nav. It was all so natural, so easy . . . so, predictably enough, I decided to mess it all up.

'James,' I said, putting my knife and fork down, 'I'm a mess.'

'You look fine to me,' he said, with the typical density of a man.

'Oh,' he added, seeing the look on my face, 'you mean you feel a mess.'

He nodded, and rubbed his hand through his hair, leaving tiny blond peaks tufted up from his scalp. 'Yeah, I get it. Truth be known, I'm a bit of a mess too, have been for a while. Cards on the table then – what do you want from me?'

I leaned forward, kissed him very lightly on the lips, then pulled back. Obviously not what he was expecting, and my ego did a little jig when I saw his pupils dilate.

'Sometimes, I want that from you,' I said, 'and a lot more than that. Because I can't deny you've flicked some kind of switch in me, and I think about you and your body and the things I'd like to do to it all the time. You're always there in the back of my mind, looking all gorgeous and hunky and making me feel . . . wiggly.'

A slow grin started to spread across his face. I guess it was his ego's turn to do a jig.

'There's a "but" coming, isn't there?' he asked.

'Yep. I like you as well. I think we could be friends. And that's probably what I need right now – friendship. I've seen what you lot have here, at the Blue Bay. The way you're woven into each other's lives; the way you're so supportive of each other. I don't really have many friends, and I'm pretty sure I need them.

'I'm looking after Ollie and Lucy on my own and probably doing a terrible job of that, and even though Simon's done this awful thing, I can't put aside seventeen years of marriage as easily as he can.

'I'm really not ready for anything new – and, I'm sorry, but I don't think I'll ever be cut out for sitting on that subs' bench of yours.'

'What makes you think that's where I want you to sit? Have I ever said that?' he answered, sounding annoyed. 'I like you too. A lot. I get a hard-on just looking at you, and you make me laugh. Being a bloke, that's pretty much the whole list of what I look for in a woman, unless you could throw in an autographed Ireland rugby shirt while you're at it.

'We've only known each other for a matter of minutes but I already feel like there's something happening here. And that worries me because of Jake. I've worked hard to keep life stable for him and, much as he loves Sally the Pirate Nurse, maybe if I use my head, I know this is wrong for us as well.'

He looked worried and angry and vulnerable all at once. Which perversely made him even sexier. I was beginning to think that even if he put on five stone and had 'my dick is two inches long' tattooed on his forehead, I'd still find something about him to fancy.

'Okay,' he said, blowing out a long breath, 'let's do this friends thing if you want. I can do that.'

I was pleased to hear it. And devastated to hear it. It felt like two different people were inhabiting my mind. If only I had two different bodies as well, the whole dilemma would be solved.

'Now hurry up, friend, because we've got to go somewhere else yet.'

Chapter 21

The 'somewhere else' turned out to be a tiny English bar tucked away in a side street, announcing in flickering neon that it served Stella Artois and Guinness. Classy. I looked at James – it didn't seem to be his kind of place. But maybe now we were just friends he was going to get hammered and talk about football all night.

'I'm sorry,' he said as he ushered me through the door, 'they made me do it.'

'Surprise!' squealed Rick, racing towards me and kissing me on both cheeks. He was resplendent in skinny jeans and a tweed waistcoat – with nothing underneath but his tan.

The others stood at the bar, toasting me with pint glasses and singing 'Happy Birthday'. It was a dingy place, with low lighting and a lot of wood panelling. The randomly scattered tables had dimpled copper surfaces and beer mats shoved under their legs to keep them stable. Someone – presumably the hairy, beer-bellied sixty-something behind the counter – had gone to a lot of time and effort to recreate a spit-and-sawdust dive from back home.

The gang was all there – Allie and Mike, Marcia, Jenny and Ian with Jake, Max; even Lucy and Ollie. There was also a cake, which looked suspiciously like it might have been borrowed from the Blue Bay restaurant.

I was touched. I liked my holiday life much better than my real life – not only did all these people think I was worth throwing a surprise party for, but I'd almost had truly excellent sex as well.

'Sal, come and meet Harry,' said Mike, waving me towards him. Harry appeared to be half man, half goat. His hair was wispy and grey, and his beard was so long it almost touched the barrage balloon that was his belly, barely covered by a Motörhead T-shirt.

'Nice to meet you,' he said, wiping his hand on Lemmy's face before reaching out to shake. 'What'll it be – Guinness or Stella?'

'Erm . . . do you have any white wine?'

'No, never touch the stuff, love. You don't get a figure like this by arsing round with spritzers, right, Mike?' he said, while lovingly stroking his gut.

'Have a lager – at least it's fizzy,' said Mike, 'you can pretend it's Bolly. And if you drink enough, it'll taste like it as well. Harry and I go way back. This is where I come when Allie's doing all that Pilates. He ran a boozer in Southampton for years before he got sick of the rain and traded up for the dolce vita.'

'Yes, I can see that,' I said, feeling the heels of my shoes sink into the sticky goo that passed as the floor.

I took the lager, and downed half of it in one go. I'd grown up in Liverpool – and it was time to dump middle-class Oxford Sally, and get back in touch with the one who cut her drinking teeth in pubs round Anfield.

Everyone else seemed half cut already, and I was grateful that my birthday had given them a good excuse, as Allie had said.

As I looked around the pub, I saw that there was only one other group in, which was comprised of exactly the same clientele I suspect Harry had back in Blighty – loud, rough, and drunk as skunks. They'd all joined in with 'Happy Birthday', and were now singing along to 'Who Let the Dogs Out?'. Rick was dancing on the top of the bar, giving it some welly, urging the others to do the same.

Most of the Ugly Bunch were looking at him, which was understandable, but I noticed that one of them was instead eyeing up my daughter, and not being subtle about it. That was pretty much the last thing I noticed before all hell broke loose, and my very eventful fortieth birthday took another resplendent turn.

The bloke staggered to his feet, ambled towards Lucy, and went straight for an arse-grab. Nice. She whirled round, eyes blazing, looking intent on causing some serious physical harm. I knew that look – and it was likely to get her in a lot of trouble.

Some stupid mothering instinct kicked in, and I ran over, slamming the pointy heel of my sandal straight down into the instep of his foot. Girl power.

He fell to the floor, howling in pain, and Lucy turned her glare to me instead. Oops. I'd clearly breached Teenaged Goth Protocol. Again.

I started to stutter an apology for daring to intervene when one of his friends lumbered over, scattering half-empty pint glasses as he came. He ran towards us, and I watched him come in something like slow motion, with all the charm of a drooling bison.

Before he managed to get within arm's reach, James landed him with an almighty left hook to the face.

The blow knocked him unsteady; he took a couple of steps back, tottered, and finally lost his balance. Landing right in the middle of my birthday cake.

'Oh you arsehole!' yelled Allie, grabbing hold of his head and twisting so he was face down, and threatened with death by icing sugar. He struggled free and looked up, dazed, pink sponge crusted to his eyelashes and white goo oozing out of his nose.

Rick was gesticulating from the top of the bar, his hands fluttering in placatory gestures, asking everyone to 'calm down, please, this is a party!'

Sadly, one of the Ugly Bunch replied with a comment which, while understandable, had some pretty dire consequences for him: 'Shut the fuck up, gay boy.'

Marcia was across the room in seconds, her six-foot Amazonian body speeding like a pissed-off leopard. She launched herself right at him with a flying tackle, growling and snarling as she pinned him to the floor, straddling him and punching him repeatedly in the face as he squealed like a girl.

Two of the others stood to intervene, but Jenny and Ian and Max lined up in front of them, looking as threatening as they could. Ollie stood next to them, gangling and skinny, whipping his hand through the air as though he was wielding some kind of sword – channelling Lords of Legend, I knew.

It had all happened so quickly, slipping from happy-happy to crazy town in a matter of minutes. The story of my life at the moment.

As I backed away from Lucy, and looked on as James took hold of Jake and lifted him over the bar to safety, the ridiculous goings-on were interrupted by the sound of a bell clanging.

'Time, gentlemen, please!' called Harry, in a town-crier voice. It had the desired effect, and everyone froze.

'Come on now, lads, off you piss,' continued Harry, making a hook-slinging gesture and pointing at the door. Covered in cake, blood, dirty footprints and clumps of Marcia's hair, they staggered to the exit, looking downtrodden and defeated. We were a strange old bunch – but we stuck together. I felt a strange thrill at being part of it – this odd gang of mismatched souls who were all so loyal to each other.

I looked around. James might have sore knuckles. Allie was covered in icing. Jake had emerged from behind the bar, giggling and apparently not at all traumatised. Marcia had lost a few clumps of hair. But we were all in one piece – the cake was definitely the worst casualty of the night.

'Well, that was entertaining,' said Mike, 'don't you think so, Harry? Haven't seen a good scrap like that for ages.'

Mike hadn't budged during the whole fracas – choosing to look on and chuckle as he supped his ale.

'You're right, mate,' answered Harry, 'that was a laugh. A bit like one of them saloon fights in the old Westerns. Would've been better if the ladies were dressed up as tarts in frilly bloomers, though, wouldn't it?'

As the dust settled, I saw Lucy gulping down someone else's Guinness. She grimaced at the taste then stormed over to me.

'What the fuck did you do that for? I'm not a baby. When are you going to get it into your tiny little brain that I can fight my own battles?' she said, poking a finger at me.

I'd almost been attacked, had my birthday cake squashed, and my date-night make-up was in ruins. I wasn't in the mood for Cruella de Vil.

'And when are you going to get it into your tiny brain that I am your mother and you are only sixteen years old? I know you wish you were an orphan, and I'm sorry to have inconvenienced you by sticking around – but I'm here to stay, so tough. If it makes you feel better, tell everyone you're adopted, I don't give a shit!'

I thought it was a great speech and I felt much better after I made it. Lucy was so impressed she gave the Vs with two sets of digits instead of the usual one.

James came and put his arms around me. I sank into the embrace, sighing and rubbing my cheek against his chest. It was solid and warm and I could feel his heart beating fast.

'Well,' he said, kissing me on the head, 'never a dull moment with you around, is there? Are you all right? You're not upset or anything?'

'You must be kidding,' I answered. 'They were a bunch of pricks and they got what they deserved. Thanks for being, you know, such a good friend. I didn't even say yes to the sex, and you still got stuck in.'

'Well, I live in hope – just put it on my account in the sex bank. Now let's get home before anything else happens.'

Chapter 22

It was our last night at the Blue Bay Hotel. Lucy had spent most of the day weeping and wailing because she was about to be parted from the love of her life.

Pointing out that he only lived a few hours away in Brighton didn't help. Trying to console her didn't help. Calling her a moody cow and sticking my tongue out behind her back didn't help either, but it made me feel better.

She'd locked herself in the bathroom again, where she was probably listening to suicide songs for beginners on her iPod.

Ollie was having a full day out with the Ginger Twins, neither of whom, he assured me, he fancied. I know one of them's a boy, but I like to be inclusive in my prying.

Which left me, funnily enough, to do everybody's packing. I stuffed everything randomly into whichever case was to hand. Folding is for losers when you're on your way home.

Within a matter of days I'd be taking it all out again, shoving it into the washer, the smell of sun cream wafting around to remind me of paradise lost. Flip-flops with sand still in them. Random foreign coins left in pockets. And a camera full of memories. I understood exactly where Lucy was coming from:

I suspected we were all heading for holiday blues that would make Ella Fitzgerald weep.

Plus back to reality for me was still a terrifying prospect: would Simon ever come back? Would he bugger off to Latvia to repair Russian mafia bosses' hips instead? Would I honestly care if he did? I'd been devastated when he left. And I still was. Two weeks away wasn't enough to cure a broken heart – but it had raised some questions. I'd been desperate for my old life back, the comfort and security of my life with Simon; but now, if I was honest, tiny doubts were creeping in.

There had been moments here – with James, with Allie, that night during the bar-room brawl with all of them – where I'd felt different. Almost happy. Where the pain that Simon's absence had caused had flickered away, even if only for brief moments. I wasn't one hundred per cent sure what I wanted any more.

There was too much to think about, especially while I was still on holiday.

And tonight, I was told by the experts, was the night to beat them all – everyone got very tarted up, including the staff, drank gallons of booze, and sang until the wee small hours.

Diane had called earlier to quiz me on how things had gone with James. When I told her we'd decided to be friends, she was disappointed. When I told her we ended the night in a knock-down fight in a fake English pub, she perked up a lot. Honestly. My family is ridiculous.

While she was on the phone she'd chosen my wardrobe for me long distance, erring very much on the side of slutty as it was time to go out 'with a bang'. She'd said that with a nudge-nudge wink-wink that managed to travel all the way from Liverpool.

So here I was, tottering down to the bar in a killer red dress and equally killer heels. The dress had been an impulse buy the day before we left, and they usually work out as well as one of Joan Collins's marriages. But this was a corker – a plunging neckline, fitted at the waist, then a gentle flare that covered a multitude of buttocks. Well, only the two that I know of, but both big enough to have their own parking spaces at the moment.

I found Allie, Mike and James deep in conversation about the Blue Bay nannies.

'What I like about them is that they're all so . . . perky,' Mike said, with a snigger.

'Oh shut up, Mike – we're talking about their personalities, not their tits,' said Allie, poking him in the gut so hard her finger half disappeared.

'That's unfair, wife! It's not like I'm obsessed with them or anything—'

'Yes it is,' she said. 'When we're out in the car you deliberately stop so pedestrians can run in front of you – but oddly enough only the girls with big boobs because you like watching them bounce as they go. Old men and children have to stand in the rain and eat your exhaust.'

'Again, unfair – it's not just the ones with the *big* boobs I let cross . . . I'm not prejudiced. Although,' he said, turning to me, 'I must say, Sally, that you have outdone yourself on the knockers front tonight. Don't you think so, James, Allie?'

Allie shook her head in disgust and announced she was going to the bar for cocktails for the girls, and Mike could fetch his own. 'I like to watch your belly bounce as you go,' she added as she walked off.

I made eye contact with James and raised an eyebrow. I was feeling shockingly foxy and in the mood to flaunt it.

'So? Anything to add?' I said, wobbling my cleavage around like a TV stripper for comedy effect.

'I don't think I'm capable of speech. And stop doing that – you're playing with fire.'

'Oooh,' said Mike, 'big words from the big man in the corner. Still time for a last-night fling, kids!'

I smiled in what I hoped was a mysterious way. I probably just looked confused.

Allie returned with two huge cocktails, off-white in colour and decorated with what looked to be chopped-up parts of Jelly Baby massacred on a bed of fluffy cream. Jenny followed behind with her own.

'Don't ask,' Jenny said, 'just drink. I asked Mehmet to do them in brandy glasses so we could get more down our necks at once. I think we're going to need them. It's karaoke night.'

'I don't do karaoke,' I said, which wasn't strictly speaking true. In fact, if I'd had enough to drink, you couldn't get me off the bloody thing. My brother Martin has a machine at home and I once woke up on his living-room floor at four in the morning, wearing his mother-in-law's girdle and still clutching the microphone. One side of my face was glued to the carpet with drool and I had 'Big Spender' on repeat.

Miss McTavish arrived, dressed in a little black dress that was way too little for her body. It was covered in sequins and tassels and would have looked OTT on *Strictly Come Dancing*.

'Oh, my dears!' she said, climbing up on to a bar stool. Her tiny legs waved around in the air, not long enough to reach the footrest. 'I've had such a day! I went off to the nudist beach – so very liberating! I felt like quite the prude putting clothes back on this evening, I really did – but I'm going commando to try and recapture the moment, if you get my drift!'

With the last sentence, she cocked her legs up so they were at right angles with her body, and did a little showgirl scissor kick. The men all averted their eyes so fast they probably got cricks in their necks.

I gulped down my drink and went in search of more.

I noticed Lucy and Max, draped around each other at their own table, gazing into each other's eyes with the dumb adoration you only experience as a teenager. And, possibly, as a forty-year-old, almost-divorcée, confronted with a sexy blond Dubliner in a well-fitted pair of jeans. They were holding hands and sipping Cokes. No fags. No booze. No biting the heads off bats. He was a bloody good influence on her. Ollie was upstairs on the pool table with Carin and Christian and a ragtag of other teens, overdosing on Red Bull and tripping over their own baggy jeans.

I stood and watched as Mehmet made the next cocktail. It seemed to consist of about seventeen different shots of spirits and liqueurs, topped off with squirty cream and sweets for nutritional value. It was practically a meal in a glass. He called it his 'wonky bonky tipsy special'.

The karaoke was starting, hosted by one of the boy-wonder reps. He kicked it off with a rousing rendition of 'Billie Jean', complete with moonwalking, followed by his colleagues, who set the tone for the rest of the night before the guests got into the swing of things. It was like an upscale version of the Pontins Bluecoats putting on a show.

Mehmet was doing his bit to help the party go with a bang, giving treble measures to everyone, including himself.

'I want hear you sing tonight, Sally,' he said with a wink as he mixed another cocktail for me, Allie and Jenny. He'd now graduated to pint glasses, which I was fairly sure should be illegal.

Next up on the karaoke stage of superstars was Rick. He was dressed, and I kid you not, in a sailor suit with a little white hat.

He looked cute as a button, and launched straight into a hypnotically bump-and-grind version of 'Livin' La Vida Loca'. His make-up was perfect. Marcia was tanked up but dignified, smoking a cigarette and applauding in support of her nautical beau.

I'd spent the afternoon with her the day before, learning more about her life and her marriage and her work as a university lecturer. She was scarily intelligent, as well as scary in pretty much every other way. I was no closer to understanding her relationship with Rick, but I did know one thing: they loved each other completely.

'Come on, we're up,' said Mike to Allie, who by this stage was so drunk she was ricocheting off the tables as they made their way up to the stage, apologising to invisible people as she went.

I almost choked laughing as I watched them do their very individual version of 'Bohemian Rhapsody'. Mike was Freddie and Allie sang all the backing vocals, doing star jumps as she 'Scaramouched' and miming thunderbolts and lightning. Awesome. They got a huge round of applause, and Mike picked Allie up, threw her over his shoulder and did a lap of victory round the pool, his belly flapping away as he galloped.

James came and sat next to me, with yet another one of those wupsy wipsy specials, or whatever they were called.

'You know, James,' I said, toasting him with the glass, 'you're looking especially lovely tonight. I don't think I've ever seen a man's arse look quite as good in jeans as yours does.'

Jenny, sitting on Ian's lap next to me, snorted with laughter and buried her face in her husband's chest to try and drown out the sound.

'You're drunk,' James answered, 'and I like it. Feel free to touch my leg under the table.'

I obliged, and gave his thigh a good squeeze.

'Oh, it's like stone . . . how did you get so hard and muscly and firm?'

'Good genes and sport. How did you get so curvy and soft?'

'Bad genes and no sport,' I said, running my hand up and down his thigh. Especially up.

He reached under the table and held my hand still in his.

'Stop that. Or I won't be able to get up without knocking the table over. And we're just friends now, remember?'

I was pretty drunk by that stage, and I don't recall it completely clearly, but I think I might have actually pouted. And possibly told him he was a cowardy-custard spoilsport, or words to that effect.

'I think I want to sing now,' I said, staggering to my feet and downing the rest of my drink.

'Mehmet!' I yelled as I passed the bar. 'Here it comes, baby!' He threw his tea towel in the air and cheered as I headed up on to the stage. Somebody had definitely added a couple of extra steps, I discovered, as I stumbled up them and grabbed the mike.

I chose my all-time 'yes, I'm a drunk old child of the eighties' song, 'Like A Virgin'. Madonna has a lot to answer for, encouraging all us middle-aged women to believe we can cavort on stage doing slutty hip wiggles and get away with it. Some of us haven't been doing power yoga for the last three decades and should really know better.

Not that I stayed on the stage. Oh no, that would have been too tame by far. I danced my way back down those steps, in and out of tables, and right up to James.

I smooched towards him, wailing for all the world to hear that he made me feel, well, like a virgin. Or a vir-ir-ir-ir-gin, to be exact. I hitched up my skirt and straddled his lap, telling him yet again, in fact a few more times than the song lyrics required. Madonna just couldn't keep up with me.

He held on to my hips as I gyrated, which was probably a good thing as I'd have fallen backwards on to my wupsy tupsy special if he hadn't.

As I bawled out my last 'heartbeat', I was dimly aware of tumultuous applause. Nothing like a drunken slapper to please the crowds; and who doesn't love a blatantly fake virgin with a squirty-cream moustache?

The applause was nice, but even nicer was the fact that I was sitting astride the rather magnificent man of my current dreams.

I threw the mike down and gave him a big hug, burying my head in his shoulder. I was feeling tired and emotional, and thought I could quite happily live there, nestled in his arms, feeling safe and warm and slightly nauseous.

'I don't want to be just friends any more,' I said, wiping my squirty cream on his shirt. What man wouldn't want me?

He locked his arms tighter around my back and kissed my shoulder.

'I know. Neither do I. But you're very drunk, and you won't be feeling especially good in the morning. I'm going to take you back to your room, okay? I'll make sure Lucy and Ollie get back safe. You get some sleep. Sound like a plan?'

'Yes . . .' I sighed, having no intention of moving. Ever again.

James stood up, hoisted my legs round his waist, laced his hands under my bottom for support, and started off towards the hotel.

'Madonna is leaving the building!' he announced as he went. 'She'll be signing autographs at the airport tomorrow!'

I waved to everyone over his shoulder, and everyone waved back. Rick looked a little tearful. Allie had physically fallen off her chair she was laughing so much. Mehmet was swigging from a bottle of vodka and giving me the thumbs-up. Miss McTavish was clapping her tiny hands in glee.

Lucy – my lovely girl – had her head flat on the table, a beach towel draped over it to shut out the whole world. She probably loved seeing my extra-special performance – isn't it every teenaged girl's dream to see her mum flashing her knickers in front of her mates?

The Birthday that Changed Everything

I remember James struggling slightly to get me up the stairs, mainly because I was trying to kiss him as he did it, and he couldn't see where he was going. And as he kicked open the door and staggered in with me, I know I tried to hold on to his neck and drag him into the bed in a very unvirginal way.

Unfortunately, that's where the memory train drew to a halt. I woke up the next morning with a banging headache and a mouth like the inside of a baboon's armpit. I was also completely naked apart from one black jelly baby, which was stuck to my left bum cheek.

I couldn't be sure, but I didn't feel like I'd had sex. It'd been a while, but I was positive I'd still be able to recognise the signs. I wriggled around a bit. No. Everything felt normal. I didn't know whether I was relieved or disappointed. Relieved, I suppose – what a nightmare if I'd finally shagged him but been too drunk to even remember it.

I scraped the jelly baby off and binned it. I planned to get up and get moving. Sometime very soon. Once the banging subsided and I regained feeling in all my limbs. I threw one arm out to the side – somebody had very kindly left a bottle of water right there on the bedside cabinet. I gulped down a few mouthfuls and felt marginally more human. Ugggh.

After a moment or two of lying there, gawping at the ceiling and practising moving my eyelids, I realised that the banging was no longer just in my head – it was on the door. I ignored it. It was probably just the window cleaner looking for his money, and he'd go away in a minute.

Except that was in a different reality, and the banging didn't stop.

'Sally! It's James!'

'Shit . . .' I muttered, swinging my legs over the side of the bed.

'Hang on, won't be a minute!' I shouted, the sound of my own voice ricocheting around in my skull like a hand grenade.

I grabbed a nightshirt and pulled it over my head, zigzagged into the bathroom and brushed my teeth at lightning speed. I wet my fingertips and rubbed them under my eyes to get rid of the thickest of the mascara. When I tried to brush my hair the whole thing got stuck in a tangle the size of the Isle of Wight, so I gave up.

I had lost track of how long the complete process had taken – somewhere between two minutes and an hour.

I opened the door and James was leaning on the frame, long and lean and every bit as luscious as usual. He was dangling one of my red high heels from his fingers.

'I thought you might want this. I found it hanging off the flagpole in the gardens.'

'Thank you. For the shoe. And for getting me back. And . . . we didn't have sex, did we?'

'No,' he said, 'we didn't. Despite your best efforts.'

He grinned and took a couple of steps towards me, putting his hands on my arms and pushing me gently back so I was resting against the wall.

'We have to leave for the airport in ten minutes,' he said, 'and I wanted to say goodbye. Properly.'

He ran his hands up over my shoulders, twining his fingers into my hair. He used his grip to tilt my head up, and I met his ocean-deep eyes. I think he was giving me a moment to make my protest. None came. I'd brushed my teeth and was ready to go. It was probably the wrong thing to do, and I was probably still drunk, but I wanted that kiss more than anything in the world. More than superpowers. More than chocolate cake. More than Simon coming home. More than my next breath. I'd figure out everything else afterwards, but for now . . . well, I was worth it.

He leaned down and kissed me slowly, deliberately, and gently. His lips were like butterflies, nibbling and teasing and provoking until I put my arms around him, holding him tighter and standing on tippy-toes to get nearer to him.

His body moved closer, his chest crushing my breasts. The bulge of his jeans was pressing into me and I rubbed myself against him shamelessly.

He trailed kisses down past my ear, nuzzling his way to that super-sensitive spot where neck meets shoulder, then pulled away. I fell forward slightly, and thought I might cry. That just felt too nice to be finished so soon.

'God . . . I've got to go,' he said hoarsely. His chest was heaving slightly and the trouser issue made it obvious he'd been a very naughty boy. I'm not sure staring at the hard points of my nipples outlined against my shirt was helping.

'All that stuff you did last night,' he said, 'try it again next year. When you're sober.'

And with that, he was gone. Walking, slowly and awkwardly, down the corridor and out of my line of vision.

Chapter 23

The airport looked like a refugee camp. Me and Lucy were sharing a seat, and Ollie had gone to get us Cokes. Nobody even had the energy to snipe at each other, which is usually cause for calling the paramedics in our household.

Lucy had stopped crying and started texting.

'Are you texting him already?' I asked. 'Haven't you ever heard of playing hard to get?'

She didn't look up or let her thumbs stop their tap-dance as she answered: 'Yeah, right, Mum, like I'm going to take relationship advice from you. Anyway, you were hardly playing coy last night, practically shagging James in front of the whole hotel, were you?

'Did you, by the way . . . you know, shag him? I know he came down and sent us to bed a bit later, but for all I know at his age it only takes a few minutes . . .'

There was so much wrong with that whole speech, I didn't know where to start.

'On second thoughts don't bother telling me. I know that technically you're only human, and Dad's at it like some demented middle-aged bunny on Viagra. So I understand if

158

you . . . do stuff. Just don't fucking tell me about it, though, 'cause it's too gross to imagine.'

'Mum! Luce!' said Ollie excitedly as he returned with cans of Coke that cost about £5 each. 'Look at them – that couple over there!'

He pointed at a well-dressed man and woman in their early sixties. She had a very tidy bun, matching pearl earrings and necklace and wore expensive-looking cream slacks. Her husband had neat grey hair, a perma-tan, and a yellow Argyll golfing sweater on. There was nothing at all to distinguish them from any other well-to-do, middle-class grey panthers enjoying an active retirement.

'What about them, dimwit? Are you hoping they'll adopt you?' said Lucy, voice dripping with sarcasm.

'Fuck off, cow-face – listen, honest, this is hilarious! I was behind them in the queue in the shop, and I got a look at the tags on their hand luggage. That's Mr and Mrs Smith from Solihull!'

'No way!' said Lucy and I at the same time, jumping up for a better look. That was just too weird.

'Do you want to go and give them their Clit Stick back? I've still got it in my bag,' I said.

'No thanks. Disgusting. They shouldn't even be having sex at their age, never mind extra-weird sex. I think I might puke if I think about it any more.'

Ollie threw himself down on his rucksack, using it as a chair for his skinny backside. He looked a little tired and deflated after sharing his revelation. He got out his phone and started untangling the wires.

He sighed like the world had just crash-landed on his shoulders.

'That was a great holiday, Mum. How many more sleeps until we can go back?'

Lucy snorted with laughter.

'God, you're such a baby Ollie . . . and anyway, retard, it's 364.'

Phones on. Ear pods in. Eyes closed. Full teenaged zombie state resumed.

I smiled to myself as I looked at them. They were happy. And so, bizarrely, was I.

PART THREE

Heading to Turkey – almost 364 sleeps later . . .

Chapter 24

'And that,' I typed, 'is what I would do to you if I had you face down on a massage table covered in baby oil. Bye for now!'

I signed off the email with a trio of winky-faces, including one with devil's horns and one wearing sunglasses. I had recently discovered emoticons, and was very much enjoying overusing them.

I laughed as I sent the e-mail, imagining poor James's reaction when he read it, and hoping he wasn't in the office when he did. It was past midnight now, so the chances were he wouldn't open it until the next day. But, I thought, leaning back and taking a probably unnecessary sip of wine, I'd keep the laptop on just in case.

Our fond farewell from Turkey had developed into an even fonder virtual relationship since we'd got home. He'd already messaged me by the time I'd unpacked the suitcases, which had certainly made the seventh load of washing go with more of a swing.

To start with, it was friendly. 'How are you?' type stuff. Enquiries about our kids. The journey. Settling in to life back home. That kind of thing.

And it stayed like that for quite a while, neither of us fully committing to anything more, but neither of us willing to quite let go of the connection. For me, it was a thread of sanity and optimism that made life back in Oxford so much more bearable.

Despite his under-the-influence birthday phone call, Simon – at first – had shown no signs of regretting his decision to leave us. He turned up on the doorstep a few days after we'd come home, looking suntanned and fit, his usual 'worried-for-the-ex's-sanity' expression on his face as I let him in.

That same look had driven me mad before the Blue Bay – the way it suggested that he still cared about me, but not enough to come back. That he felt sorry for me, more than he saw me as a life partner. It made me feel – simultaneously – hopeful that there was still some underlying affection, angry that he'd left me, and pathetic for still wanting him back.

But, as he wandered in behind me and took in the heaps of laundry with a raised eyebrow, stroking the dog (who was always the most pleased to see him) and asking how I was, I felt different. It wasn't just the messages from James. It was the fact that Allie had called the night before, and we'd chatted for hours. That Jenny had tagged me in a load of photos of us all from the holiday. That Rick and Marcia had joined in a lengthy and hilarious Facebook conversation about our last-night karaoke, and what we should sing next year.

That they were already assuming I'd be there next year made me feel part of something – something that hadn't just disappeared the moment we all got on our respective planes back to the UK. They'd all urged me to book again straight away, and I started to understand the way they were all so close. Two weeks in Turkey – and the rest of the year to look forward to the next trip.

For the first time since I'd met him, Simon *wasn't* at the centre of every single part of my life. I still missed him – there's only so much that a group of long-distance friends can compensate for – but it was less raw. Less desperate. When I felt the black moods descending, as I settled in for yet another lonely night in front of the TV when the kids were out, I had something to help me snap out of it.

I had people to e-mail, to call. I had James to fantasise about. I had an alternative reality that I could dip into when I needed it – it wasn't only about Simon, and what Simon might do next.

He noticed the slight difference in me straight away, and I think at first he was relieved. Felt as though some of the burden of worrying about me had been lifted, freeing him up to enjoy his newfound liberation with Monika even more.

As the months went by, though, and especially in the run-up to our first Christmas apart, he seemed to not only notice, but be slightly more curious. He was asking more questions, showing more interest. I had a weekend away with Allie – an alleged spa break in Hampshire that actually turned into a giant piss-up – and I had one delicious day in London with James. Both events prompted a flurry of messages from Simon, on various blatantly made-up pretexts, usually involving the kids.

Lucy's continuing romance with Max gave him the apparent reason to be so nosy – but I sensed it was more. Slowly, but very surely, the balance of our relationship was changing.

With typically frustrating timing, the less I cared about what he was doing, the more he cared about what I was doing.

He'd turned up on 1 December, looking as though he'd been dressed by Lumberjacks R Us, and announced that he'd come so we could go and choose our Christmas tree. This had been a family tradition for as long as I could remember – he, the kids and I piled into the car, heading to a forest in the Oxfordshire countryside where we squabbled over which pine to strap to the top. It had been lovely when the kids were little, but over the years it had descended into an annual grump-fest.

The Christmas before he'd left, Lucy had sulked for the whole journey, Ollie had sprained his ankle when she'd pushed him out of the car, and I'd been overly bright and chirpy, desperately trying to compensate for it all. Simon had sullenly followed us around, clearly hating every minute of it. Now, with the clarity of distance, I could see how miserable he'd actually been. It was still, after all this time, a memory that could provoke me to tears – a parody of a happy family outing.

So to say that I hadn't expected a repeat performance now he'd actually left the marital home was something of an understatement. I'd broken the news to him that we'd bought one already, and invited him in when I saw the forlorn expression on his face. In fact, I'd felt so sorry for him, he'd stayed for dinner – a takeaway in front of the telly, laughing our backsides off at a Will Ferrell movie.

Ollie had joined us, Lucy luckily hadn't, and it had felt . . . nice. Enjoyable. Almost normal – apart from the fact that we hadn't spent pleasant nights like this together for a long time before he left. When he finally drove away, and Ollie went up to bed, I'd smiled at the whole thing. At the fact that it possibly – just possibly – showed a way that we could be in each other's lives without him feeling trapped, or me feeling desperate to have him back.

If that evening had happened without me going to the Blue Bay, I'd have probably begged him to stay. Clung on to him on the doorstep. Spent the whole night lying awake, wondering if it meant he was coming home.

But I had better things to do by then. Like send my Irish cyber-boyfriend rude e-mails. We'd progressed to that stage within a month of coming home – and now, with just a few days to go until we all returned to the Blue Bay, we were still going strong.

I heard a ping from my laptop. Smiled as I opened his reply.

'Dear Sally,' it said. 'I was very much intrigued by your plans for an alternative massage, and also by your masterly use of emoticons. Would you care to log on to Skype to discuss this matter further?'

I finished my wine. Realised I was grinning at the prospect. Why, I thought, clicking the Skype icon, the hell not?

Chapter 25

'Have you seen this?' said Allie, throwing a paperback down on the table in front of me.

I'd been back at the Blue Bay Hotel for all of twenty minutes and was already at the bar. Allie had a mostly empty bottle of white wine in front of her, so I was guessing she'd been there at least ten minutes longer.

I picked up the book and glanced at the front.

'Look at the title. And look who wrote it,' she instructed.

'*Shag Yourself Happy* by . . . by . . . Jane McTavish! Bloody hell! Is that our Miss McTavish?'

According to the cover, it was a global bestseller – a guaranteed guide to 'finding your inner goddess through mind-blowing sex'. Jesus. I flicked to the inside blurb, which informed me that Jane McTavish was one of the most respected relationship coaches in the world. She'd written several self-help books before her current multimillion-selling smash hit, and lived in Edinburgh.

She was also, if you believed the accompanying photo, a drop-dead gorgeous blonde of about thirty-five. Either the art of airbrushing had been elevated to new heights, or Miss

McT had wisely decided she'd sell better as a sex guru if she wasn't known as a wrinkly old gnome.

I quickly thumbed through the book, reading chapter titles about nudism, loving your own body, and dressing up for role-play. It was like a flashback to the horrors of last year.

'Oh the cow! She's even got a chapter in here called "The Missing Sock"!' I said, recalling our conversation about mine and Simon's sex life. What a nerve – I didn't even get a credit, and instead the case study was based on 'Nancy, 40, a nurse'.

'Unbelievable, isn't it?' said Allie. 'And this was the last copy at the airport – everywhere I looked there were women reading it, nodding, and husbands looking more and more twitchy. We were nothing but guinea pigs for the old perve – she's not back here this year, I asked Tarkan on reception. She only came the once, presumably for research . . . well, at least you were interesting enough to make it in there. Mike feels quite insulted. You can borrow that if you like – I read it all on the plane.'

I tucked it into my bag to gag over later. I'd have to send a copy to Diane, with my sections highlighted – she'd be so proud.

'So, what's been going on with you since we last spoke?' I asked. As we'd last spoken about a month ago, I was guessing not that much. I had some funny news for her, and I'd resisted the temptation to tell her on the phone – it was so juicy I had to deliver it in person.

Allie thought for a moment, looked as though she was about to say something important, then shook her head. 'Nothing much . . . work, Mike, life . . . getting Max ready to start at

Oxford in October. Promise me you'll keep an eye on him and make sure he eats something other than Pot Noodles?'

'But of course,' I replied. 'At the very least I'll encourage him to eat different flavours so he gets a balanced diet.'

'Seriously?' she said, leaning forward and frowning, 'you will look out for him, won't you?'

'You know I will, you silly moo!' I replied. 'I'll care for him like he's my own. Probably better.'

Allie slid back into her seat, her whole body relaxing. She seemed a bit edgy – probably a combination of the journey, her prospective empty-nest syndrome, and the wine.

'Great. Thank you. So what have you been up to? Apart from sexually harassing James?'

I giggled, in a way an almost-forty-one-year-old woman really shouldn't, before I replied.

'Well,' I said, 'I did meet Monika the husband-stealer last week . . .'

'No way! Tell me all! What did she say? Did you pull her hair and hit her with your handbag?'

'She said – and I don't know if I can get my voice low enough for this: "Hees deek, it dos not dance." But she said it more scarily.'

'She said *what?* And does she really sound like a Bond villainess?' said Allie, sitting forward with excitement.

'She sounds more like a Bond villain, actually. I'd finished work and she ambushed me in the car park, saying we had to talk. I did have a mad few seconds where I considered running her over, but in the end curiosity got the better of me, so we went for a coffee. There's no way I was taking her back to the house – she might have left with the dog as well.

'Turns out the love match of the decade is falling a bit . . . floppy. "I am vorried," she says, "early days, deek always like happy little soldier. Always dancing. Now, ees sad. Vy ees thees? Thees ever happen vith you?" I almost choked on my cappuccino. Unbelievable.'

'What a cheek,' said Allie, 'coming to you for sex counselling – maybe we could refer her to Miss McTavish. What did you tell her? And what *does* she look like?'

'I told her no, it had never happened with us – which is true, but probably only because we hardly ever had sex. He could have had erectile dysfunction for the last six months for all I'd have noticed. Obviously I didn't add that bit, because I'm a petty-minded bitch and I quite enjoyed seeing her suffer. For a few minutes at least.

'As for what she looks like, well . . . no getting away from it, she's young and gorgeous. And . . . okay, I know this makes me super-pathetic, but I did feel sorry for her. It was obvious she wasn't quite the money-grabbing little whore I wanted her to be – she seemed to be genuinely devastated about what was going on with her and Simon. Or what was not going on, anyway.'

'So how does it make you feel, then, knowing there's trouble in paradise?'

It was a good question. And I admit it. I'd felt a bit smug about the non-dancing-dick thing – technically, he was still *my* husband . . . at least for the next month or so. And I'd suspected there was trouble in paradise long before I met her.

As well as the Christmas-tree thing, he'd just been coming round more. Saying he was there for the kids, but staying for a cup of tea. Even asking if I needed any jobs doing round the house – which in itself was enough to make me wonder if he needed to seek psychiatric help.

'You know, Allie,' I said, 'if it'd happened sooner, I might have been pleased. I'd probably have considered giving Mr Floppy the kiss of life to get Simon back. But now . . . I just don't know. It's been over a year. It's not been easy, but we've all survived it. I've got used to having the whole bed, and not rinsing his shaving foam out of the sink, and changing light bulbs myself. I'm not saying I'm glad it happened, but I'm okay with it. I've moved on.'

'And that moving on would have nothing at all to do with James?' she asked, immediately seeing through my bravado. 'Because last time I saw you two together, you were dry-humping him in front of two hundred strangers . . . I hope that didn't happen when you met up in London.'

'No,' I replied, 'Covent Garden wasn't ready for that. We just had lunch . . . and maybe a big snog as well.'

Allie raised her eyebrows and grinned, pouring another glass of wine for us both. She was hitting it pretty hard by her standards, and it seemed rude to let her drink alone.

'Anyway, it was lovely to see Max when he came to stay in December,' I said, changing the subject. 'Lucy's been unbearable the last few weeks waiting to see him – and she's got a bit of a surprise for him.'

'Is she pregnant?'

'I bloody well hope not! No, it's her hair – she's decided she's had enough of being Madame Midnight, and she's gone back to blonde. I know she's nervous about what Max is going to think – I can tell 'cause she tried to push me down the stairs this morning. With both hands.'

'Oh,' said Allie. It was a meaningful 'oh'. As in, 'Oh – there's a giant iceberg straight ahead, Captain.'

'What's the problem?' I asked, feeling my own throat go dry. If Max was going to chuck her, he could at least have let me know in advance – I'd have brought body armour.

'Here he comes, you can see for yourself . . .'

I turned round to see what all the fuss was about, half expecting him to have had a sex change.

'Oh,' I said. Max – buff, toned and smiling as ever – walked towards us. He'd grown an extra inch and added another instalment on that six pack, from the looks of it. His green eyes were lively, scanning the terrace for Lucy, and he was in his usual outfit – bare chest and surfer shorts.

The only thing that had really changed, in fact, was his hair. It used to be a gorgeous, glinting auburn brown. It wasn't that colour any more. It was dyed a shade I was very familiar with – midnight blue-black. And he'd even had his eyebrows done to match.

Oh indeed.

Chapter 26

'Hi Max – you look . . . different,' I said. And awful, I thought – it really didn't suit him. On Lucy it had worked in a weird way. It suited her satanic nature. But on Max it was just wrong.

'I know – do you think she'll like it?' he said, like an eager puppy dog. 'Last year she felt like she didn't fit in and, well, I wanted to show her she does with me . . .'

God, he was so sweet, you could make candyfloss from him. Allie and I made eye contact and smiled. Young love at its best.

Ollie arrived, swigging an energy drink and bopping to his iPod. He sat down and nodded at us all, stopping dead when he saw Max. He pulled out his earphones and stared at him.

'Holy cow, Batman,' he said, 'wait till she sees that.' He shook his head in disbelief and went back to his drink.

We were all watching for her to emerge from the hotel. I saw Max looking confused as a blonde with Lucy's slender body and fuck-you-very-much walk headed towards us.

Lucy stopped in her tracks as she got close enough to see us properly. Hands on hips, eyes narrowed as she zoned in on Max and his jet-black mop-top, she didn't say a word. He in return gaped at this slightly pissed-off platinum-blonde goddess standing before him.

Twenty, thirty seconds passed, as they both presumably worked out what was going on, and what their motives had been.

'Fancy a swim?' she said.

'Yeah!' he answered, jumping up and running over to her. They walked off hand in hand.

'Phew,' said Ollie, 'that could have got nasty. I thought she was going to scalp him with her nail file for a minute. I s'pose it'll all grow out – he looks really bad with black hair.'

Allie laughed and poured yet another glass. Ollie looked at the two of us, debated if he was about to get told off for being rude or not, then started fiddling with his iPod.

'Have you been telling Allie about how you got sacked this year, Mum?' he said innocently, before plugging back in. The little shit. He was just as evil as Lucy, only cleverer.

'Oh yes? You didn't mention that, Sally! Hang on a minute, here comes Mike – I'm sure he'd want to hear!'

'Hear what?' said Mike, settling his bear-like body into a chair and leaning back so far I heard the legs creak. His hair was losing its battle against the grey, and I think his beer belly had visited a few new breweries since last year. I knew from my phone chats with Allie that he was considering taking semi-retirement from his engineering business, and presumed he'd started in on his leisure plans already.

Ironically, it was Allie who was drinking us all under the table just then. I caught his eye as he checked out how much booze Allie had already put away. He gave me a little 'haven't got a clue' shrug.

'Sally got sacked,' said Allie. 'She's just about to tell us all about it, as she neglected to mention it on the phone.'

'Did it involve going into school dressed as a slutty nurse?' Mike asked, rubbing his hands together and wriggling his bushy eyebrows suggestively.

'No . . . it's worse than that. I got sacked for indecently assaulting the lollipop man,' I said. I could tell from Ollie's snigger that he could still hear me, even though he was pretending to listen to Led Zeppelin.

'Saucy Sid, we call him. He's a seventy-two-year-old with severe halitosis, and he's as randy as a goat. We've all suffered at his hands – literally. For years he's been pinching my arse as we cross the road. You get ready to hop forward whenever you get near him and his giant yellow stick. Don't ask me why, but when I went back after Easter I'd had enough. I marched straight over and grabbed him by his scrawny geriatric back-side instead, and gave him a good squeeze.

'I thought it'd be a bit of a laugh, but he made an official complaint of sexual harassment. There were loads of witnesses and some of them were only four, so there wasn't much I could do . . .'

'The lucky bastard,' said Mike, 'I wish you'd come and grope me in the workplace, Sal – I'd pay good money for it. So what are you up to now? Massage parlour, is it? Any happy endings?'

'No, Mike, I am currently working as a very respectable doctor's receptionist.'

'You can't be – you're not rude enough. Haven't they sent you on the training course in how to be obstructive yet?'

'Stop being a wanker, Mike. Some of my best friends are doctors' receptionists. Go get us some more wine,' said Allie, putting her feet up on the chair opposite her. For a moment I thought he was going to comment, but he hoisted himself up and ambled to the bar.

'You okay?' I said cautiously after he'd gone.

'Yeah, why wouldn't I be? Anyway, I'd have thought that was the last thing on your mind, as I've just seen James and Jake arrive.'

My eyes widened and I jolted upright. He was earlier than I'd expected, and a whole family of butterflies had instantly made their home in my tummy.

'Don't worry, you look fine,' said Allie. 'Gorgeous, in fact.'

I could have sworn there were tears in her eyes, but I didn't have time to worry about that right now. Usually it was from laughing at one of my horror stories, anyway – sometimes I felt as if I was put on this planet purely to provide entertainment for my friends and family.

'James! My good fellow!' bellowed Mike, greeting him with a man-hug and a slap on the back. 'I see you're still in rotten shape – have you ever considered getting some exercise?'

Jake ran over at the speed of light and threw his arms around Allie, then me. I stood him back to get a good look at him.

'Jake! I think you've grown about six inches since last summer!' I said. 'I bet you're almost as tall as me!' I stood up to check, and sure enough he was working his way higher, especially as he was on tiptoes.

'Can I listen to your music?' he shouted to Ollie. Ollie didn't break a beat in his toe-tapping, but nodded, patted his lap, and gave Jake one earpiece once he was settled.

James was standing with his back to us, chatting to Mike at the bar. He was wearing a pair of dark jeans and a black short-sleeved T-shirt. His golden hair was cut slightly shorter than usual. He still had a tan, from a winter work trip to Brazil, and his rear view was as awesome as I remembered it.

He sensed me watching, or possibly heard me spluttering, and turned round. Our eyes met across a not-so-crowded bar, and his face broke out into a broad smile.

Mike gave him a shove in the back and he staggered forward a few steps, regaining his balance and walking over to our table.

'Hi, Allie,' he said, not taking his eyes away from mine.

'Hi, James,' she said, 'and bye, James! Husband – come and drink this with me down at the beach!'

She wouldn't win any prizes for subtlety, but I appreciated it nonetheless. Even Ollie looked up and said he was going to take Jake to play on the swings, and fifteen-year-old boys are not renowned for their sensitivity. Must be the collection of 'vintage' Mills & Boons of mine he'd found in the garage and read voraciously over the summer.

James stopped just in front of me. Close enough that our fingertips reached out and touched. I was sure if I looked down I'd see sparks. He ran his fingers gently up my bare arm, caressed the side of my neck, and leaned in for a little kiss. It looked polite enough on the surface, but I could practically hear my knees knocking.

'You're doing it again,' he said.

'What?'

'Looking up at me with those big brown eyes and forcing me to imagine you with no clothes on . . .'

'And it's not even via Skype,' I said, moving forward slightly so I could feel more of his body pressing against mine. Some bits were already more pressing than others.

He blew out a long breath and hugged me closer, resting his chin on my head.

'I think we might both die if we have another fortnight of this, Sally. Tonight I need to settle Jake in. Tomorrow, my phone-sex friend, is all ours.'

Chapter 27

'So,' said Lucy that night at the bar, 'I think it's about time we had The Talk. You know, The Sex Talk. Don't be embarrassed – there comes a time in every mother's life when she needs to learn about the birds and the bees . . .'

'What the fuck are you talking about?' I asked, hackles immediately on alert. She'd eaten dinner with Max, and I hadn't seen her all day. I wasn't sure I liked blonde Lucy – she was even more cocky than Goth Lucy.

'I saw you earlier, with James. And pretty disgusting it was too, let me add. But it's pretty obvious there's been something going on, and maybe there'll be a lot more going on this holiday, so—'

'Stop! I'm not listening! I'm not listening! Tra la la la!' I shouted, holding my hands over my ears in terror.

Shouldn't this be the other way round? Okay, so I'd skipped The Sex Talk with Lucy. But that's because she knew more than I did by the time she was eleven, and looked at me like dog poo the day she figured out I'd 'let Dad put that thing there'.

Her mouth had stopped moving. I took my hands away.

'Let's talk condoms!' she said immediately.

'Let's not!' I replied, looking around for rescue – where the hell was Max when you needed him? She'd probably sent him out to buy me a pack of Durex and a diagram of the human reproductive organs.

'Mum, just listen!' she said, loudly – in the tone I associate with a potential escalation in violence. It was the same way she said 'Die, fuckers, die!' when she killed wasps with streams of hairspray.

'I'm talking sense here. And you're always going on about wanting us to be friends.'

'No I'm not. I said that once when you were fourteen and you threw an ashtray at my head. I'm happy with our distance. I prefer remembering you when you were seven. Look, I'm forty years old, Lucy. I think I know a thing or two about sex.'

'Okay, maybe you used to be a bit of a slapper when you were younger, but let's face it, you've been Mrs Mouse for the last God-knows-how-many years. And if you'd pay a bit of attention and listen to the *subtext*,' she said this with the assumed superiority of an A level English student, 'you'd see that what I'm trying to fucking do is let you know we're all right with it – with you and James. Me and Ollie both think he's okay, as old men go.'

'He's forty-three, for Christ's sake! But, well, thanks . . . I think,' I said. 'But you know, Luce, nothing's happened anyway . . . not much. Nothing full-on. Just a bit of snogging and a bit of feeling. Nothing I'd need condoms for.'

Lucy screwed up her face and threw her hands over her ears. 'I'm not listening! Tra la la la!' she said, 'and I was only fucking kidding when I said I wanted to talk about it – don't make me chuck by telling me the gross details, that's TMI!'

'Well, what about you and Max?' I asked, as soon as her hands were back down. I should have asked ages ago but I was afraid of the answer.

'What about me and Max? Are you asking me if we're having sexual intercourse, Mother?' I felt myself blushing bright red.

'Well, that's none of your frigging business, is it? I'm seventeen, I can shag whoever the fuck I want to. But if we are at it, believe me I know all about how babies are made, and how you catch chlamydia, and when to take the morning-after pill, if that puts your sordid mind at rest. And I bet that's a lot more than you know – there are probably STDs out there now that didn't even exist last time you had sex!'

She flounced off, spinning her golden hair behind her like a supernova. I was left sitting on the bar stool, wondering if she was right, and whether I should sign up for a sex-education class for middle-aged born-again virgins. And as for all that experience I'd allegedly gained while I was a young slapper, in reality I'd only ever slept with two-and-a-half men.

One was my boyfriend Lee, who I went out with when I was eighteen. We'd lost our virginity together in the back of his dad's fruit and veg van, parked up by Anfield – not on match day, I might add. At university there was Archie, the heart-throb captain of the rugby team, for one night only after a yard-of-ale contest. But he'd had such a bad case of brewer's droop it'd been like trying to straddle a willie made of Play-Doh, so I count him as the half.

Then, of course, there was Simon, whose super-fit sperm wasted no time at all swimming up to my ovaries, saying 'Hey, how *you* doing?' Not an impressive tally, really.

'That sounded like an interesting conversation,' said Jenny, who'd arrived a couple of hours ago with Ian. She'd already been for a bike ride and done a yoga class. The cow. I forgave her when I saw she was drinking pints of lager to offset the damage.

'Yes. It was. If your idea of interesting is abuse and humiliation. My daughter just tried to fill me in on the birds and the bees. How are you, anyway?'

'Great!' she said, her usual answer – I'd never met anybody so unswervingly cheerful. I knew from talking to Allie that she'd been having surgery that year, to try and improve her fertility, so it seemed unlikely that she felt as cheerful as she sounded.

'Really?' I asked, meeting her eyes, and noticing a slight tremble in the hand that was holding her beer.

'Well, maybe not that great,' she replied, her eyes filling up a little. 'In all honesty, Sally, it's been a shit of a year. When we first met you, we were coming to terms with the diagnosis – severe endometriosis. At first we just tried to accept it, but neither of us was happy giving up. So this has been the Year of the Cyst Removal, which is about as much fun as it sounds.

'We've seen loads of specialists, but nobody seems to know what's going on – and whether I can have kids or not. Believe me we've been trying – but, so far, nothing. And no answers at all.'

I recalled from my dim and distant past training that endometriosis often affected fertility in mysterious ways. Not, of course, that that was any help at all to Jenny, who was now swiping tears from her eyes to stop them spilling on to her cheeks.

I reached out and touched her hand, wanting to let her know it was okay.

'And I'm sure the uncertainty isn't helping anything, is it?' I asked.

'No! That's the thing – every time we have sex, we have no idea if it's worked, or if it's pointless, or if we should try and adopt or . . . God, I'm sorry to cry on you, I know it's pathetic, but it all just makes me feel like such a failure as a woman!'

'Jenny, sweetheart,' I said, heart breaking for her. 'You mustn't see yourself like that. I'm sure Ian doesn't. And it's all right to get upset about it – that's what friends are for. Any time you want to talk, any time at all, just come and find me. We'll go for a walk, or a drink, or go and start a fight in a bar if you feel like it . . . whatever you want.'

She squeezed my hand back, and managed a smile.

'Thanks, Sally,' she said. 'I really appreciate that. Ian and I just can't talk about it any more; it's like it's taken over our whole lives. He's so stressed. Anyway. We're here. On holiday – and whatever else is going on, I'm going to at least try and enjoy myself.'

I nodded, patting her hand as I saw Ian wandering over towards us. She was right – he looked as though he'd aged ten years in the one since I'd last seen him. The poor loves.

As well as Ian and Jenny, Rick and Marcia had also arrived at the Blue Bay. Marcia had assumed her usual position, regally drinking cocktails and smoking the occasional Gauloise cigarette in a Marlene Dietrich style. Rick was buzzing about like a firefly, catching up with everyone, and making the acquaintance of the brand-new waiter, Hakan.

Hakan couldn't have been older than twenty-one, and had a smile so big and dazzling it could have stopped warring nations in their tracks. Seriously. It was impossible not to feel really, really good about yourself whenever he looked at you. Rick, wearing a fluorescent orange muscle top and a pair of white linen trousers, was clearly feeling really, really good about Hakan as well. He was following him around the restaurant, helping him collect in plates and giggling at his every word. Crikey – that was trouble in the making.

Marcia didn't seem to be reacting at all, but I wondered if she was going to wander over and stub her Gauloise out in his eye at some stage. Of all of the Blue-Bayers, she was the one who still remained the most mysterious. Even though she seemed to be drunk pretty much all the time, she never gave much away when she was in her cups.

James had been down at the beach with Jake and his new friend Matthew, whose parents were here for the first time, collecting driftwood. The kids were ecstatic to be up so late and trailed back after him barefoot, carrying piles of twigs, clumps of seaweed and an old whisky bottle.

James had his trouser legs rolled up and his face was covered in smudges of sand. He gave me a wink as he passed by. Yum. Against the odds I managed to stay upright.

'Off for an early night, Sally . . . busy day tomorrow.'

Double yum, with a side helping of nerves – I wondered if there actually was a condom machine here . . .

Chapter 28

'Did you bring any condoms?' I said to James the minute we tied up the boat.

'What?' he said, laughing. 'Where's the romance in that, you beast? Can't we even eat lunch first? You won't respect me if I give in too soon!'

'Sorry. I'm nervous.'

'Well don't be. It's not like having a tooth pulled out. Relax and enjoy the day. There's no kids, no people, no noise – just us. Nothing's going to happen that you don't want to happen.'

That, of course, was the problem – there was all sorts of stuff I did want to happen. Stuff we'd talked about while holding the phone with one hand. Stuff I'd never done before and ached to try with him. But I was scared witless and focusing on the practicalities to distract myself.

James had made good on his promise from last year and taken me out on a bigger boat. Some kind of speedy affair with an engine. He'd brought us over to a tiny island an hour away, which was, he assured me, always totally deserted.

He'd packed a picnic hamper. He'd remembered blankets and towels and booze and bottles of water. He'd brought himself, dressed only in a pair of black swimming trunks. He'd thought of everything. So surely he'd have remembered the condoms?

All I'd brought to the party, on the other hand, was a tense silence and a packet of mints. I'd been chewing on my lip so hard in the night it was bleeding. Ollie had asked if I'd been eating glass at breakfast, and Lucy smiled like a snake and mouthed the word 'gonorrhoea' over the coffee pot. I dropped my cup, I was so jumpy.

I hadn't been able to enjoy the journey at all, even though part of my brain recognised how beautiful it had been. The island itself was perfect – no buildings, no people, just a hill in the middle surrounded by a fringe of sandy beach so fine and soft your feet sank into it, warming your toes.

James threw down the blanket, opened the hamper, and pulled out a bottle of chilled champagne. It couldn't have been nicer if he'd scattered rose petals on the ground and coated himself in chocolate.

'Drink this,' he said, passing me a glass, 'you look bloody terrified. Would you prefer to go back to the hotel and call me on your mobile instead? Come on, what's the problem?'

'Oh fuck. I'm sorry, James – you've made all this effort and I'm acting like an idiot. I'm just . . . a bit freaked out. I've hardly ever slept with anyone at all compared to you, and not with anybody for ages, and only with Simon really, and . . . well, maybe I've forgotten what to do. Or maybe I'll be rubbish at it and you'll be disappointed. And what about all those STDs that are out there these days?'

He shook his head, took a deep breath in and whistled it back out in a lengthy sigh. He rubbed his hands through his hair like he always does when he's frustrated or upset. It's a gesture I've seen a few too many times – I can't be good for his mental health.

'Okay,' he said, after he'd gathered his thoughts, 'let's go through that list one at a time, because you're clearly not going to rest until we have.

'First up, yes, I've slept with a lot of women, I'm not going to lie about that. I haven't kept count but it's more than a few. But guess what? There is a plus side – I've picked up some tips along the way. As for not having sex for ages, neither have I. For just over a year, in fact. Which, dimwit, was when I met you.'

'What about your subs' bench?' I bleated, hardly daring to believe what I was hearing. I suppose I'd categorised James as my fantasy man, and Simon as real life – and part of my current anxiety was based on James moving into reality, before I was even divorced from Simon.

'I retired it. I was too busy talking dirty to you every weekend. My body has remained pure for twelve whole months. And I'm pretty sure you haven't forgotten what to do – if you have, I'll give you a few lessons to bring you up to date. Now, saving the best for last, all those STDs . . . what a lovely thought. You really know how to capture the moment, don't you?

'I don't have any, end of story – I got tested for everything when Jake came along, and I've been careful ever since. Baby-making, though, is a different matter – still fully loaded on that front. Okay, little Miss Practical – your turn.'

'Erm . . . nothing to declare on the disease front, which is nice, isn't it? And probably not on the baby-making front at the moment as I've still got one of those coil doo-dahs in. Sorry about all this James . . . it just felt so easy when you were—'

'In another country?'

'Um . . . yes. Am I a complete nightmare? Do you want to go back?'

'Yes, you are a complete nightmare, and no, I don't want to go back. What I want to do is to shut up, lie down in this sunshine, and enjoy being here with you. We have a whole day together, during which we don't need to have sex, if you're so stressed about it. In fact, let's not.'

He shoved a T-shirt under his head as a makeshift pillow and stretched himself out on the blanket. He was still wet from splashing on to the beach and mooring the boat, and as he lay back tiny droplets of sea water trailed through the light hair on his thighs and calves. His chest was wide and hard and golden. He crossed his arms above his head and closed his eyes. His biceps were rippling, and his mouth relaxed into a hint of a smile.

I couldn't help noticing as he lay there that those trunks were quite small. And tight. And there were still parts of him I hadn't seen and would really quite like to.

I sat and stared for a while. I was starting to feel a little hot. Some of it was because of the sun. Some of it was because of the big slab of perfect lying there in front of me. I looked at the hill. Then at him. I looked at the sea. Then at him. I looked at the boat. Then at him.

Eventually, looking just wasn't enough. I finished the champagne, snapped off my bikini top, and climbed on top of him.

'I knew that'd work . . .' he said, then opened his ice-blue eyes. They almost fell out of his head when he saw what I was wearing, or wasn't, and I felt an instant and very gratifying response in the trouser department.

'Bloody hell . . . I think I've died and gone to heaven,' he said, stroking the sides of my thighs and hips, circling his hands up to my waist, where his fingers fluttered tantalisingly short of anything too rude. He edged slowly upwards, tracing the lower curve of my breast, then down again.

I could feel his hard outline beneath me, in exactly the right place to be sending sparks all through my body. I slowly moved my hips back and forwards, shamelessly using his hard-on to pleasure myself with. James groaned and arched upwards slightly, before grabbing my arms and pulling me down on to his chest. He rolled me over so I was lying on my back, spreading my legs with his until the length of him was between my thighs.

He stroked my hair back off my face and traced the outline of my lips with his fingers. I darted my tongue out to lick them. He nuzzled the side of my neck, kissed me hard, then pulled back, laughing.

'Let's slow this down. We have all day. And don't forget – no sex. Not proper sex, anyway.'

'I've changed my mind,' I said. 'I want to have sex. And I want it right now.'

I wrapped my thighs around his back and tried to lever him down, but he resisted.

'No. I'm going to make you wait. You deserve it for being such a nightmare. Now just stay still, I want to look at you . . .'

He couldn't have said anything scarier if he'd tried. It was a real Hammer House of Horror moment. Look at me? Like this? On my back, in daylight? My boobs are fine when I'm upright – but lying down there is a slow roll to the hills, it has to be said. And then there's the stretch marks. And the flabby bump on the front of my tummy. And those bits of cellulite on my thighs . . .

This was the body that Simon had lost interest in. The body he'd left for a younger, tighter one. So far, James had done nothing to make me believe he found me anything other than sexy – but still . . .

'Stop it,' he said quickly. 'I know what you're thinking, and you need to stop thinking it. You look beautiful to me, so relax and let me do all the things I've been wanting to do to you since we met.'

He leaned forward and kissed my left breast, teasing the nipple until it was rigid, then taking it into his mouth and gently sucking. His hand worked on the other, squeezing and teasing until I was desperate for him to get to that one too. I arched my back and held his head down to get as much of myself into him as I could, feeling dizzy with the unfamiliar sensations shooting in a direct line from my boobs to other places. God, who knew? I'd always thought of breasts as fun for the boys, but the way he was treating them was driving me crazy.

He pulled his head away, looking down at me hazily, holding one in each hand and rolling my nipples between his thumb and forefinger. There was a slight edge of pain, swamped in the pleasure. He made a noise low in his throat and his groin was pressed hard into mine.

He circled both nipples with his tongue once more, then moved his head further down, slowly licking and kissing his way to my stomach. I knew where this was heading and it was going to be good. I'd forgotten about the stretch marks and flabby bits by then, as I felt his fingers start to work over the fabric of my bikini bottoms, slowly stroking the moist groove between my legs.

He lifted away from me long enough to pull my pants down and over my ankles, then went back to my tummy, working his way lower and lower until he was almost exactly where I wanted him to be. He kissed the inside of my thighs, his breath warm and intimate, driving me insane. He paused, using his fingers to spread me wide, as I wriggled around impatiently, desperate to feel his mouth on me.

When I did, it was electric. He licked the nub of me, slowly and deliberately, in long, steady strokes until I couldn't keep still. He held my hips down with his hands, and carried on teasing me until I thought I might scream. He moved his tongue at a faster pace, until I finally shook and juddered and jerked and yes, probably screamed as well. I swear I almost blacked out, it felt so good – my body had no energy left to think or breathe or stay conscious. I'd never, ever experienced anything like it, and I couldn't move for a minute afterwards as the aftershocks rocked through me.

As I calmed, I blinked my eyes clear and looked up. He was kneeling in front of me, a lazy smile on his face and a huge erection in his pants.

I reached up and laid my hand on his groin, felt him twitch in response.

'Stand up,' I said. He did, and I kneeled in front of him, pulled out his cock, and licked it from shaft to tip before closing my lips around it. I felt him tangle his hands in the back of my hair, and heard him moaning. He was big, and more than ready, and it was over in seconds.

We both collapsed back on to the blanket, and James rolled me into his arms so my head was scooped on to his chest.

'Jesus,' he said, laughter in his voice. 'That didn't take long. I suppose we'd been storing it up for over a year.'

'I know,' I said letting my hands roam across his muscles, all embarrassment gone – however temporarily. 'In the words of Miss McTavish, I think I just found my inner goddess. And she's a bit of a slut.'

Chapter 29

'Told you we weren't having sex,' he said, as we arrived back on dry land. It was late afternoon, and James needed to get Jake from kids' club. I needed a shower and a screaming phone call to Diane.

After our initial and rather fabulous fumble, we'd entertained ourselves eating, drinking, and messing around with each other's body parts. True enough, no sex – or 'intercourse', as Lucy had put it. But lots of other lovely stuff; stuff I'd never even known could feel that good.

'Didn't any of that count, then?' I asked.

'No – that was just foreplay. You're in for a lot of trouble over the next couple of weeks. I hope you packed your vitamins.'

A random thought raced across my mind: what happens after that couple of weeks? When the holiday's over, and reality bites? Will it be back to Saturday-night smut and long-distance lust? Or will that be it for us – a fortnight of fun then we go bye-bye?

Either I've got the most transparent face in the world, or James can read my mind. He'd done it a few times already. He put his arm round me as we walked, hefting the hamper along with the other.

'We're here, and we're together, Sal. It's taken us a year to get this far . . . let's not worry about what happens next just yet.'

I nodded. He was right. And he was touching me again, so that was okay.

As we neared the turn-off to the hotel, I spotted Marcia striding along the shore, dressed in a diaphanous multicoloured wrap that swirled around her awesomely long legs. I was about to shout hello to her when I noticed she was meeting someone – Hakan, the new waiter. He cracked open one of those special grins, and reached out to embrace her. He was at least thirty years younger and half a foot shorter, but that didn't seem to be bothering either of them. They hadn't even noticed us.

'Holey-moley,' I said, quickly averting my eyes, 'I wonder what's going on there?'

'I don't know,' James replied, frowning. 'Rick and Marcia are a mystery to us all – I love them to bits, and I'd have Marcia on my side in a fight any day, but I couldn't even begin to guess the rules of their relationship. So I'm going to do the mature thing and pretend I didn't see it. Right, I'm off for Jake . . . shall I text you? Turn up at your door at midnight naked with a rose in my teeth?'

An enticing thought, but probably not a good idea. Ollie and Lucy might be okay with it – but that doesn't mean they'd want to listen to it.

'No. I'll come round to you, about three tomorrow. Stick to the naked thing, though. That works for me.'

I thought my face might break in two I was smiling so wide. What a day.

Chapter 30

'One day, when you're older and have kids of your own, you'll need me again you know – for babysitting.'

I waved a fork at Ollie triumphantly – I don't know why; all I'd done was establish that, for the next twenty years, he probably wouldn't need me at all. It was lunchtime, and we were eating together in the open-air restaurant. He'd just told me he'd be AWOL for the night as he was off with the Ginger Twins, who'd also returned to the Blue Bay.

'Don't be daft, Mum,' he said. 'By the time I have kids, I'll be able to download a babysitter from my phone, or buy one from the Apple store. Sorry, but you're completely obsolete.'

I stared at him. Maybe he was right. One day, he'll even be capable of washing his own socks. Ollie laughed out loud, and said 'Gotcha!', pointing a finger at me.

'You think you're a funny fuck, don't you, Ollie? Well, you're not.'

'I'm not?'

'No, you're not funny at all.'

'Oh. So I'm just a fuck then, is that what you're saying?'

'Yep, that's about the size of it . . . what are you up to with them, anyway? Something exciting?'

He pulled a bit of a face and explained probably not, 'cause Christian had gone all girl-mad and was intent on pulling Rosie, this new 'chick' who'd arrived the day before.

'What's she like?' I asked.

'She's all right, if you like that kind of thing – blonde, pretty, you know. Not my type, though.'

'Oh? What is your type? Carin? Christian?'

Ollie sighed, and put his knife and fork down. 'Mum, I'm not gay . . . don't interrupt! Yes, I know it would be perfectly all right if I was. I know you wouldn't mind. I know you'd be great about it – you've been letting me know that since I was a kid, and you probably even think you've been subtle. But stop – you don't need to make me feel comfortable with it, 'cause *I'm not gay*. If I fancied boys, I'd tell you, okay? I don't. I fancy girls.'

Oh. Well. That straightened that up, so to speak. He was right – I did always tag on a slightly probing reference at the end of sentences. What a very silly mummy I was.

'Okay . . . well, that's fine. It's just that . . . I never see you take any interest in girls . . .'

'Or boys, I hope,' he said. 'Mum, I'm really not that bothered yet. I know I'm sixteen next month and maybe I've got a bad case of arrested development, but at the moment girls are friends. Some of them are nice to look at. That's it. I'm not like Dad – I don't think with my dick. Is that enough for you? Or do you want to know who I masturbate about at night?'

'No! God no! That's more than enough, thanks . . . sorry, Ollie,' I said, reaching out to give his arm a sneaky pat. My lovely boy.

'Right,' he said, standing up and stretching – he was up to six foot now and still growing. I sometimes wondered how his skinny body didn't collapse in on itself.

'I'm off then – going to chill with my girlfriends and boyfriends. If I find myself sexually attracted to any of them, I'll let you know. I've been reading those Mills & Boons of yours, I know the signs. Anyway, Jake's in kids' club – I thought you'd have better things to be up to yourself,' he said with a knowing smirk. Sometimes it was hard to figure out who was the teenager in our relationship.

He was right, actually – I did have better things to be doing. I had a hot date with the hottest man in Hotsville. I'd been sunbathing all morning and had a nice warm glow going on. My tan was halfway to chocolate, my dark hair was shining, and my mind was already rolling around in a mud bath of filth.

I had plenty of time to go back to the room, shower, rub in lotions and potions and lie in front of the mirror naked, trying to see what gravity did to my body in different sexual positions.

I was pondering this rare burst of luxury when Jenny appeared by the side of the table, plonking herself down and sloshing coffee all over the place. Her normally glowing skin was verging on the gray, and there were dark circles under her eyes. She had her T-shirt on inside out and her short dark hair was plastered to one side of her head.

'God,' she said, gulping down the caffeine, 'I feel like poo. Allie was really going for it last night. I literally can't believe how much that woman can put away.'

'Ah,' I replied, sympathetically. 'You made the mistake of trying to keep up, did you?'

'I did. Schoolgirl error. Allie's on a mission this year. I've only just got up, Ian's still in bed, and I missed my Pilates class.'

She was right. Allie was on a mission this year – a mission, it seemed, to give every guest at the hotel their worst hangovers ever. I screwed my eyes up a little, feeling a twitch of anxiety about it.

'Do you think she's okay?' I asked. 'Allie?'

Jenny paused mid-slurp, and thought about it. It looked like it hurt.

'I don't know. She's definitely more party animal than she's been before. Maybe we should just keep an eye on her, make sure she doesn't go water ski-ing when she's tanked up or anything?'

I nodded. That sounded like a plan.

'Good,' I replied. 'Now I need to leave you alone with your misery, and head up back to my room. Take paracetamol and stay out of the sun.'

She laid her head flat on the table, groaned, and waved goodbye as I left. I was off for a pampering session.

The plan was a teensy bit spoiled by the fact that Lucy was there. I'd expected her to be out with Max at this time of day, but she was lounging around, writing in her journal and eating grapes. What a life.

'Hi!' I shouted through the interconnecting door.

'Dear Diary,' she said, in a loud stage voice, 'today my mother was even more irritating than usual, ruining my perfect moment of solitude and blocking all natural light with her big fat arse . . .'

I slammed the door shut. Cow. One day, she'd put on an ounce of weight, and when she did, I'd . . . probably console her and tell her she's gorgeous. Because I am a much nicer person than she is. So was Stalin, and Genghis Khan and Vlad the Impaler.

I got into the shower, and tried to put her out of my mind. I replaced her with James, who was a much more appropriate shower companion.

By the time I got out, I was smiling and happy again. Sadly, she was still there.

'Mum,' she said, 'you know Max is starting at Oxford in October? Can he come and stay with us for a few days again beforehand?'

'Yes of course he can. So . . . still going strong then?'

She shrugged, faking nonchalance. 'S'pose so, yeah. But hopefully next year I'll be off to uni in Liverpool, so we'll see what happens. Okay. There's my soul all exposed. Your turn – and I have a question to ask. What happens after this holiday? Are you going to carry on seeing James? Because I'm not moving to fucking Dublin just so you can keep getting your menopausal end away, you know.'

Charming as ever. I don't remember girl-talks being like this when I was younger. When I was a teenager I spoke to my mother about nothing more overtly sexual than the fact that we both liked Ronan Keating's hair.

'Nobody's moving anywhere, Luce. And I'm *not* menopausal.'

I'd been rubbing cream into my legs, but I put the pot down and sat next to her. Lucy might display all the tenderness of a pickaxe to the skull, but she also had a habit of getting straight to the point.

'I don't know what's going to happen after this holiday. After what happened with Dad, I'm not that confident. I really like James and, to be honest, I'm a bit scared of it all. So there. Go on then – do your worst with that.'

I was expecting a tirade of abuse or hysterical laughter, but for a fraction of a second her face softened. She looked almost . . . human. It must have been a trick of the light.

'Dad behaved like a prick, Mum. I know I blamed you at the time, but the last year, in the house with just us, it's been fine. It's been better. Let's face it, there's only room for one prima donna in our lives, and that's me – he was always way too much competition, with his cologne collection and tie rack and never-ending stories about his surgical brilliance . . . wanker. But the thing with James? You should talk to him about it. That's what you always tell me to do when I'm worried about something with Max. When are you seeing him next?'

'In about an hour. But I don't plan on doing much talking—'

'Shut up! Shut up right now! I don't need to know the details. When are you next going out alone, then; somewhere your hideous geriatric sex drives won't get the better of you?'

'Night after tomorrow. Jake's at the video club. We're going for dinner.'

'Well what you need is a plan. If you could ask him anything, what would it be?'

'I don't know – how he feels about me? What he wants to happen next? Whether we'll see each other again? That type of stuff.'

'Yeah. Predictably lame,' she said, back to normal. 'You always tell me to be honest and discuss my feelings. In fact I get sick of hearing that particular gem. So why not be a big girl for once and follow your own advice?'

Chapter 31

'Fancy a shag?' I said, as he opened the door. Well, why mess with a classic?

'Come in, Sally. Nice to see you too,' he said.

He'd obviously just had a shower himself. His hair was tousled and damp, and he smelled of that gorgeous spicy stuff that always makes me want to sniff him. He was wearing nothing but a clean white towel, hanging low on his hips and loosely knotted. I could have that off with my teeth in two seconds flat.

I let my eyes roam up and down his body, drinking it all in. I couldn't believe my luck – he was perfect; all taut golden muscle and hard edges. I also couldn't believe he wanted me as much as I wanted him. Against the odds, that seemed to be the case, and it was turning me into a shameless floozie. I reached out to trace the contours of his chest, whispering the palms of my hands over his nipples.

'You really are a fine physical specimen, Mr Carver,' I said, pushing him back so he was leaning against the wall.

'Are we playing doctors and nurses?' he asked.

'Just doctors. And it's time for an examination. Let's have a look at you then . . . Yes, magnificent deltoids,' I said, reaching up to caress the broad expanse of his shoulders, then his drool-inspiring arms. 'Mmm. Nicely bulging biceps. And then we come back to pectoralis major, one of my personal favourites.' I leaned forward to kiss his chest, then let both my hands roam downwards to the solid wall of his stomach. The towel was starting to twitch, like a magic trick in an X-rated stage show.

I leaned in close, put my arms around him, and massaged the ridge of muscle at the top of his back. 'All very satisfying in the trapezius area . . . solid lats . . . Now let's do the rest of you . . .'

I ran one of my hands down his side, then slipped it under the bottom edge of the towel. He spread his legs obligingly and I stroked his inner thigh, downy with hair. He was quivering under my touch. I knelt down in front of him, and the magic towel almost poked me in the eye. I untied it and let it drop to the floor. Oh yes. A fine physical specimen indeed. My hands got busy to his rear, enjoying the firm curves of those world-beating glutes, and my mouth got busy on the equally impressive front view.

He slouched back against the wall, groaning slightly as I licked and sucked, encouraging him on with my hands on his backside. When I could feel the pressure building along the ridge of his penis, and knew he was near to coming, I ran my tongue around him once more then pulled away. I looked up at him, and saw the mist clear from his eyes.

'Fuck,' he said, pulling me up so I was facing him, 'were you trained in a bordello or what?'

He threw me back on to the bed, and pulled my top off over my head. The skirt quickly followed, and I kicked off the sandals myself. I'd taken the sensible precaution of wearing no underwear at all, and had lived in fear of a sharp breeze on the walk over.

He smiled as he saw me naked, then climbed on top of me and kissed me, letting his hands roam down over my sides, my hips, and slowly back up to my neck. My breasts were crushed up against his chest, and he felt deliciously heavy along the line of my body. I was clinging on to his back, and spread my legs wide, more than ready for nature to take its course by that stage.

He paused for a second and looked at me, blue eyes luminous in the dim, curtained light.

'Are you okay with this?' he asked.

I responded by thrusting my hips up to meet his, and squirming around until the angle was just right. I nodded. The time for talking was gone, and he pushed himself inside me, hard.

At first it was a shock – he was big, and I am a born-again virgin after all – but that passed in the blink of an eye. He put his hands under my bottom, raising me slightly so he could go even deeper. So deep I thought he might come out the other side. It felt wonderful.

I reached up to twine my fingers into his hair and pull his mouth down for a kiss. It was hard and hungry and turned me on even more. He grabbed my wrists, held my arms back over my head, moving so fast and with such a rhythm I could feel tingles pulsing between my legs as our sweat and flesh mingled together. A second before it happened, I realised I was about to come. It came as quite a shock, and I held on to his hands so hard I left crescent-moon marks with my fingernails. I felt my muscles squeezing hard around him as I climaxed, and that was all the encouragement he needed.

Afterwards he fell on top of me in a damp, lifeless heap. His head rested on my chest and his breath was coming in hot gasps. I stroked his hair and wrapped my legs over his derrière to keep him inside me for a few moments more.

'That's never happened to me before,' I said.

'What do you mean? That happened to you on the island. A few times at least,' he replied, his voice muffled against my boobs.

'No. I mean that's never happened to me during sex-sex before. Sometimes in the bit before sex, sometimes after, but never actually during . . . I didn't think it was possible.'

He looked up from his nest of breasts, hair spiked up all over the place and eyes shining.

'Well, now you know it is possible – I've ruined you for other men. There are lots of other ways we can make it happen too – over and over again,' he said, running his hand up the length of my inner thigh and giving me a clue about at least one of those ways.

Chapter 32

'I'm having *déjà vu* here, Sal,' said Diane over a crackling phone line. 'You're off to dinner with the same bloke from the same hotel at the same time of year? This is the fella you've been shagging on the phone, isn't it – the one you sent me the photo of, the blond with the big guns?'

'Yeah. James. He's lovely.'

I suspected I sighed as I said his name, and wasn't even ashamed of it. He was lovely – and, for the rest of the holiday at least, he was all mine.

'And now he's been shagging you senseless in real life, I deduce from your soppy tone of voice. Don't keep me waiting – is he any good?'

'He's the best ever. In the whole world. I've spent the last few days practically blind from orgasms.'

'Fuck. That is good. I take it you don't want me to repeat that last sentence to your father or your brothers?'

'Best not, Di – don't want Dad to drop dead of a heart attack, do we? Anyway, I've got to go – Mr Orgasm's waiting downstairs. And don't worry, I'm looking slutty.'

I galloped down the steps, eager to see him, trailing a

cloud of perfume.

James was leaning against a bar stool, talking to Jenny. He was wearing a deep blue shirt. His arms were crossed firmly in front of him, and the short sleeves were stretched tight around his flexed biceps. I knew exactly how he'd smell before I even got there, and couldn't resist lightly trailing a hand over his bottom as I approached from behind.

I leaned in, and kissed the face off him.

I heard Jenny laughing in the background, and was glad I'd cheered her up at least. She and Ian had been trying their best so far – up to their usual sporty activities, romantic dinners, and public displays of affection. But if you ever caught either of them alone, it was easy to see the mask slip, and the strain of their situation peek through. Just then, though, she seemed nothing less than tickled pink. They all knew about me and James – they'd have to be idiots not to – but this was the first time I'd displayed it so vividly.

'Come on, let's go,' I said, taking him by the hand and leading him towards the promenade.

'That was . . . interesting,' he said. 'Am I to take it that we are now going public?'

'We always were public. It was one of those secrets that everyone knew. My crap sex life was in a bloody bestselling book – I don't see why my awesome sex life should be hidden away! Where are we going?'

'Same place as last time? That night we decided we were just going to be friends.' His hand wandered down to my bum, resting it there as we walked, in a decidedly more-than-friends way.

'Okay. As long as we don't have to go to Harry's and have a scrap afterwards. I'd rather do other things afterwards, if we have the time.'

'Jesus, woman . . . you're insatiable. Talk about making up for lost time.'

We strolled along to the restaurant, settled down and ordered. I drank a glass of wine in one gulp. I'd decided that Lucy was right, the cow. It was time to be a big girl. James and I had been bonking each other senseless for days now, but it was more than that. We spent our evenings together, with the rest of the group but always sitting next to each other. Always within touching distance. Sharing smiles and laughs and looks when Mike said something especially outrageous, or Allie replied with something especially cutting.

We'd joined Jenny and Ian on a sailing trip; we'd taken Jake to the water park; we'd even played cards with Rick and Marcia.

The sex had been amazing – but the friendship was growing, too. I felt – for the first time in years – like part of a couple. Even with Simon, if I was honest, I didn't feel like that towards the end.

This was different; it was pretty much magical. And if it was all going to finish on the last day of our holiday, I wanted to know in advance. I couldn't afford another man-related near nervous breakdown. If I tried to keep all these feelings inside much longer, I might spontaneously combust on my sun lounger.

'James,' I said, 'do you mind if I ask you a question?'

'No. Go ahead.'

I took a deep breath, said a little prayer. Wondered what Lucy would do, and then realised that she was a very inappropriate role model to choose. Another breath. Here we go . . .

'Okay then. I was wondering what's going to happen next with us. Is this a holiday shag and nothing more? Am I anything more to you than a nice pair of tits and a quickie? Will we ever see each other again after next Thursday?'

He closed his eyes, put two fingers to his forehead and rubbed, the way you do when you feel a headache coming on. Good to see I still had the old magic.

'Christ . . . Sally, I have to say your tits are very nice, but it's not your chest I've been e-mailing for the last year, is it? And we've shared a lot more than a quickie, which I hoped you'd noticed.

'I know you've been through the mill with Simon, but you've got to stop letting that get in the way of this. No, I don't know what's going to happen next – who does? But I'm loving every minute I spend with you. Isn't that enough for now?'

I nodded, incapable of actually replying. I could feel tears stalking the back of my eyes. I felt like an idiot now, embarrassed on top of everything else. So much for being a grown-up.

'It is,' I finally murmured. 'It is. I'm just being a train wreck, as usual – you know what I'm like.'

'Yeah, I know what you're like – and I love that too. So don't feel embarrassed,' he said, lifting my chin up until I was looking into his eyes. 'If I wasn't such a macho beast, I'd probably be asking the same things myself. Let's finish our dinner, then head back – if we're lucky we can go back to my room for an hour before I pick up Jake. I'd like to lie down with you and snuggle.'

'Snuggle?' I said. 'What kind of word is that for a macho beast?'

'Shut up and eat, woman – is that better? Do you want chocolate cake?'

Of course I did. And I felt so much better after it – he knows me so well.

Chapter 33

When we got back to the hotel, there was some kind of Bacchanalia going on.

Allie was cavorting on the stage singing Pharrell's 'Happy', slapping herself vigorously on the backside as she danced to the chorus. Ian and Jenny were cheering Allie on, obviously hammered themselves, and Mike . . . Mike was sitting sipping a pint. Which was worrying, as he never normally sips anything – he normally inhales it all in one gulp before shouting, 'Next!'

The music was poundingly loud, and disco lights were lasering in on a sea of very hot, very drunk faces. The waiters were all getting in on the act, even the ones with a night off were joining in the party. Rick was pirouetting in the middle of them like the dancing queen he was, clapping his hands above his head in delight. Marcia looked on, glugging wine straight from the bottle, three cigarettes burning in the ashtray at once.

A man I'd never even seen before staggered over and grabbed me, trying to drag me off for a dance.

'Come on, gorgeous – come and shake your tail feather with me!'

James reached out and pulled his fingers from my arm, his face stern. The man laughed, held up his hands in apology, then skipped off to the next woman, who happened to be Marcia. I hoped he had good insurance.

'What the fuck's going on here?' James wondered out loud. I was thinking exactly the same thing.

'Go get Jake,' I said, kissing him, 'I'll be with Mike over there. He looks like the world's coming to an end.'

James nodded and headed off to the kids' club. I squeezed my way through the rampaging mass of writhing bodies. It was like doing an assault course with a squadron of horny octopuses.

'Bloody hell . . . my arse is going to be black and blue in the morning after all that groping . . . Is everyone on drugs?'

'Don't know, Sal,' said Mike as I sat down next to him. 'But there's definitely something in the air, isn't there? Allie started it, if I'm honest. And it's not even the last night . . .'

Mike had been staring at his wife as she built up to her finale, and moved right on to the next song – the 'Cha Cha Slide'. She was dancing it like a pro up on the stage, shouting at everyone to join in down below. They did, but the vast majority were too drunk to know their right from their left, and ended up knocking each other over with flying hips.

He shook his burly head and turned to face me. He looked as serious as I've ever seen him.

'What's up with her, Sal? There's something wrong – she's hardly spoken to me since we got here, and she avoids being alone with me as much as she can. If she's met someone else,

I wish she'd tell me. Lord knows I deserve it, the way I've behaved in the past. But all this crap isn't good for her. She's trying too hard – looking like the party queen up there, but she's not right inside. I caught her crying in the bathroom the other day. She wouldn't tell me what was wrong – just slammed the door in my face and locked it. All I can come up with is that she's having an affair.'

I reached out and held one of his enormous hands in mine. He was built like a bear, but looked like a lost child.

'Mike, I'm sure there's nobody else – even if she has read Miss McTavish's book. She loves you, and she'd never do that to you. I've noticed as well – from that first day, she's seemed . . . off. And since then, she's avoided being on her own with me, even though I thought she'd be gagging to pick my brains about James. You're right – she's upset about something, but I'm one hundred per cent sure it's not another man. Do you want me to have a word with her?'

'If you would, Sal, that'd be grand. I'd really appreciate it. She might open up a bit more to you.'

He gave my hand a squeeze and went back to his beer. He drained almost a full pint in one slurp, so he must have been feeling better. I promised myself I'd pin Allie down the next day. I might be enjoying my big romance, but my friend clearly needed me, whether she was willing to admit it or not. Allie had been there for me last summer, all the way from Naughty Nurse Nancy onwards. Now it was my turn.

James emerged from the kids' club complex, holding Jake by the hand. He lifted him up and Jake wrapped his little legs around his waist, his arms clinging to his dad's neck. They made their way through the crowds towards us.

I gave Mike a kiss on the cheek, and walked over to a quieter table near the back. James sat on the chair next to me, Jake still on his knee.

'Daddy, can I sit on Sally's lap? She's way more comfy than you,' he said, yawning.

'Yeah, she is, isn't she?' said James, as his son scampered over and settled himself in my arms. He wriggled down and nestled his face up against my chest with a contented sigh. Like father like son. His eyes were barely open and I could feel his small body slowly going floppy.

'Are you tired, sweetie?' I asked.

'No, don't be silly! I'm going to stay up all night!'

'Okay, darling, you do that,' I said, kissing his head. I felt my heart swell with fondness for him. I loved my kids, for all their flaws, but nothing quite beat the feeling of a little one collapsed in your arms.

'I'll get us a drink,' James said, smiling at us both as he stood up, 'I think I need one.'

'Me too. Allie's gone nuts, and Mike's worried sick about her. Jenny and Ian aren't themselves. And Marcia and Rick . . . well, let's not even go there. I never thought I'd say this, but I feel pretty sane in comparison to everyone else this year.'

'You're right,' he replied, grinning. 'It must be bad.'

He headed off to the bar, waylaid en route by Jenny, insisting he gave her a tango dip. He flipped her down as if she weighed as much as a bag of sugar, then pulled her back to her feet and into his chest with a dramatic slam. She screamed with laughter, and ran off to find other partners in her quest for ballroom excellence.

By that point Allie was reaching the end of a rousing solo performance of 'I Will Survive', yelling, 'Come on, Blue Bay! Make some noise!' into the microphone.

James returned, placed our drinks on the table, and shook his head in amazement, staying quiet as he examined Jake for signs of sleep.

As if sensing his scrutiny, Jake shuffled his head up and opened one eye. He was winding a piece of my hair around his fingers as he spoke.

'Dad, Matthew said he saw Sally kissing you earlier, and that Sally's your girlfriend now. Is that true?'

I locked eyes with James and waited. It wasn't my question to answer.

He pulled his chair right next to us, and reached over to ruffle Jake's hair. Then he settled back and put his arm around my shoulders as we sat there. I pretended I was breathing normally and stared off into the distance. No pressure here, no sirree.

'Yeah, Sally is my girlfriend, Jake. Is that okay with you?'

'Course it is. She's really soft and squishy. Sally, does that mean you'll come and live in our house? Will Ollie come too? He's so cool . . .'

'Well, maybe we'll just come and visit,' I said.

'To start with,' added James.

Jake nodded, content with all our answers, and went to sleep almost immediately. He was warm and snug and just right.

The Birthday that Changed Everything

The music had quietened. The stars were shining. James's thigh was pressed against mine and his fingers were absently caressing the back of my neck.

I was so happy, it scared me.

Chapter 34

It was my birthday. Again. Weird how that kept happening. I was indulging in my traditional birthday breakfast of Turkish delight, sitting with Allie, who this morning seemed manically happy – a bit of a surprise considering the way she'd behaved towards me when I'd tried to talk to her the day before.

I'd spent ages trying to find her, and being told she was water-skiing, playing tennis, doing yoga – anything, in fact, other than sitting still. It was like tracking the Scarlet Pimpernel, if he went on posh package holidays.

By the time I'd found her, determined to fulfil my promise to Mike, the sun was slithering low over the distant island, and her long, lean body was striped with shade as she lay stretched out on a sun lounger by the pool.

I'd sat down next to her, and passed over the drink I'd brought from the bar.

'Is everything okay with you, Allie?' I'd asked, once we'd made our greetings and she'd slurped down half the G&T. 'You seem a bit . . . intense this year.'

She'd slipped her sunglasses on, which was completely unnecessary at that time of day. Dusk was coming in fast, and the hazy natural light was starting to be replaced by the lamps and lanterns that were already fluttering into life.

'Yeah. I'm okay. I'm sorry if I've been a bit off with everyone. I know Mike's worried, and Max thinks I'm going through my change of life. That's probably it; it'll be wonky woman hormones. Please don't worry about me. I'm absolutely fine.'

She'd stood up abruptly, gathering her towel and book and sun cream up in her arms.

'Got to go Sal, I'm freezing out here. See you later.'

It was nowhere near freezing. And it was nowhere near sunny enough for shades. And Allie was nowhere near fine – but she didn't seem to want to talk about it. Mike was right – something was definitely off, and I felt both worried about Allie, and a bit hurt that she wouldn't talk to me about it.

Last year, she'd been my best Blue-Bay friend, and over the intervening months, it had been her friendship and phone calls and our weekend away that had helped me recover from Simon as much as James had. Now, she was closed off, evasive, manic. She hadn't even asked what James was like in bed, which was very unlike her.

This morning, she was like a different person, though – humming with excitement.

'We've planned a birthday surprise for you,' she said, beaming. 'I've told James and he thinks it's the best idea ever.'

'Go on then,' I said, 'the suspense is killing me.'

'We're going away for the night – well, not you or James, just the rest of us. We've hired a *gulet* – that's one of those wooden cruise boats. We're going after lunch and we won't be back till tomorrow.'

That sounded very nice, but I couldn't understand why it was a present for me. They weren't even taking me on their fabulous trip.

'Mike and I are going, and Max. And Lucy, and Ollie, and Jake, and Rick and Marcia, and Jenny and Ian . . .'

The only names that registered on that list were Jake, Lucy and Ollie. That meant all three of our kids. Gone, for the whole night. The light slowly dawned and I jumped up to give her a hug.

'Allie, you are the best! Thank you so much, that's amazing. I can't wait to . . . to—'

'I can imagine. So, anyway, I'm off to pack for the night.'

She held my hands in hers, and gave me a small, sad smile. Even now, when we were alone, and when she was clearly keen to give me a happy birthday, she was retreating back into her uncharacteristic solitude.

'Enjoy every minute of it – life's too short to waste the good things, and James is definitely one of the good things.'

That sounded ominous, and my anxiety levels in relation to Allie ratcheted up another notch. She'd looked happy enough, but those words . . . they didn't sound it.

Still, I knew she was right. Whatever her state of mind, and I *would* get to the bottom of it, she was right.

James was one of the very best things. He'd built me back up after Simon knocked me down. He'd helped me see my own worth at a time when nobody else did. And he'd made me come more times in two weeks than I had in the last decade.

We'd had mornings here, afternoons there, but never a whole night. Jake was occasionally at Matthew's for a sleepover, but

The Birthday that Changed Everything

I always had to drag myself away from James's arms and go back to my room in case one of my overgrown babies needed me – mother first, sex slave second.

But tonight, with all of them away and happy and taken care of, we could celebrate my birthday in style. Stay together. Sleep in the same bed. Wake up next to each other in the morning . . .

Hmmm. Shit – what if I snored? Or drooled? Or talked about pepperoni pizza in my sleep? I might even fart out loud.

I'd stopped eating, I was so caught up in my thoughts, and had a piece of Turkish delight paused halfway to my lips.

James sat down opposite me, bringing his coffee with him. He looked at me, with my gaping mouth and frozen hand.

'Are you playing musical statues by yourself?' he said. 'Or are you lost in Crazy Town? I know Allie's told you about the trip. So, by now, I'm guessing the happy's worn off, and you're starting to worry about whether I'll still fancy you before you brush your teeth in the morning.'

Bugger. I hadn't even thought of that one.

'How do you know all this stuff? It's very annoying.'

'Psychic powers. Sally, I do actually know you are a real-life woman. I don't care if you snore, and I look forward to our first communal fart. It's a rite of passage. I just want to wake up with you still there – I get very horny first thing in the morning. Anyway, here's your present – happy birthday, gorgeous.'

He kissed me and left. There was a small box lying on the table. I tore it open, and inside found a beautiful gold necklace with a delicate Celtic knot pendant, nestled on a crinkly red tissue paper. I put it on straight away and held the pendant in my hands, grinning like an idiot. I planned to keep it on for ever.

That afternoon we stood down by the shore and waved everyone off. Jake was sick with excitement, clinging on to Ollie's hand as they trotted along the jetty to the boat, three skipping steps to each one of Ollie's strides. Everyone else trooped along, carrying overnight bags and beer and snorkels and fishing rods. The only one left behind was Rick, who'd cried off with a sore stomach.

James and I stood on the edge of the beach, waving for what seemed like an eternity. When they finally drifted off out of sight, we held hands and walked back towards the hotel.

'So . . . what shall we do now then?' I asked, pretty sure what the answer was going to be.

'Well, we could lie in the sun eating ice cream and only moving when we've run out of gin. Or go back to my room. Your choice.'

I wound my arms round his neck and kissed him slowly, for a very long time, melding my hips into his.

'Can we take the gin and ice cream with us?' I said. He nodded, hands roaming over my body.

We spent the rest of the afternoon rolling around on the bed, kissing, talking and making each other go cross-eyed. Later, James went down to the restaurant, and came back bearing gossip as well as a loaded tray.

'Rick's down there. He's made a miraculous recovery. He was drinking cocktails with Hakan, that new waiter, and I swear they were playing footsie under the table. He winked at me and said: 'James, what happens in the Blue Bay, stays in the Blue Bay.' I didn't know what to say to that so I ran off. Here, most of this is for you,' he said, putting the tray down.

After the food and a little resting of my eyes, James woke me up by pulling the covers off me. I was getting over the self-consciousness of being starkers in front of him, but still instinctively tried to grab them back to hide myself.

'No,' he said, 'time for a shower together. This has been a secret fantasy of mine since I met you. Come on, you know you want to.'

I watched him walk away to the bathroom, naked as the day he was born but a whole lot bigger. The muscular rise and fall of his backside looked so good I wanted to crawl after him on all fours and bite it. Instead I jumped up and followed.

He was already in, standing under a steaming jet, rubbing his hair. I faced him, watching the water splash on to the bulk of his shoulders and stream down over the golden plane of his chest. I reached out to touch him, still amazed I was allowed to.

'Like what you see?' he asked, his voice strained. I nodded and moved closer, putting my arms around his waist and pulling him to me. I gently sucked his rigid nipples and felt him spring to life between us. He sighed and pushed me away slightly, smoothing my wet hair away from my face.

'Not yet,' he said.

He squeezed shower gel into his hands – the same smell I always associated with him, and which was usually enough to kick-start my libido all on its own. He soaped it on to me, paying an inordinate amount of attention to my breasts.

His hands worked their way down my body, in between my legs, over the curves of my back and bottom and thighs. By the time he finished, I was not only very clean indeed, but horny as hell.

He stepped forward until I was backed against the wall, then lifted me up, my legs automatically wrapping around his waist. For once I didn't even wonder about being too heavy – I was too turned on, and I knew now he was more than strong enough.

Within seconds he was thrusting inside me, his hands on the small of my back for support. It was hard and fast and my flesh was slapping against the tiles of the shower wall as he did it. He was murmuring my name over and over, his mouth buried in my neck and my shoulders, biting me and kissing me.

I was screaming with pleasure and had my fingers wound in his hair so tight it had to hurt. The shower pounded on to his back as he pounded into me, a waterfall flowing over the muscles of his back, knotted with effort. My hips rose and fell to meet him, urging him on, a fiery heat spreading through me.

When it was over for both of us, I stayed wrapped around him, his head collapsed on to my breasts. I could feel his panting breath as he nuzzled into me, holding me tighter. I'd left scratch marks on his back, and reached down to soothe them with my fingers. Mercy, what a perfect moment.

'God, I love you James,' I whispered.

Well, somebody had to go and spoil it.

Once the words were out, I don't know who was more shocked – me or him. Both our bodies went suddenly tense, then I slid down from him and walked wordlessly out of the shower, grabbing a towel.

Fuck, fuck, fuck, I thought as I dried off, why did I have to go and do that? Even if it was true, I didn't intend to say it out loud. I don't think I even realised it until the words escaped. But it was true – this was more than a fling for me. Whether the timing was right or not; whether I was still harbouring feelings for Simon or not, it was true. I loved James. And now I'd gone and said it.

I walked back into the room and started gathering up my clothes. Maybe it was time to make my excuses and leave. If only because I thought I might cry.

'Where do you think you're going?' he asked as he walked back in, towel tucked round his waist.

'I . . . well . . . you know, I have things to do . . . We're leaving in a few days so I thought I'd start the packing, and I need to call the dog-sitter to check everything's okay, and—'

'No,' he said, 'you're not going anywhere. I'm not going to let you run away from this. Get into bed.'

'But my hair's still wet. I'll make the pillow soggy.'

'Get in.'

I did as he said, shaking as much from my emotions as the mild chill of the air-conditioned room. He climbed in next to me, rolling on to his side so we were face to face. I didn't want to be, and tried to avoid meeting his eyes. I was forty-one, for Christ's sake – way too old for all this crap. Meeting James had made me feel young again – like I'd discovered sex and men and love for the first time. Feeling like a humiliated teenager who'd overused the 'L' word was the downside.

He held the side of my face with his hand, stroking my hair back behind my ears. When the tears fell, he kissed them away.

'Don't cry, Sal. I love you too. I just wasn't brave enough to say it. You were more honest, as usual. But I've been thinking it, for a long time now. I love you. Okay? I love you. Does that make things better?'

For some reason, instead of making me smile, that made me cry even more – I should have been on diazepam. I nodded, and hid my face under the sheets.

He turned on to his back and scooped me into his arms so my head was lying against his chest. He held me tight and told me he loved me again and I slid one of my legs over his. Eventually the crying stopped, and the happiness started.

We were quiet for a moment, and he fingered the Celtic knot necklace I was wearing.

'I'm glad you like it,' he said, 'I don't usually go in for all this professional Irish stuff, but this is supposed to symbolise endings and beginnings and how one leads to another. That seemed right for us. Are you okay now? You're not crying any more, are you?'

'For that last bit, I was crying 'cause I was so happy. I'm female – don't try and understand it, just accept it. And now I'm even more happy. And, well, a bit sleepy. Must be all that food and sex and emotional trauma . . .' I yawned as I said the last words, covering my mouth with my hand.

'Then sleep,' he said, 'stay where you are, and sleep.'

And I did. We did. Wrapped in each other's arms, warm and safe and sated. Knowing we could stay like that all night made it even better, as did being able to say I loved him rather than avoiding it like a dirty secret. I don't think I'd slept so well for years.

Right up until the moment the phone started to ring, that is. Loudly and insistently and at just before midnight. I needed to get rid of that *William Tell* overture – it was way too brutal.

'God, not again,' muttered James, pulling the covers over his head to shut out the noise.

I stretched my hand out into the darkness and blindly felt about with my fingers, until I scooped the phone up and answered with a groggy hello.

'Sally, it's me,' said the voice on the other end. Flashback time, except this year I had a lot fewer clothes on. 'You sound sleepy, love, hope I didn't wake you up – I wanted to wish you a happy birthday.'

Simon. Again. At least he sounded sober this time. And at least he'd got the day right – just about.

'Simon, thanks, that's really sweet, but this isn't a good time—'

James reached out and took the phone from my hand.

'She's busy,' he snapped, 'call back in daylight.'

He disconnected, and put the phone down, turning to me with an irritated gleam in his eyes.

'I'm sorry, Sal, I know that was rude, but . . . well. Like you said about being female? I'm male, and sometimes we're irrational too. You're in bed with me right now, and I'm not willing to share with your ex-husband.'

Almost ex-husband, I wanted to say. But didn't.

James pulled me to him, and I wriggled down into his embrace, and within minutes he was asleep again. It took me longer to drift away, and when I did, Simon was right there in my dreams. Where he had no right to be.

Simon, who'd got the day right this year. Simon, whom I'd once loved as well, back then, in a distant land.

Chapter 35

I was back in my own room after a blissful few hours with James. Waking up with him had been everything I'd hoped it would be – and yes, he did get very, very horny in the morning.

But in the back of my loved-up brain was Simon – and the way our conversation had ended last night. As soon as I was alone, I dialled his work number, half hoping he was in surgery.

He already had an idea who I'd been with. He referred to him confusingly as 'the fridge man', because of a photo of James and Jake I had tacked under the magnet that Jake had given me last year. When I confirmed that it was indeed the fridge man, he paused, regrouped. Possibly felt slightly sick – it was an especially flattering photo of James and his Big Guns.

'I see. Sal, I know I have no right to even ask, the way I've treated you, but . . . do you love him? Or is it just a holiday thing?'

'No, you don't have any right to ask, Simon, and I'm not going to discuss it with you. You made your choices. I'm happy, and the kids are happy, and I hope you are too. We'll see you when we get back.'

229

'Of course. You're right. Would you like me to pick you all up at the airport? It's no problem, really.'

'And what would Monika think about that?'

'Monika's not . . . well, we'll catch up when you're home. Give me a bell when I can come round and see you. And the kids. I'm sorry, Sal. Love you.'

I put the phone down, shaking my head – the man really was unbelievable. Sorry for what? Never once loading the dishwasher during our entire marriage? Treating me like a nobody for the last ten years? Shagging around behind my back? Dumping me for a nineteen-year-old lap-dancer? The list was endless. I don't know why I'd even bothered calling.

Except . . . except he was Simon. He was the father of my children, the man I'd been happily – or at least satisfactorily – married to for seventeen years. He'd always be in my life one way or another, and we were all going to have to work around that.

I put it to the back of my mind and carried on getting ready. The boat-trip gang had arrived back safe and sound and full of tall tales, and there was a barbecue on the beach.

'Mum!' said Ollie, popping his head round the door. 'Just came up to get my Frisbee. How're you? Did you have a nice time? Did James kiss you punishingly?'

'Ollie, you've really got to stop reading those Mills & Boons, love . . . Come on, let's go down together.'

Mehmet and Adnan had set up a grill on the beach, and the smell of lamb and chicken was wafting up into the sky mixed with curls of black smoke. There were buckets full of ice with wine and beer chilling in them, and an ancient ghetto blaster was pumping out Enrique Iglesias.

Allie was umpiring a game of rounders. Jake and his pal Matthew were paused on their bases, waiting to run, and James was bowling. He was wearing a pair of khaki shorts with pockets on the front and was bare-chested.

Lucy was in to bat, hair tied back in a wild blond ponytail, giving him the eye of the tiger and skipping from toe to toe in anticipation.

'Don't break him, Lucy!' I yelled. 'I need him later!'

James laughed as he ran, and threw a distracted ball that Lucy whacked with all her strength, jumping a foot off the ground with the effort. It flew high into the sky, inches over the reaching fingertips of Ian and Jenny in field, and right out into the bay. Jake and Matthew legged it as fast as they could, both coming back to base and high-fiving each other so hard they fell over into the sand.

'Come on, Sally,' shouted Jenny, 'we need you!'

Ha ha. As if. I'd settled myself down on a blanket to watch, and that was as close as I planned to get – I had no intention of bouncing my boobs round the beach for their entertainment. Mike was obviously of the same opinion about his budding man-breasts, and he lowered his bulk next to me, cracking open a new can of lager.

'That's a shame, Sal. I was looking forward to seeing you in action.'

'Bet you were, you old pervert – how was Allie?'

'Hyper,' he said, 'and still not talking. I know you tried, so thanks for that. I s'pose she'll tell us when she's good and ready. You're right, though, there's probably not another man on the scene. How could he compete with this?'

He stretched out and rubbed his beer gut lovingly, downing his drink in one swig.

The game, and the eating and the drinking and the laughing, went on all afternoon. Even Lucy seemed relaxed and happy. I didn't hear her swear once, and at one point she passed me a can of Coke. Voluntarily, and without spitting in it.

The sun was fading out on the horizon, sliding down into the sea and shimmering a golden light over the waves. It was slightly cooler, and there was talk of starting a campfire so we could stay out and tell each other scary stories.

James was next to me, lying down with his eyes closed, his head resting on my thighs as I sat up watching Ollie and Jake play Frisbee. I was stroking his hair and he was making a man-purr. Max and Lucy were sitting cross-legged, talking animatedly and eating ice-cream cones.

I never, ever wanted to go home. This was as perfect as I could ever remember life being.

Out in the distance, a sleek wooden sailing boat was heading towards shore. It looked like the *gulet* the others had taken their trip in.

It headed straight for the wooden jetty in front of us, and I strained my eyes to watch. A man jumped out and tied it secure, then a woman followed. She made her way alone along the jetty, and as she got nearer and her figure got bigger, everyone stopped what they were doing to look on in curiosity. Apart from James, who was snoozing away in my lap.

The woman was tall and slim and had long jet-black hair, gleaming in the dimming light of the sun. She was wearing minuscule denim shorts and a tight black vest top that left no doubt at all that she had dispensed with the services of a bra.

'Crikey . . . who's that? She's a bit of all right,' said Mike, shading his eyes with his hand and staring out at her.

'Yeah, she's a mega-babe – she looks like Lara Croft,' added Ollie, gazing at her in a very non-gay way.

Even the little boys were fascinated. They stopped their game of tag to look, then Jake started running frantically along the jetty towards her.

'Mummy!' he shrieked, throwing himself into her arms.

Chapter 36

'James! Wake up!' I muttered urgently, shaking him awake by his shoulders.

'What? What's the emergency? Do you need more sex already?' he murmured, opening one eye as he came to, flipping over on to his stomach and looking up at me.

'Ah, no. This really wouldn't be the right time.'

'Daddy! Daddy! It's Mummy!' shouted Jake, moving so fast his feet looked as though they were flying over the sand. Mummy followed, holding his hand and smiling down at us. Up close she was even more stunning, with huge, slanted green eyes and the kind of deep tan you get from spending most of your life outdoors. Eventually it might look old and leathery – but she was still young enough to pull it off. Of course.

James jumped quickly to his feet, rubbing his hands through his hair and looking deeply unsettled.

'Lavender,' he said. 'What are you doing here?'

I saw Lucy's eyes go wide, and she mouthed 'Lavender?' to Max. He shook his head and shrugged. It was a pretty silly name – down to those hippy-dippy parents, I supposed. At least I'd known it in advance.

She reached out and pulled a bit of stray grass out of James's hair. Everyone was staring at the two of them, then at me, then back at them again.

'Well I was in the area,' she said, in a sexy, sultry American drawl. 'We were doing some filming of the sea turtles – it's hatching season. And I knew you were here, so I thought I'd cruise along and see you. And Jake.'

I didn't miss the emphasis on that, and I'm pretty sure James didn't either. I could sense the tension coming off him in waves. I sat still and silent – this wasn't my move to call. I was the one who'd been on the phone to her bloody ex this morning, so I was in no position to throw a tantrum.

'Isn't it brill, Daddy? And she says she can stay for the rest of our holiday if we want!' said Jake, clinging to her leg.

Oh goodie, I thought. What fantastic news.

'Mummy – this is Sally,' he said, pointing down at me. 'She's Daddy's girlfriend now.'

I gave her a little wave with my fingers to be polite. She looked down at me with those cat eyes, and I knew that in one glance she'd checked me out, summed me up, and filed me under 'N' for 'Nobody'.

'Sally, it's great to meet you,' she said, 'and I hope I get to know all of Jake's friends while I'm here. But right now, would you mind too much if I hijacked James for a while?'

She flicked her eyes back up and smiled at him like he was the only person in the entire world. 'We should talk,' she added. Maybe she'd decided to join the French Foreign Legion and had come to say her goodbyes.

James snapped out of his paralysis and turned to me. His face was a mess of emotions.

'Is that okay with you?' he asked quietly. As if he needed permission. As if I wanted to give it. I nodded, not trusting myself to speak in case I screamed at him. He reached out to hold one of my hands in his, then raised it to his mouth and kissed the palm. He was staring into my eyes, apparently trying to send me some kind of message, but my psychic skills had fallen flat just when I needed them.

Lavender walked off towards the hotel, Jake hanging off her arm. James followed a few paces behind, glancing back at me over his shoulder.

'What the fuck was that all about?' said Lucy, as soon as he'd gone.

'That, ladies and gentlemen,' I said, feeling a chill run through me, 'was Lavender Breeze, James's ex and Jake's mum.'

'Lavender Breeze? What the fuck kind of a name is that? It sounds like something you'd clean the toilet with.'

God bless my daughter. She was the bitch from hell to live with, but I was glad I had her on my side. The rest of the gang gathered in and sat around me, murmuring their surprise and support. I don't think anybody really knew what to say, it was such a strange situation.

Jenny sat by my side and held my hand, and Allie was stroking my back as though I had indigestion. Mike handed me a can of lager. I stared out into the bay, and cracked it open. Everyone followed my lead and stayed quiet for a few blessed seconds.

'She does have lovely hair, though, doesn't she?' asked Rick in a wistful voice. Marcia kicked him on the thigh and he squealed like a girl.

'It's probably fake,' he added, apologetically, 'or stolen from some poor Russian peasant girl who swapped it for a turnip.'

'Yeah, I'm sure you're right,' I said, finding a smile to reassure the assembled support group that I wasn't about to stab myself with a kebab skewer.

But deep down, I knew it wasn't going to be all right. I knew, in fact, that it was going to be very, very wrong.

Chapter 37

By dinner I still hadn't heard from James. I sat with Mike and Allie and pretended to eat, too nervous to take any real interest. I was sick of waiting for the phone to ring or a text to land. I was sick of looking up every time I heard footsteps, hoping it was him, smiling and holding out his arms. I was sick of wanting to be told everything was going to be all right. I was just very, very sick.

No matter how much my friends tried to make light of it for my sake; no matter how many times Allie told me it'd be fine, or Jenny hugged me, or Marcia offered to go and find them, I knew there was something badly wrong. After my last catastrophe I'd learned to trust my instincts; James had been healing the wounds Simon left, but now I felt them all over again – vivid and searing and bloody and twice as painful.

We were all sitting on the terrace when they finally emerged. Jake had gone to watch a movie with Matthew. Ollie and Lucy were hovering around me protectively. Everyone else was there, talking about any topic under the sun apart from what was happening. I couldn't even drink, my stomach was so queasy, and I was planning an early escape as soon as I'd been out long enough to preserve my dignity.

I heard her laughing before I saw them. Like she didn't have a care in the world. I couldn't even look up and meet his eyes, I felt so bad. I pretended to be fastening my sandals for a minute or two as they joined us, wondering if I could just crawl between everyone's legs and escape without them noticing.

I saw James's feet planted in front of me. I looked up at his legs, then the rest of him, and eventually his face. He looked exhausted and drawn and maybe a decade older than he had when he was playing rounders earlier.

'Hi,' I said, with my usual stunning wit.

'Hi yourself. Are you okay?'

No, I was not okay. I was a lifetime from okay. The man who hours before had been proclaiming his love for me was standing there looking like boiled shit after spending the evening holed up with the woman who broke his heart. I thought I was about to die of sheer misery, and the woman in question was busily flipping her hair around and telling gripping stories about her time among the gorillas of Uganda.

'Okay I am. Yes,' I said, sounding like Yoda after a few shandies. He sat next to me and held my hand, our arms dangling loosely between the two chairs, like neither of us had the energy to hold them up.

'What's going on? Is she joining the French Foreign Legion?' I whispered.

'What? No. It's . . . it's complicated. Can I see you later? Just to talk?'

Just to talk? Since when had James and I been on a 'just talking' basis? We'd spent the entire holiday tearing each other's clothes off, and the night before enjoyed a marathon bonking frenzy interrupted only by declarations of love. Now here we were, holding hands with as much passion as a pair of four-year-olds on a school trip, and planning a 'just-talking' session. I thought I might throw up.

I nodded and looked on as Lavender held court. James was right: she was charming. And beautiful. And busy making friends and influencing people. She talked to Ian and Jenny about rock climbing. To Mike about a brewery she'd visited in South Africa. To Rick, she could have been talking about crocheting socks, he was so enraptured by Lavender's every word.

'So,' said Rick, leaning forward on his chair and unable to quite shake the look of adoration off his face, 'you spend your entire life travelling round all these beautiful places taking photos of animals?'

'That's about the size of it,' said Lavender, 'and I know how lucky I am. This latest shoot is for a calendar for an international wildlife charity. It's going to be accompanied by a DVD, so we're doing video as well. Then I'm taking some time off.'

I felt James tense next to me, and saw Lavender shoot him a look from her shining green eyes.

'So where's the best place you've ever been?' asked Rick, oblivious to the tension. The others couldn't help but listen, even though I knew they were on my side. Deep down.

'Oh, I couldn't say, Rick. I've been all over the world – the Amazon, Africa, months shooting the birds of southeast Asia.

I guess I'm just like anybody else, though – home is where the heart is. It just makes you appreciate it even more when you're away.'

She looked across at me, and I knew she'd noticed my hand in James's.

'So, Sally – what do you do?' she asked.

I'm a spy, I wanted to say. I work for MI6 and if I tell you any more, I'll have to kill you. I'm a porn star. I'm a genetic engineer. I'm a Pierrot clown playing the international circus circuit. I'm a back-up singer for Bruce Springsteen.

'I'm a doctor's receptionist,' I said.

No way I was going to be able to glam that up with a trip to waterfalls of Zambia. The furthest I ever went was to the local pharmacy dropping off prescriptions. And I'd been happy with that – until now. Now I felt small and provincial and dull and way too boring for a man like James, when he had this bird of paradise strutting her colours for him.

'Which is a very useful job,' interjected Marcia, looking ferociously at Lavender from behind a curtain of steel-grey hair. 'I think the world needs efficient medical administration more than it needs pictures of turtles' arses.'

Bless her: so scary – and so loyal. Lavender just nodded in reply, not at all fazed by Marcia's display of aggression. Perhaps it was down to her time with the gorillas in Uganda.

Lucy had been standing on the edge of the crowd, perched on a bar stool, arms folded in front of her chest and toes tapping furiously. I knew that sound. It was never a sign of contentment.

Allie had been quiet, looking around her and sizing up the mood. She stood up, holding Mike's hand.

'Come on, big man, time for me to thrash you at pool. Again. Anyone else up for it? Winner gets to see me naked. Same prize for the loser. See you all upstairs.'

One by one they all followed, traipsing up the steps to the pool room. Rick had to be dragged away by Marcia – I think he wanted to sit on Lavender's lap and sniff her hair.

Lucy and Ollie stayed, evening up the odds, and Lavender pulled her chair in closer to me and James. I felt him stroking the palm of my hand with his fingers, but he still didn't say a word.

'That's a pretty amazing career you have,' said Lucy, sweetly. Ollie grimaced slightly and glanced around, possibly looking for an umbrella to use when the shit started flying.

'You must have started early – is that why you dumped Jake and did a runner?'

Lavender smiled, equally sweetly. 'Oh Lucy, I can't possibly expect you to understand – you're only a baby! I love Jake, I always have. But I was too young, I was only twenty-three. Now I'm thirty, I see things differently.'

'Only twenty-three,' said Lucy, eyes narrowed. 'That's about the same age my mum was when she had me. She had a career too. The difference is she loved me enough to stay with my Dad and raise me.'

'Oh yeah?' replied Lavender, arching her eyebrows. 'And how'd that work out for her?'

She clearly knew all about my hideous past. I felt a jab of anger shoot through me – why had he told her? He had no right. That was my business, not hers.

'It was working out just fine until you arrived, you—'

'Lucy! That's enough!' I said.

Lavender laughed, genuinely amused. 'Sally – this girl of yours has real spirit, real fire. She's a credit to you.'

I saw Lucy reflexively gripping a pot of cocktail sticks on the table. Probably pondering how many she could stick in Lavender's mocking eyes before someone restrained her.

'Yes, she is, Lavender, I'm very proud of her,' I said, 'and Jake is a credit to James.'

That shut her up, no matter how temporarily. I seized the opportunity to stand up and make my exit.

'Come on kids,' I said, 'let's go play pool with our friends. James, if you want to see me later, you know where I am.

'The door will always be open,' I added significantly, hoping it gave the bitch something to think about.

Chapter 38

I was a tiny bit inebriated by the end of the night. I can't play pool unless I'm drunk, for some reason – the balls fly into the pockets with much more ease if I've had a bottle of wine. I beat Max, Mike and Ollie all in a row – unlucky in love, lucky in meaningless pub games, as the old saying doesn't go.

The talk was all of Lavender as we played. She'd stayed down on the terrace with James, their heads bent deep in conversation. Not that I was looking.

'Stop looking at them,' said Allie, after my third trip to the balcony to spy. 'You've done well so far, kept up a dignified front under pressure. Leave it alone until you know what's going on.'

'I know. You're right. But if I see her touch him, I'm going straight down there and sticking this pool cue right up her jacksie. I might even be able to hit her with the white ball from here if I angle it right – she'd look much better with a broken nose.'

I held the ball up, closing one eye to get her shiny black head in my sights.

'Don't worry,' Allie said, 'she's clearly a mega-bitch. One of those women who hate other women. Miss McTavish would have despised her, unless she gave her an interesting chapter on the sex lives of gorillas.'

After an hour or so of surreptitious spying, I saw Lavender stand up to leave. She headed off in the direction of the kids' club and I presumed she was picking up Jake. James stayed where he was, holding his head in his hands for a moment before he stood and stretched. He looked up at the balcony, trying to spot me. I dropped the cue and ran down the stairs two at a time – so much for dignity.

'Come on then. Let's talk,' I said. He followed me to my room, and I let us both in. I flicked on the light, and sat down on the bed, kicking my sandals off. My heart felt so heavy I thought it was in my ankles, and all the masterful little speeches I'd planned earlier drained from my mind when I looked up at him.

James was wearing his Levis and a white shirt with three buttons undone. He looked wonderful – apart from the red-rimmed eyes and the fingers clenched into tight, tense fists. It seemed unlikely that we were going to end this particular bedroom session with a mind-blowing orgasm or six. I'd probably never have one again, come to think of it – because if this went the way I thought it was going to, that was it for me and men. For ever.

'You can sit next to me, you know,' I said, 'unless you suddenly find me physically repulsive.'

His eyes flashed and he shook his head.

'Don't be stupid. Don't ever think anything like that.'

He sat down by my side and took my hands in his. 'I could never find you anything other than gorgeous and hard-on inducing.'

I glanced down at his crotch. No sign of any action there.

'James, just tell me what's going on,' I sighed. 'This morning you loved me. Tonight you're on a different planet. I'm always honest with you and I deserve the same. I'm a big girl, I can take it.'

'You're not that big, and you're probably lying . . . but yeah, you're right. We do need to talk about it.

'Seems that Lavender's had some kind of epiphany. She wants to come back to us, give it another try. She's cancelled all her projects for the next year. You don't know her, but that is a huge deal for her. She says she's done it because she wants to live with me and Jake in Dublin. Be a proper mum to him, and a . . . well, be with me too.'

I bet she did. I mean, who in their right minds wouldn't? Oh yes – her. Seven years ago. But now she was a big, grown-up thirty-year-old, fed up of playing the field, and she wanted her man back. Or my man, as I'd foolishly been thinking of him.

'That's quite an offer,' I said sarcastically. 'Shame it's taken her this long to come up with the idea. So what did you say to her?'

'I haven't said anything yet!' he half shouted, angry more at himself than me, I think. 'It's all too fucked-up for words. I had no idea this was coming. She invited me to stay with her when Jake went at Easter . . . but I didn't analyse it. I'm a bloke – I didn't poke at it and look for ulterior motives. It was just Lavender, being as unpredictable as usual. She's always been like that, does everything on a whim.

'And this last year I was too busy thinking about you, Sally, and getting to know you, and imagining what might happen here. Maybe she picked up on that. I don't know. But whatever the fuck was going on in her head, I didn't pay it any attention.'

'And now? Now you *do* know what's going on in her head?'

'Well, Jake's over the moon to see her, and it's pretty damn hard not to pay her any attention now she's actually here! She seems so serious about it. More than I've ever seen her, turning up here like this. Cancelling work – she's never done that before. I don't know, Sal, it's all so . . . screwed.'

He rubbed his hands over his face and kept them there. I wondered if he was crying underneath. I didn't care. I was getting sick of men doing this to me. Second-choice Sally, every bloody time.

'Part of me knows she's manipulative and hates not getting what she wants, but part of me wonders if . . . if this might be a chance for Jake to have his mother around full time, and if I owe it to him to at least *think* about it.'

I wondered where I fitted into all this. Into his misguided vision of happy families. Me, the woman he said he loved. The woman who most definitely loved him. Was it all so meaningless that he could throw it aside like this? What did he expect me to do? Fight for him? Get down on my hands and knees and beg? Or make it easy for him, give him my blessing?

'Why aren't you saying anything?' he asked, the blue of his eyes intense on mine as he faced me. 'I do love you, Sal. None of it was a lie.'

I could feel a tide of bitterness rising up in my throat. Oh yes – he loved me so much he was thinking of running off into the sunset with another woman. It was all starting to sound sickeningly familiar.

'Talk to me!' he said desperately, trying to put his arms round me. I pushed him away and stood up.

'No. I won't talk to you. And don't touch me. You don't have the right, James. You can't be the man who hurts me and the man who comforts me as well, just to make yourself feel better. It doesn't work like that. I survived before you, and I'll survive after you. Now I think you'd better go. Piss off back to Lavender and your bright shiny future.'

He stood, his eyes desperately sad, and reached out for me again. A quick hug to make everything all right.

'No! Just go!' I shouted. He closed his eyes for a beat, then walked out of the door, shutting it quietly behind him.

As soon as he was gone I pulled my clothes off, threw them in a heap on the floor, and collapsed into bed. I was exhausted and angry and desperate all at the same time. My head was on backwards, and my stomach was inside out. I wanted him and hated him and was so washed out I couldn't even cry. So I did what my body was telling me to do: switched off from it all, and fell asleep.

When I woke up, I found my ability to cry had been magically restored. And from the feel of the pillows, I'd been crying all night in my sleep. I had a raging headache and one look in the mirror made it worse.

I stared at my reflection as I splashed water on my face and my swollen eyes. I looked like poo. I looked like a woman who'd lost the love of her life the same day she'd found him. The necklace James had given me was glinting under the spotlights. Beginnings and endings. I felt the sting of more tears welling up.

I clamped my eyelids shut and squeezed to stave them off, then went through the motions of brushing my teeth and trying to comb the tangles out of my hair.

I put on shorts and a vest top and sat on the edge of the bed, resting my hands on my knees. I felt miserable. I couldn't help wondering if I'd made a terrible mistake last night, shouting at him and kicking him out – wasn't that just pushing him into her arms? He said himself he hadn't made his mind up – had I made it up for him by telling him to leave? Should I have seduced him and told him I loved him and kept him by my side; reminded him of how very good it was between us?

My pride hadn't allowed me to even consider that. I'd felt as if I was in a time machine, listening to Simon and his lies the year before. The rejection of that was still stinging, and I'd mentally rolled it all into one big ball of crap.

But James wasn't Simon, and there were no lies – just a truly crappy situation for everyone. All he'd said was he wanted to listen to her, for Jake's sake. As a mother, I could understand that. If my kids had been younger, and Simon had come crawling back, wouldn't I have heard him out because of them? Yes, I would – and, being me, probably taken him straight back and made him *coq au vin* for his tea as well. If he'd wanted to come home, I'd still be ironing those five work shirts every week.

And what I'd felt for Simon looked like a chip-pan fire in comparison to the blazing passion I had for James. I'd never been this swept away by a man before – and I'd certainly never known what good sex was. He'd been nothing but honest and kind and patient while I worked through my own issues. Yet, last night, I'd pushed James away. Kicked him out of the room without even really hearing him out.

It had been some twisted kind of pride. But, I reminded myself, I was both Simon's rejected wife and Lucy's mother. That meant I was a dab hand at coping with humiliation. It must be worth risking a little bit more, surely?

Mind made up, I jumped to my feet and dashed out, as quietly as I could so I didn't wake the kids. I headed for his room, and knocked firmly on the door. He was always horny in the mornings – it might be the best time to catch him. I'd drive her out of his mind with sex.

No answer. I banged again, and again. Nothing. I stood in the hallway for a minute, nodding politely at the cleaners as they went past with mops and buckets, feeling like a lemon.

There was nobody in. I'd woken up pretty much everybody else in the corridor, but he wasn't there.

I walked through the restaurant, in case he was having breakfast, but there was no sign of him, just Marcia drinking coffee and smoking. I joined her for a moment, wondering if I should take up cigarettes to release the tension.

'Are you all right?' she asked gruffly from behind a grey cloud.

'I don't know yet,' I replied, coughing as the fug hit my throat. 'Have you seen James?'

'No. But when you find him, don't let him go. All kinds of people try and get in the way of love – but don't you let them, Sally. You tough it out.'

I nodded and stood up to leave. I was fairly sure her relationship with Rick hadn't been obstacle-free, and she was right. I needed to tough it out. And I would – if I could only find him.

Maybe he was out on a run – he did that sometimes in the morning, before it got too hot. But then where was Jake? Could be with Matthew and his parents. Could be out with James somewhere. Could be with his hellfire bitch of a mother.

I felt deflated – all the energy fizzed out of me, leaving me saggy and shapeless, like a balloon that had been popped with a pin. I'd been focused and determined and full of adrenaline. Now I just felt tired and hungry, so I picked up a doughnut from the buffet and strolled down to the beach to watch the sun on the waves.

We were going home tomorrow, and my horizons would be back to other people's driveways and passing Nissan Micras and old men walking labradors. No more golden sunrises or blue water or gently bobbing boats.

I sat down on one of the loungers, still damp with morning dew, and nibbled my doughnut. Some things never let you down.

Lavender's *gulet* was still moored to the end of the jetty. I wondered if I could slip out there unnoticed and slash the rope with a butter knife.

As I gazed out at it, hatching my evil plan, I saw figures moving about on deck. Lavender, I supposed, perhaps with her fellow Horsemen of the Apocalypse.

They climbed over, and started walking up the jetty towards the beach. It was her, wearing some kind of transparent white dress that clung to her thighs and made her look like one of the illustrations in *Shag Yourself Happy*. Next to her was James, my James, who I knew full well could shag me happy. And in between them was Jake, holding on to both their hands as they swung him up and down into the air. I could hear him giggling from here. So that's where he'd been all night – straight from my room to her cabin.

I stared at them in horror, almost choking on my doughnut. The bastard. I snapped out of my trance, and looked around for somewhere to hide. They were almost here and I couldn't bear to see that familial happiness and pretend I was okay with it. I wasn't okay with it. I hated them both. I'd cry or scream or burst out into a chorus of 'It Should Have Been Me', and that wasn't fair on Jake.

There was nothing big enough to shelter me, so I shoved the rest of the doughnut into my mouth, and dropped down to my hands and knees.

I started to shuffle myself headfirst under the sun lounger, which seemed like a really great idea until my arse got stuck. It wouldn't fit under, no matter how much I flattened myself to the ground or wriggled around or swore. I tried to dig myself a hole in the sand, like a huge burrowing rabbit, but I didn't have time. The rest of my body was safely concealed, but the sun lounger was lifted half a foot into the air, floating on the ginormous island of my backside. I could hear them close now, so I stayed very, very still, and hoped they wouldn't notice.

'Sally? Are you okay?' I heard James say to my bottom. Shit. No way out now. I did an awkward reverse crawl back into the daylight, catching my hair in the hinges of the seat and ripping a chunk out as I came. I climbed up on to my feet, covered in sand from nose to toes, and smiled.

'Hi! Yes, I'm fine – I just . . . er, dropped my doughnut,' I said.

'I think it's there,' said Lavender, pointing to a greasy piece of pastry squashed flat against my cheek. I wiped it off and brushed some of the sand from my knees. Why did I always make it so easy for people to see me as a total buffoon? Maybe it's because I am one.

'Silly Sally!' said Jake, getting in on the act. I ruffled his hair and gave him a smile.

'Go get a table, I'll join you in a minute,' said James, gesturing to the restaurant. Lavender looked from me to him, then smiled and nodded – and why wouldn't she? It wasn't like she had anything at all to fear from the likes of me, was it? A mammoth-arsed, doughnut-scoffing, sand-coated human rabbit.

Before she left she leaned in and kissed him on the lips. Properly, like you would your boyfriend or your husband. Or someone else's boyfriend or husband, as usually seemed to be the case with the women I came across. He didn't respond, or put his arms around her, but he didn't push her away either.

The pain was so ferocious and so instantaneous I thought someone might have shot me through the heart with an air rifle. My hand flew to my chest and my breath froze in my throat. God, I'd rather scoop my own eyes out with a dessert-spoon than see that again.

'I'm sorry, I didn't know she was going to do that,' said James, as soon as Jake and his mother had moved out of earshot. I turned to go, not even meeting his eyes, but he grabbed hold of my arm. 'Keep still for a minute; you've got sand right in your eye. Not to mention all over your cleavage.'

He gently held my chin with one hand and wiped the sand away with his fingers. Well, the sand on my eyes, anyway – wisely he left the cleavage well alone.

'What were you really doing under there anyway?'

'I was hiding. I hoped you wouldn't see me.'

'Really?' he said, his voice thick with amusement, which I didn't think very appropriate under the circumstances. 'I'm afraid that's a rear view I'd recognise anywhere. How are you today?'

Oh just fucking brilliant thanks, I thought, having ten seconds ago watched you snog the face off your ex. Or current. Or future. Or whatever she was.

'Did you sleep with her?' I blurted out, with my usual tact.

He looked exasperated and annoyed, and rolled his eyes heavenward.

'No, of course I didn't sleep with her. Jake wanted to spend the night on the boat, and we were talking. What do you think I am?'

Male, I thought.

'Sally, I love you. And I don't hop from one woman's bed to another like that. But I do have feelings for her – she's Jake's mother, for Christ's sake. He's ecstatic at having the two of us together, even for a few days. I've never seen him so happy. I have to see where this goes. Tell me, honestly – what would you do if Simon turned up; if Lucy and Ollie wanted him back as well?'

I felt my lower lip start to tremble like a baby before it cries, so I closed my eyes, then stared at my feet. I didn't want to look at him. Even now, as the cracks spread across my heart, he still looked beautiful, standing there in the sunlight, messy-headed and bare-chested.

I wanted to tell him I'd send Simon straight back home. That I'd kick his arse on to the next flight and settle right back down to 24/7 sex with my new lover. But it wasn't true, and the lie wouldn't come out of my mouth.

'Lucy and Ollie would barricade the door if he tried to come back – they've already taken over the garage and sold his golf clubs on eBay . . . but, oh, I don't know, James! You're probably right – maybe I'd do the same. We're parents, we do anything we can for our kids.

'But that doesn't mean I have to watch. It's killing me, even if I can understand why you're doing it. It hurts too much. And you'll never make it work with her if I'm hovering in the background. So let's cut our losses. You do your thing. I'll do mine. We're going tomorrow, and we don't ever need to see each other again.'

I kissed him quickly, then turned away before he could argue, walking briskly back up to the hotel.

I needed to get back to my room, where I could have my meltdown in private. I was stumbling along blindly, eyes blurred with unshed tears and breathless from the choking sobs I was trying to control. I bounced off a wall or two, tripped over a sprinkler and terrified the gardener on my way. I ended up sitting down at the bottom of the stairs, unable to take a single step further.

A shadow fell over me and I looked up to see Marcia again. She sat down next to me, and pulled a pack of Gauloises from her pocket.

'Have one of these,' she said, handing me a cigarette. I put it in my mouth, and she lit it with her Zippo. I started choking as soon as I inhaled, and stubbed it out, coughing. Well, it was worth a try. Maybe I'd do heroin next.

'I was waiting for you to come back, after I saw *her* arrive. Come on, I'll walk you up to your room,' she said, pulling me to my feet. 'It's absolutely shit, loving someone that much, isn't it?'

Chapter 39

'Come on – time to get ready,' said Lucy, shaking my arms and hissing into my face. I knew there'd be a slap next, maybe a small electric shock from her portable torture kit.

'I don't want to come, and you can't make me,' I said, childishly. It was last-night-party time at the Blue Bay – and I felt about as much like partying as eating a Tupperware bowl of pickled pig's testicles.

'I *can* make you – I can do fucking anything,' she replied, 'but first we're in hair and make-up. And if you don't like it, tough.'

She waved a spiky hairbrush at me like she was planning to impale me with it.

I sat and winced as she worked on my hair. I had no idea what she was doing, but it involved a lot of back-combing, burning my ears with the straighteners, and blasts of hairspray so toxic they formed mushroom clouds. She pulled and prodded with her fingers, was finally satisfied, then started rooting around in her make-up bag.

'You have to go down there looking gorgeous, or at least as gorgeous as you can at your age, and show that twat what he's missing. You don't have any choice. It's the law.'

'Easy for you to say, Luce. You are gorgeous. But with me, there's always someone younger and better-looking round the corner – first Monika, now Lavender. Seems to be my fate to always be the trade-in model. Ouch!'

She'd poked me in the eye, accidentally on purpose, with an eyeliner pencil. It occurred to me that I hadn't worn eyeliner since 1991 and should possibly be feeling the fear at this point.

She was making 'O' gestures at me with her mouth while doing things with lip gloss.

'Stop feeling sorry for yourself, it's pathetic,' she said, smearing another layer on. 'And there isn't someone better round the corner – just some man stupid enough to behave like there is. It's not you; it's them – they're natural-born pricks.'

I waited for the punch line – the bit where she put the boot in, and told me once was a mistake, twice made me an undesirable cretin who was fated to die alone in a puddle of my own pee. But strangely, it never came. Either she meant it, or she'd been distracted by the pot of purple eye-shadow she was slathering over my lids.

'There you go – fantastic, if I do say so myself. I am so frigging talented, it defies belief. If only there was an A level in creative hair-straightening.'

I wandered into the bathroom and looked in the mirror. I wasn't there. I'd been replaced by a large-breasted middle-aged Goth with hair so tall she'd have problems walking through doors. A whole colony of guinea pigs could have lived in there. My eyes were stripes of purple and black, and my lips were coated in thick violet goo. She'd used white face powder that didn't cover my tan, just decorated my cheeks with streaks of pale frosting, as though I'd let shaving foam dry on. I looked like Amy Winehouse's grandma.

Yep, Lavender would eat her heart out once she got a load of this. James would probably dump her on the spot and ask me to marry him. I'd be Frankenstein's bride.

The upside was, maybe nobody would even recognise me. I was almost past caring.

The party was in full swing by the time we got down there. The staff had expanded their repertoire, and Tarkan from reception was up doing 'Born To Be Wild', straddling an imaginary motorbike, holding on to the handlebars and thrusting with his hips. It looked as if he was shagging the Invisible Woman from the rear.

Allie was already well on her way to hammered, and threw her arms around me as soon as I arrived, leaving lipstick smudges all over my cheeks. Which was great, because I needed more make-up.

Mike eyed my face and hair and burst out laughing.

'Oh piss off, Mr Universe,' I said.

Mehmet behind the bar didn't recognise me at first, and did a cartoon-style double take once he did. He mixed me a killer cocktail without asking and handed it over to me, shaking his head.

'Sally, looking good tonight . . . like *Rocky Horror Show*! "Time Warp" later, yeah?'

I got through about six cocktails in the space of an hour – they kept appearing magically on the table in front of me, delivered by Ian, by Jenny, by pretty much anyone who wanted to show their support but didn't know what to say. Kindness through alcohol.

I could see James and Lavender on the other side of the terrace, and I sincerely hoped they stayed there. She was leaning in close to him, whispering into his ear over the noise of Adnan oozing his version of 'Careless Whisper'. James looked stiff, and not very happy, and that was absolutely fine by me. I didn't want him to be happy. I wasn't that big a person. I wanted him to be sad and empty and have two-foot-tall hair and make-up that Adam Ant would be ashamed of.

My phone beeped in my bag. A text from Simon. 'Offer still open if you want lift from airport. xxx.' What the hell – it would be one less thing to worry about at the other end. 'Yes please,' I replied. No kisses. I'd rather remove my own lips with a cheese grater than kiss another man.

I looked up as Rick took to the stage, dressed in a pair of blue Speedos and a pink silk pashmina. Hakan climbed up next to him, and they launched into a duet of 'Summer Nights', with Rick as Sandy. They held hands at the end and gazed into each other's eyes as the final 'tell me more' faded into the distance.

Marcia, watching from the wings, was not a happy woman. She stubbed her cigarette out furiously, like she was trying to kill the ashtray, and stood up.

As soon as they were off the stage she marched over to them and picked the hapless waiter up by the scruff of his shirt. His feet were dangling and kicking into thin air as she carried him off, like a pterodactyl bearing a field mouse. Mike was busting a gut laughing, and even in my depressed state it looked comical.

Rick ran after them, flapping his hands and crying, swatting her arms to try and get her to let go. When she did, Hakan fell to the floor in a crumpled heap, his head wrapped in his hands.

'Marcia! What are you doing!' Rick shrieked, mascara running down his cheeks.

'He's not worth it, Rick. He's . . . he's been with both of us, the little shit . . .' She kicked Hakan in the ribs and he started to crawl off into the bushes, bottom in the air. She gave that a kick as well and he scooted forward, falling flat on his face in the dirt before recovering enough to run off into the darkness.

'You? You . . . and him? How could you, Marcia?'

'Well it's not like you're interested, is it?' she answered, 'and I'm only human. Much as I love you, I have needs. I only realised what was going on when I saw the way you were looking at him at the end of that song. He's not good enough for you, Rick, and I won't let anyone make a fool of you.'

Rick held his face in both his hands and cried some more. Then he used his pashmina to wipe his eyes, and held out his arms to her. They clutched on to each other like the last two in the lifeboat. It was so sweet I started to fill up too, but then I remembered how much eyeliner I had on.

'Bloody hell – nothing but drama here tonight, eh, Sal?' said Mike. 'Pulling at the old heart strings, those two. How are you holding up anyway, love? For what it's worth, I think

James is going to live to regret what he's up to. From the look on his face, I think he probably already regrets it.'

'Don't be nice to me, Mike,' I said, ''cause you'll make me cry and then my whole face will fall off. Look – Allie's getting up. I'm amazed it's taken her this long.'

'This one's for my burning hunk of love, Mike,' said Allie, swaying in time to the opening chords of 'Can't Take My Eyes Off You'. As she sang, the crowd joined in, waving their arms from side to side in the chorus. I noticed tears streaming down Mike's craggy face. It was like watching rivers flow through the Grand Canyon: this big, gruff, bear of a man sobbing with love for his wife.

'That was our wedding song,' he said, 'both times. Oh God – what's wrong with her, Sal? I love that woman so much, even if she can't sing to save her life!'

That was it. I was gone. It was like *Four Weddings*, *Titanic* and the bit where you think E.T.'s dead, all combined. We sat there together, sobbing and weeping and producing enough moisture to cause a flood alert.

Allie took her bows and walked over to our table, giving Mike a big sloppy kiss. He clutched on to her back and told her he loved her.

'I love you too, you big sentimental fool. Now bugger off for a bit – girls' talk time. How do you expect me to tell Sally what a fantastic lover you are if you're sitting right there? Go talk to James and Lavender. Tell them Sally's just broken the news she's got herpes or something, will you?'

He shambled off, and I knew he'd do exactly that. It would be interesting to keep an eye on that far table for the next few minutes. James wouldn't believe him, but it might wipe the smile off *her* face.

'Are you okay?' she asked, settling in next to me.

'I'm fine, Allie – just, you know, tired and emotional. But listen – and don't try and run away – I've been worried about you all holiday. There's something wrong and we all know it, so you might as well tell me. In fact you have to – I'm sick of being the centre of the trauma police's attention. What's going on?'

She paused, and stayed silent for a second, gazing off into the distance at Mike. She grimaced once, then turned back to look at me.

'Okay. I was going to anyway. But I warn you, you're going to need more of those tissues.'

She suddenly sounded serious, and sober, and sad, and the selfish part of me wished I hadn't asked. I had so much to cope with at the moment, I wasn't sure I could be much help to anybody else. As if everything wasn't bad enough, I could hear someone slaughtering 'Wind Beneath My Wings' in the background as I waited for her to speak.

'I've got breast cancer,' she said, 'and it's not looking good. It's my own fault. I felt something ages ago – almost a year, in fact. I put off getting it looked at, kept convincing myself it was gone or it was a cyst. I was too busy. I came up with all kinds of excuses. I had a biopsy and some other tests done before we came and the results aren't exactly optimistic. They think it might have spread. I'll start treatment as soon as I get back but . . . well, I wanted one really brilliant holiday first. I don't know what's going to happen, and I needed this. Before everything turns to shit.'

Even as she spoke the words, I realised that I'd been suspecting something like this all along. It explained her mood swings, and her insane lust for life, and the fact that she'd been so careful to avoid being alone with anyone she'd be tempted to confess to.

'Oh, Allie,' I said, clutching her hand in mine. 'You poor, poor thing. When are you going to tell them?' I asked.

'When we get home. I didn't want to spoil the holiday. And listen, I don't want to spend all night talking about this to you either – I'll be in touch when we're back. I swear I will. But I want you to promise me two things.'

'Anything, Allie, anything at all.'

'Next year, promise me you'll come back here. I know it's all gone tits-up with James, but I'm going to book ours anyway, and if I'm not here, I want to know you and Lucy will be. It'll help them. And promise me you'll look after Max. He'll be there in Oxford from October and I'll . . . rest better knowing you're keeping an eye on him.'

'Allie, stop it!' I said, squeezing her hands. 'Don't think like that! Of course you'll be here!'

'Yeah. Hopefully so. But promise me anyway.'

I nodded, and recycled an already soggy tissue. I wasn't sure if it was my own snot or Mike's.

'Now,' pronounced Allie, extricating herself from my grip and standing up, 'I'm going to circulate, and sing, and drink, and have fun – and whatever you do, woman, don't get up and start sobbing now. I don't want Mike to know yet. So laugh. Look joyous. Think of Lavender with dysentery in the middle of the Sahara Desert, forced to use cactus spikes for loo roll.'

The Birthday that Changed Everything

Sure enough, I managed to crack a smile at that, as she stood up, saluted me, and walked away.

Fuck. I couldn't cry. I'd promised. Although everyone would assume it was about my tattered love life anyway. I grabbed my bag and ran – the party, such as it was, was over.

Chapter 40

I ignored the knock on the door for as long as I could. I knew who it would be, and I didn't want to answer. I'd hardly slept.

Ollie popped his head through the connecting door. His hair was flat on one side and fright wig on the other; glasses shoved crookedly on the end of his nose.

'Mum, it's James. What do you want me to do? Do you want me to hit him for you? Set Lucy on him?'

'No, sweets, it's fine – go back to sleep. I'll sort it out. If Lucy wakes up, muzzle her.'

I swung my legs out of the bed. I was wearing a pair of old pants that had been through the washer a million times and a T-shirt from a pharmaceutical company that Simon got for free. I didn't give two hoots. There was no washing of face, no brushing of teeth, and no look in the mirror. The grim reality of Sally Summers in the morning.

I snatched the door open and presented myself in all my glory. Maybe I could give him a heart attack. He did jump back slightly, but that might be because I snapped 'What?' in his face as soon as I appeared.

'Erm . . . I wanted to say goodbye. And to ask if I can call you when I get home?'

'Is Lavender moving in?'

'I don't know. I'm so sorry. This is killing me . . . but maybe. At least for a while to see how it goes.'

'Then no, you can't fucking call me when you get home. You can't call me ever again. It's over. Don't phone, don't e-mail, don't exist.'

He looked so crestfallen I almost felt sorry for him. I wish some mad scientist would invent an on/off switch for loving someone. It'd make life so much easier. And when would I ever stop wanting to reach out and touch him? Probably when I went blind, lost my sense of smell, and had all my limbs amputated. Even then I'd want to lick him.

'James, I'm sorry,' I said, backtracking. 'I'm just angry and hurt. I don't hate you. I hope you'll be happy. But seriously – don't call me. I couldn't cope with it.'

'That's the thing,' he said. 'I don't know if I can be happy without you any more, Sally.' As he spoke, he reached out and stroked my hair. Looked like he had the same problem with the touching as I did.

'But you're going to try, aren't you?' I replied.

He nodded, leaned in, kissed me softly on the lips. I grabbed the back of his head and pulled him down closer, kissing him harder. His arms snapped round my waist, crushing me to him. By the time I broke away he was breathless and flustered and erect. Ha. Let him stagger back to Lavender with that in his pants and explain it all away.

'That was one for the road,' I said, shutting the door in his face.

PART FOUR

Endings and Beginnings

Chapter 41

'Sally, are you okay?' he shouted, knocking on the bath-room door again.

I dragged my face out of the toilet bowl for long enough to reply. I knew he'd just keep banging if I didn't. He'd been on some kind of semi-suicide-watch for a long time now, and took his caring duties seriously.

'I'm fine, Simon!' I yelled back. 'I'll be out in a minute, all right?'

'All right,' he replied. 'Just let me know if you need any help.'

Ha, I thought, standing up straight and looking in the mirror. I was perfectly capable of throwing my guts up without anyone's help. I grabbed the toothbrush and went to work, staring at a reflection that I hardly recognised any more.

To say that I'd lost weight would be something of an understatement. I'd lost several stone, and several dress sizes, and several months of my life. When I'd arrived back home from Turkey, almost a year ago, I'd been a mess. Now, as I was about to return to Turkey, I felt almost as bad.

Last August, Simon had met us at the airport, taken one look at me, and told us to wait while he drove the car round to the front from the multistorey. I obviously hadn't even looked capable of walking that far.

When I'd remained near catatonic for the drive back to Oxford, he'd carried the bags in, and taken me up to bed so I could 'catch up on some sleep', tucking me in like a child.

I'd lain there, staring at the ceiling, listening to the sounds of him talking to the kids downstairs. Eventually, I heard the traditional rise in volume that signified Lucy getting her knickers in a twist, then the delicate stomping sound of her running up the steps. The door to my room had edged open, and I shut my eyes quickly, pretending to be asleep. The last thing I needed was a row with Lucy – or, even worse, her showing concern about me.

Eventually, I had passed out. Not slept exactly – that implies rest. It was more a case of slipping into an unpleasant coma for a few hours. When I woke up, Simon was still there. He'd slept in the spare room, had collected the dog from the sitter, and had been to the shops to get fresh milk and supplies. By the time I made it down the stairs, there was toast and coffee and orange juice waiting. None of which I could face.

He'd tried to engage me in conversation, having gained a broad outline of what was going on from Ollie and Lucy – but that was another thing I couldn't face. Everything, in fact, felt too hard.

Simon stayed on for a couple of nights, cooking dinners I never ate, making conversation I never took part in, checking up on kids who were perfectly capable of checking up on themselves – until, eventually, I was able to function well enough to ask him to leave.

'Are you sure?' he'd said, taking in my haggard face and dirty hair and unusual lack of interest in the Ben's Cookies he'd gone all the way to the Covered Market to fetch for me.

'Yes. I need to start again, Simon, and I won't be able to do that if you're here. I really appreciate everything you've done, but I need some time alone. To get my balance back.'

The reality of getting my balance back consisted of bone-numbing depression, eating barely enough to keep me alive, and only speaking to people I absolutely had to speak to – which meant work colleagues who thought I was on an extreme low-carb diet and kept congratulating me on the weight loss, the kids to reassure them I wasn't about to top myself, and Allie.

Allie, who went through brutal chemotherapy and lost her lovely curly hair. Allie, who stayed brave through everything, so much braver than me, trying to make things right for Mike and Max. Allie who, after the most ferocious of fights, had finally died earlier in the year.

I'd visited her in the hospice during her last few days, horrified at her wasted form and papery skin; even more horrified at how selfish I'd been – sliding into a pit of despair because of a man, when she'd been facing this.

Despite it all, she'd still been Allie. Lying there, holding my hand, she'd said: 'Look after Max for me, Sal. And don't forget you promised to go back to the Blue Bay – someone's got to keep Mike from drinking himself to death. And you and James . . . don't write it off just yet. Give him a chance. Give yourself a chance.'

She'd paused, and looked me up and down through narrowed eyes.

'And for God's sake eat some Turkish delight while you're there, will you?'

Her funeral had been held on a vivid January day near her home in Brighton. The eternal rain we'd been enduring held off for one morning only, replaced by bright sunshine and a crisp, cold wind that blew the tears across our faces.

It had been hell for everyone, especially Mike, stumbling through the day with false jollity and a stock of dirty jokes he'd churned out to anyone who'd listen. Marcia and Rick had book-ended him through most of the wake, protecting him from anyone they thought might push him over the edge, or not laugh at his jokes. If they didn't react properly, one look at Marcia's face made them suddenly think the gag about the nuns and the bar of soap was perfectly appropriate for a funeral.

I'd sat with Jenny and Ian during the service, all three of us in floods of silent tears as we listened to the eulogy from Allie's sister Helen, and the poem that Max read out. I think we were crying for Allie, crying for Max and Mike, and crying for ourselves – Jenny and Ian were still mourning the loss of the babies they'd never have; and I was still in a state of quiet crisis, a downward spiral I didn't seem quite capable of pulling out of. The loss of Allie had left a monumental hole in lives that were already less than perfect, and I suspected we'd never be the same again.

James had been there, but I'd avoided him as much as I could. I saw his eyes widen when he looked at me, doing a double take and walking in my direction, face grim, body wrapped up against the wind in a long black greatcoat. I'd headed immediately for Marcia, somehow knowing that she'd keep me safe – which she did, not leaving my side until James had got the message and moved on to talk to someone else. Ollie also stood with me throughout, subtly heading off any of James's attempts to talk to me alone. It was all very polite, very civilised, but brutal in its own way as well.

Despite everything that had happened between us, when I first saw him, I wanted nothing more than to go to him, lay my head on his chest, feel his arms around me while I wept. He'd be feeling Allie's loss, hard, and he knew how much she meant to me – but again, the man who'd destroyed me couldn't be the man who consoled me as well.

Lucy had stayed in Brighton with Max, waving me and Ollie off as we drove out of their garden and back towards the grim slog of the motorway. It had been the day from hell. The year from hell, in fact.

And now here I was. Bags packed. Sun cream bought. Flip-flops ready to rock. Throwing up in my bathroom at the very thought of heading to Turkey again; of being there without Allie. If I was honest, being there without James. Being there without any of the joy and hope and sense of change that I'd experienced there for the last two years.

My mind didn't want to go. My body, I thought, splashing my face with cold water, really didn't want to go.

But Allie wanted me to. So I was going.

Chapter 42

We were back. Most of us were, anyway. One year, and a whole world of pain, later. A new arrival, and a missing face. None of us, I suspected, thought we'd be able to enjoy the Blue Bay without Allie. And the only reason I was putting myself through it was that promise I'd made, all those months ago.

A promise to Allie, with her sparkly green eyes and her long limbs and her filthy sense of humour. Allie, whom we'd all lost. I glanced around the bar, and everything reminded me of her: the sun loungers where she'd first met Nurse Nancy. The stage where she did her karaoke. The shady spot in the garden where she did her Pilates. The restaurant where we'd sat together, talking about Max and Lucy and life in general. And mainly, the big man sitting opposite me.

'There she is, the old girl,' said Mike, producing a huge jar of Kenco from his rucksack. I stared at it, wondering what he was up to – I'd never seen Mike willingly drink anything other than lager.

He nudged the jar towards me with his finger.

'You know, my Coffee-Mate,' he said, winking.

'No. Still no clue, Mike. Do you want a coffee? Is that what you're saying?'

He leaned forward across the table, as far as he could get with his belly in the way. There was a lot less belly this year, though. The weight had fallen from the lines of his face, leaving folds of skin that made him look like an old man.

'No, Sal. It's her. It's Allie – I smuggled her through Customs in disguise! Genius, eh? Couldn't be arsed filling all the forms in.'

I leaped back from the coffee jar and stared at it like it might be about to sprout teeth and bite me.

'Mike! Isn't that kind of . . . macabre?' And gross, and disgusting, and stomach churning. How could our beautiful, vivacious Allie be reduced to that? Dust in a pot. It made no sense at all.

'It's what she wanted, love. We had a long talk about it before she even went into the hospice – you know what she was like; always one eye on the next party. She didn't specify the coffee jar, mind. She'd have preferred Fair Trade, now I come to think of it . . .'

She would, I thought. But at least she was here . . . in a strange way. I couldn't imagine the Blue Bay without Allie, but if Mike was willing to give it a go, so was I. Besides. I'd made that promise, hadn't I? A promise to a dying friend. It was sacred.

'Earth to Sally,' said Mike, waving his fingers in front of my face. 'What were you thinking about? George Clooney?'

'As if. Why would I think about him when I have a real-life sex god sitting opposite me?'

'True enough, Sal, true enough. I'm so svelte these days I could pass for his better-looking brother anyway. You're a bit on the skinny side as well, love. Been a rough year for you, hasn't it?'

'Not as rough as yours, Mike. I'm fine.'

Not quite fine. But alive. And definitely a lot thinner. James had succeeded where no man, woman or beast had ever succeeded before – he'd put me off my food. The kids had done their best – Lucy heaping sugars in my tea and hoping I wouldn't notice, Ollie spending all his dinner money buying chocolate from the corner shop to tempt me with – but nothing had worked. The side of the sofa was now terminally stained from me hiding Mars Bars and pretending I'd eaten them, and I was half the woman I used to be.

'So,' I said, staring at Kenco, 'what's the plan then? Are we scattering . . . that . . . somewhere?'

'Yes. Out at sea in the bay. She gave me very strict instructions, and even told me how to avoid the wind blowing it back in my face. What a woman. So we'll be out tomorrow, then James and Ian are going to sail us to the island for a bit of a knees-up. It's all sorted, pie and a pint, just how she'd want it.'

'Um . . . did you say James? Is James here? I thought he was going to New York for the summer? God, I'm sorry, Mike – ignore what I just said, it doesn't matter.'

The poor man was planning how to scatter his wife's ashes, and I was acting like a fifteen-year-old drama queen. Self, self, self. But still . . . fuck. I'd counted on never seeing James again after the funeral. It was the only way I'd survived. The prospect of spending a fortnight up close and personal with him and Lavender was as appealing as brewing myself a mug of Mike's coffee.

I'd worked bloody hard to scramble back to sanity, and I'd had help from the most unlikely of sources, but it was a sanity built on sand. Even the thought of seeing them was making my throat close up in panic. To my utter shame, my thoughts raced straight away from Mike and Allie, and back to seeing James. I couldn't do it. I might actually die if I did.

I started to formulate a plan for catching an earlier flight home. Or a train. Or a very long walk – anything that got me away from the happy couple.

'I think that was in July, Sal, the New York thing, and I'm not sure if he went in the end. You can ask him yourself when you see him later.'

I blinked steadily at Mike, trying not to sink under the tsunami of anxiety I could feel swamping me. I'd promised Allie I'd come back and, as far as I'd known, James was playing happy families in the States. It should have been safe. It should have been all right. But now, my pounding heart and cold sweat told me, it wasn't.

I was glancing around nervously, wondering if I was going to need to do a drop-and-roll under the table any time soon.

'Don't worry, love, it won't be as bad as you think,' said Mike, reaching out to grip my hand. 'She always hoped it would work out between you two, you know? She always did.'

I didn't reply. I loved Allie – I was here because of Allie. But on that point, she was wrong.

'How're those nippers of yours anyway?' he asked, changing the subject. 'Your Lucy, you know, she's a diamond. She's stuck with Max through all of this. Lord knows I've been bugger-all use to him; too busy wallowing in my own misery. And he's been a pain in the arse as well – but she's never once lost that temper of hers. That's 'cause she's loyal, like her mum.'

Max had started at Oxford in October, even though he hadn't wanted to. He'd wanted to put it off to be with Allie, but she'd insisted. So he'd come to the city, forlorn and lost, staying with us as much as in his college, and had made the trek back to Brighton every weekend. It was hardly the carefree undergraduate life Allie had imagined for him – but at least he'd done it. With, as Mike had said, the unexpectedly calm support of Lucy. It had been a crazy year for us all.

Mike gave my clenched hands a squeeze, and I relaxed them enough to stop my nails drawing blood from the palms of my hands. The grieving widower was comforting the fruit-and-nut-cake sitting opposite him. I needed to get a grip. And a wig. And a new hotel.

'Right, Sal – I'm off for a swim,' he said, standing up and stretching.

I was so shocked I thought my eyeballs might fall out and roll round the table. For the last two years I'd never seen him lift anything heavier than a tray of beer, or walk further than bar to chair.

'Don't look so surprised. It was one of those things she made me promise her – that I'd lose a bit of bulk and get fitter. Not keen myself, but I'm a man of my word. I'm going to start off with one width of the pool and take it from there. Get the paramedics on standby.'

The Birthday that Changed Everything

As he ambled off, coffee jar tucked under his arm, Lucy scurried towards me from the opposite direction. She was less blonde this year, as her naturally fair hair grew back. My battle against the nose stud had been lost, and there'd been a trip to the tattoo parlour the month before. I knew this because she'd stolen my credit card from my purse to pay for it, having long ago detected the fact that my PIN number was her date of birth. I still didn't know where the tattoo was. Either I'd see it on this holiday, or I didn't want to know.

'How's Max?' I asked as she sat down. I'd missed him since he went home at the end of summer term. I'd been doing his washing and feeding him and letting him store his sports gear in the garage. I don't know what Lucy did for him – and I didn't ask, as I respected her privacy as a young adult. Plus I was scared she might actually tell me.

'Max is fine. Mum – do you know James is here? He's looking for you. What the fuck's that all about? Are you going to be okay? You're not going to turn into little Miss Lobotomy again, are you?'

'I wasn't that bad!' I said, biting the inside of my cheek so hard I tasted blood. 'Listen, I've got a few things to do. Unpacking and stuff. Will you be all right on your own?'

What a stupid question. Lucy had been all right on her own since she was eight and worked out how to use the TV remote control. Lucy would be all right on her own if she woke up one morning as the sole survivor in a post-Apocalyptic world.

She could drive as well these days, so I didn't even have the privilege of her sitting next to me in the passenger seat, cross-armed and sullen, pretending I didn't exist as I chauffeured her around.

Ollie was almost seventeen, and was never in the house unless he was hungry. I think he spent a lot of time at the library, and with his friends, and in the cinema. Or possibly roaming wild in the wastelands of Oxfordshire, turning into a werewolf on the full moon. I hadn't got clue about either of them any more.

'Yeah, I think I'll cope,' she said sarcastically, giving me a look that let me know I was about as necessary to her well-being as Bubonic plague.

I wanted to head for our room and lock myself in the wardrobe with the spare pillows, but it wouldn't be safe. Too easy to find me there. I decided to hide out in the gardens for a bit while my brain simmered down from boiling point. I could cover myself with leaves and twigs and sit camouflaged in the corner for hours.

As I made my way over, Ollie lolloped up to me, out of puff and red in the face, a nervy gleam in his hazel eyes.

'Mum! I've been looking everywhere for you!'

'I was at the bar, where I usually am, Ollie. What's up?'

'Do you know that James is—'

'Yes! I do! And it's no big deal. I'm fine with it. There's nothing for you and Lucy to worry about. Now bugger off and play with your sister – I'll be back down later.'

I don't think he believed me, and looked so concerned it hurt my stomach – I didn't want my kids fretting over me like this. It wasn't right. I should be the one stressing about them.

There was a section of the gardens the reps used for storing equipment and stuff that needed repairing. You had to force your way through some fairly dense foliage to get to it, but it was the perfect temporary sanctuary.

I pushed through the greenery headfirst, clamping my eyes shut so I didn't get blinded by a whiplashing branch, and emerged into a graveyard of punctured exercise balls and cracked paddles.

There was a hammock that still looked functional, so I grabbed a frayed yoga mat and climbed in, pulling the mat over me. I curled up into a foetal ball with my knees hugged in to my chest. Only my feet were poking out. If I stayed here long enough the grass might grow over me. Some archaeologist could dig me up in a hundred years and put me on display in a museum – scared English woman mid-panic-attack.

Truth be told, I was terrified of seeing James again. The only way I'd coped last year was to erase him from my memory. I'd cleared out the photos, put Jake's fridge magnet away in the attic, and given the necklace to the charity shop. Okay, I went and bought it back the next day, but it was safely locked in a box now. I'd put James in a box, too, mentally. Ideally I'd have put Lavender in one as well – a pine one about six feet long – but I tried not to dwell on her too much.

I knew I'd have to face him at some point – if not before, then tomorrow, on our ashes-scattering trip. That wouldn't be at all emotional. I might as well punch myself in the eyes now so they could swell up in advance.

I heard footsteps swishing through the grass and a few swear words as the bushes trembled. I was being followed.

'Sally? Is that you? Are you all right?'

Shit. I stayed very still. I'd watched a lot of David Attenborough on the telly over the years. I knew better than to make any sudden movements. The predator would eventually move on to a softer target as long as I didn't reveal my hiding place.

'What are you doing under there?' said James, pulling the yoga mat off me so the sunlight came streaming down on to my face. Bloody David Attenborough. Shows what he knows.

I blinked my eyes a few times, shocked by the sudden blast of light, and sat up suddenly. That was a big mistake. The two supporting poles of the hammock shook, then came crashing down, crossing over each other in the middle and slamming to the floor. It was a broken hammock, after all.

I was squashed inwards like a concertina, wrapped up in the string of the swinging seat so tightly that parts of my flesh were squeezing through the gaps.

I was lying in a hog-tied heap on the grass, with one foot and one hand poking out and waving. The rest of me was stuck. If the sun caught me I'd have stripes for the rest of the holiday. I couldn't talk, because my lips were twisted up against the ropes, holding my mouth open like a horse baring its teeth.

'Keep still, stop wriggling around,' said James, kneeling down by my side and trying to untangle me. I did as he said and tried hard not to cry. It hurt, and it was uncomfortable, and it wasn't the ideal way to present yourself to a former lover.

Bit by bit, he untied me, and I crawled out. I had grass stains on my shorts, my knees were bleeding, and I swear a pair of thrushes were sizing my hair up as the ideal starter home.

'Thanks, James – and what a surprise to see you,' I lied, smoothing my hair down and hyperventilating a bit.

He looked at me cynically and shook his head.

'Those poles could have crushed you. What are you doing back here anyway?'

'Erm . . . I saw a really interesting bird scuttling off into the undergrowth and I was just following it. I've taken up bird-watching as a hobby this year. I'm a twitcher.'

'Really? And what did this bird look like?'

'Like a . . . pheasant. Yes, like a pheasant.'

'Right. That sounds likely. Are you hiding from me?'

'What if I am? And how did you find me anyway?' I asked, sitting down on the grass. The shorts were already knackered, and my legs were rubbery with nerves. James sat next to me. I tried not to notice, but he was looking as gorgeous as ever; jeans tight over his thighs and a pale blue T-shirt stretching over his shoulders. I fought off the image and replaced it with one of Dame Edna Everage naked in the shower.

'Process of elimination. I checked beneath the sun loungers, and looked in the pool in case you were underwater and breathing through a straw. I even went in the ladies to check, which caused a stir. Here, I brought you some Turkish delight from the restaurant.'

He put a small plate in front of me.

'Right. Great. Thanks – I feel so much better now. Did you think that was going to help? I don't even eat stuff like that any more.'

He looked me up and down and nodded.

'I see that,' he said. 'I noticed at the funeral, when you weren't hiding behind Marcia. I can't imagine you not eating cake . . .'

'Well, this is the new and joyless life I lead, James. No cake. No Turkish delight. My only vice is crack cocaine, but hey, at least it keeps me thin.'

I was sounding like a shrew, and I didn't care. At first I'd been scared. Now I was getting angry. I was here on holiday with my family – my whole bloody family – and to mourn Allie. Seeing him was simply not on the itinerary.

'Look, what do you want, James? I didn't know you were coming, and I'm not very happy about it. I thought you were in New York, or I wouldn't have come. Can't we just politely avoid each other? Can't you and Lavender just . . . bugger off?'

'Lavender's not here. Just me and Jake. And I was looking for you because I need to talk to you. I would've been in touch earlier except you seemed to have gone under the radar like some kind of retired intelligence agent. Changed your phone, bounce-backs from your e-mail. I could've tracked you down through Mike, but in the end I decided it was better to see you face to face. Sally, we need to—'

What? What did we need to do? Drink Cosmopolitans on the beach? Have sex? Build seaworthy yachts from newspaper and balls of string? I never found out, because we were very noisily interrupted.

'Sal! Are you out there in that bloody jungle? Did you pack any insect repellent, this place is swarming,' came an annoyed voice. A voice that I recognised, but James clearly didn't.

He crashed through the trees as though he was Humphrey Bogart in *The African Queen*. Except he was wearing a white polo shirt and a pair of tennis shorts. He stopped dead and stared at us both, raising his eyebrows to ask me what was going on.

'Simon, meet James. James, meet Simon,' I said. They stared at each other warily, and James eventually held out his hand to shake.

'Nice to meet you at last, Simon. I think we spoke once on the phone.'

Chapter 43

Rick had joined us for dinner. He was looking at Simon as if he was the second coming, and Simon was receiving his adulation like a benign deity. If he was at all disconcerted by the eye make-up, he didn't let on.

'So, what do you wear for work in the hospital, Simon?' Rick asked, holding his chin in his hands, elbows resting on the table. I suspect he was hoping for 'nothing at all, Rick – I go in stark naked and covered with baby oil'.

'For consultations I wear a shirt and tie, and for surgery I wear scrubs.'

'Oooh! Like in *ER*?' said Rick, excitedly.

'Yes, I suppose so. But honestly, it's nowhere near as glamorous as that . . . the nurses aren't as good-looking, for a start. There are some similarities, though – the tension, the life-and-death situations . . .'

I considered pointing out that Simon specialised in sports injuries – hardly a matter of life and death. If Simon had to hold someone's intestines in after a gunshot wound he'd probably pass out, or call for one of those ugly nurses he worked with. He fainted when I was in labour with Lucy, and had to be propped up on the waiting-room chairs while I got on with it.

But he was enjoying himself, and so was Rick, so what was the harm? His own ego had taken a battering after Monika dumped him for one of the bouncers at the club where she worked. Mainly because of the non-dancing-dick situation, I learned – which in turn had been caused by Simon's increasing realisation that a middle-aged father of two had no place in a nineteen-year-old lap-dancer's social life.

The sex, drugs and rock 'n' roll all became too much for him. Eventually he started popping paracetamol, pretending they were Ecstasy so he'd fit in, then faking hands-in-the-air joy until dawn. Shame he didn't have the brains to realise all this before he walked out on me. He'd really been a rock throughout the last year, but still . . . some wounds take a very long time to scab over.

Lucy was ignoring us all, reading a book on literary criticism. She was off to Liverpool University to study English in September. I wasn't sure if I'd miss her or not. That probably makes me a terrible mother, but sometimes the daily death threats got a little tiring.

'Oh Simon, I'm overwhelmed – your work is so important! Saving lives like you do! Your family must be so proud!' said Rick, clapping his hands together in pleasure.

'Yeah,' said Lucy, not looking up from her book, 'he's fucking amazing. Sometimes, Rick, at home, I have to wear shades in the house because of the sun shining out of his bloody arse.'

We all fell silent for a minute. Simon looked angry and perplexed and helpless.

'Welcome to my world,' I said, secretly enjoying it. At least she had a different target these days. She wasn't happy about Simon spending more time with us. She wasn't happy about Simon being on holiday with us. She wasn't happy about Simon, full stop.

It had come as a bit of a surprise to me, as well. The way he'd come back into our lives – sneaking through the back door while I was mid-nervous breakdown. But I couldn't complain – because he was the one who got me through it. His brutalisation at the hands of his Latvian lover had lent him a new air of humanity; an empathy that had always been missing before.

He was the one who constantly called in, making sure I was okay. He was the one who once found me sitting catatonic in a bath full of cold water while the dog was eating our dinner off the kitchen table. He was the one who talked, who listened. Who looked at my photos of Allie and handed me tissues when I cracked. Unlikely as it might have seemed this time last year, he helped. And now, he was here on holiday with us, playing Dr Feelgood to his brand-new audience.

'So, Rick, what have you been up to,' I asked, 'and where's Marcia tonight?'

'Oh, she'll be down soon – she's upstairs with our friend Andrew. We met him at a special party. He's a *firefighter*,' he said meaningfully. Excellent. A firefighter – irresistible to both sexes, and very handy to have around while Marcia chain-smoked her way through a crate of wine every night.

'Has he brought his uniform?'

'Oh, Sally, don't be naughty, of course not – although he does keep a spare at our house! He's fabulous, darling – wait and see!'

I was looking forward to it already. Any man with a hose flexible enough to satisfy both Marcia and Rick had to be worth meeting.

'So what's the plan for tomorrow?' asked Simon.

'Well, we're going out to the island and scattering Allie's ashes, then we're having a . . . party?' The word didn't sound quite right.

'A celebration of her life,' said Rick firmly – which was just perfect. That was the way we had to view it.

'You're not coming,' said Lucy, slamming her book face down on the table and glaring at Simon. 'You never even met her. I don't want you there with your fake sincerity, talking about yourself all the time. No fucking way. If you even try and come, I'll push you off the boat.'

She stood up abruptly and stalked off, 'accidentally' knocking over his wine glass with her hip as she went. It soaked into the tablecloth, spreading a red stain over the linen.

This time Simon looked genuinely hurt. I reached out and held his hand.

'Don't take any notice. She's upset, and she needs someone to take it out on. We're her parents and that's our job. But she may be right – not about your fake sincerity or anything, but about not coming. I know I've talked about her a lot, but you didn't know Allie, and I think it'll be an intense day.'

'Is *he* going?' Simon asked. Gosh, I wonder who he could mean – Denzel Washington? Prince Albert of Monaco? Or James Carver, the man he perceived as his rival for my affections. I'd been rebuilding my relationship with Simon over the last year, but he still hadn't made it back into my bed. He'd been hoping this holiday would be the time it would happen, and seeing James here had thrown a serious spanner in the works. He was worried on behalf of both his own libido, and my mental health.

'Yes, he is. But so is everybody else. Rick, what do you think?'

'I think she's right, Simon – you'd feel out of place. And Andrew's staying here – maybe the two of you could get to know each other while we're gone.'

From the distracted look that swam across his mahogany face, I suspected Rick had a vivid image of how Simon and Andrew could get to know each other, and ideally there'd be a professional cameraman around while it happened. I glanced at Simon. He was handsome, I thought, with his floppy fair hair and his long, lean physique. Once upon a time I'd thought he was Adonis incarnate.

Simon nodded in agreement. I could tell he wasn't happy about it, but he'd stay. Maybe he was getting more mature in his old age. Or maybe he was just scared of Lucy.

Chapter 44

Mike managed the whole ash-scattering thing without falling in, getting any stuck in his eye, or crying. All of which was remarkable, as the wind was blowing strong and the waves out on the bay were choppy. Even under the blistering sun you could feel the chill scorch of the breeze on your skin.

It was a relief for everyone to be back on dry land, as we splashed out of the boat and on to the island.

We were greeted with a makeshift sign made of an old bed sheet, tied to two rickety poles shoved in the sand. 'Allie's Palace – this way', it said in black magic marker, with a red arrow pointing round the corner to the sheltered side of the shore.

Harry had closed down his pub for the day, and transported it all here. The tables and chairs were scattered around at improbable angles, legs sinking into the sand. There was a bar, made of old crates and pallets, and casks of ale with screw taps on the front. Three enormous chiller boxes held wine and spirits and mixers. A wonky trestle table was lined up with rows and rows of pies, all slipping precariously to the right.

He'd set up a sound system, which was currently belting out Billy Joel doing 'Uptown Girl'.

We all wandered round, getting drinks and settling ourselves in for the party. I held back until I saw where James was going to sit, then made sure I was as far away as possible. He shot me a look that told me he knew exactly what I was doing. He was always good at getting inside my head – but this year, he wasn't welcome.

I sprawled on the sand with Jenny and Ian. I'd been in fairly close contact with Jenny all year. We'd offered each other support and shared memories of Allie; she'd talked about the strain their fertility situation was putting on their marriage; I'd very occasionally confessed to the fact that losing James had made me feel like my whole life had ended. And that every now and then – if I was brutally honest – I wished that it had.

It was good to see her in the flesh, but I couldn't help noticing the changes in her. Where I'd lost weight, she was out of shape. She was usually so clean and fresh and sporty. Now, she looked grungy and greasy and unhappy. Her hair was longer and unstyled, and her eyes were glassy and crusted. Ian just looked helpless.

Max and Mike stood at the bar, and Harry clanged a fork against a glass to get everyone's attention. We stopped chatting and drinking and looked up.

Max stepped forward and cleared his throat. His hair was back to its usual colour, but his eyebrows had retained a bit of midnight blue-black. It was an interesting look. Mike slapped him on the back and he started to speak.

'Me and my dad want to thank you all for coming. We want you to get drunk, sing, dance and have fun. You all knew Mum and you know that's what she'd have wanted. She was . . . she was the best . . .'

He started to choke up, and lowered his eyes to the floor. Mike was rubbing his shoulders and whispering his support, but he couldn't go on. Lucy stepped forward and stood next to him, long and lithe and protective as a tiger with newborn cubs.

'Cheers to Allie!' she said simply, swigging straight from a bottle of wine. We all joined in, a chorus of ragged salutations as we swallowed back our own tears and followed the toast. Harry chose that moment to pump up the volume on 'Don't Stop Me Now'.

'Come and get your pies!' he bellowed over the music. 'Before the salmonella sets in!'

I could see Max, folded up into Lucy's arms. She held his head on her shoulder, and was stroking his back reassuringly, whispering to him. All the times I'd wanted to throttle her melted into the background, as I watched this gorgeous, grown-up girl taking care of her man.

She spotted me watching, and gave me the Vs behind Max's back.

'Sally!' shouted Mike as I tried to sneak off. 'Come here!' He was at the pretend bar, with Harry and James. Harry nodded to me, and handed me another plastic cup.

'Have a pie as well, love,' he said. 'You look like you need feeding up.'

'No thanks, Harry, I'm . . . I'm a vegetarian,' I lied, not wanting to hurt the hairy old biker's feelings.

He made the sign of the cross over his body. 'It's worse than I thought then,' he said, shaking his head in sympathy.

I ignored James. I was pretending he wasn't there. Mike stood between us, putting one arm over each of our shoulders.

'Come on, you two – go and talk to each other. Can't you act like grown-ups about this? Sit down, have a drink, remember the good times.'

I wasn't budging, just staring straight ahead and thinking of how many nights of this hell I had to put up with. James looked hurt and pissed off and exasperated. Any minute now he'd be rubbing his hair with his hands and sighing, the predictable shit.

'Go on,' said Mike, pushing us away, 'it's what Allie would have wanted.'

The magic words. I looked at him suspiciously, but his face was a picture of innocence. I nodded and gave James a flicker of a smile. He returned it, and we sat down by one of the wonky bar tables. It reminded me of that ridiculous fight in Harry's bar on my birthday. And of last year, when James and I had visited this place alone. It was like taking a trip down Memory Lane and getting mugged on the way.

There was so much to remember, and it all cut like glass scraping across my skin. I'd been pretending I was okay all year. But pretending wasn't the same as feeling, even if everyone else accepted it.

'Do you remember the last time we came here?' said James, sounding off-balance himself.

'Why? Did something significant happen?' I asked. I'd agreed to talk to him. Not to be nice.

'It did for me,' he replied quietly, staring back at me. Yeah, I was significant to him for about five minutes, as I recalled.

'Well, that was a lifetime ago, wasn't it, James? We were different people then. You have Lavender now.'

'And you have Simon. Where is he today? Chatting up one of the nannies? A few of them only look nineteen, just his type.'

I sucked in a quick breath. It felt like he'd slapped me. Oh, that was harsh. Spiteful and painful and deliberate. Nothing at all like the James I used to know. It may also, of course, have been true.

'Oh God, I'm sorry,' he said, touching my wrist with his fingers in apology. I snatched it away and rubbed it like he'd burned me. Any part of my body was a no-go area for him. I'd drown before I let him give me the kiss of life.

'I'm sorry, Sal. I don't want us to be like this, hurting each other. You're just so different, and I don't know what to do to reach you. We need to talk. I need to explain. You need to know things. You need to know that Lavender's gone. It's over.'

Chapter 45

'It didn't work,' he said, when I failed to respond. I was too busy trying to stay upright.

'It was never going to work – because I was always thinking about you. I tried for Jake, but in the end he was unhappy as well, because all we did was argue. I was wrong. I was stupid. I loved you then, and I love you now. Is there any way we can get over this?'

I closed my eyes and tried to blank it all out. This was too much. This was the speech I'd spent months wanting to hear when I got home last year. This was the speech I played over and over in my mind for hours on end, lying sleeplessly in my bed, feverish with pain and need. This was the fantasy I woke up with every morning, before the reality crashed back in and crushed me afresh. This should be making me happy.

But it wasn't. I wasn't sure I was capable of being happy any more. I'd gone into hibernation a long time ago and didn't want to come out again. I couldn't hate him – but I couldn't open myself up to his love again, and take the risk that all the fragile safety I'd built around myself would crumble.

'I don't want us to hurt each other either, James,' I finally said. 'But I can't pretend it never happened – you can't come running back to me because Lavender didn't work out. And then there's Simon.'

'Yeah. Then there's Simon,' he replied, his lips twisting in bitterness. 'What's going on there, Sal? After everything he did to you, how bad he made you feel about yourself – how could you take him back? I couldn't believe it when I saw him here.'

'I don't owe you any explanations, James. But how would you like it if I told you I love him? That I'd taken him back for the sake of my family? That we're having wild, crazy sex every hour of every day and it's the best I've ever had? How would that feel?'

He shut up, sat back. He looked shocked. Stunned. In physical pain. His eyes clouded and his lips clamped shut, as if they were trying to stop words he'd regret from escaping. I'd hurt him and I had enjoyed it. Jesus. We needed to stop this – it was no way to celebrate Allie's life, or carry on with ours.

'God, I hate this,' I said. 'It's like a party without the guest of honour. I really, really miss Allie. And we need to stop doing this to each other. It's over. It's too late. Can you please leave me alone?'

I started crying and he reached out to console me. I slapped his hand away and stood up.

'Alone doesn't mean touching me.'

Chapter 46

We avoided each other for the rest of the day, and I made sure I was nowhere near him when we all piled off the boat. Instead I pleaded a headache and went straight to bed for an early night.

The next morning, I stuck to my own corner of the pool, where I was determined to practise my specialist sport – lying very still and frying. I wanted to forget about James, and being anywhere near him was going to spoil that plan. Hard to forget about someone when you are constantly having to suppress a mixture of lust and anguish.

I stuck to the schedule for the next few days, with limited amounts of success, depending on whether I was conscious or not. And holiday life went on steadily around me – including the ever-developing vision of Simon the Macho Super-Surgeon.

He was currently walking dejectedly towards me, dripping wet and stone-faced. His arms drooped at his sides, and there was blood seeping out of a gash on his knee. He trailed water over to my sun lounger and sat down beside me, soaking the paperback I had stowed at my feet.

I sat up, propped my shades on to my forehead. The sun was scorching, and until he'd arrived, I'd felt relatively peaceful.

'What happened?' I asked.

'Nothing. I bashed my knee sailing. There was a race, and I thought I'd give it a go. You know I used to row at college.'

Hmm. For one term. Usually with a hangover.

'I'm guessing you didn't do as well as you'd hoped?' I asked, patting him on the arm. Simon was super-competitive – and, in his world, he usually won. He was a superstar in surgery, a guru at golf, and Favourite Son with his whole family. He hated losing, and he hadn't had enough practice at it to ever get any better.

'No. I didn't win. *He* did,' he replied.

Ah. Everything became clear. Simon's alpha male was on the loose, and I seemed to be spending a lot of this holiday chasing it around with a lasso. He was obsessed with James, with the way James looked, the things James could do, and how James had made me feel. With the things James and I had done together the year before, none of which I had told him, of course.

He'd started going to the hotel's gym and pumping iron every day in an effort to bulk up his naturally lean physique. He was running five miles before breakfast to boost his already good cardio-fitness. And he was entering every silly contest on offer, all in an attempt to match up to the shoes he assumed he needed to fill.

James, naturally enough, wasn't helping. He was already bigger, fitter, faster and even more stubborn. He wouldn't budge an inch, on anything. In short, they were both acting like a pair of dickheads.

'Simon. How many times have I told you to stop this? You don't need to compete with James.'

He turned to face me, reaching across to stroke my cheek. He looked indescribably sad. It wasn't a look I was used to seeing on his face and it unsettled me. I wanted life to continue on its nice, smooth, unexciting path. Why did other people keep trying to change things when I wasn't looking?

'I do need to, Sal. I know it was all my fault things went wrong with us, but the thought of you with that . . . that big *oaf* drives me insane. I want us to get back together. Properly – not just for nights in with a curry, or a trip to the cinema. But I don't seem to be getting anywhere, and I think it's because of him. He's not good for you. He made you so ill, I didn't know if you'd ever be all right again. I stuck with you through that, and I'll always be here for you. I promise I'll never hurt you again. We've got a lot of years behind us, Sal, and I don't want them to end now.

'I just want to come home. To you. To the kids. For good.'

Chapter 47

I didn't know what to say to all that.

Yet again, a man was standing before me giving a speech I'd once been desperate to hear. First James telling me it was over with Lavender. Then Simon saying he wanted to come home.

What was it with them both? And why hadn't either of their speeches made me happy? I knew why with James – I was frankly too scared to consider going near him again. I'd almost lost my mind last time, and I wasn't willing to chance it again.

And with Simon . . . well, yesterday's philandering bastard was today's security blanket. It kept me warm, but I didn't want to have sex with it. I liked having him around, but I didn't want him back full time. I liked it just the way it was – a lot of companionship, a few dates every week, and the occasional snog on the doorstep as I insisted he went back to his own flat.

'The thing is, Simon,' I said, carefully, trying to find a way to say all of this without hurting him unnecessarily. 'I—'

'Never mind,' he said, interrupting me. I could tell from the focus that had snapped back into his features that he was now thinking about something else entirely.

'Never mind,' he repeated, grinning at me, 'there's always the tennis. You know I'm good at tennis. I'm off to find that coach, Heather, and practise my serve. See you later, Sal.'

And he was gone, limping purposefully towards the tennis courts, watery blood running down one leg. Nutter.

Ollie had been sitting on the edge of the pool eating an ice cream, studiously looking in the opposite direction. He stood up and came over to me.

'Want a lick?' he asked, holding the cone towards my face.

'Erm . . . no, though it's very kind of you to offer. Were you ear-wigging on all that, you nosy little shit?'

'Mother! Language please! Of course I was. So what're you going to do? Are you going to let him move back in?'

'What do you think?'

'I don't think you should be asking a sixteen-year-old boy for advice on your love life, for a start. But as you are – it's a bit like a Mills & Boon, isn't it? The hunky Irishman and his punishing kisses versus the suave, debonair surgeon – and you stuck in the middle. Not that you look like a Mills & Boon chick, though, you're too old. You need to be twenty years younger and a governess, really.'

'Thanks,' I said, knocking the ice cream out of his hands so it splashed in a pink puddle on the floor, 'and I think you should stop reading those bloody books – sexual politics have moved on since the 1970s.'

'I've moved on too,' he replied. 'I'm into Jackie Collins and Jilly Cooper now. Then I've got *Bridget Jones* lined up – by the end of all this I'll be a world expert on women. I'm giving *Fifty Shades* a miss 'cause it might traumatise me, though.

'But honestly, Mum,' he said, 'I don't know. I wouldn't object to Dad coming back – but I'm not arsed if he doesn't either. I like James, and when you were happy with him it was the happiest I'd ever seen you. But when it all went wrong, well, it was crap, wasn't it? I just want you to be okay, 'cause you're better than the two of them put together.'

I filled up a bit, and felt guilty about the ice-cream thing. I'd get him another later.

'That's very sweet, Ollie. And I think you're already an expert on women – at least the old ones like me. Look, here's Jake. He'll be after you.'

Jake was now eight, and obsessed with Ollie, the coolest boy in Christendom. And after that little speech, I couldn't argue.

'Hi, Sally! Hi, Ollie!' he squeaked, scampering up to sit next to us.

'Do you want to play hide-and-seek with me?' he asked.

'Sorry, sweetie, I'm busy right now,' I said, stretching back down.

'You don't look busy. You're just lying in the sun.'

'I know that's what it looks like. But in my head, I'm creating a new chemical formula that makes cabbage taste like chips.'

He giggled.

'I'll play with you, Jake, as long as you promise not to go in the ladies like last time – I can't get away with it like you,' said Ollie, 'and Mum'll give us the money for some ice cream, won't you, Mum?'

'You know where the purse is – you're in it often enough,' I said, gesturing under the sun lounger with my head. Ollie leaned down to pick it up, then paused mid-stretch and mid-breath, his mouth hanging open.

I followed his gaze across the pool. A-ha. The female of the species. She was short, maybe a shade over five foot, with a long black ponytail bouncing from the top of her head. About the same age as Ollie, from her face, but about twenty-two, from her body. If she was mine I'd have locked her in a cupboard until she was old enough to know what to do with those boobs.

'Who's that?' said Jake. 'She's really pretty.'

'That's Tabitha,' replied Ollie. 'She's like the hottest girl ever. I'm going to ask her out.'

I did a double take at my beloved son. Six foot two, scrawny, glasses, floppy hair, and a T-shirt that said 'Geeks do it in binary'. Then I looked at her – drop-dead gorgeous and clearly the coolest girl in school.

'Go for it, son. She'd be mad to say no.'

Chapter 48

'Where are you going this early?' said Lucy, yawning and foggy-eyed. She'd heard me pottering around and come through to investigate the noise. She looked at the unmade bed.

'And where's the prick?'

'If you're referring to your father, he's gone to the gym.'

'God, he's so dumb. He's never going to look like James, no matter how much time he spends there. How can you bear to be near him? And doesn't it freak you out being in the same bed as him after all this time?'

Yes, it did. But all the interconnecting rooms had double beds in one section, so I was living with it. Every night I barricaded myself in on one side, with the sheets shoved down the middle like a checkpoint. There had been a few security breaches, but nothing a good slap couldn't sort.

'Are you offering to swap rooms? Then you'd have to share this with me, and I can't see that happening.'

'Fuck no. It's bad enough I even have to be in the same room as the geekazoid. If I come next year, Max and I are getting our own room.'

She'd fallen backwards on to my bed and was stretching out like a very long cat.

'Right. So you'll be paying for it as well, will you?' I asked, tying my hair back into a ponytail and doing up my laces.

She snorted and ignored me, rolling round so she was face down in the pillows.

'Where *are* you going, anyway?' she said again, her voice muffled, the back of her head a mop of tangled blond hair.

'I'm going for a bike ride. With Mike.'

I heard her laughing into the mattress. She sat up and turned round, pointing an accusatory finger at me. 'You? On a bike ride? With Mike? That's fucking hilarious. You must be the two biggest couch potatoes on the entire planet. I know you're not fat any more, which is annoying, but you're still a slug. It'll be like Little and Large on a road trip. I wonder how many times you'll fall off. Can I come? I could be like the official first-aider, and carry water and those foil blankets . . .'

'No you can't come, you cheeky cow. And I'll tell Mike you said all that. He's trying to get fitter, that's all. He wants me to go with him, so I'm going. Now bugger off back to your own room.'

As usual, though, Madame Malicious did have a point. I tended to wobble and topple an awful lot when I rode a bike. We went to Center Parcs once and it was disastrous. I had permanently skinned knees and pine cones up my bum for days. I ended up getting a comedy tricycle instead, and rode it round, ringing my bell, like a physically incompetent Mary Poppins.

Mike was probably the perfect companion for me. We could do half a mile, downhill, then go the pub. That sounded like an excellent plan.

I skipped down the stairs and headed for the restaurant for a quick coffee before I left. Marcia and Rick were there, with their Greek God. Or Andrew, as they called him. I went to join them while I drank. My libido might be in retreat, but I wasn't dead – Andrew was foxier than Basil Brush.

'Morning!' I said, sitting down and gazing at him over his waffles. Marcia and Rick were doing pretty much the same. It was a meeting of the Andrew Fan Club. He was even taller than Marcia, which put him well over six foot, all of it made up of long, lean muscle. He had deep brown eyes, shiny dark hair, and Hollywood teeth. He lived near them in Surrey, but had the sexiest Newcastle accent I'd ever heard.

'Morning!' they all chorused in response. Andrew smiled his magnificent smile and I looked at him some more. He didn't mind you looking. Or touching, I suspect, from the time he'd caught me eyeing his bum in shorts. He'd grinned and said: 'Feel free. Rick and Marcia won't mind sharing if you're interested.'

I shoved an apple in my pocket for later, reluctantly made my farewells, and went to meet Mike at the bike sheds.

When I got there, he was lying on the floor. At first I assumed he was drunk, but then I noticed he was clutching his left foot. He was perfectly still until he saw me, then he started writhing around in the dust and groaning as though he was trapped under a heavy goods vehicle.

'Mike! What's up!' I said, running over and crouching down next to him.

'Oh, Sal, it's my ankle – I twisted it on the stairs. Is it broken?'

I supported his foot in my hands and took off his trainer and sock. I rotated it as gently as I could, and moved his toes. No swelling, no bruising, no heat. No Odor-Eaters either, from the pong. Mike yelled with every touch, holding his head in his hands. I looked up at him and smiled.

'You're an old ham, Mike. There's bugger-all wrong with this ankle. I'm an almost-trained professional and I can tell. If you don't want to go on a bike ride, just say so. I don't either.'

'No, honest, love, it really hurts. I don't want to disappoint you, I know how much you've been looking forward to this—'

'No I haven't. I'd be happier if I was still in bed. I was only doing it to keep you company.'

'I know how much you've been looking forward to this,' he repeated, completely ignoring me, 'why don't you go with James instead? Look, here he comes – what a coincidence.'

'Yeah, what a coincidence,' I said, dropping his foot from my hands without warning, so it slammed hard on to the floor.

'Ow! Careful, Sal, that bloody hurt – you could give a man a sprained ankle like that,' he said, sitting up and straining over his belly to put his sock back on.

'Are you all right?' said James as he approached. 'You did say nine, didn't you?'

He nodded at me and I nodded back. Gone were the days when we greeted each other with love bites and lusty kisses. Now we were like a pair of nodding dogs.

'He's fine,' I said, 'apart from a really bad case of lying bastard-itis. The only cure is a good kick up the backside, and I know exactly the person to administer it.'

'Oh, don't be like that, Sally – I'm still grieving, you know. Can't be held accountable for my actions. Go on – go for a little bike ride with James. It's what Allie would have wanted.'

I'd heard that one too many times now. I was about to object when I saw the pleading look in his eyes, and felt him squeeze my hand. Jesus Christ. He actually meant it.

'Okay. Mike, you'd better go rest that foot – I'd suggest putting it up on a bar stool. James – shall we? I must warn you I'll probably fall off at some point, so don't come too close or I'll take you down with me. You know what to expect by now.'

We pushed the bikes to the hotel exit, and I strapped on my helmet. James did the same, and threw one leg over his saddle. Just once, it would've been nice if he was rubbish at something. If he careened sideways on to the pavement, or crashed into a tree, or tried to do a wheelie and landed on his awesome arse. But no, as usual, he was all grace and power, effortlessly pushing off as the pedal bashed the bony bit of my ankle.

'Shall we go to Leyla's?' he shouted over his shoulder.

'Isn't that . . . up a hill?' I replied, weaving from side to side as I followed.

'Not much of a one – come on.'

And he was away. I tried to keep up, and must confess to a few less-than-platonic thoughts every time I was within sight of him. He was leaning over, bum inches from my face when I was close enough, the muscles in his calves bunching and knotting as he pedalled.

When we arrived, I lowered my bike down to the ground, then took off my helmet. James stared at me.

'Yeah? So I have huge helmet hair. Do you have a problem with that, golden bollocks?'

'No! Not at all. It looks lovely,' he said, pulling a face that said just the opposite. Well, frankly, he could go screw himself.

Leyla dashed out, looking as harassed as the last time. She was also about eight months pregnant and the size of a submarine. I felt guilty making her move at all. She was so big she should be on wheels.

'It didn't seem to take as long to get here this time,' I said, looking down at the azure blue of the bay.

'That's because you were on a bike. It's faster. And you're, well, you know, thinner.'

'Yep. I finally got rid of those wobbly bits.'

'I liked the wobbly bits. I liked you just the way you were.'

'That's touching. Especially as you liked me so much you buggered off with another woman by the end of the holiday.'

Leyla brought the tea and cakes, took one whiff of the atmosphere, and scurried back into the house. I didn't blame her – you wouldn't want your unborn child exposed to this kind of karma.

'I always loved you. I was an arsehole, and I've paid the price for it.'

'We all paid a price, James. I did, Lucy and Ollie did as well. Even Simon got dragged into the fallout. What happened, anyway? Did she get an offer she couldn't refuse and dump you all again?'

'No . . . no, she didn't,' he said, sighing out his anger. 'She's back in New York. From day one I made it impossible for her. She tried, really hard, but my heart was always with you.

I picked on her. I found fault with everything she did. I'm not proud of any of it; I was a bastard to her as well as you. Eventually we decided we had to call it quits or we'd end up hating each other. So she packed up and left in June.'

I knew he was trying to explain, to make things better between us – but it wasn't working.

'June. She was there for a while, then. Did you find so much fault that you didn't sleep with her, or did you manage to overcome your repulsion on that front? Your heart might have been with me, but I'm assuming your dick was with her?'

He looked off over my shoulder and I saw his nostrils flare in shock. He paled slightly under the tan as he sipped his drink, ignoring me. I wondered if he was formulating a lie, but that wasn't James's style. He could be as much of a blunt instrument as me.

'Yes. I did sleep with her. But not for months after we got back, and only a few times, and it was never any good for either of us. Does any of that make you feel better?'

I'd tortured myself with images of him and Lavender for a long time when we got home. My memories of James naked and James having sex were all too vivid – but in my mind, I'd replaced myself with her, which drove me half mad. I didn't answer.

'Okay. I've been honest with you, and it's probably done me no good at all. Now you tell me – what's going on with you and Simon? You're sharing a room. Are you sleeping with him? I don't believe he can be in the same bed as you and not want to.'

'He does want to. I don't. Yet. That might change.'

'Even though he left you? Even though he chose another woman over you? Why does he get a second chance and I don't?'

I looked at him, that beautiful face, the golden hair shining in the sun. The magical hands that could turn me to jelly. The broad, muscular shoulders. And I imagined it all rolling down the hill, faster and faster, until it landed in the middle of a road and got run over by a melon truck. Splat.

'Because he was there for me, James, and you weren't. You destroyed me, and he cleaned up the mess. When I couldn't get out of bed because I was so depressed, he was there. When I couldn't eat without throwing up for months on end, he was there.

'When you were busy forcing yourself to have sex with Lavender, he was holding my hair back while I was sick in the toilet. He cooked for me and made me drink Lucozade. He phoned work and pretended I had swine flu. He looked after the kids and came round every single day to walk the bloody dog while I sat in my pyjamas, having my nervous breakdown. He did it all – the dirty stuff, the nasty stuff – because he cared about me. So I'm not bothered if you think he's a knob. Sometimes he is. But I wouldn't have survived the last year without him.'

He looked sick himself by the time I'd finished. He reached out a hand to mine, thought better of it when he saw my expression, and pulled it back. His blue eyes were vivid with tears.

'I'm so sorry, Sally. If I could take it all back, I would, I swear. I'd give anything for things to be the way they were. I made the biggest mistake of my life. I love you, I never stopped. Is there any way you can ever forgive me? I'll do anything it takes if you'll just give me a chance.'

'I'd recommend giving up now,' I said, coldly. 'I can't imagine a situation where I could allow myself to come back to you.'

'Because of Simon?'

'No. Because of me.'

Chapter 49

'What are you reading, Lucy?' asked Simon at breakfast. He was making an effort to be civil with her. He had a lot to learn.

Lucy was angry this morning. I could tell, because she was awake. She carried on reading, and answered in a dull monotone while still staring at the page.

'It's the *Kama Sutra*, Father,' she said. 'I'm going through all the sexual positions that I've tried and giving them marks out of ten.'

He spluttered his coffee out of his mouth in a brown jet, choking as she continued: 'Mmm . . . up the arse . . . only a six for that, I think . . .'

I put a calming hand on his arm.

'Ignore her. She's just winding you up,' I said. At least I thought she was.

Simon wiped the dripping coffee from his chin and looked at Lucy warily. Maybe considering a DNA test.

'And what are you up to today, Ollie?' I asked, changing the subject. Ollie was listening to his iPod and reading Jilly Cooper's *Riders*, underlining important sections in pencil.

I waved my fingers in front of his face and he looked up, pulling the earpieces out and smiling at me.

'I said, what are you up to today?'

'Oh. Well, today I'm going to pull Tabitha. I've laid the groundwork. She's already interested, I just have to throw the final hook. I've been basing my lines on Rupert Campbell-Black out of this book. He's a handsome cad with a sex appeal no woman can resist. Shouldn't be too hard to pull off.'

He shoved his too-long hair behind his ears, folded his too-long body forward over the table, and knocked his glasses back on his nose. I remembered devouring *Riders* as a teenager. Rupert Campbell-Black was the kind of man who made you wriggle on the seam of your jeans while you read about him. I couldn't quite see Ollie in the same way. But then again, I was his mother, and that was probably a good thing.

'Here she comes,' I whispered, spotting Tabitha, Queen of Cool, approaching with her disciples. She was wearing a pink sarong that only just covered her bottom, and a barely there bikini top over her Page-Three-girl boobs. Her hair was a black sheet shimmering down her back, and close up she had dimples, and big, round brown eyes. I noticed Simon do a surreptitious double take and kicked his ankle under the table.

She walked past us, slowing down her pace. She was looking at Ollie's chestnut head, which was still bent over his book. He was deliberately ignoring her.

'Hi, Ollie,' she said quietly as she stopped in front of us. 'Do you want to eat breakfast with us?'

He still didn't look at her, and only acknowledged her presence by holding his palm up in a 'not just now' gesture. Her cheeks flushed pink and I thought she might cry. The little shit – he was turning into his father's son. Eventually he folded the corner of his page over, closed his book, and raised his head.

'Sorry, Tab – I had to finish that chapter. What were you saying?'

He sounded bored beyond belief. Like he was being forced to talk to his ninety-year-old grandmother about her haemorrhoids. His eyes were flicking back to his book, as though he was desperate for her to bugger off and leave him to it.

'Erm . . . nothing. It doesn't matter. I was going to ask if you wanted to join us for breakfast.'

He glanced at her friends, sitting around a table chattering and laughing and flicking bits of toast at each other's heads.

'Don't think so, Tab. Doesn't look like my scene. I'm not a group person. I might have an hour or so free later, if you want to do something then.'

Her face lit up, and for a second I thought she might actually jump into the air and clap her hands like a very happy, very busty fairy.

'Okay! That sounds great! I'll come and find you, shall I?'

'Yeah, if you like,' said Ollie, already back to his book, 'I'll try and remember. Chill if I'm not around, though. I get busy.'

Tabitha smiled at us all, waved with her fingers, and bounced off to her pals, looking like she'd just won a EuroMillions rollover.

'See,' said Ollie, 'she's mine. Easy. Now I'm off back to the room to try on all my clothes and see what looks best for later. Dad, can I borrow some of your aftershave? Not that I need to shave, but the chicks love it.'

And off he shambled, Ollie Campbell-Black – an irresistible cad in flip-flops.

'Aw, look, Mommy,' said Lucy, smirking, 'our baby's finally located his balls. And it's really quite disgusting.'

Simon was gazing after him in amazement. He looked over at Tabitha, the very definition of jailbait, then back at Ollie's skinny figure, playing air guitar and tripping over his own feet as he went.

'That was interesting,' he said, 'and I don't think I could be prouder.'

Lucy threw her fork on the table, clattering it deliberately against her juice glass, then leaned back in a huff, arms folded in front of her chest. She stared at Simon.

'Well, isn't that fucking typical?' she said, in her quiet-but-deadly tone. 'You've ignored him for the last sixteen years because he's shit at rugby, but now suddenly you're *proud*?' The last word went up a few decibels, and I noticed Adnan standing by with a dustpan and brush. He'd seen all this before, and knew it often ended with the smashing of crockery.

'That is so fucking typical of you,' she screeched. 'You've treated him like he has special needs his whole life, but as soon as he starts getting led round by his dick, you're proud? You frigging loser – it says it all!'

She lobbed her toast at him, stuck her fingers up at us both, one hand for each, and made her exit. The people who knew Lucy were smiling into their cups. The people who didn't were looking terrified and probably wondering if they could get a refund on the price of their holiday.

Simon looked at me. The toast had stuck, buttered side down, to his forehead.

I sipped my coffee.

'Harsh but fair,' I said, suppressing a smile.

Chapter 50

We were up bright and early the next day for a trip to the ancient city of Ephesus. I'd wanted to go there in previous years, but was always too busy falling off surfboards, or having sex, or getting my heart smashed up into tiny pieces. This year, as I was doing none of the above, I'd booked the trip.

Ollie was staying behind to play hard to get with Tabitha, who had now succumbed completely to his charms. He'd obviously not mentioned his Pokémon card collection.

Lucy and Max were coming with us, despite initial objections.

'Why do you want to go all the way there?' she said when I first asked. 'If you want to see an ancient ruin, just look in the mirror.'

She went on to complain for the entire journey about the coach being too hot, too small and too smelly, then shut her trap for about two minutes once we walked into the site. I knew she wanted to claim it was boring, but she couldn't, because it was jaw-droppingly beautiful.

It would have been a wonderful day out – if I'd been on my own. Unfortunately I was surrounded by a pack of feral circus clowns all going for cheap laughs at each other's expense. Mainly Simon and Lucy, but even Max was infected by it, and called her a 'bitchy bell-end' at one point.

'Did you know that this was the second city of the Roman Empire,' said Lucy, reading from the guidebook as we stumbled along, 'and St Paul and St John both visited here?'

'Yes we do, Lucy,' said Simon, 'because some of us paid attention at school.'

'Oh fuck off, fathead,' she answered, perfectly mimicking his pompous tone. '*Some* of us didn't go to school during the Boer War. Just think, your mater and pater wasted all that money educating you in how to be a condescending prick – when you didn't need lessons at all.'

I sighed and wandered off on my own.

Max joined me, fleeing the snipe-fest.

'That's brilliant, isn't it, Sally?' he asked, gazing at the reconstructed ruins. 'This must have been awesome back in the day.'

'Yeah. It's fantastic. And it'd be even more fantastic if we could dump Dumb and Dumber back there and see it all on our own.'

He grinned at me, and nodded. I really hoped he still visited me when Lucy was off at Liverpool. It was, to use a popular catchphrase, what Allie would have wanted.

'Yeah. Let's do it. Lucy'll kill me later, but I'm sick of listening to the two of them. I know he's upset her, but he's her dad, and I wish she'd appreciate him while he's still around.'

I linked his arm and we headed off around the corner without Simon and Lucy, too fast for them to notice.

The rest of the day was much nicer. We visited the House of the Virgin Mary, and the hillside homes of the ancient

Ephesians. As I looked at the mosaics and friezes and the way their central heating worked, I wondered if women then had the same problems as women now. Like annoying kids and man troubles. And getting hold of an Ancient plumber to fix the Ancient heating when it broke.

Near the end of the day, we stopped by the souvenir shop and waited for them. Lucy sat down next to us, and Simon stood in front, fanning his face with the tour guide and looking as if his head had been dipped in a pot of boiling water. His naturally fair complexion didn't take too well to all this heat.

'Your daughter,' he said – of course, she was my daughter now – 'is a foul-mouthed harridan. It's got to be down to your side of the family – nobody in mine behaves like this.'

I was saved the trouble of thinking of a suitable retort as Lucy jumped back up, bashing me on the head with her bobbing rucksack, and getting right up into his lobster-red face.

'That's because your side of the family froze in time in the frigging 1930s. All they do is eat cucumber sandwiches on the lawn and call for Jeeves to wipe their arses. How *did* they react to you shacking up with a nineteen-year-old prostitute, by the way?'

'She wasn't a prostitute!' he blurted out, almost screaming with frustration. Every English-speaker within a two-mile radius turned to stare at us. I felt all the peace and calm of the last few hours drain out of me, replaced by a nerve-racking tension that made my bones shake.

I stood up, dusted myself down, and gave Max a kiss on the cheek.

'I've had enough of you two,' I said to Simon and Lucy. 'I'll see you back on the coach later. Feel free to sit on different seats. Or entirely different vehicles.'

I made my way through the milling crowds to the coach park, waved at the driver till he buzzed open the doors for me, and climbed on.

I sank down into the soft back of the seat, flicking on the air-conditioning and closing my eyes. I was hot, dirty, and sick of my entire life. Everything was a mess. I wanted to move to a small island in the Outer Hebrides where my nearest neighbours were a ferry ride away. I could weave my own clothes and make friends with sheep.

I let myself slowly relax, planning to sleep all the way home – or at least pretend to so I didn't have to speak to anyone.

As soon as the coach arrived back at the hotel, I shuddered awake, and looked around me. Sadly they were all there: Max snoozing gently on Lucy's shoulder, Lucy and Simon still glaring at each other. The journey took more than two hours – they'd displayed amazing stamina.

I wasn't ready to face up to them again. Or to James. Or to the mess that my entire life had become. So I sneaked off the bus, shouted something vague about going to buy some apples, and legged it – all the way into the nearby village, where I found myself a nice, comfy spot in a bar, and got merrily shitfaced.

It was almost three in the morning when they finally kicked me out. The English owners poured me into a taxi, and then probably retired to Tuscany on the night's takings.

It had been so long since I'd done that. On my own, away from my alleged 'loved ones'. And I bloody well enjoyed it.

I enjoyed it so much, in fact, that when the cabbie pulled up at the hotel and kindly helped me out (I was feeling a tad wobbly by then), I snogged him as a thank-you. A proper, full-on snog, with a middle-aged man with a handlebar moustache. What can I say? I've always been a generous tipper.

I staggered towards the lobby, slightly confused as to where my room was. What I wanted to do was walk to reception and get Tarkan to help me. He was a very nice man who always stayed up late studying his university textbooks. He was also quite handsome and I thought I might snog him too. In fact, I thought I might snog every man I came across on the way back to my room. Possibly some of the women as well.

Unfortunately, as I headed in what I thought was the right direction, a lemon tree in a huge terracotta pot appeared from nowhere and jumped right out in front of me. I tumbled over it like a blind rag doll and fell with a bang on my side. Luckily I was very drunk and very relaxed and landed as smoothly as an SAS paratrooper out on manoeuvres.

I turned over on to my back and looked up at the stars. They were so beautiful. It was still so warm. Why would I want to move from here anyway? I didn't want to go back to my room; it was full of Simon's farts and fumblings and he'd have peed on the floor round the toilet again. I could spend the night here, then I'd be handily placed for breakfast. I shoved my bag behind my head as a pillow and closed my eyes.

I was settling in for my alfresco night when cruel hands reached down, taking hold of mine and pulling me up. I flew into the sky a few inches before landing shakily back on to my feet. James. Looking very pissed off.

I snatched my hands away from him. A bit too quickly, as it turned out. I wobbled for a good ten seconds before almost keeling over again, then leaned on him to keep myself upright.

'I can do just fine without you, you know,' I said.

'Yes. I can see that,' he replied, holding me steady. 'Everyone's been worried about you. Simon's going demented, calling hospitals. Then you roll up, pissed, and snogging a stranger.'

He stared straight ahead and shoved his hands in his pockets, like he was stowing them there to stop himself from strangling me. Mr Mad, Bad and Dangerous to Know.

'Oh. You saw that. Well, you and Simon can both bugger off. I'm technically still single, thanks to you two and your roaming penises. Or penii. Whatever. I can snog whoever I like. It's about time I did more of it. You're not the only two men in the world. And a lot of people happen to think I'm a very attractive woman!'

Speech safely delivered, I pulled free of James's arm, and vomited straight into the lemon-tree pot.

Chapter 51

I felt like microwaved dog poo the next morning. My mouth was furry, my tongue was swollen and my stomach was churning. I rolled over, falling out of the bed and on to the ground with a thud. Ow. My knees were broken. I crawled into the bathroom, and rooted round in my toilet bag for painkillers. I chugged a couple down without water, then sat very still next to the loo, in case anything untoward happened.

When I felt confident enough to move, I did a Bionic Man-style slow-motion walk back into the bedroom, holding on to the walls as I went. I looked in the fridge, the light stinging my eyes as I opened the door. Simon had taken the last bottle of water. Bloody typical. I needed coffee. Diet Coke. A bacon butty. And possibly a head transplant.

I dressed very, very slowly, then splashed my face with cold water. I made my way down the steps and into the restaurant, hoping the others had already eaten and buggered off.

James passed me by as I went, dressed in his tennis whites, giving me nothing but a frosty nod. There was a little flutter down below as I watched his rear strut proudly across to the gardens. I must still be drunk.

Lucy was still in the restaurant, holding Ollie in a head-lock, battering his skull with a rolled-up newspaper. Simon was screaming ineffectually at them to stop.

'Kids! Pack it in!' I said as I reached the table. I grabbed the newspaper out of Lucy's hand mid-flight and gave them both a whack with it. Lucy let Ollie go and he sat up, rubbing his head and glaring at her. Simon breathed a sigh of relief and poured me a coffee.

'Lucy's been unbearable,' he said, straight away.

'No I haven't,' she snapped. 'I've been my usual charming self. Sitting with you two Neanderthals drove me to it, talking about Tabitha like she's a fucking Barbie doll. I hate you both. You'd be much nicer if you had your balls amputated.'

She turned to look at me, taking in the shaky hands and bloodshot eyes and hair that had been touched by neither comb nor man.

'I believe you were a naughty little girl last night, Mother. Daddy darling was most distressed.'

Bugger.

I looked up apologetically at Simon, who wouldn't meet my eyes. Lucy carried on regardless.

'And as for James, he's been walking round like someone stole his back copies of *Playboy* all morning. So, well done, I say.'

Simon slammed his cup down so hard coffee spilled over the edge. We are a very messy family at mealtimes. We should have a specially reserved table coated in plastic, standing on a tarpaulin.

'Simon, it was nothing,' I said. 'I was just drunk and acting like I was at a school disco. I'm sorry if I upset you.'

He nodded, tersely. Lucy pretended she hadn't noticed, but she was taking sly peeks at him from under her lashes to see how high she was scoring on the wind-up-ometer. Abruptly, she changed the subject, asking Simon if he'd bought me a birthday present. I felt my hackles rise – something bad was coming.

'James's birthday is in November, you know,' she added, all innocence. That was true, but we'd never been around him for it. At least I hadn't wasted money as well as time on the bastard.

Simon tried to look uninterested, but as ever was desperate to pick up bits of information on James. Perhaps he thought if he knew his birthday, he could hire a voodoo priestess and curse him until his testicles shrivelled up like raisins.

'Yeah. Do you know what Mum got him for his birthday the other year?'

Nothing. I got him nothing. Ever. She was about to tell a big fat lie and I hadn't got the energy to stop her. My brain was bouncing off the wall of my skull and the coffee tasted like liquid tar. I wanted to die.

'She bought him a penis reduction, Dad – 'cause his cock is so awesomely large!'

She held her hands about two feet apart, and cackled with laughter so hard I thought she might go up in a puff of smoke. I unscrewed a bottle of water and threw it in her face to shut her up. She spluttered and choked and howled, and eventually did shut up. I wondered briefly if she'd melt as well.

'Stop being so rude to your dad. That was out of order. Now go away and torment someone your own age.'

She glared at me, water dripping down her cheeks and on to her neck. She flounced off, wringing her hair out and muttering under her breath.

Simon stood up, his back rigid. 'I'm off for a tennis lesson with Heather. We'll talk about this later,' he said.

Ollie pulled a face, switched on his iPod. Communication central.

I lay my head flat on the table. Hopefully a giant anvil would come falling from the sky and put me out of my misery.

'Wakey-wakey, Sal! Time for our match!' said Mike, bouncing the strings of a tennis racquet up and down on the back of my head. I yelped like he'd poured acid on my skin, and raised my aching skull as slowly as I could to avoid a brain rupture.

He sat opposite me, wearing a scary Hawaiian shirt and a pair of cut-down jogging pants. His legs stuck out of them like hairy Cumberland sausages.

'What?' I snapped. 'What do you want?'

'Oh dear. Like that, is it? Hangover, Sal, or time of the month?'

I glared at him, for a very long moment.

'Come on. I brought you this,' he said, pointing to a glass of chilled Diet Coke on the table. 'I know what women need in times like these. Drink up. You said you'd be my partner for the tennis tournament.'

'No I did not.'

'Yes you did.'

'No, I didn't. Fuck off.'

'Sally! Shocking! Well, I thought I'd asked you, and I thought you'd said yes. Must have all been in my mind. But you won't turn an old man down, will you, love? It's what Al—'

'Mike, if you say it's what Allie would have wanted one more time, I'm going to swing for you. It's not what Allie would have wanted. Allie would have wanted me to be living a different life than this. In a house with a swimming pool as Bradley Cooper's sex slave. Or, at the very least in bed, sleeping off this bloody hangover.'

He sighed, loudly, and the breeze rippled the pink straw round in the glass. All the fight seemed to go out of him and his body sank a few inches lower into the chair.

'You're right, love. I'm sorry. I shouldn't keep doing this to you; I know you've got your own problems. Truth be told, it's not what Allie would have wanted. It's what I want. I just miss her so much, Sal. I'm here because she wanted me to come, but I feel like a spare part without her. Max is happy with your Luce, and I'm . . . well. I'm trying to keep myself busy so I don't lie down and die. 'Cause that's all I really want to do. I'm not even alive without her.'

His eyes were crumpled into the folds of his face and I knew he was trying not to break down in public. He reached out to pat my hand. 'Not to worry, love. I'll take myself off to my room for a bit, I think. All this talking lark's quite tired me out.'

He aimed for a smile, and tried to stand up. I grabbed hold of his hand and kept it in mine. I missed her so much it ached, and that was a fraction of what Mike must be feeling. He looked at me and made a funny choking sound in his throat, then started crying. Obviously I joined in. We sat there like that for maybe five minutes, clutching each other's hands and weeping like a pair of blubbering jellyfish. Is this what Allie would have wanted? I wasn't sure, but it would have made her laugh, at least.

I wiped my eyes and my nose and sucked up the Diet Coke through the pink straw.

'Come on,' I said, 'I feel better already. Let's go kick some tennis ass.'

Chapter 52

We were knocked out in the first round. By Jake and his best holiday friend Matthew. Outclassed even by eight-year-olds, Mike resorted to faking a hamstring injury so we could retire early after twelve long minutes of humiliation.

'Better luck next time!' said Heather, as I half carried Mike off the court. Heather was about twenty and looked like a *Sports Illustrated* calendar girl – all legs and teeth and long blond hair. I hated her.

I was relieved beyond words to get out in one piece. The sun was spreading across the court, chasing the shady patches away and replacing them with a ferociously hot, cye piercing glare. I was fighting back waves of nausea and my head was thumping so hard it felt like there was a rabbit in there trying to kick its way out.

'Thanks for that, Mike. I thought I might die if I had to run another step. Those little bastards are so fast.'

'I know,' he said, 'I could feel a heart attack coming on. Now we can just watch the rest of the idiots run themselves ragged. It'll be beer o'clock soon as well. I'll go and get us some in. Hair of the dog and all that.'

I glanced at my watch. It was 11 a.m. Fair enough.

The doubles final ended up as Marcia and Rick against Andrew and Ian. I was a few bottles in and feeling much better. Mike passed me a refill, and I concentrated on the match. Well, I concentrated on Andrew, who moved around so beautifully it could be classed as an art form. He should get a grant for it. It was one of the few small pleasures left to me in life – drinking warm bottled lager and leching over a bisexual Geordie firefighter.

The singles matches were going on in adjacent courts. I noticed Simon marching around, practising shots without a ball, like he was playing air tennis. And James, sitting silently under the shade of a pine tree, drinking water and staring off into the distance. He looked sad. Like someone should go and sit on his lap and cheer him up . . . *No!* Inappropriate thought alert! I dragged my eyes away from him, and slapped myself physically round the head. Hopefully anybody watching would think I was killing a fly.

As we sat, Ian came and joined us, still hot from his match. He usually partnered up with his wife, but today he was alone, and he seemed distracted, jumpy. I hadn't seen much of Jenny all holiday, after the day we scattered Allie's ashes. She'd not been in the restaurant or bar, and when I'd knocked on the door a few times there'd been no answer. I asked Ian how she was, and his face immediately fell.

'She's not very sociable at the moment, Sally,' he said apologetically. 'Don't know what's wrong with her, to be honest. It's been a hard year. She lost interest in running, and dropped out of our badminton team. So she's put a bit of weight on, and she keeps saying she looks like a beached whale and feels too tired to move. She's been sitting in the room, in the dark, eating chocolate and watching Turkish game shows all day.'

Oh dear. That didn't sound good.

'Sorry to hear that, Ian. I'll pop up and see her some time; maybe I can tempt her out to play.'

'That'd be great, Sally, thanks. Look – it's the singles final. James and Simon. That's . . . weird, isn't it?'

Weird, yes. But totally predictable. Obviously I was fated to be attracted to men who were incapable of staying faithful, but who were very good at tennis. I'd tick different boxes on my cosmic compatibility questionnaire next time round: 'Must be able to keep dick in pants. Tennis skills optional.'

Mike was chuckling away next to me, like a satanic Cabbage Patch doll.

'What are you laughing at?' I said.

'Those two swaggering about.'

Simon was limbering up like he was about to run the 100 metres in the Olympics, with Heather giving him some last-minute coaching.

James was ignoring him and firing practice serves across the court so hard they were lodging in the netting. There was a buzz in the air as the crowd picked up on the tension. I immediately felt self-conscious, as though everybody knew I was the third part of some comedy love triangle, and they were all staring at me.

The match started. James was serving. He fired one straight past Simon, who tried so desperately hard to reach it he overstretched and fell over. Without giving him any time at all to recover, James moved across the service box, aimed, and sent another scorcher humming over the net. Simon just about managed to get his racquet to the ball, bouncing it back loose and high. James moved forward and smashed it as hard as he could. The ball hit Simon in the groin and he doubled up in pain. Ouch.

'Oh, for fuck's sake,' I muttered to Mike, 'what a pair of dickheads. It's going to be like this all the way through. Simon'll be just as bad. I'm off. If anybody asks, tell them I've gone to Istanbul to watch a cock-fight. It's less bloodthirsty and the cocks involved are more intelligent.'

'Will do, Sal. Careful you don't bewitch any more men while you're gone – you temptress, you. Wouldn't want anyone else peeing on the trees, would we? Not in this heat.'

Chapter 53

I retreated to my room for a couple of hours, for a little restorative snooze, and to call Diane in Liverpool for a good, old-fashioned whinge.

She'd taken Simon off her 'shit list' at last – but had no useful advice to offer about the James situation. Other than 'follow your heart'.

Follow my heart? I thought not. My heart never led me anywhere good. Neither did the other body parts that sometimes shouted out instructions. I needed to use my head for once.

Could I make a go of it with Simon? Maybe I could. Or maybe I should at least try. He was a different man these days. He'd waited, been patient, and he even ironed his own shirts. I should stop messing around and give him a proper chance. And probably a shag as well. He wouldn't wait for ever – and we'd had a decent life before Monika shimmied her way into his knickers. Maybe we could have a decent life again.

It was making my head hurt thinking about it, so I decided to go and obtain alcohol. I cut through the restaurant and over to the gardens on my way. It was much noisier than usual, and a small crowd had gathered near the cluster of pine trees in the middle. I could hear some yelling, and a high-pitched female voice trying to shout over the top of everyone else.

It sounded like Lucy. Maybe she'd finally gone over the edge and had someone pinned to the floor with a scimitar. Any minute now, I'd see her arm raised in triumph, a still-beating heart pulsing between her fingers.

I ran over in panic, pushing my way through the crowd. The good news was, Lucy was fine. No knives, no blood, no potential jail sentence. Phew.

The bad news was Simon and James. Squaring up to each other like a pair of prizefighters. Or a pair of prize pricks, depending on your point of view. Mike grabbed hold of my arm as I moved towards them.

'Don't spoil the fun, Sal! It was always going to come to this at some point, wasn't it? My money's on James – he's shorter than Simon but he's got more bulk. I'll go a tenner on a knockout. What do you say?'

'Are you nuts? This isn't funny! What the fuck's going on?'

'It all started when James won the tennis. They insisted on playing the whole five sets, and Simon disputed the final line call. James said, "Are you calling me a cheat?" and Simon said, "Well, if the cap fits", and that was that. They pushed and shoved their way over here, and we came with them. It'd be rude not to watch when they've put so much effort in.'

Simon gave James a vicious shove in the chest. He stepped back a few paces, regrouped, and then punched Simon in the jaw. I saw blood seep from his lips and he went white with pain. Simon was not a man used to the physical rough and tumble of life. The only time I'd known him come to blows was with a heart specialist over a reserved parking space at work. Porsche versus Bentley. He was a sixty-eight-year-old with a glass eye, and he still won. I was going to have to intervene or he'd die.

I was about to step forward when Lucy beat me to it. She stood in between them, and I held my breath. Both of them were mid-swing and men could be dumb when their blood was up. I hoped she could duck fast or she might be needing a new set of teeth sometime soon.

'Stop!' she shouted. 'Stop and listen to me, you fuckwits!'

She held one hand out on each of their chests, holding them back with sheer strength of will rather than her skinny wrists.

'Dad – grow up, will you? Do you think Mum would appreciate this? She'd bloody hate it, and you'll be in deep shit if she finds out.

'And, James – if you do kick the crap out of him, avoid his hands. He's a surgeon, for fuck's sake. Leave the hands alone, or he can't work, and if he can't work, I can't go to university – understood?'

James dropped his fists to his side, and nodded. I could see his breathing regulate as he tried to calm down. Simon was still springing around on the balls of his feet, blood smeared across his face, pretending he was tough enough for round two.

'Anyway, there must be a better way to settle this,' she said, pretending to think about it. 'Tell you what, why don't you both just get your cocks out, and we'll measure them?'

'I'll do it!' shouted Rick from the crowd, fluttering his hand in the air to show he was ready and willing. He probably had a special Tackle Tape in his pocket for just these kinds of occasions.

'Great. Then whoever has the biggest wins!' said Lucy. She noticed me in the crowd and her eyes zeroed in. I knew something bad was coming next. She made Ming the Merciless look like a nun when she was in this mood.

'Unless you want to save Rick the trouble and just tell us, Mother – you have got first-hand experience of both the cocks in question, haven't you?'

She stared at me. Simon stared at me. James stared at me. Everybody else stared at me. Rick looked especially interested in what I was going to say.

'Oh, piss off, the lot of you,' I shouted, heading back to the room.

They could both chop their cocks off and stir-fry them, for all I cared.

Chapter 54

I tried to eat dinner on my own, but Simon stubbornly insisted on playing happy families. I knew full well he was doing it in case James was there – he wanted to gloat about being in my favour. Which he wasn't. I was still seething with him and his stupid swollen lip.

'I don't know what you're sulking about,' he said, cutting his pork chop up into perfectly equal one-inch cubes, 'he's been asking for it all holiday. If Lucy hadn't interfered, I'd have taught him a lesson.'

Yeah, right. Like a lesson in how to cry like a baby, and take a beating until your brains dribbled out of your ears.

'You behaved like an idiot and I don't want to talk about it any more,' I said.

'Fine. Suit yourself. I'll sit here and read. I found this fascinating book on the shelves in reception – have you seen it?'

He was holding up a dog-eared paperback of *Shag Yourself Happy*. I wasn't sure I'd want to touch a copy that well used without plastic gloves on.

'Yeah, I have. Hope you enjoy the bit about Nurse Nancy.'

He looked confused, but went back to his reading. Maybe

he'd pick up a few tips. My plan for carnal reunion had been put on hold because he was acting like such a knob. It might be on hold for a while on current form.

After dinner I sat with Mike, getting mildly smashed – it was, we both decided, what Allie would have wanted.

Just after ten, Ollie walked into the bar. Or fell into the bar, to be more precise. He was so drunk his knees wouldn't lock properly, and when he came to stand in front of us, his pipe-cleaner legs kept buckling beneath him. Eventually Mike held a chair in place to catch him; next time he slumped, his bum made contact with the seat and he stayed down.

'Oh. That's better. What happened?' he said.

'You sat down, sweetheart. Where have you been? Have you been drinking? Drinking something purple maybe?'

There was no maybe about it. He stank of stale cider and cream, like an apple crumble that's rotted and been eaten by maggots. There was an open vodka bottle peeping out of his jeans pocket and stains I didn't want to analyse too closely on the legs.

'Of course not, Mum. You know I don't drink.'

It was less than convincing, especially as he went glassy-eyed and fell straight forward with the final word. Mike caught his shoulders and straightened him back up, patting him on the cheek.

'We've all been there, son,' he said, taking the vodka bottle out and examining it. Empty. Cripes.

'No, honest, I haven't had a thing to drink. But I think I'll go to bed now. Fancy an early night.'

He stood up, wobbled, and fell back down on to the chair.

'Is there something wrong with my glasses?' he asked, taking them off and staring at them with booze-fogged eyes.

At last, he'd noticed. We'd been staring at them since he arrived, trying not to laugh. They were completely covered in dried-up purple sick. Crusted on, and totally obscuring the little round lenses. Splashback, I suspected. So much to learn.

'Come on, mate, I'll walk you home,' said Mike, putting his hands under his armpits and hauling him up. Ollie threw an arm round his shoulder and they staggered off together, like they were taking part in a drunks' three-legged race.

It was my bedtime as well, I thought. Simon was busy holding court with a pair of ear, nose and throat specialists from Kent. They'd spend hours discussing the pros and cons of different anaesthetics and swapping hospital horror stories. I'd had my fill of that boring crap at the works parties he'd dragged me to over the years.

I got up to leave, and felt a bit of a tremor in my legs. I'd possibly had a few more drinks than I'd realised. I decided to go for a nice sit in the gardens before bed. Ten minutes' peace and quiet to gather my thoughts would be good. I was likely to be awake for much of the night anyway, listening for the telltale sounds of my second-born choking on his own vomit.

I settled in under the big pine tree, watching bats wheeling and circling overhead. I hugged my wrap around my shoulders and tried closing my eyes, first one at a time, then together. Good. Nothing was spinning around too much. A cup of coffee back in the room and I'd be fine.

'Can I join you?'

I jumped a couple of inches and my eyes snapped open. James. Poo. We hadn't shared a civil word for days and I didn't really want to start now.

'No,' I said.

'Well I am anyway,' he replied, sitting down next to me. Jeans and an open-necked shirt. An oldie but a goodie. Not that I was looking, of course.

'I just wanted to apologise about earlier. With Simon. The man is an absolute cretin and was asking for everything he got, but I shouldn't have risen to it. It was childish and unnecessary and I should've walked away. I'm really sorry if we embarrassed you.'

Oh, for fuck's sake, I thought. Why couldn't people ever do what you wanted them to do? Just once? If Simon had made that little speech, had showed even an ounce of remorse, I'd have got down on one knee and asked him to re-marry me. But no, he was too busy being a macho twat, with all the charm of a mud-flap.

And now, here was James, looking all blond and gorgeous and touchable, saying exactly the right thing when all I wanted to do was hate him.

'Okay. Well. Thanks for that,' I said, huddling down even deeper inside my wrap. I had to keep my hands tied up in case they started straying, like in those horror films where transplanted fingers have a life of their own.

'Sal, I'm sorry about all of this. Everything. I've acted like an arsehole this holiday. You have every right to see other people. Even him,' he said, his face twisting with distaste, 'if it makes you happy.'

He turned towards me, held my face by the chin and tilted it up so I was looking into his eyes.

'But does he make you happy? You don't seem happy to me.'

'I'm not . . . unhappy,' I said.

I now had that bloody wrap twisted round my wrists so tightly I was starting to lose all feeling in my hands. I wished I could do the same with my brain, and stop looking at James like he was dessert.

He took the fact that I didn't punch him, knee him in the balls or scream as a sign of encouragement, and leaned in to kiss me. Tentatively at first, then harder, his arms going behind my back.

That was it. The hands were out. They could resist no more, and reached up to tangle into James's golden hair, pulling his mouth even closer to mine. He made a strange 'ug-gug' noise in the back of his throat and lowered me down on to the ground.

I could feel the dampness of the grass and the hardness of his body on mine, the scent of pine needles around us. My hands were all over him – his shoulders, his arms, his bottom, clinging to him, spreading my legs so he could nestle into me. He was squeezing me to him and kissing my neck in such a nerve-tingling way I felt myself going cross-eyed. We were as close to having sex as you could be without taking your clothes off, and I had about a year's worth of orgasms stored up and ready to burst out in glorious Technicolor.

Who had I been kidding? There was no way anything was ever going to come close to this, I thought, as his hand found its way under my bra and made me yelp with pleasure. God, it felt good.

We were so busy getting reacquainted, we didn't notice we had a visitor. A very small visitor. We wouldn't have noticed if the entire London Gospel Choir had turned up to sing backing vocals, to be honest, never mind one very quiet eight-year-old boy.

'What are you doing? Are you *kissing* each other?' Jake said, in disgust. 'And does this mean you're my dad's girlfriend again?'

Chapter 55

I was woken up early next morning by the sound of Ollie retching into the toilet. At least I hoped it was the toilet.

I wiped my eyes, moved Simon's leg away from its unlicensed position splayed across my hip, and pulled on some clothes. I eased open the connecting door as quietly as I could, and found Ollie, ashen-faced, on the bathroom floor.

'You okay, love?'

He nodded, too miserable to speak. I squatted down next to him and patted his shoulder. His breath was so foul I pulled my head back a few inches. Even I didn't love him that much.

'Don't worry, Ollie, you'll be fine in a few hours. Drink some water – but not too much 'cause it'll make you sick again. If you can keep them down, take some painkillers. I'll check in on you later, all right?'

I stroked his forehead with the back of my hand. Clammy with sweat that had chilled on his skin. Poor lamb. The first time's always the worst.

'Do you think Tabitha will still fancy me?' he asked, his voice small and sad and pathetic.

Not in a million years, I thought, if she could see you now.

'Course she will, sweetie. Don't worry.'

'Happy birthday, Mum,' he said, as I got up to leave. Aaah. Even in his hour of need, he'd remembered.

'And, Mum?' he said, as I reached the door. 'Could you sort my glasses out for me? There's something stuck on them and I can't get it off . . .'

That was less of an 'aah'. As a special birthday treat this year, I got to wash crusty purple puke off my 16-year-old son's specs. It just got better and better, it really did.

Simon was stirring when I returned. I didn't want to get back into bed with him. I knew what would be lurking under those covers and I wasn't quite ready to face it. Last night had shown me there was still a sex drive hidden under my layers of denial, but whether it wanted to motor in Simon's direction remained to be seen.

He sat up, belched, and said: 'Happy birthday, darling.'

I averted my eyes as he got out of bed with a bulge tenting out his pants, and rooted around in the wardrobe. He eventually produced a gift-wrapped package done so prettily I knew he'd paid extra for it. Or got Jean, his secretary, to do it for him.

Before he handed it over, he put his arms round me and gave me a kiss. A longer one than we'd shared for over a year. With a bit of tongue. It felt . . . okay. Pleasant enough. It didn't make my knickers fall off with lust, but it was nice. Maybe we could work at it.

I smiled and took the present. It was well taped down and I thought I was going to break a nail getting into it. Lucy had wandered through, and sat on the bed yawning as she watched me struggle.

'Oh, for fuck's sake give it here,' she said, grabbing it out of my hands and ripping the wrapping off in one vicious tear.

The contents fell out on to the bedclothes and she grabbed them a fraction of a second earlier than I could. She held up a pair of exceptionally skimpy black lace panties on one finger. If your arse was the size of a tangerine, they'd be perfect. There was a matching black bra to go with them. They wouldn't have looked out of place in Mr and Mrs Smith's suitcase of smut.

She examined the labels, and I could feel Simon tensing with anger next to me.

'Size eight,' she said. 'Even the new you is way too fat for these. I'm not, but I wouldn't be seen dead in them. Maybe we could donate them to the Home for Needy Hookers when we get back? I'm sure there are women in King's Cross who'd kill for these. Hang on, there's something else here.'

She held up the second present. A DVD. 'Perfectly Toned: The Pilates Way'. A blonde woman who even had Perfectly Toned Teeth smiled out at us.

'Ha! At least he's thought ahead,' said Lucy, throwing the DVD back down. 'All you need to do is go back to starving yourself for another year, and do this stupid shit every day, and then you *might* be able to squeeze yourself into his fantasy whore slut-wear. Men are such fucking wankers.'

On that note she slammed the door behind her. I heard Ollie groan at the noise. I looked at Simon, and stood on tiptoe to give him a peck on the cheek. As ever, he'd not got it quite right. But, looking on the bright side, it was a damn sight better than the effort he put in for my fortieth.

'Thanks, Simon. They're lovely. Look, we're up nice and early, so I'm going to go for a bit of a walk. Blow away the cobwebs. Meet you downstairs for breakfast?'

He nodded and gave me a pat on the bum. I paused, wondering whether that was acceptable or not, but thought better of it and left. I'd figure it out later. I needed to process what had happened last night, grateful that Jake had interrupted us and that there wasn't even more to process. I'd practically fled the scene of the crime as soon as he'd arrived.

By the time I'd made it back to the restaurant, after spending a good hour on my own down at the beach, I was feeling dazed. I'd consoled my sixteen-year-old alcohol-poisoned son as he threw up; been bought a pair of knickers that wouldn't look out of place on a porn star, and spent forty minutes watching two crabs fighting.

It has to be said, my birthdays were never, ever dull.

Simon was waiting for me, sitting at a table for two, reading a three-day-old *Telegraph* and stirring his tea. He looked red-faced and was wearing his workout clothes.

'Hi,' I said, 'have you just got back from the gym?'

'Yes – feel the power.'

He flexed his arms and I dutifully squeezed them, making appreciative noises.

Simon went back to the paper, holding it full-sized in front of his face so I couldn't see a thing. I poured myself some coffee and stared at the back pages. Ugh. Cricket. He could at least have folded it on to the telly reviews for me.

Jake appeared and came running over, his feet skipping and his face flushed with excitement. He threw himself on to my lap and gave me a hug. I was hoping he didn't mention what he'd seen last night; I hadn't even figured out what it meant myself yet, and had no desire for Simon to find out until I had.

'Sally! Happy birthday – again! You always have a birthday here – you must be about a hundred by now!'

Simon snorted on the other side of his paper. I considered sticking a knife through it.

'About that, yes, Jake.'

'We've got you a present,' he said, 'and it's very special.'

James arrived, and Simon at last folded the paper down. Typical. I – the alleged love of his life and mother of his children – wasn't interesting enough to talk to. But the minute his arch-enemy turned up, he was all ears.

James was carrying a cake on a plate. He laid it down carefully on the table in front of me. It was a sponge, covered in haphazard icing in psychedelic colours, a flickering candle planted inch-deep.

'I did the icing!' said Jake, proudly, 'and Daddy baked the whole thing!'

'You bake?' I asked, looking at James in amazement.

'Yes. I find it very therapeutic. Why, don't I look like someone who bakes?'

I gave him a quick up and down. He was wearing that skin-tight sailing gear and had muscles busting out of all the right places. His hair was cut brutally short, and his face still had a slightly battered nose in the middle of it. No. He didn't look like he baked.

'I know you don't eat cake any more,' he said, 'and it got a bit mashed. But it was made with . . . love,' he said, staring Simon right in the eye as he said it.

'And a LOT of sugar!' said Jake. 'Can I have some?'

'Course you can, sweetie. Here.' I cut him a slice and put it in his hand. He shoved it all in his mouth in one go, his face smothered in red and yellow icing. Without thinking, I reached a finger out to the cake, and scooped up a bit of cream. I licked it off while I laughed at James trying to wipe Jake's face with a napkin.

'Are you sure you want to be eating that?' said Simon, looking from the cake to me with surprise. I blushed, and pushed the plate away from me. He was right. Of course I shouldn't be eating it.

But should he be the person telling me not to? Was he simply concerned about me, and wanting me to stay healthy? Or did the cake veto – along with the slutty knickers – mean that he was more concerned with keeping me skinny? Simon had been an absolute godsend in the last year – he'd changed. Grown up. Or at least I thought he had. Now, though, as I pushed the cake to one side, I started to wonder how much had really altered between us.

He folded his paper, stood up, and announced that he was going for a run. 'Just a quick ten-miler.'

'I'll be off as well,' said James once he'd left, 'I'm taking the kids kayaking for an hour. Have a happy birthday, Sal. And take no notice of him, he's a prick. Eat the bloody cake. You know you want to.'

He leaned down and kissed me, briefly, but right on the

lips, before walking off. I watched him and his bottom go. I blew out my candle and made a very rude wish.

He was right. I did want to eat it.

And the cake.

Chapter 56

I ate some cake. And boy, did it feel good. Only a tiny piece, but it was the most decadent I'd been since . . . well, my last birthday.

Afterwards I felt a warm glow in my tummy, and couldn't get the smile off my face. It was like I'd had really terrific sex.

I checked in on Ollie – still alive – and took myself off for some emergency sunbathing. We were going home soon and I could be several shades darker if I tried really hard.

Lucy and Max were splashing around in the pool. Simon was doing something else somewhere else. I didn't really care. I had sunshine, water, and the most fantastic sugar-rush going on. Happiness is birthday cake. It's that simple. James was a heck of a lover – but he was possibly an even better baker.

I drifted off to sleep, pondering the possible combinations of the two, and slipped into a luxuriant dream about icing nozzles in personal places. I don't know how long I was under, but when Ian woke me up, shaking my shoulders, I tried to lick his face.

He looked terribly shocked and jumped back so far and so fast he almost fell into the pool.

'Sorry!' I said, mortified. 'I'm so sorry! I was dreaming about . . . well, ice cream. Yes. Ice cream.'

'That's okay. Sally, can you come with me and see Jenny? She's been ill all night and I don't know what's wrong with her. She won't let me call the doctor; she keeps saying it's wind. Last time I tried to persuade her, she threw her shoe at me.'

I'd tried to see Jenny, as I'd promised him on the day of the tennis tournament, but she'd just shouted at me through the door to come back later because she'd got the runs. It was too much information, and probably not even true – she just wanted to get rid of me. Or maybe, I thought, listening now to Ian's description, she did have the runs. Or appendicitis. Or something worse.

'Of course,' I said, getting up to follow him. He was practically running and his face was pallid. Shit. I hoped I wasn't on my way to a real emergency. Just in case, I shouted over my shoulder to Lucy and Max, telling them to go and look for Simon, or James. Simon was a doctor and James was . . . well, an architect, but I knew he'd be good in a crisis.

Ian pushed the door open so hard it banged back on its hinges, slamming into the wall behind it. I took one look at Jenny and I could see why. Her eyes were rolling in her head with pain, and sweat was beaded down her contorted face. She was yelling, and squatting down on her feet, holding her stomach with her arms. She looked up at me with pleading eyes.

'Sally! Kill me now!' she said, meaning every word.

'How long has this been going on?' I said to Ian, as we helped her on to the bed.

'On and off for a couple of days, but really bad overnight, and like this for the last hour or so. Sally, what should I do?'

Jenny calmed momentarily, sucking up air in huge gasps and clutching the pillow in her arms so tightly it started to burst at the seams.

'What's happening to me? Am I dying?' she said, wailing the last word. 'It keeps going away for a bit then coming back! I can't stand it – and I feel like I need a poo really badly but nothing's happening!'

Oh . . . oh! My mind did the symptom sums and came up with a very strange answer. Weight gain. Grumpiness. Championship-level chocolate-eating. Intermittent hellish cramps . . . and the telltale need for a number two.

I lifted her nightie up for a quick look. Nope. I wasn't wrong.

I took in a few deep breaths of my own, then turned to Ian. I held his shoulders and tried to sound as reassuring as possible.

'Ian,' I said, 'you need to go to reception and get them to call for an ambulance. Tell them Jenny's in labour and the baby's about to arrive.'

He stared at me like I was talking to him in Croatian. Eventually it sank in, and he shook his sandy-haired head.

'No, Sally, that's not it. We can't have kids. We had tests and everything. And anyway, she's been normal – you know, periods and things. And – look – she's not pregnant! You must have made a mistake!'

Jenny started screaming again and the pillow disintegrated in her hands, showering feathers into the air like she'd slaughtered a duck.

'No, Ian, it's not a mistake. Look.'

I lifted the nightie again, and he saw the blood, gore, and the faintest hint of a tiny, pulsating head. I thought for a moment he was going to pass out.

'Somehow,' I said, 'one of your little swimmers found its way to the right place. As for the rest of it, that happens sometimes – more women than you think end up having babies without even knowing they were expecting. Weight-wise, though, she is small. I think the baby's coming early. If it's premature, it's going to need special care, and fast – so go, now, and sort that ambulance out.'

He looked at Jenny, writhing in agony and exhaustion, then looked at me. He ran as fast as his legs could carry him out of the door. He bumped into Lucy on the way in. James was behind her.

'What is it?' he said, 'what can I do?'

'She's in labour. Luce, go downstairs to the kitchens and ask them if they can boil some string in hot water. And some scissors.'

'String? What do you want that for?' she asked, staring at Jenny in morbid fascination.

'Because I want to fly a fucking kite! Just do it!' I yelled, dashing into the bathroom to scrub my hands.

When I came back she was between contractions, and I helped her sit up. James made an ice pack with a towel, and used it to stroke her forehead and face to cool her down.

'Jenny,' I said, 'look at me. Now breathe, nice and deep. You're having a baby and you need to trust me. It'll all be okay. Now, when the pain comes, tell me if it stings. And don't push until I tell you to. Okay? Do you want to stay there, or get up?'

'I want to get up. I want to die. I can't stand it any more!' she screeched pitifully.

Between us, we got her upright. She squatted back down into the same position I'd found her in.

'Towels, clean ones,' I said to James, lying down on the floor myself to take a better look.

James came back with the towels and we spread them out beneath her.

'It stings! It's burning! I've got to push!' she yelled, grabbing hold of James's shoulder and gripping it so hard I saw him wince.

'Jenny,' I said, my voice low and even, 'you need to let me see what's going on.'

She stared at me and nodded. Keeping my voice calm was working. Good job she couldn't see inside my head – where I was screaming, 'Help! Help! We're all going to die!'

James mopped her down again, and she started sobbing as I took a quick look down below. Fuck. She was crowning. This baby was coming, and it was coming now. She spread her legs wider and let out an ear-splitting scream.

'Jenny, pant – pant fast and push really gently when you feel the pain coming again. The baby's going to be here in the next few pushes and this will all be over.'

As she pushed, Ian ran back into the room, then fell to his knees by our side.

'Ambulance is on the way. How is she? How are you, Jen?'

'How do I fucking look?' she hissed, clenching her teeth against the pain. I saw James bite back a smile. He held one of her hands, and Ian held the other. I was at the business end, hoping for the best. I could see a tiny blood-capped head peeking out and it was my job to get it safely into the world. No pressure then.

'Sally! Lucy said you needed me – what is it?' said Simon, running into the now quite crowded room.

Oh, thank God. He was here. A real, proper, qualified doctor. I could hand over to him and just stand by with blankets and water and words of encouragement.

'Simon! I'm so glad you're here – I don't know what the hell I'm doing!'

Jenny glared up at me sharply. Ian gulped. James got busy with the towel again. Oops. So much for my calm and reassuring exterior.

'Simon?' I said, glancing behind me. Simon was rooted to the spot, white as a sheet, staring in absolute terror at the baby emerging from Jenny's pain-racked body. Oh no. Please, no, not now. He staggered, held the wall, then fell. Thud. He was down and out for the count.

'Oh you shit!' I yelled, kicking him in the ribs. Lucy and Max arrived back, breathless and confused.

'They're cooking the string,' she said, then stopped and stared. Her eyes were the size of steering wheels and Max looked as if he might hurl.

'Guys, could you drag your dad out, then go wait for the ambulance at reception?'

They nodded, grateful for an excuse to make their getaway, then hauled Simon's limp and lifeless body out into the hallway. 'Useless fuck,' Lucy muttered, giving him another kick for good measure.

'Okay. Look,' I said, 'we're going to do this, and we're going to do it now. And when it's over, you're going to have a beautiful baby to show for it.'

'I don't give a shit about that! I just want the pain to stop!' yelled Jenny.

'It will. Now, come on, next contraction, gentle pushes – let's get this head out.'

I lay down on the floor in front of her, manoeuvring myself as close as I could. James was murmuring his support, and stroking her head. His fingers were so red and swollen from her grip I thought they might be broken. Ian looked shell-shocked and as though he might be about to follow Simon into the hallway.

She pushed. The head popped out. I put my hand under it for support. It looked small, but okay. Another contraction.

'A bit more Jenny. The head's out. Shoulders to go, then it's almost done. Come on now.'

She grunted like a pig, bearing down and pushing a bit too hard, her panic so fierce it was hovering in the air.

'No! I can't! Just cut it out of me!'

James took hold of her chin, turned her face up so he was looking into her eyes.

'Jenny, you can do this – you're having a baby. You've always wanted a baby. This is a miracle. You're creating a miracle here. Now, look at me, trust me, and stay calm. I've known you for a long time, Jenny, and you can do anything. You can do this. We're all here to help you. So just look at me, and breathe.'

She stared at him, tears flooding from her screwed-up eye sockets, and nodded. Sucked in another breath. Contorted her face as she pushed, gazing at James all the time as she crushed his fingers.

It worked. One shoulder was out, then another, then the whole body slipped out like a fish. I caught it, pulling it up to check it over, clearing its nose and trying to remember what else to do. Smack its arse? No, that was just in films.

I looked down at the tiny scrap of life in my hands. Definitely premature, its face waxy and blood-stained and screwed up like a desiccated apple. But breathing, and waving its tiny hands around and letting out whimpers, the poor little soul.

'Is it okay? What is it?' said Jenny, trying to lean forward.

'No, stay there Jen. It's okay. It's a –' I took a quick look in the relevant place – 'boy! Here you go.'

I laid the baby on her tummy, and she looked at him in wonder. Like she'd never seen anything so beautiful in her whole life. She picked him up nervously, and he slipped in her hands until she got a firmer grip and lifted him to her face. Ian was weeping by her side, and James was stroking her hair, murmuring calm words of congratulations.

I heard the sound of footsteps pounding up the stairs. The cavalry had arrived, at bloody last. The professionals took over, clamping the cord and getting both Jenny and the baby loaded into the ambulance. No need for the boiled string after all.

When they were gone I fell back on to the bed. I was covered in blood and goo and other organic substances I couldn't wait to wash off. I could hear Simon groaning in the hallway. He'd been as much use as a chocolate fireguard, as my nan would have said.

James lay down next to me. We both stared at the ceiling, catching our breath.

'That was amazing,' he said, turning to look at me, 'you were amazing. I love you.'

I closed my eyes. Remembered the feel of his fingertips on my body, the lush touch of his tongue. His humour and kindness and strength. The calm way he'd helped Jenny get through it all.

Then I remembered the way I'd felt for the last year of my life, when all those things were taken away from me.

I still loved him. I couldn't hide from it any longer.

I kept my eyes closed tight, and wept. When he reached for my hand, I pulled away.

Because loving him didn't fix anything.

Chapter 57

'I was thinking,' said Simon, as we strolled along the beach, 'that when we get back, perhaps I could start staying over again – just for a night a week, maybe, to see how it goes?'

The sun was setting over the bay. We'd just had dinner together. He was holding my hand. It was pleasant. I didn't answer straight away, which he took as a sign to continue.

'I know we've got a long way to go, but maybe this is a place to start?'

'Let's wait and see, shall we?' I said, squeezing his hand in what I hoped was a reassuring way. 'I've had a really nice holiday with you, Simon, but I don't want to rush things. Can we take it slowly?'

'Sal, if we take it any more slowly, we'll be dead. But all right, if that's what you want, we'll talk again when we're back.'

He was probably right. He couldn't be expected to wait for ever. But a few more days wouldn't hurt, surely? A few more days for me to get James out of my system before I faced up to the reality of never seeing him again?

When we were back in Oxford, things would be different. I could love Simon again. He was attractive and clever and he wanted me. He'd learned his lesson, hadn't he? And when I looked at him, when I touched him, I felt warm and quite content. And warm and content didn't threaten to set you on fire, the way that James's heat did.

We'd go home. It would all be different there. At least, that's what I told myself. The Blue Bay and its crowd had been a blessing in my life when I'd first found it. Now, it was starting to feel like more of a curse.

It was last-night party time. My third, unbelievably. Tomorrow was home. And a nice, new, calm beginning.

We went back up to our room to get ready. I made a quick call to the hospital, to check on Ian and Jenny and the Baby With No Name. He'd been about eight weeks early, but with well-developed lungs, and was going to be fine. I cried every time I thought about it. Not just because of the memory of his birth, but because that part of my life was over and I'm a sad old moo.

Jenny and Ian were at the start of the adventure. They'd be the centre of that child's life for a long time to come – at least while he was still pooing in his own pants and getting garden peas stuck up his nostrils.

I was like an old armchair to mine – comfy but barely noticeable. One day, when they've really had enough, they'll leave me outside in the front garden and get the Council to come and take me to the tip.

I'd never hold another baby of my own in my arms; and I'd have to stick pins in Lucy's condom collection until I got some grandchildren.

She waltzed into our room, and I felt a twinge of guilt for planning to turn her into a gymslip mum. For tonight's look, she'd stolen Tina Turner's hair and Dusty Springfield's eye make-up. She was wearing a T-shirt that had 'Bored To Tears' written across the chest and a skirt that seemed to be made out of a bin bag. She looked me up and down and sneered.

'You look shit. Why don't you let me style you again?'

'No!' I said, locking the bathroom door so she couldn't get at me. I was wearing a bit of make-up. I'd brushed my hair. And I had a nice white sundress on. She could fuck right off.

'Coward!' she yelled through the door. I considered barricading myself in with the rubbish bin and the cabinet, but I heard her do a stage sigh and flounce off, slamming the door behind her. I opened up, and cautiously peeked my head out.

'Got ya!' she shouted, leaping out from behind the wardrobe. She'd bluffed me, the cow. I screamed and threw my arms over my face, but it was too late – she had indeed got me. With a fluorescent pink spray can. There was a huge glittering streak of the stuff zigzagged all over my hair. I looked as though I'd been ambushed by Graffiti Artist Barbie.

'That's better,' she said, with a smug smile. I tried to kick her up the bum as she went but she sensed it coming and dodged, laughing as she ran away. I looked in the mirror. Brushed my hair. Fluffed it up a bit. It wasn't too bad. Anyway, people here were so used to me turning up in fancy dress of one kind or another, they wouldn't even notice. I could go to karaoke night naked wearing a rubber Ronald Reagan mask and they'd all nod and say, 'Interesting look, Sally.'

By the time I'd walked through to the terrace, the usual hellish noise was booming from the speakers. Three of the female tennis coaches were doing 'When Will I See You Again'?

They sounded awful, but they looked great. Heather was on lead, throwing her hair around, teeth glinting like an advert for whitening paste.

I sat down with Mike. He was looking on appreciatively, with his fingers in his ears to block out the caterwauling.

'She's a sight for sore eyes,' he said, nodding towards Heather. 'Exceptionally nice boobs on her. Not that I'd kick any of them out of bed. That one on the left has the best legs, and the one on the right looks like she'd be a bit of a handful in the—'

I grabbed his hands and pulled his fingers away from his ears.

'Mike,' I said, 'I am not one of your male friends. We are not in the pub after the match. This is not an appropriate conversation to have with me. Do you want me to start talking about throbbing cocks and the best way to lick a clitoris?'

'I'd be more than happy to listen, Sal – I'm an equal opportunities pervert. Let's start with Lucy's question the other day about Simon and James, and who had the biggest dong.'

'I'm not going to discuss their dongs,' I said firmly. I was trying to stay annoyed but I couldn't help smiling at the dirty old bastard. 'Anyway,' I added, 'depends on whether you're talking length or girth . . .'

'That's the spirit, Sal! Nice hair, by the way. Bit restrained by your usual standards. Look – there's Dong Number One up on stage now.'

I looked over. Simon. On stage. Doing karaoke. If his mother could see him now, she'd probably have a heart attack. Especially as he was throwing his arms into the air with gay abandon doing all the actions to 'YMCA', along with Rick,

Marcia and Andrew. He looked mighty fine up there – handsome enough to hold his own with Andrew, even. Yes. I could do this.

They came over to us when the song had finished. Simon was flushed with adrenaline. 'That was fantastic!' he said. 'I don't know why I've never done that before!'

Because you're a reformed stuck-up pillock who once said karaoke was for drunk lorry drivers, footballers' wives and Scousers, I thought. How times change.

Rick was practically shimmering with excitement as he bopped over to join us.

'Let's do it again next year!' he trilled. 'But let's dress up! Andrew – you've already got a firefighter's outfit, and Simon, darling, you could be a dishy doctor. Typecasting! I'm a HR manager, which is a bit rubbish, but I'd *love* to be the Red Indian!'

'I'll be the motorcyle cop in leathers,' volunteered Marcia, lighting up her post-karaoke fag.

Simon was leaning back in his chair, tapping his toe on the floor, looking as if he wanted to go straight back up and do 'Flashdance'.

'I've got so much energy, Sal, I'm going for a wander. I need to get some more cash from upstairs anyway. And what happened to your hair? It's pink.'

'Lucy happened to my hair – and be careful, she's still out there somewhere.'

He nodded and ambled off, hands shoved into his pockets, humming 'YMCA' to himself. He was on a real high, I could tell, and it wasn't only down to the beer. He'd been infected by the Blue Bay madness. Maybe we could buy a karaoke machine of our very own when we got home – it could be our new baby.

'He seems a happy boy,' said Mike, coming back with a fresh tray of drinks. Two each, to save him getting up again for a while.

'Yeah. He does. I think I'm going to let him move back in.'

He raised a tufted grey eyebrow at me.

'That so? You sure about that, love?'

'No. I'm not sure about it. But I don't want to spend my whole life wondering what might have happened with James. James was for the holidays. Not to make him sound like a rescue dog, but Simon is for life. I need to get back to reality.'

'Always thought reality was overrated myself,' Mike said, peering over towards the stage. He squinted his eyes together.

'Hey, Sal. Look. It's Dong Number Two. Can't say that I've ever seen that before, in all the years we've been coming here. Allie would've peed herself.'

I turned round to see what he was ranting about. Fucking hell. He was right. Super-cool James Carver, or Dong Number Two as we knew him, was standing there on stage, looking about as comfortable as the cast of *Watership Down* on a greyhound track. He was staring up into the lights like he was about to be questioned by the Gestapo, sweat beading his forehead, and even from this distance you could see his hand trembling on the mike.

He cleared his throat as the intro to the song started, and looked out into the crowd.

'Um . . . this is for Sally,' he said.

I recognised the song straight away. Sinead O'Connor. Oh shit. Wasn't that taking national loyalties too far? He might be Irish, but he came without the bald head or ovaries or the talent. This was going to be terrible. Mike was chortling away, settling in for the disaster unfolding before our eyes.

As James started wailing along to 'Nothing Compares 2 U', I realised it was going to be even worse than I'd imagined. This wasn't terrible. It was catastrophic. I'd finally found the one thing that James was bad at. He had the kind of voice that could unblock drains at fifty paces. Every note he hit was the wrong one. Every word he sang, he shouted. Every time he should have gone up, he went down.

It was absolutely the worst karaoke performance I have ever seen in my life, and that includes Yates's Wine Lodge in Liverpool on a Saturday night.

'No-thing compares,' he yelled, 'no-thing compares . . . to you!'

I felt the table rocking next to me, followed by a muffled thud. Mike had overturned his chair from laughing so much. He stayed down, chortling.

By the time the song finished, the place was half empty. Even the traditionally tolerant Blue Bay karaoke crowd had snapped and felt a sudden urge to check on their packing.

He dropped the mike and walked off stage, looking wobbly on his legs. I saw him pick up his pint and down it in one, hands still shaking, as he came towards us.

'Why's Mike on the floor?' he said.

'He's pissed, or hopefully dead,' I answered, booting Mike under the table to stop him contradicting me.

'Oh. Right. I know that was awful, Sal. Singing is not one of my skills. But I meant it. Every word. I'm going to get Jake now, and we'll be off early in the morning. You know where I am if you change your mind.'

I looked up at him and shook my head slightly. No going back. I'd made my decision, and all I craved now were the predictable rhythms of my old life coming back to me. I needed to heal, and move on, and stay safe. I couldn't do that with him, no matter how much he meant it.

'I'm sorry, James, I really am. But I won't be changing my mind. I'm going back to my real life.'

He nodded once, said a curt goodbye to the others, and left, marching a little unsteadily towards the kids' club. I felt a sickening lurch spread through my stomach. This might be the last time I ever saw him. Was I making the right choice? I never even wanted a choice. Why was life so fucking complicated?

I stood up and grabbed my handbag. It was time to go. I was tired. And sad. And worried that if I drank too much, I'd climb through James's bedroom window in the middle of the night.

I headed back to our room through the darkened gardens, staring at my feet, lost in thought. My brain was hurting, which didn't seem fair as I wasn't even drunk.

I stopped and blinked when I realised there was somebody else in the garden with me. I could hear footsteps, and panting. I looked up and around. My mental health must be worse than I thought – there was a pair of fluorescent pink hands flying towards me in the dark. And a shiny pink head darting from left to right. Neither was attached to a body.

They were bobbing around in the blackness, like someone had chopped them off and attached them to strings. Yikes. Maybe Mehmet had taken the party-night cocktails to new extremes and started spiking them with acid.

The creepy head and the hands came nearer, and I realised they were in fact attached to Simon. He was dashing around like a parrot with its tail on fire, zigzagging through the trees, high-stepping for speed. His body was in darkness, but his head and hands were completely fluorescent. I could hear him screaming 'Stop it! Leave me alone! It wasn't what it looked like!' as he ran.

Lucy was chasing him, shooting jets of pink spray from her aerosol, calling him names that would make a docker blush. When the stream of spray slowed to a jerky trickle, she threw the can viciously at his head. It crunched between his eyes and he fell to the ground, where she kicked him, hard, in the balls. He clasped his hands to his groin, leaving giant pink finger marks all over the crotch of his shorts.

'You fucking unbelievable bastard!' she said, going in for another kick. I grabbed hold of her arms and tugged her back, her legs dragging along the floor as she shouted obscenities at him. Simon stayed where he was, snivelling and wiping at his eyes with the corner of his T-shirt.

'What is it?' I said. 'Calm down and tell me!' I held her face steady in my hands so she was forced to look at me.

'Him. I found him with Heather, that pneumatic tennis bitch. And he wasn't practising his fucking serve!'

She tried to break free to get at him again, but I managed to keep hold of one arm and pull her back.

'It wasn't what it looked like!' shouted Simon miserably, who'd struggled upright. He had two round white patches on his face where he'd managed to wipe his eyes. They stared out, blue and watery with tears. The rest of his head – including all his hair – was solid pink.

'Really?' she yelled back. 'You had your hand up her skirt and your tongue down her fucking throat. What was it then?'

'I . . . I . . .' he stuttered. His brain couldn't think up a lie fast enough, which was unlike him.

'Lucy,' I said firmly, 'leave us alone.'

She scowled, and kicked a big clod of grass up with her Converse, then skulked away. Every now and then she looked back and stared at him over her shoulder. He winced every time.

I sat down next to him, passing him a tissue so he could wipe some of the spray from his face. He scrubbed away at it, but it was already dried on.

'Okay, Simon. Time to be honest. I won't kick you in the balls again, I promise. But I have to know. We've not made any commitment to each other yet, so you can still get away with this one. But don't lie to me, or I'll chop them off.'

He stared off into the night for a moment. His luminous head was glowing in the dark. He sighed and his pink shoulders sagged lower.

'I did . . . kiss her. I was drunk and happy and she's always so sweet to me and tells me how good I am at tennis. Which sounds so pathetic now I'm saying it out loud. I didn't plan it. I was only going back to the room, and she was there, on the way to hers, and . . . God, Sal. Lucy's right. I'm just an arsehole. But I've felt so bad about myself since we've been here. Since *he's* been here. I know you've said you'll think about us trying again, but you don't really want to, do you?

'I know you're fond of me, but you jump away every time I try and touch you. And I see the way you look at him. You still want him, more than you want me. I'm never going to win, no matter how much we both try. We'll just end up friends who sleep next to each other. That's not enough for me, even if it is for you. I don't want to be second best, my ego's not tolerant enough. I'm so sorry. Do you understand?'

I stood up and looked down at his face, shining up at me like a wide pink moon. His glowing hands were gripping his knees, and he was crying again. I recalled how easy it had been to snog a random cabbie after a few drinks, and how little it had actually meant to me. Recalled kissing James in these very gardens just nights ago. Was I really in a position to judge?

'Yes. I think I do understand,' I said. 'And maybe you're right. But I wish you'd held it together till we'd got home. Now I'm going to have to sit next to you on the plane looking like that. And Simon? I was lying.'

'About what?'

'About this.'

I left him groaning in the grass, and walked off to the stairs feeling very odd indeed. Satisfied with the kick, hurt at his betrayal, and overwhelmingly relieved that it was finally all over. That Simon's natural inclinations had stopped me from making the wrong choice. Saved by the bell-end.

Lucy was waiting for me in the doorway.

'I saw that,' she said, 'nice one. He won't be pissing straight for days. Look, Mum – you've got to get rid of him. I know you've been thinking of taking him back, but you can't.'

'And why not?' I said, letting us both into our room. 'You just can't bear the thought of him living in our house again.'

'That's not true! I'm off to Liverpool next month, and I'll have better things to do with my spare time than visit you losers! How selfish do you think I am, anyway?'

'Do you really want me to answer that?' I said. She glared at me, stormed off into her own room, and slammed the door behind her.

'I'm going out again!' she yelled through. 'I've got things to do – and you were a lot more fun when you were fucking James!'

Chapter 58

When I woke up the next morning, Simon's long, pale body was stretched out on the bed, legs spread, one hand stuck down the front of his white boxer shorts. His head was still bright pink. He looked like a masturbating matchstick.

I felt an unexpected rush of warmth towards him as I watched his leg twitch, like a dog dreaming about rabbits. He might be a macho fuckwit incapable of keeping his penis in his pants, but he was right – I didn't really want to try again. I was only doing it because I was a great big wuss using him as a human shield.

When I'd heard he'd been locking lips with Heather, I'd been angry and hurt. For about thirty seconds. Because he didn't have the power to hurt me any more – I didn't care enough. I'm no expert on these things, but that didn't seem like a solid basis for a life partnership.

I sat beside him on the bed and gave him a little shove.

He opened one eye, still bloodshot from Lucy's attack. I smiled and gave him a quick kiss on one very pink cheek.

'Hi,' he said, 'are you all right? You were dead to the world when I got up here last night. What time is it anyway? Am I still pink?'

'It's early, and yes, you are. Look, I want to thank you, Simon.'

He looked shocked, perplexed, and a little hopeful. I swear there was an extra twitch in the boxers as I said it. For goodness' sake. Did they really never think about anything else?

'For what?'

'For being so good to me this last year. I wouldn't have got through it without you. You saved me. But you were right last night – it's not going to work. It wasn't fair of me to lead you on, and there would always have been a Heather at some point down the line, wouldn't there? We both deserve better than second best. So let's call it quits and try and be friends. How does that sound?'

'It sounds awful. And it's not what I want. But you're probably right, and I'll try. But . . . what about him? Are you going back to him? Please be careful, Sal. Remember what he did to you last time.'

No need to ask who 'him' was, or why I needed to be careful.

As for whether I was going back to him . . . it was an excellent question. The one I'd stumble on in *Who Wants to Be a Millionaire*. I'd already tried the 50-50, and there wasn't an audience.

Could I go back to him? Could I ever forgive him, or feel safe enough to try? It was easier to hate him.

But I knew, deep down, that Lucy was right. I was a lot more fun when I was fucking James. Because I'd been happy with him. I'd loved him. I still loved him.

If I didn't even try to make it work, I'd be living life on half-power, always wondering how happy I could have been in a parallel universe. He'd made a mistake. A huge one. But he'd apologised a million times, and I'd never let myself listen. I'd sent him away last night as if he was peddling life insurance on the doorstep. As though he didn't matter. He did matter, and if I let him walk away now, I'd be the one making a huge mistake.

I was a coward, and James had never been that. He'd tried to work things out with Lavender for the sake of his little boy. He'd told me he loved me over and over. He'd helped me deliver a baby. He'd sung on the bleeding karaoke. And still, I'd hardened myself to him, convinced myself that Simon was the safer bet. The better bet.

And that's why I thanked Simon. For showing me how wrong I'd been, on all counts. Simon wasn't a safe bet – and who wanted safe anyway? I wanted James.

I looked at my watch. I still had my nightshirt on. It was short and white and had patterns of tiny red Scotty dogs all over it. But who cared, really?

Without answering his question, I scooted to the door, opened it, and dashed out. I galloped barefoot down the stairs, jumping the last three and landing with a heel-jarring wallop on the concrete floor. I ran down the corridor, out into the gardens, and followed the path to reception.

Panting and exhausted, I ran inside. Tarkan stared at me, wild eyed and half dressed, and smiled cautiously.

'You okay, Sally?' he asked. I caught my breath and shook my head.

'No. Yes. Maybe . . . have they gone?'

'Have who gone?'

'The Dublin people, of course!' I yelled, angry at his lack of psychic powers.

He nodded, and looked nervous. I wondered if he kept a syringe full of elephant sedative behind the counter in case he needed to control crazy English chicks in Scotty-dog nighties.

'Yes. A while ago. Their flight leaves in maybe one hour.'

Shit. I collapsed on to the floor of reception, feeling the cold stone chill against my thighs and spread all through me. He'd gone. And I wouldn't blame him if he never spoke to me again. I was dimly aware of Tarkan dashing over and trying to lift me, then giving up and dropping me to the floor again. He ran out for help, looking terrified.

'Sally! What's up? What's wrong?' said a voice from the doorway.

Marcia. He'd found Marcia. She was always an early riser, needing to get a head start on her nicotine consumption. She lifted me up as though I weighed as much as a chihuahua and sat me down on the bench.

'Are you ill?' she said, feeling my forehead with the palm of her hand to see if I had a temperature.

'No! But he's gone!' I wailed, tears rumbling up and erupting down my cheeks.

'Oh. You mean James?'

'Yes! Who else would I mean?' I sobbed, which wasn't quite fair.

She nodded her understanding, then grabbed Tarkan by the arm and shook him. The poor man had gone rigid with fear at all the female hysteria.

'What time does their flight leave?' she asked. When he didn't reply, she shook him so hard his moustache wobbled.

'In about forty minutes!' he said, glancing at the clock.

'Come on – we can make it,' she said, pulling me to my bare feet and giving me a shake as well. It bloody hurt, and she left vivid red fingerprints in the flesh of my arms.

'Sally, stop blubbering. And you, Tarkan, give me the keys to your motorbike. Move it, we haven't got all day!'

He jumped like he'd been blasted with an electrified cattle plod, and fished around in his pockets. Marcia grabbed the keys from his hand, and dragged me outside to the courtyard.

'Put this on!' she said, thrusting the spare helmet into my hands. She straddled the bike, and stared back at me.

'Well, get on. Do you want to see him or not?'

'But I've got no pants on! And how are you going to drive this thing?'

'Piece of cake – I used to be in the Hell's Angels, you know. Leatherhead branch. Now come on!'

I climbed on, wincing slightly at the feel of cool leather on my overexposed nether regions, and grabbed hold of Marcia's waist. The tyres spun and kicked up a dust cloud before we zoomed off and out into the road. We skidded, and swerved so low we almost came off. Hell's Angels, my arse. The woman could barely ride. And she was probably pissed as well.

We flew along on to the main road to the airport, over-taking trucks, vans and possibly Formula One racing cars. There was a lot of honking of horns and swarthy Turkish lorry drivers leaning out of their cabs to get a better look, at both Marcia's driving and my bare backside.

In the end we made it in under forty minutes instead of the usual hour and a half. Thanks to Evel fucking Knievel in front of me. Marcia skidded the bike to a screeching halt right outside the terminal.

'Go on,' she said, 'I'll wait for you.' She pulled a packet of Gauloises out of her pocket and lit up. I saw the security guards eyeing her suspiciously and hoped she'd be okay. They had guns and everything.

I ran into the building, which was jam-packed with crispy-fried tourists waiting to go home. Everywhere I looked there were family groups like mine: bored teens, stressed mums, dads reading the sports pages. Babies crying. Toddlers screaming.

After several failed attempts at finding the right screen, I pushed my way to the front of a small crowd studying the departures board. One of them made noises like she was going to object, but took one look at my bare feet, Scotty dogs and fright wig and decided it wasn't worth the trouble.

Dublin flight, Dublin flight, where the fuck are you? Manchester, Milan, Azerbai-effing-jan . . . where was Dublin? My eyes flickered over the list three times before I spotted it. My heart was racing as I scanned across the find-the-gate-number, even though I had no idea what I was going to do then. Scream my everlasting love from passport control? Tell the Customs guards he had a kilo of cocaine packed in his pants and get him strip-searched?

In the end I didn't need to. Because there was no gate number. There was only one word: departed. It was gone. I was too late. I'd missed him, despite risking life, limb and a severe chill to the cheeks to make it.

I wandered through the crowds over to the viewing window. I squashed my face and hands against the glass, wondering if by some freaky coincidence his plane was out there, and whether he'd miraculously turn round and see me. Making pig faces and steaming up the window.

I had no idea which plane was his, and watched forlornly as they lined up to taxi down the runway. Next to me, a concerned mother shepherded her young child closer to her legs, away from the scary lady.

Well, I thought, turning back into the noise and bustle of the airport. That was the end of that stupid idea. I walked back towards the exit, noticing for the first time that my feet were bleeding. It didn't hurt at all in comparison to the fierce ache in my heart, and the sense of depression that was settling on my shoulders.

I spotted Marcia in the car park. She was leaning against the bike, smoking a ciggie and drinking from a hip flask.

She looked up expectantly and I shook my head. She passed me the helmet and I got back on. Marcia was a woman who always knew when to stay quiet.

Tarkan was waiting for us when we got back, his dark eyes huge with worry. I thought he might cry with relief when Marcia handed him the keys back.

'We need to go and get ready for our own flights, Sally. You tried. And if you want me to tell him that, I will.'

I nodded and hugged her, and started limping back towards my room. I saw Mike at the bar, reading a paperback and supping a refreshing morning pint of lager.

'Aren't you supposed to have gone home by now?' I asked, sitting down opposite him. He looked up, assessing my sartorial state and raising an eyebrow.

'I'm not going home,' he said. 'There's nothing to go back for just yet. Maybe ever. The business ticks over without me these days. Max doesn't have to be at college till October. And Harry's invited us to stay at the pub with him – so we are. What have you been up to? You look like you've been attacked by a flock of rabid seagulls.'

'I'm all right. Well, no, actually, I'm not all right. Give me a drink.'

He passed the glass over and I took a long, cool swig. That was better. Morning drinking could be the way forward.

'I hared off to the airport. On the back of a bloody motorbike, with Marcia. I was trying to catch James before he left, so I could, you know—'

'Declare your eternal love? Have a quickie in the bogs?'

'Yeah. Those things. But he was gone, and he thinks I hate him, and there's no hope, and he'll probably forget all about me now. He'll fall in love with one of the air hostesses on the way home and they'll get married and have seventeen children. 'Cause that's the way my luck seems to go.'

'My my,' he said, retrieving his drink before I drained it, 'we are feeling sorry for ourselves, aren't we? Chin up. Just phone him when you get home. It's not the end of the world.'

'Didn't you hear what I said about the fucking air hostess, Mike? I've missed my chance.'

Mike held his hands in front of him in surrender, knowing better than to argue with a woman in the grip of a major melodrama.

'Okay Sal,' he said, 'I get it. Your life's over, you'll never be happy again. But look. Here's Lucy. She'll cheer you up.'

Yeah. Like a dose of the clap.

She spotted me sitting with Mike and ran over. Her cheeks were flushed and her hair was flying.

'Mum!' she said, 'thank fuck you're back! We've got a problem – we've lost your passport. We were hoping you had it with you, but as you're practically naked as usual, I suppose not. Unless we find it in the next hour, you're screwed.'

So what was new there?

Chapter 59

The passport was nowhere to be found. I'd assumed I'd see it in plain sight as soon as I entered the room – one man and two teenagers searching for it was about as much use as putting the three blind mice on the trail.

Simon had all the drawers out and turned upside down, the clothes from the suitcases scattered over the floor, and was barking commands at Ollie, telling him to check in the toilet cistern. Of course, that's where I usually keep my passport.

'What have you done with it, Sally? We need to leave soon; this is ridiculous! Where've you been anyway – and what happened to your hair?'

'Simon, have you looked in a mirror this morning? I don't think a man with a fluorescent pink head is in any position to comment. And my passport was in the bottom of the wardrobe, along with everyone else's!'

'Well, ours are all there – it's only yours that's missing.'

His tone made it sound as if it was all my fault. Like I'd accidentally sold my passport to a troupe of wandering gypsies with a dancing bear and forgotten to tell him.

'Look,' I said, 'you and the kids will have to go, and I'll get a later flight. It's not a disaster.'

'Yes it is!' said Lucy, skulking through the interconnecting door, 'and if you think I'm going home with him, you must be off your medication. If you stay, I stay. Max is here anyway. Maybe I'll stay for the whole month.'

'Well, help us look then – I haven't seen you lift a finger.'

'How's this?' she said, lifting a finger. But not in quite the way I meant.

I closed my eyes and counted to ten while I tried to calm down.

When I opened my eyes she'd disappeared off with her bags, I assumed to find Max. Ollie was looking at me quizzically.

'No! You're going back with your dad,' I said. 'I don't care if Tabitha's asked you to marry her – you've got school next week.'

'Nah,' he said, 'I dumped her. She just wasn't cool enough for me. And I want to go home anyway – there's a fancy-dress triple-bill of the old *Star Wars* films on in town.'

Right. Of course. Tabitha wasn't cool enough for him.

'Okay, good. Simon – you and Ollie go on ahead. You've got keys. Just buy a load of pizzas or something, you'll be fine. Now come on, let's get you sorted.'

We repacked the scattered clothes, and I kept enough for a couple of days just in case, before heading down to reception to meet the transfer coach. Simon loaded the bags on, and we waited until everyone else was aboard.

'See you soon, Mum,' said Ollie, hugging me. 'Don't talk to any strange men.'

Simon kissed me on the cheek, joined Ollie, and waved through the window as they drove off. I waved frantically back, missing them already. I wanted to go home too. I wanted to sleep in my own bed and walk the dog and watch *Coronation Street* and have a Chinese on my lap in the living room. Instead I was stuck here with Lucy, wondering if James would even remember my name by the time he got home. It had been a shit of a day, it truly had.

I trudged back to reception, and noticed Tarkan hiding behind the desk. Can't say that I blamed him.

'Come out! I can see you! Don't worry, I just need a bit of help. And Marcia's not here.'

He peeked his head up cautiously and smiled. I explained about the passport, and he said he'd get the staff to search for it as well. And if it didn't turn up, he'd make me an appointment with the Consulate to get an emergency replacement.

I got changed into more respectable clothes, and went back out to find Mike. He had three empty pint glasses lined up in front of him and was snoring gently in the midday sun.

I sat down with my own drink and looked around. It was quite eerie here on changeover day. Most of the old guests had gone and the new ones hadn't arrived. Everything was being cleaned and polished and scrubbed, and the staff were in their civvies. Hopefully, somewhere upstairs, one of the old Turkish ladies with faces like dried-up orange peel would be discovering a British passport lurking inside a pillowcase.

'So. I see you're still here. What's the plan?' said Mike, without opening his eyes. 'Do you want to stay with Harry? He won't mind.'

'Yeah, that'd be great. As soon as I'm sorted, I'll book us new flights. Lucy's gone AWOL; I suspect she'll be with your son somewhere. I might go and visit Jenny and Ian and the baby as well.'

'Well, tonight you can come to the island with us. Harry's doing a barbecue. We can get shitfaced and play strip poker. Meet us at the beach at about eight and we'll all go over. What do you say?'

'Sounds good,' I said, 'as long as you promise to wear plenty of layers.'

Chapter 60

'How was the baby?' asked Mike, bumping around in the back of the boat. Harry was at the wheel, and we were bouncing over waves so hard that Mike's belly was wobbling up and down like a big hairy jelly.

'Oh, gorgeous,' I said, 'just beautiful.'

'Are you sure? You look like you're going to cry – not that ugly, is it?'

'Oh shut up you pig! He's lovely. Putting on loads of weight, feeding well. Honestly, Mike, you've never seen two happier people. Knackered, but over the moon.'

I blinked the tears away. I was tired. I was lonely. I had no idea where my life was heading. And my feet were sore.

'Good luck to 'em, eh? I'll visit myself soon. Anyhow, here goes, Sal. You get off first and we'll unload the stuff. Then we'll go back for Max and Lucy.'

We moored the boat, and I climbed out. I tucked my skirt into my knickers and splashed down in my flip-flops. Once I was steady, Mike passed me my bag. I waded through the shallows and up to the beach, putting the bag down and turning back to see how I could help.

There were chiller boxes and charcoal and probably a brewery's worth of beer to bring back up. And I was going to need it all if they seriously expected me to play strip poker with them, the old perverts. A good booze-up was probably just what I needed. It wasn't only the baby making me cry – it was the sense that I'd let love walk out of my life, and I might never get the chance to find it again.

As I neared the boat, Mike stood up. I held my hand out to help him over the side, but he waved me away.

'Just stand back a bit, Sal!' he said. I did, wondering if he was going for a splash landing.

'A bit further!'

I budged back some more.

'Okay, off we go, Harry! See you later, Sal!' he yelled, waving. Harry saluted me. He was wearing one of those giant felt hats shaped like a pint of Guinness, and he was laughing.

He started the engine, and before I could ask what was going on, they were off. Mike was sitting in the back, still bouncing, toasting me with a can he'd just opened.

'What the hell . . .' I muttered, walking back up to the beach and sitting down by my bag. All men were clearly insane. I shrugged, and rooted in my bag. A Snickers bar. Well, why not?

I unwrapped it and took a bite. Delicious. If only there were another six, I'd be set for the night. I looked out at the bay. Okay, I seemed to be stranded on a desert island with no apparent means of getting off. The sun had almost set, and it was going to get cooler soon. But, on the plus side, I had chocolate, a bag full of clothes, and . . . a bottle of wine. What was that doing in there? I pulled it out and looked at the label. Pretty nice wine too.

I'd started to unpack the bag, wondering what other little gifts Mike had left me, when I heard a noise nearby. It sounded like bottles clinking together. I couldn't see anyone, but it was coming from nearby. Had one of the others been here all along? Had Mike and Harry come back and landed at the other side for some reason? Or was I about to meet my end at the hands of a crazed island-hopping serial killer carrying a crate of milk?

I edged back, pulling my bag with me, and plastered myself flat against the steep side of the hill. Ouch. There were prickles and shrubs and all kinds of pointy objects now poking in places that shouldn't be poked. I saw a shady figure emerging, and knew straight away it wasn't Mike or Harry or Max. And definitely not Lucy, unless she'd overdosed on steroids this afternoon. I gripped the wine bottle by the neck, in case I needed to clock anyone.

I squinted my eyes to see in the fading light of the sun as he got closer. Then I squeaked. It was James. My James. And he was absolutely stark-bollock-naked.

He whirled round at the noise, and stared at me with equal surprise.

'Sally?' he said, 'what are you doing here? I thought your plane left ages ago?'

'Well, what about you? Shouldn't you be in Dublin snogging an air hostess by now? And why haven't you got any clothes on?'

'You're rambling. I don't know any air hostesses. Come away from that hill, there's all sorts of insects on there you don't want crawling on you.'

I said something eloquent like 'erk!' and jumped away, brushing down my back and my bottom with jerky hands. I pulled my tucked-up skirt out of my knickers while I was at it. This was a situation that called for some dignity, although I did at least have the advantage over a man with his schlong hanging out.

Shit, I thought – how do I handle this? A few hours ago I was practically streaking through the airport ready to give him a blow job on the runway. Now he was here, I felt . . . embarrassed. Nervous. Tongue-tied.

'So why are you still here?' he finally said, as I tried not to look at his dangly bits.

'Lost my passport,' I mumbled. It was such a bloody typical me thing to do, and I did get tired of being such a joke. 'What about you? And where's Jake?'

He started pulling little twigs out of my hair, and then he started stroking my cheek, and then his hand trailed down to hold mine. I linked my fingers into his and squeezed them. Now that felt good.

'My flight was cancelled until tomorrow morning. We hung round for an hour, then Mike said we could bunk down at Harry's. Max was playing with Jake and Mike said they were having a—'

'Barbecue on the island? With strip poker?'

'Yes! Not the kind of thing I'd normally do with blokes, but we were betting for quite a bit of cash. They were cheating somehow, and I lost every hand for . . . well, ever. Then they grabbed all my clothes and legged it. You wouldn't believe how fast those fat bastards can run when they want to.

They just left me this bag, which is full of some very weird stuff.'

I sat down on the soft sand. It was getting really dark now. In the distance I could see the twinkling lights of the towns and villages dotted around the bay. There'd be a whole new intake of Blue-Bayers there now, getting to know each other and drinking themselves stupid.

James sat down beside me. Still naked. His thigh was pressed against mine, and I realised he was shivering. I put my hand on his leg and rubbed, trying to warm him up. His cock pinged straight up into the air, so I guess it worked. He looked a bit embarrassed and tried to cover himself up with his hands.

'Here,' I said, emptying the contents of my bag out on to the floor and picking up a nice silk wrap, 'put this on.'

'I don't think so,' he said, squinting at it, 'it's got sequins.'

'Right. Sorry. Is it too gay for you? I mean, if I'd known I was going to meet you out here starkers, I'd have packed something more appropriate! For fuck's sake, stop being such a dick – you'll freeze.'

He threw it round his shoulders and hunkered down. I found a long white skirt and passed it to him. He shot me a look.

'No, I don't expect you to put it on. It won't fit over your thighs.'

Your gorgeous, muscular, super-sexy, crushed-right-up-against-mine thighs, I thought, as I draped it over him. The penis problem had faded slightly, just a little bump in the fabric now. That was probably a good thing. I'm not sure how I'd handle it if James got turned on by wearing women's clothes.

'Who told you the flight was cancelled anyway?' I said as I tucked him in. 'Because it wasn't.'

'Lucy told me. Well, she brought me the notice they'd left at reception for me. It was nice of her – saved us dragging all the bags downstairs when we didn't need to. And what makes you say it wasn't cancelled?'

I sighed and nodded. Everything was beginning to slip into place now. It was a great big jigsaw with a picture of my daughter in the middle of it, holding up two fingers.

'I think we've been set up,' I said. 'I know your flight wasn't cancelled because I saw it had left. Apparently without you on it, but I didn't know that at the time. And I know for a fact that Tarkan on reception didn't type up a notice for you about the flight being cancelled – which just leaves Lucy. She disappeared off saying she had things to do, and now I know what – I think it was Lucy who typed up that notice, printed it off, and brought it up to your room to stop you leaving. You should know by now she wouldn't do anything from the kindness of her own heart.'

'You were at the airport? Why? How?'

'Because I thought you were leaving. And I wanted to, erm, have a quickie in the bogs.'

His skirt bobbed up and down. Primitive response to the mere mention of sex.

'Oh. Well. In that case I'm sorry I missed you. We could always—'

'What do you have in your bag?' I said, cutting him off before we both ended up naked.

He emptied it out. Lighter fluid and a lighter. Presumably for a fire, as neither of us smoked.

More chocolate. Good. More wine. Better. A corkscrew. And a packet of condoms. Right. No mixed messages in that agenda, then. I'm surprised they hadn't drawn some stick figures having sex in an instruction manual.

I rooted through the debris in front of me. As well as my own clothes, and the wine, there were a couple of blankets, and a white envelope with my name written on it. I tore it open, but I already had a suspicion as to what I was going to find.

My passport tumbled out on to my lap, along with a note in Lucy's scrawl.

'See you in the morning, you old bag. Don't fuck this up.'

'This is what I think happened,' I said. 'She faked you into thinking your plane was cancelled. Sucker. Then Mike got you and Jake out of the way and over to Harry's, and she stole my passport. Then we both got kidnapped at different times, and dumped here. At least I managed to keep my clothes, I suppose.'

He nodded as he thought about it, running through events in his mind.

'You have to admire it, don't you? It's bloody clever,' he said. 'And it does mean we're here. Together. For what looks like the whole night. What happens now?'

'Well, I think we should talk. Then, depending on how that goes, maybe do some sex stuff. What do you think?'

'I think that I love you, Sally. I never stopped. I never will stop. If your run to the airport was any sign you're willing to try again, I'll be the happiest man in the world. Please, Sally – give me another chance.'

I looked at him. He might be dressed in a skirt and a sequined silk wrap, but he was still the most desirable hunk of manhood I'd ever clapped eyes on. And he loved me. It was there, in his eyes, so bright and so warm. He loved me, and I loved him, and it was time to be brave. Time to trust. I let my hand creep into his.

'Yes,' I said, 'I love you too. And yes, I'll give you another chance. It's all I've been thinking about. I'm sorry it took almost losing you to make me realise. I'm sorry even Lucy knew more about what I needed than I did. I was just . . . scared.'

'I know. And that's my fault. I'll never do anything like that again, believe me. So . . . have we done the talking now?'

I nodded. The skirt was off in a flash, and the wrap got thrown to the wind. My top followed suit. He pushed me down on to the sand and rolled on top of me. He kissed me and I reached up to touch the bare skin of his shoulders. God, it had been so long. I'd almost forgotten how absolutely perfect he was.

He laughed and his blue eyes crinkled round the edges. I moved one of my hands from his arse to his shoulders. There was so much of him I wanted to touch, all at once. I just didn't have enough hands.

'Let's make it more than tonight,' he said, nuzzling my neck. 'Let's make it for ever. We've messed this up enough. I've never loved anyone like this before, and I don't want to live without you. I can move. You can move. Whatever it takes – but let's be together. We can get married. Or shack up. Or have a Wiccan handfasting at Glastonbury. Whatever you want – but please, please say you'll give it a go.'

He pushed himself up with his arms, and got down on one knee. He was sinking into the sand, and his man parts were blowing in the breeze, but it's the thought that counts.

'Will you marry me, Sally?' he asked.

I was about to answer when I was suddenly blinded by a dazzling beam of light shining into my eyes. We both shielded our faces and looked out to the bay. All we could see was a giant ray of white cutting through the water and pinning us in a spotlight. Any minute now they'd let the hunting dogs loose and we'd have to run through a swamp with our legs chained together.

'What the hell?' muttered James, standing up to try and get a better view.

'Mother!' boomed Lucy's voice through some kind of loudspeaker, 'say "yes" and put your knickers on immediately!'

She moved the flashlight around for a second and waved at us. Harry was at the helm, and she was hoisting the light in one hand and the hailer in the other. The boat was chugging in to moor, engine humming.

'Get dressed and board the boat in an orderly fashion!' she barked, like a demented drill sergeant. 'We planned to leave you here all night, but then Harry remembered the tide comes right in and you'd both drown. So hurry up! James, I can see your bottom!'

He jumped up and out of the reach of the flashlight, tying the skirt lengthways around his waist. I crawled round on my hands and knees, grabbing my discarded top and pulling it on as quickly as I could.

I stood up, and looked at James bursting out of my skirt. In the background, Lucy was shouting, 'Left, right, left, right!' and clapping her hands in time.

'Let's go and chuck her in,' I whispered, reaching out and putting my arms round his waist, being careful not to dismantle his makeshift manhood protector.

'I'll happily tie her feet to the boat and drag her all the way back with you, Sal. But first – answer my question.'

I tied the sequined wrap round his neck, and trailed my hand over the contours of his chest. I never could resist a man in a nice scarf.

'Yes, James. The answer's yes.'

His face exploded into a smile and he crushed me to him, kissing me so hard I forgot we had an audience and slipped my hands under his skirt for a little feel.

'Was that a yes?' Lucy boomed at us from the boat.

I kept my arms round James's neck and, behind his back, gave her a very special message. It involved two of my fingers and the letter between U and W.

PART FIVE

Turkey – two years later

Chapter 61

'Happy birthday, Sal!' rumbled Mike as he walked towards me. He was lugging a crate of beer with him, and stopping every five seconds to catch his breath. He dragged it the last few feet, and dumped it at the bottom of my sun lounger. I looked from it to him and smiled. I hadn't seen Mike for two years, but some things never changed.

I stood up and hugged him. The belly was definitely blossoming, as was the rest of him.

'Mike! How are you?' I said. He'd sold his business last year and retired permanently to Turkey, buying a share of Harry's bar.

'Brilliant, love. I get paid to sit in a pub all day. Couldn't be better. I've made a few changes, though; introduced a few cosmopolitan touches.'

'Yeah? Like what? Are you doing food? Entertainment?'

'No. Boddingtons. Anyway, enough of my jet-set lifestyle. Have you heard from our kids?'

'Yes. They're currently in Amsterdam, doing God knows what, and they're getting a flight over in a couple of days. Simon felt so guilty about the fact that he's got yet another young girlfriend on the go that he paid for the whole trip – Lucy played him to perfection . . . Ollie's in the games room, you'll see him later. He's loving uni. Rick and Marcia are around somewhere, too – no Andrew this year, sadly. It's a Graham instead. Nowhere near as fit.'

'Sorry to hear that, love. I know you were always a fan. I saw Jenny and Ian on my way over to you, with little Clark Kent.'

'He's called Ethan,' I replied, poking him in well-hidden ribs.

'I know. But I always think of him as Superbaby. Cracking little lad, he is – and she's expecting again now! Bloody wonderful. The gang's all here again, eh?'

I nodded, and felt my eyes unexpectedly fill with tears.

'The gang's all here apart from one, Mike. I still miss her, and I know you do. How are you, really?'

'I really am good, Sal. Not a day goes by I don't wish she was here with me, but I'm building something new here. Max is well set up, and I couldn't face staying in our house without her. Here, with Harry . . . well. He's not as good at Pilates, but he does a mean fry-up. I'm moving on as best as I can. And, that, as you know, is—'

'What Allie would have wanted!' I finished for him, laughing. He was right. She would.

'Anyway,' said Mike. 'Where is she then? Where's Daisy?'

'She's just finishing her lunch,' I said, waving my arms frantically at James to let him know Mike had arrived. He waved back, and headed in our direction.

'Bloody hell,' Mike said when the two of them got closer, 'she's a corker. Look at those blond curls. Just like Jake's.'

The Birthday that Changed Everything

Daisy was one now, beginning to say a few words and stumble round the furniture. We'd started trying for a baby almost straight away once James had relocated, thinking it might take a while because of the advanced age of my ovaries. In the end it had taken about an hour. She'd turned our whole lives upside down, and I couldn't think of anything that had been more welcome.

James clapped Mike on the back in greeting, and handed Daisy over for him to hold. Mike cuddled her up into his arms, and she immediately gripped his beard with her podgy hands. She gazed up at him with very serious brown eyes, twining sticky fingers into his facial hair, fascinated by it.

'Fuck,' she said, and pulled, hard.

James and I both winced. Sadly, that had been her first word. With 'shit' as a close second.

Mike disentangled his beard and looked up, laughing.

'Am I right in guessing that Lucy's been doing some babysitting, then?'

Acknowledgements

I love holidays – I can spend hours fantasising over them, and planning them, and researching them. I even enjoy going on them. There's just nothing quite like getting away from it all with friends and family and seeing a different part of the world, or a different side to life.

So writing a book based around a holiday was the perfect concept for me – and was inspired by a real life resort I visited with my husband and kids, where we soon realised that the same people did in fact come back year after year, just like they do in this book. Nothing very dramatic happened – just a lot of fun, and catching up, and sunbathing. But it was enough to spark this whole idea, and begin Sally's story.

I, like Sally, had a lot of help along the way – it took several years for *The Birthday that Changed Everything* to see the light of day, and I have a few people to thank for that. My agent, Laura Longrigg of MBA, has always believed in me and worked tirelessly on my behalf. She also taught me the London girl secret of hiding your flats in your handbag and changing your shoes halfway through a party.

Kimberley Young and Charlotte Ledger at Harper Collins/ HarperImpulse gave me the chance to join their team, and then gave me the chance to take it to the next level – thank you so much for your faith in me. The super-talented and generally awesome Alexandra Allden has consistently come up with the most beautiful covers around – and we all know that people do, in fact, judge a book by its cover (including me!).

I've had a lot of personal and professional support from other authors, who are generally a wonderfully wacky bunch. So thanks to the HarperImpulse ladies and gents, in particular Jane Linfoot, and also to the ever-supportive Jane Costello – as good a friend as she is a writer. Milly Johnson not only took the time and effort to read this book for me, but also does some amazing dancing when she's drunk at weddings – my thanks and love, Milly.

As I started writing this back in 2010 – when I was forty as well as Sally – a few people have helped shape it along the way. Celine Kelly rounded it out beautifully with her editorial advice, and several friends also read early versions – including Sandra Shennan, Caroline Storah, Rachael Tinniswood and Ann Potterton. Thanks for all your feedback, even if it was just 'I nearly peed myself laughing at that bit' (Sandra).

My friends in general are a wonderful gaggle – so big thanks to Pam Hoey, Louise Douglas, Helen Shaw, the Barbie Quiz Night Gang, Jane Murdoch, Vikki Everett, Paula Woosey, and my former colleagues at the *Liverpool Echo*, who never fail to come out dancing when I need them to. If I've forgotten anyone, I'm sorry – I blame my age.

Last but most definitely not least, my family – both my parents have passed away, so my in-laws, Terry and Norman Newton, and the rest of the Newton tribe, are especially appreciated. And to my husband, Dom, and my kids, Keir, Dan and Louisa, all the love in the world – what would holidays be without you lot??

Laugh out loud with more romantic comedies from

Debbie Johnson

'A sheer delight'

— *Sunday Express*